About the A

Sarah Morgan is a *USA Today* and *Sunday Times* bestselling author of contemporary romance and women's fiction. She has sold more than twenty-one million copies of her books and her trademark humour and warmth have gained her fans across the globe. Sarah lives with her family near London, England, where the rain frequently keeps her trapped in her office. Visit her at sarahmorgan.com

Carol Marinelli recently filled in a form asking for her job title. Thrilled to be able to put down her answer, she put writer. Then it asked what Carol did for relaxation and she put down the truth – writing. The third question asked for her hobbies. Well, not wanting to look obsessed she crossed the fingers on her hand and answered swimming but, given that the chlorine in the pool does terrible things to her highlights – I'm sure you can guess the real answer.

Jane Porter loves central California's golden foothills and miles of farmland, rich with the sweet and heady fragrance of orange blossoms. Her parents fed her imagination by taking Jane to Europe for a year where she became passionate about Italy and those gorgeous Italian men! Jane never minds a rainy day – that's when she sits at her desk and writes stories about far-away places, fascinating people, and most important of all, love. Visit her website at: janeporter.com

European Escapes

July 2023
Madrid

February 2024
Prague

August 2023
Sicily

March 2024
Athens

September 2023
Sweden

April 2024
London

January 2024
Paris

May 2024
Berlin

European Escapes:
Sicily

SARAH MORGAN

CAROL MARINELLI

JANE PORTER

MILLS & BOON

First Published in Great Britain 2023
by Mills & Boon, an imprint of HarperCollins*Publishers* Ltd,
1 London Bridge Street, London, SE1 9GF

www.harpercollins.co.uk

HarperCollins*Publishers*
Macken House, 39/40 Mayor Street Upper,
Dublin 1, D01 C9W8, Ireland

European Escapes: Sicily © 2023 Harlequin Enterprises ULC.

The Sicilian Doctor's Proposal © 2006 Sarah Morgan
The Sicilian's Surprise Love-Child © 2019 Carol Marinelli
A Dark Sicilian Secret © 2011 Jane Porter

ISBN: 978-0-263-31961-3

MIX
Paper | Supporting
responsible forestry
FSC
www.fsc.org
FSC™ C007454

This book is produced from independently certified FSC™ paper
to ensure responsible forest management.

For more information visit: www.harpercollins.co.uk/green

Printed and Bound in the UK using 100% Renewable Electricity
at CPI Group (UK) Ltd, Croydon, CR0 4YY

THE SICILIAN DOCTOR'S PROPOSAL

SARAH MORGAN

For the Blue Watch at Bethel Street
with many thanks for the tour and the talk!

PROLOGUE

'I DON'T believe in love. And neither do you.' Alice put her pen down and stared in bemusement at her colleague of five years. Had he gone mad?

'That was before I met Trish.' His expression was soft and far-away, his smile bordering on the idiotic. 'It's finally happened. Just like the fairy-tales.'

She wanted to ask if he'd been drinking, but didn't want to offend him. 'This isn't like you at all, David. You're an intelligent, hard-working doctor and at the moment you're talking like a—like a...' *A seven-year-old girl?* No, she couldn't possibly say that. 'You're not sounding like yourself,' she finished lamely.

'I don't care. She's the one. And I have to be with her. Nothing else matters.'

'Nothing else matters?' On the desk next to her the phone suddenly rang, but for once Alice ignored it. 'It's the start of the summer season, the village is already filling with tourists, most of the locals are struck down by that horrid virus, you're telling me you're leaving and you don't think it matters? Please, tell me this is a joke, David, please tell me that.'

Even with David working alongside her she was

working flat out to cope with the demand for medical care at the moment. It wasn't that she didn't like hard work. Work was her life. *Work had saved her.* But she knew her limits.

David dragged both hands through his already untidy hair. 'Not leaving exactly, Alice. I just need the summer off. To be with Trish. We need to decide on our future. We're in love!'

Love. Alice stifled a sigh of exasperation. Behind every stupid action was a relationship, she mused silently. She should know that by now. She'd seen it often enough. Why should David be different? Just because he'd *appeared* to be a sane, rational human being—

'You'll hate London.'

'Actually, I find London unbelievably exciting,' David confessed. 'I love the craziness of it all, the crowds of people all intent on getting somewhere yesterday, no one interested in the person next to them—' He broke off with an apologetic wave of his hand. 'I'm getting carried away. But don't you ever feel trapped here, Alice? Don't you ever wish you could do something in this village without the whole place knowing?'

Alice sat back in her chair and studied him carefully. She'd never known David so emotional. 'No,' she said quietly. 'I like knowing people and I like people knowing me. It helps when it comes to understanding their medical needs. They're our responsibility and I take that seriously.'

It was what had drawn her to the little fishing village in the first place. And now it felt like home. And the people felt like family. *More than her own ever had.* Here, she fitted. She'd found her place and she couldn't imagine living anywhere else. She loved the narrow cobbled streets, the busy harbour, the tiny shops selling shells and the trendy store selling surfboards and wet-suits. She loved the summer when the streets were crowded with tourists and she loved the winter when the beaches were empty and lashed by rain. For a moment she thought of London with its muggy, traffic-clogged streets and then she thought of her beautiful house. The house overlooking the broad sweep of the sea. The house she'd lovingly restored in every spare moment she'd had over the past five years.

It had given her sanctuary and a life that suited her. A life that was under her control.

'Since we're being honest here…' David took a deep breath and straightened, his eyes slightly wary. 'I think you should consider leaving, too. You're an attractive, intelligent woman but you're never going to find someone special buried in a place like this. You never meet anyone remotely eligible. All you think about is work, work and work.'

'David, I don't want to meet anyone.' She spoke slowly and clearly so that there could be no misunder-standing. 'I love my life the way it is.'

'Work shouldn't be your life, Alice. You need love.' David stopped pacing and placed a hand on his chest. 'Everyone needs love.'

Something inside her snapped. 'Love is a word used to justify impulsive, irrational and emotional behav-iour,' she said tartly, 'and I prefer to take a logical, sci-entific approach to life.'

David looked a little shocked. 'So, you're basically saying that I'm impulsive, irrational and emotional?'

She sighed. It was unlike her to be so honest. *To reveal so much about herself.* And unlike her to risk hurting someone's feelings. On the other hand, he was behaving very oddly. 'You're giving up a great job on the basis of a feeling that is indefinable, notoriously unpredictable and invariably short-lived so yes, I suppose I am saying that.' She nibbled her lip. 'It's the truth, so you can hardly be offended. You've said it yourself often enough.'

'That was before I met Trish and discovered how wrong I was.' He shook his head and gave a wry smile. 'You just haven't met the right person. When you do, everything will make sense.'

'Everything already makes perfect sense, thank you.' She reached for a piece of paper and a pen. 'If I draft an advert now, I just might find a locum for August.'

If she was lucky.

And if she wasn't lucky, she was in for a busy summer, she thought, her logical brain already involved in making lists. The village with its pretty harbour and quaint shops might not attract the medical profession but it attracted tourists by the busload and her work increased accordingly, especially during the summer months.

David frowned. 'Locum?' His brow cleared. 'You don't need to worry about a locum. I've sorted that out.'

Her pen stilled. 'You've sorted it out?'

'Of course.' He rummaged in his pocket and pulled out several crumpled sheets of paper. 'Did you really think I'd leave you without arranging a replacement?'

Yes, she'd thought exactly that. All the people she'd ever known who'd claimed to be 'in love' had immediately ceased to give any thought or show any care to those around them.

'Who?'

'I have a friend who is eager to work in England. His qualifications are fantastic—he trained as a plastic surgeon but had to switch because he had an accident. Tragedy, actually.' David frowned slightly. 'He was brilliant, by all accounts.'

A plastic surgeon?

Alice reached for the papers and scanned the CV. 'Giovanni Moretti.' She looked up. 'He's Italian?'

'Sicilian.' David grinned. 'Never accuse him of being Italian. He's very proud of his heritage.'

'This man is well qualified.' She put the papers down on her desk. 'Why would he want to come here?'

'You want to work here,' David pointed out logically, 'so perhaps you're just about to meet your soulmate.' He caught her reproving look and shrugged. 'Just joking. Everyone is entitled to a change of pace. He was working in Milan, which might explain it but, to be honest, I don't really know why he wants to come here. You know us men. We don't delve into details.'

Alice sighed and glanced at the CV on her desk. He'd probably only last five minutes, but at least he might fill the gap while she looked for someone to cover the rest of the summer.

'Well, at least you've sorted out a replacement. Thanks for that. And what happens at the end of the summer? Are you coming back?'

David hesitated. 'Can we see how it goes? Trish and I have some big decisions to make.' His eyes gleamed at the prospect. 'But I promise not to leave you in the lurch.'

He looked so happy, Alice couldn't help but smile. 'I wish you luck.'

'But you don't understand, do you?'

She shrugged. 'If you ask me, the ability to be ruled by emotion is the only serious flaw in the human make-up.'

'Oh, for goodness' sake.' Unexpectedly, David reached out and dragged her to her feet. 'It's out there, Alice. Love. You just have to look for it.'

'Why would I want to? If you want my honest opinion, I'd say that love is just a temporary psychiatric condition that passes given sufficient time. Hence the high divorce rate.' She pulled her hands away from his, aware that he was gaping at her.

'*A temporary psychiatric condition?*' He gave a choked laugh and his hands fell to his sides. 'Oh, Alice, you *have* to be joking. That can't really be what you believe.'

Alice tilted her head to one side and mentally reviewed all the people she knew who'd behaved oddly in the name of love. There were all too many of them. Her parents and her sister included. 'Yes, actually.' Her tone was flat as she struggled with feelings that she'd managed to suppress for years. Feeling suddenly agitated, she picked up a medical journal and scanned the contents, trying to focus her mind on fact. Facts were safe and comfortable. Emotions were dangerous and uncomfortable. 'It's exactly what I believe.'

Her heart started to beat faster and she gripped the journal more tightly and reminded herself that her life was under her control now. She was no longer a child at the mercy of other people's emotional transgressions.

David watched her. 'So you still don't believe love exists? Even seeing how happy I am?'

She turned. 'If you're talking about some fuzzy, indefinable emotion that links two people together then, no, I don't think that exists. I don't believe in the existence of an indefinable emotional bond any more than I believe in Father Christmas and the tooth fairy.'

David shook his head in disbelief. 'But I *do* feel a powerful emotion.'

She couldn't bring herself to put a dent in his happiness by saying more, so she stepped towards him and took his face in her hands. 'I'm pleased for you. Really I am.' She reached up and kissed him on the cheek. 'But it isn't "love".' She sat back down and David studied her with a knowing, slightly superior smile on his face.

'It's going to happen to you, Alice.' He folded his arms across his chest and his tone rang with conviction. 'One of these days you're going to be swept off your feet.'

'I'm a scientist,' she reminded him, amusement sparkling in her blue eyes as they met the challenge in his. 'I have a logical brain. I don't believe in being swept off my feet.'

He stared at her for a long moment. 'No. Which is why it's likely to happen. Love strikes when you're not looking for it.'

'That's measles,' Alice said dryly, reaching for a pile of results that needed her attention. 'Talking of which, little Fiona Ellis has been terribly poorly since her bout of measles last winter. I'm going to check up on her today. See if there's anything else we can do. And I'm going to speak to Gina, the health visitor, about our MMR rates.'

'They dipped slightly after the last newspaper scare but I thought they were up again. The hospital has been keeping an eye on Fiona's hearing,' David observed, and Alice nodded.

'Yes, and I gather there's been some improvement. All the same, the family need support and we need to make sure that no one else in our practice suffers unnecessarily.' She rose to her feet and smiled at her partner. 'And that's what we give in a small community. Support and individual care. Don't you think you'll miss that? In London you'll end up working in one of those huge health centres with thousands of doctors and you probably won't get to see the same patient twice. You won't know them and they won't know you. It will be completely impersonal. Like seeing medical cases on a production line.'

She knew all the arguments, of course. She understood that a large group of GPs working together could afford a wider variety of services for their patients—psychologists, chiropodists—but she still believed that a good family doctor who knew his patients intimately was able to provide a superior level of care.

'You'll like Gio,' David said, strolling towards the door. 'Women always do.'

'As long as he does his job,' Alice said crisply, 'I'll like him.'

'He's generally considered a heartthrob.' There was a speculative look on his face as he glanced towards her. 'Women go weak at the knees when he walks into a room.'

Great. The last thing she needed was a Romeo who was distracted by everything female.

'Some women are foolish like that.' Alice stood up and reached for her jacket. 'Just as long as he doesn't break more hearts than he heals, then I really don't mind what he does when he isn't working here.'

'There's more to life than work, Alice.'

'Then go out there and enjoy it,' she advised, a smile on her face. 'And leave me to enjoy mine.'

CHAPTER ONE

GIOVANNI MORETTI stood at the top of the narrow cobbled street, flexed his broad shoulders to try and ease the tension from the journey and breathed in the fresh, clean sea air. Above him, seagulls shrieked and swooped in the hope of benefiting from the early morning catch.

Sounds of the sea.

He paused for a moment, his fingers tucked into the pockets of his faded jeans, his dark eyes slightly narrowed as he scanned the pretty painted cottages that led down to the busy harbour. Window-boxes and terracotta pots were crammed full with brightly coloured geraniums and tumbling lobelia and a smile touched his handsome face. Before today he'd thought that places like this existed only in the imagination of artists. It was as far from the dusty, traffic-clogged streets of Milan as it was possible to be, and he felt a welcome feeling of calm wash over him.

He'd been right to agree to take this job, he mused silently, remembering all the arguments he'd been presented with. Right to choose this moment to slow the pace of his life and leave Italy.

It was early in the morning but warm, tempting smells of baking flavoured the air and already the street seemed alive with activity.

A few people in flip-flops and shorts, who he took to be tourists, meandered down towards the harbour in search of early morning entertainment while others jostled each other in their eagerness to join the queue in the bakery and emerged clutching bags of hot, fragrant croissants and rolls.

His own stomach rumbled and he reminded himself that he hadn't eaten anything since he'd left Milan the night before. Fast food had never interested him. He preferred to wait for the real thing. And the bakery looked like the real thing.

He needed a shower and a shave but there was no chance of that until he'd picked up the key to his accommodation and he doubted his new partner was even in the surgery yet. He glanced at his watch and decided that he just about had time to eat something and still time his arrival to see her just before she started work.

He strolled into the bakery and smiled at the pretty girl behind the counter. '*Buongiorno*—good morning.'

She glanced up and caught the smile. Her blue eyes widened in feminine appreciation. 'Hello. What can I offer you?'

It was obvious from the look in those eyes that she was prepared to offer him the moon but Gio ignored the mute invitation he saw in her eyes and studied the pastries on offer, accustomed to keeping women at a polite distance. He'd always been choosy when it came to women. Too choosy, some might say. 'What's good?'

'Oh—well...' The girl lifted a hand to her face, her

cheeks suddenly pink. 'The *pain au chocolat* is my favourite but the almond croissant is our biggest seller. Take away or eat in?'

For the first time Gio noticed the small round tables covered in cheerful blue gingham, positioned by the window at the back of the shop. 'Eat in.' It was still so early he doubted that his partner had even reached the surgery yet. 'I'll take an almond croissant and a double espresso. *Grazie.*'

He selected the table with the best view over the harbour. The coffee turned out to be exceptionally good, the croissant wickedly sweet, and by the time he'd finished the last of his breakfast he'd decided that spending the summer in this quaint little village was going to be no hardship at all.

'Are you on holiday?' The girl on the till was putting croissants into bags faster than the chef could take them from the oven and still the queue didn't seem to diminish.

Gio dug his hand into his pocket and paid the bill. 'Not on holiday.' Although a holiday would have been welcome, he mused, his eyes still on the boats bobbing in the harbour. 'I'm working.'

'Working?' She handed him change. 'Where?'

'Here. I'm a doctor. A GP, to be precise.' It still felt strange to him to call himself that. For years he'd been a surgeon and he still considered himself to be a surgeon. But fate had decreed otherwise.

'You're our new doctor?'

He nodded, aware that after driving through the night he didn't exactly look the part. He could have been evasive, of course, but his new role in the community was hardly likely to remain a secret for long in a place this small. And, anyway, he didn't believe in being evasive. What was the harm in announcing himself? 'Having told you that, I might as well take advantage of your local knowledge. How does Dr Anderson take her coffee?'

All that he knew about his new partner was what David had shared in their brief phone conversation. He knew that she was married to her job, very academic and extremely serious. Already he'd formed an image of her in his mind. Tweed skirt, flat heels, horn-rimmed glasses—he knew the type. Had met plenty like her in medical school.

'Dr Anderson? That's easy.' The girl smiled, her eyes fixed on his face in a kind of trance. 'Same as you. Strong and black.'

'Ah.' His new partner was obviously a woman of taste. 'And what does she eat?'

The girl continued to gaze at him and then seemed to shake herself. 'Eat? Actually, I've never seen her eat anything.' She shrugged. 'Between the tourists and the locals, we probably keep her too busy to give her time to eat. Or maybe she isn't that interested in food.'

Gio winced and hoped it was the former. He couldn't imagine developing a good working partnership with someone who wasn't interested in food. 'In that case, I'll play it safe and take her a large Americano.' Time enough to persuade her of the benefits of eating. 'So the next thing you can do is direct me to the surgery. Or maybe Dr Anderson won't be there yet.'

It wasn't even eight o'clock.

Perhaps she slept late, or maybe—

'Follow the street right down to the harbour and it's

straight in front of you. Blue door. And she'll be there.' The girl pressed a cap onto the coffee-cup. 'She was up half the night with the Bennetts' six-year-old. Asthma attack.'

Gio lifted an eyebrow. 'You know that?'

The girl shrugged and blew a strand of hair out of her eyes. 'Around here, everyone knows everything.' She handed him the coffee and his change. 'Word gets around.'

'So maybe she's having a lie-in.'

The girl looked at the clock. 'I doubt it. Dr Anderson doesn't sleep much and, anyway, surgery starts soon.'

Gio digested that piece of information with interest. If she worked that hard, no wonder she took her coffee strong and black.

With a parting smile at the girl he left the bakery and followed her instructions, enjoying the brief walk down the steep cobbled street, glancing into shop windows as he passed.

The harbour was bigger than he'd expected, crowded with boats that bobbed and danced under the soft seduction of the sea. Tall masts clinked in the soft breeze and across the harbour he saw a row of shops and a blue door with a brass nameplate. The surgery.

A few minutes later he pushed open the surgery door and blinked in surprise. What had promised to be a small, cramped building proved to be light, airy and spacious. Somehow he'd expected something entirely different—somewhere dark and tired, like some of the surgeries he'd visited in London. What he hadn't expected was this bright, calming environment designed to soothe and relax.

Above his head glass panels threw light across a neat waiting room and on the far side of the room a children's corner overflowed with an abundance of toys in bright primary colours. A table in a glaring, cheerful red was laid with pens and sheets of paper to occupy busy hands.

On the walls posters encouraged patients to give up smoking and have their blood pressure checked and there were leaflets on first aid and adverts for various local clinics.

It seemed that nothing had been forgotten.

Gio was just studying a poster in greater depth when he noticed the receptionist.

She was bent over the curved desk, half-hidden from view as she sifted through a pile of results. Her honey blonde hair fell to her shoulders and her skin was creamy smooth and untouched by sun. She was impossibly slim, wore no make-up and the shadows under her eyes suggested that she worked harder than she should. She looked fragile, tired and very young.

Gio's eyes narrowed in an instinctively masculine assessment.

She was beautiful, he decided, and as English as scones and cream. His eyes rested on her cheekbones and then dropped to her perfectly shaped, soft mouth. He found himself thinking of summer fruit—strawberries, raspberries, redcurrants…

Something flickered to life inside him.

The girl was so absorbed in what she was reading that she hadn't even noticed him and he was just about to step forward and introduce himself when the surgery door swung open again and a group of teenage boys stumbled in, swearing and laughing.

They didn't notice him. In fact, they seemed incapable of noticing anyone, they were so drunk.

Gio stood still, sensing trouble. His dark eyes were suddenly watchful and he set the coffee down on the nearest table just in case he was going to need his hands.

One of them swore fluently as he crashed into a low table and sent magazines flying across the floor. 'Where the hell's the doctor in this place? Matt's bleeding.'

The friend in question lurched forward, blood streaming from a cut on his head. His chest was bare and he wore a pair of surf shorts, damp from the sea and bloodstained. 'Went surfing.' He gave a hiccup and tried to stand up without support but failed. Instead he slumped against his friend with a groan, his eyes closed. 'Feel sick.'

'Surfing when you're drunk is never the best idea.' The girl behind the desk straightened and looked them over with weary acceptance. Clearly it wasn't the first time she'd had drunks in the surgery. 'Sit him down over there and I'll take a look at it.'

'You?' The third teenager swaggered across the room, fingers tucked into the pockets of his jeans. He gave a suggestive wink. 'I'm Jack. How about taking a look at me while you're at it?' He leaned across the desk, leering. 'There are bits of me you might be interested in. You a nurse? You ever wear one of those blue outfits with a short skirt and stockings?'

'I'm the doctor.' The girl's eyes were cool as she pulled on a pair of disposable gloves and walked round the desk without giving Jack a second glance. 'Sit your friend down before he falls down and does himself more damage. I'll take a quick look at him before I start surgery.'

Gio didn't know who was more surprised—him or the teenagers.

She was the doctor?

She was Alice Anderson?

He ran a hand over the back of his neck and wondered why David had omitted to mention that his new partner was stunning. He tried to match up David's description of a serious, academic woman with this slender, delicate beauty standing in front of him, and failed dismally. He realised suddenly that he'd taken 'single' to mean 'mature'. And 'academic' to mean 'dowdy'.

'*You're* the doctor?' Jack lurched towards her, his gait so unsteady that he could barely stand. 'Well, that's good news. I love a woman with brains and looks. You and I could make a perfect team, babe.'

She didn't spare him a glance, refusing to respond to the banter. 'Sit your friend down.' Her tone was firm and the injured boy collapsed onto the nearest chair with a groan.

'I'll sit myself down. Oh, man, my head is killing me.'

'That's what happens when you drink all night and then bang your head.' Efficient and businesslike, she pushed up the sleeves of her plain blue top, tilted his head and took a look at the cut. She parted the boy's hair gently and probed with her fingers. Her mouth tightened. 'Well, you've done a good job of that. Were you knocked out?'

Gio cast a professional eye over the cut and saw immediately that it wasn't going to be straightforward. Surely she wasn't planning to stitch that herself? He could see ragged edges and knew it was going to be difficult to get a good cosmetic result, even for someone skilled in that area.

'I wasn't knocked out.' The teenager tried to shake

his head and instantly winced at the pain. 'I swallowed half the ocean, though. Got any aspirin?'

'In a minute. That's a nasty cut you've got there and it's near your eye and down your cheek. It's beyond my skills, I'm afraid.' She ripped off the gloves and took a few steps backwards, a slight frown on her face as she considered the options. 'You need to go to the accident and emergency department up the coast. They'll get a surgeon to stitch you up. I'll call them and let them know that you're coming.'

'No way. We haven't got time for that.' The third teenager, who hadn't spoken up until now, stepped up to her, his expression threatening. 'You're going to do it. And you're going to do it here. Right now.'

She dropped the gloves into a bin and washed her hands. 'I'll put a dressing on it for you, but you need to go to the hospital to get it stitched. They'll do a better job than I ever could. Stitching faces is an art.'

She turned to walk back across the reception area but the teenager called Jack blocked her path.

'I've got news for you, babe.' His tone was low and insulting. 'We're not going anywhere until you've fixed Matt's face. I'm not wasting a whole day of my holiday sitting in some hospital with a load of sickos. He doesn't mind a scar. Scars are sexy. Hard. You know?'

'Whoever does it, he'll be left with a scar,' she said calmly, 'but he'll get a better result at the hospital.'

'No hospital.' The boy took a step closer and stabbed a finger into her chest. 'Are you listening to me?'

'I'm listening to you but I don't think you're listening to me.' The girl didn't flinch. 'Unless he wants to have a significant scar, that cut needs to be stitched by someone with specific skills. It's for his own good.'

It happened so quickly that no one could have anticipated it. The teenager backed her against the wall and put
a hand round her throat. 'I don't think you're listening to
me, babe. It's your bloody job, Doc. Stitch him up! *Do it.*'

Gio crossed the room in two strides, just as the
teenager uttered a howl of pain and collapsed onto the
floor in a foetal position, clutching his groin.

She'd kneed him.

'Don't try and tell me my job.' She lifted her hand to
her reddened throat. Her tone was chilly and composed
and then she glanced up, noticed Gio for the first time
and her face visibly paled. For a moment she just stared
at him and then her gaze flickered towards the door,
measuring the distance. Gio winced inwardly. It was
obvious that she thought he was trouble and he felt
slightly miffed by her reaction.

He liked women. Women liked him. And they usually
responded to him. They chatted, they flirted, they sent
him long looks. The look in Dr Anderson's eyes suggested that she was calculating ways to injure him. All
right, so he hadn't had time to shave and change, but did
he really look that scary?

He was about to introduce himself, about to try and
redeem himself in her eyes, when the third teenager
stepped towards the girl, his expression threatening. Gio
closed a hand over his arm and yanked him backwards.

'I think it's time you left. Both of you.' His tone was
icy cool and he held the boy in an iron grip. 'You can
pick up your friend in an hour.'

The teenager balled his fists, prepared to fight, but
then eyed the width of Gio's shoulders. His hands relaxed
and he gave a slight frown. 'Whazzit to do with you?'

'Everything.' Gio stepped forward so that his body was between them and Dr Anderson. 'I work here.'

'What as?' The boy twisted in his grip and his eyes slid from Gio's shoulders to the hard line of his jaw. 'A bouncer?'

'A doctor. One hour. That's how long I estimate it's going to take to make a decent job of his face. Or you can drive to the hospital.' Gio released him, aware that Alice was staring at him in disbelief. 'Your choice.'

The teenager winced and rubbed his arm. 'She…' he jerked his head towards the doctor '…said he needed a specialist doctor.'

'Well, this is your lucky day, because I am a specialist doctor.'

There was a long pause while the teenager tried to focus. 'You don't look anything like a doctor. Doctors shave and dress smart. You look more like one of those— those…' His words slurred and he swayed and waved a hand vaguely. 'Those Mafia thugs that you see in films.'

'Then you'd better behave yourself,' Gio suggested silkily, casting a glance towards his new partner to check she was all right. Her pallor was worrying him. He hoped she wasn't about to pass out. 'Leave now and come back in an hour for your friend.'

'You're not English.' The boy hiccoughed. 'What are you, then? Italian?'

'I'm Sicilian.' Gio's eyes were cold. '*Never* call me Italian.'

'Sicilian?' A nervous respect entered the teenager's eyes and he licked his lips and eyed the door. 'OK.' He gave a casual shrug. 'So maybe we'll come back later, like you suggested.'

Gio nodded. 'Good decision.'

The boy backed away, still rubbing his arm. 'We're going. C'mon, Rick.' He loped over to the door and left without a backward glance.

'*Dios,* did he hurt you?' Gio walked over to the girl and lifted a hand to her neck. The skin was slightly reddened and he stroked a finger carefully over the bruising with a frown. 'We should call the police now.'

She shook her head and backed away. 'No need. He didn't hurt me.' She glanced towards the teenager who was still sprawled over the seats of her waiting room and gave a wry shake of her head. 'If you're Dr Moretti, we'd better see to him before he's sick on the floor or bleeds to death over my chairs.'

'It won't hurt him to wait for two minutes. You should call the police.' Gio's tone was firm. He didn't want to be too graphic about what might have happened, but it was important that she acknowledge the danger. It hadn't escaped him that if he hadn't decided to arrive at the surgery early, she would have been on her own with them. 'You should call them.'

She rubbed her neck. 'I suppose you're right. All right, I'll do it when I get a minute.'

'Does this happen often? I imagined I was coming to a quiet seaside village. Not some hotbed of violence.'

'There's nothing quiet about this place, at least not in the middle of summer,' she said wearily. 'We're the only doctors' surgery in this part of the town and the nearest A and E is twenty miles down the coast so, yes, we get our fair share of drama. David probably didn't tell you that when he was persuading you to take the job. You can leave now, if you like.'

His eyes rested on her soft mouth. 'I'm not leaving.'

There was a brief silence. A silence during which she stared back at him. Then she licked her lips. 'Well, that's good news for my patients. And good news for me. I'm glad you arrived when you did.'

'You didn't look glad.'

'Well, a girl can't be too careful and you don't exactly look like a doctor.' A hint of a smile touched that perfect mouth. 'Did you see his face when you said you were Sicilian? I think they were expecting you to put a hand in your jacket and shoot them dead any moment.'

'I considered it.' Gio's eyes gleamed with humour. 'But I've only had one cup of coffee so far today. Generally I need at least two before I shoot people dead. And you don't need to apologise for the mistake. I confess that I thought you were the receptionist. If you're Alice Anderson, you're nothing like David's description.'

'I can imagine.' She spoke in a tone of weary acceptance. 'David is seeing the world through a romantic haze at the moment. Be patient with him. It will pass, given time.'

He laughed. 'You think so?'

'Love always does, Dr Moretti. Like many viruses, it's a self-limiting condition. Left alone, the body can cure itself.'

Gio searched her face to see if she was joking and decided that she wasn't. Filing the information away in his brain for later use, he walked over to retrieve the coffee from the window-sill. 'If you're truly Dr Anderson, this is for you. An ice breaker, from me.'

She stared at the coffee with sudden hunger in her eyes and then at him. 'You brought coffee?' Judging from the expression on her face, he might have offered her an expensive bauble from Tiffany's. She lifted a hand and brushed a strand of hair out of her eyes. Tired eyes. 'For me? Is it black?'

'*Si.*' He smiled easily and handed her the coffee, amused by her response. 'You have fans in the bakery who know every detail of your dietary preferences. I was told "just coffee" so I passed on the croissant.'

'There's no such thing as "just coffee". Coffee is wonderful. It's my only vice and currently I'm in desperate need of a caffeine hit.' She prised the lid off the coffee, sniffed and gave a whimper of pleasure. 'Large Americano. Oh, that's just the best smell…'

He watched as she sipped, closed her eyes and savoured the taste. She gave a tiny moan of appreciation that sent a flicker of awareness through his body. He gave a slight frown at the strength of his reaction.

'So…' She studied him for a moment and then took another sip of coffee. Some of the colour returned to her cheeks. 'I wasn't expecting you until tomorrow. Not that I'm complaining, you understand. I'm glad you're early. You were just in time to save me from a nasty situation.'

'I prefer to drive when the roads are clear. I thought you might appreciate the help, given that David has already been gone two days. We haven't been formally introduced. I'm Gio Moretti.' He wanted to hold her until she stopped shaking but he sensed that she wouldn't appreciate the gesture so he kept his distance. 'I'm your new partner.'

She hesitated and then put her free hand in his. 'Alice Anderson.'

'I gathered that. You're really *not* what I expected.'

She tilted her head to one side. 'You're standing in my surgery having frightened off two teenage thugs by your appearance and you're telling me *I'm* not what *you* expected?' There was a hint of humour in her blue eyes and his attention was caught by the length of her lashes.

'So maybe I don't fit anyone's image of a conventional doctor right at this moment...' he dragged his gaze away from her face and glanced down at himself with a rueful smile '...but I've been travelling all night and I'm dressed for comfort. After a shave and a quick change of clothes, I will be ready to impress your patients. But first show me to a room and I'll stitch that boy before his friends return.'

'Are you sure?' She frowned slightly. 'I mean, David told me you didn't operate any more and—'

'I don't operate.' He waited for the usual feelings to rise up inside him. Waited for the frustration and the sick disappointment. Nothing happened. Maybe he was just tired. Or maybe he'd made progress. 'I don't operate, but I can certainly stitch up a face.'

'Then I'm very grateful and I'm certainly not going to argue with you. That wound is beyond my skills and I've got a full surgery starting in ten minutes.' She looked at the teenager who was sprawled across the chairs, eyes closed, and sighed. 'Oh, joy. Is it alcohol or a bang on the head, do you think?'

'Hard to tell.' Gio followed her gaze and shook his head slowly. 'I'll stitch him up, do a neurological assessment and then we'll see. Is there anyone who can help me? Show me around? I can give you a list of what I'll need.'

'Rita, our practice nurse, will be here in a minute. She's very experienced. Her asthma clinic doesn't start until ten so I'll send her in.' Her eyes slid over him. 'Are you sure you're all right with this? We weren't expecting you until tomorrow and if you've been travelling all night you must be tired.'

'I'm fine.' He studied her carefully, noting the dark shadows under her eyes. 'In fact, I'd say that you're the one who's tired, Dr Anderson.'

She gave a dismissive shrug. 'Goes with the job. I'll show you where you can work. We have a separate room for minor surgery. I think you'll find everything you need but I can't be sure. We don't usually stitch faces.'

He followed her down the corridor, his eyes drawn to the gentle swing of her hips. 'Do you have 5/0 Ethilon?'

'Yes.' She pushed open a door and held it open while he walked inside. 'Is that all you need?'

'The really important thing is to debride the wound and align the tissues exactly. And not leave the stitches in for too long.'

Her glance was interested. Intelligent. 'I wish I had time to watch you. Not that I'm about to start suturing faces,' she assured him hastily, and he smiled.

'Like most things, it's just a question of practice.'

She opened a cupboard. 'Stitches are in here. Gloves on the shelf. You're probably about the same size as David. Tetanus et cetera in the fridge.' She waved a hand. 'I'll send Rita in with the patient. I'll get on with surgery. Come and find me when you've finished.'

'Alice.' He stopped her before she walked out of the door. 'Don't forget to call the police.'

She tilted her head back and he sensed that she was wrestling with what seemed like a major inconvenience then she gave a resigned sigh.

'I'll do that.'

CHAPTER TWO

ALICE spoke to Rita, called the police and then worked flat out, seeing patients, with no time to even think about checking on her new partner.

'How long have you had this rash on your eye, Mr Denny?' As she saw her tenth patient of the morning, she thought gratefully of the cup of coffee that Gio Moretti had thought to bring her. It was the only sustenance she'd had all day.

'It started with a bit of pain and tingling. Then it all went numb.' The man sat still as she examined him. 'I suppose all that began on Saturday. My wife noticed the rash yesterday. She was worried because it looks blistered. We wondered if I'd brushed up against something in the garden. You know how it is with some of those plants.'

Alice picked up her ophthalmoscope and examined his eye thoroughly. 'I don't think it's anything to do with the garden, Mr Denny. You've got quite a discharge from your eye.'

'It's very sore.'

'I'm sure it is.' Alice put the ophthalmoscope down on her desk and washed her hands. 'I want to test your vision. Can you read the letters for me?'

The man squinted at the chart on her wall and struggled to recite the letters. 'Not very clear, I'm afraid.' He looked worried. 'My eyes have always been good. Am I losing my sight?'

'You have a virus.' Alice sat down and tapped something into her computer. Then she turned back to the patient. 'I think you have shingles, Mr Denny.'

'Shingles?' He frowned. 'In my eye?'

'Shingles is a virus that affects the nerves,' she explained, 'and one in five cases occur in the eye—to be technical, it's the ophthalmic branch of the trigeminal nerve.'

He pulled a face. 'Never was much good at biology.'

Alice smiled. 'You don't need biology, Mr Denny. But I just wanted you to know it isn't uncommon, unfortunately. I'm going to need to refer you to an ophthalmologist—an eye doctor at the hospital. Is there someone who can take you up there?'

He nodded. 'My daughter's waiting in the car park. She brought me here.'

'Good.' Alice reached for the phone and dialled the clinic number. 'They'll see you within the next couple of days.'

'Do I really need to go there?'

Alice nodded. 'They need to examine your eye with a slit lamp—a special piece of equipment that allows them to look at your eye properly. They need to exclude iritis. In the meantime, I'll give you aciclovir to take five times a day for a week. It should speed up healing time and reduce the incidence of new lesions.' She printed out the prescription on the computer as she waited for the hospital to answer the phone.

Once she'd spoken to the consultant, she quickly

wrote a letter and gave it to the patient. 'They're really nice up there,' she assured him, 'but if you have any worries you're welcome to come back to me.'

He left the room and Alice picked up a set of results. She was studying the numbers with a puzzled frown when Rita walked in. A motherly woman in her early fifties, her navy blue uniform was stretched over her large bosom and there was a far-away expression on her face. 'Pinch me. Go on, pinch me hard. I've died and gone to heaven.'

Alice looked up. 'Rita, have you seen Mrs Frank lately? I ran some tests but the results just don't make sense.' She'd examined the patient carefully and had been expecting something entirely different. She studied the results again. Perhaps she'd missed something.

'Forget Mrs Frank's results for a moment.' Rita closed the door behind her. 'I've got something far more important for you to think about.'

Alice didn't look up. 'I thought she had hypothyroidism. She had all the symptoms.'

'Alice…'

Still absorbed in the problem, Alice shook her head. 'The results are normal.' She checked the results one more time and checked the normal values, just in case she'd missed something. She'd been so *sure*.

'*Alice!*' Rita sounded exasperated. 'Are you even listening to me?'

Alice dragged her eyes away from the piece of paper in her hand, still pondering. Aware that Rita was glaring at her, she gave a faint smile. 'Sorry, I'm still thinking about Mrs Frank,' she admitted apologetically. 'What's the matter?'

'Dr Giovanni Moretti is the matter.'

'Oh, my goodness!' Alice slapped her hand over her mouth and rose to her feet quickly, ridden with guilt. 'I'd *totally* forgotten about him. How could I?'

Rita stared at her. 'How could you, indeed?'

'Don't! I feel terrible about it.' Guilt consumed her. And after he'd been so helpful. 'How could I have done that? I showed him into the room, made sure he had what he needed and I *promised* to look in on him, but I've had streams of patients this morning and I completely forgot his existence.'

'You forgot his existence?' Rita shook her head. 'Alice, how could you *possibly* have forgotten his existence?'

'I know, it's dreadful! I feel terribly rude.' She walked briskly round her desk, determined to make amends. 'I'll go and check on him immediately. Hopefully, if he'd needed any help he would have come and found me.'

'Help?' Rita's tone was dry. 'Trust me, Alice, the guy doesn't need any help from you or anyone else. He's slick. Mr Hotshot. Or I suppose I should call him Dr Hotshot.'

'He's finished stitching the boy?' She glanced at her watch for the first time since she'd started surgery and realised with a shock that almost an hour and a half had passed.

'Just the head, although personally I would have been happy to see him do the mouth as well.' Rita gave a snort of disapproval. 'Never heard such obscenities.'

'Yes, they were pretty drunk, the three of them. How does the head look?'

'Better than that boy deserves. Never seen a job as neat in my life and I've been nursing for thirty years,'

Rita admitted, a dreamy expression on her face. 'Dr Moretti has *amazing* hands.'

'He used to be a surgeon. If he's done a good job and he's finished, why did you come rushing in here telling me he was having problems?'

'I never said he was having problems.'

'You said something was the matter.'

'No.' Rita closed her eyes and sighed. 'At least, not with him. Only with me. I think he's fantastic.'

'Oh.' Alice paused by the door. 'Well, he arrived a day early, brought me coffee first thing, sorted out a bunch of rowdy teenagers and stitched a nasty cut so, yes, I think he's fantastic, too. He's obviously a good doctor.'

'I'm not talking about his medical skills, Alice.'

'What are you talking about, then?'

'Alice, he's *gorgeous*. Don't tell me you haven't noticed!'

'Actually, I thought he looked a mess.' Her hand dropped from the doorhandle and she frowned at the recollection. 'But he'd been travelling all night.'

'A mess?' Rita sounded faint. 'You think he looks a *mess?*'

Alice wondered whether to confess that she'd thought he looked dangerous. Strangely enough, the teenagers hadn't bothered her. They were nothing more than gawky children and she'd had no doubts about her ability to handle them. But when she'd looked up and seen Gio standing there...

'I'm sure he'll look more respectable when he's had a shower and a shave.' Alice frowned. 'And possibly a haircut. The boy was in such a state, I didn't think it mattered.'

'You didn't even notice, did you?' Rita shook her head in disbelief. 'Alice, you need to do something about your life. The man is sex on a stick. He's a walking female fantasy.'

Alice stared at her blankly, struggling to understand. 'Rita, you've been married for twenty years and, anyway, he's far too young for you.'

Rita gave her a suggestive wink. 'Don't you believe it. I like them young and vigorous.'

Alice sighed and wished she didn't feel so completely out of step with the rest of her sex. Was she the only woman in the world who didn't spend her whole life thinking about men? Even Rita was susceptible, even though she'd reached an age where she should have grown out of such stupidity.

'He doesn't look much like a doctor,' she said frankly, 'but I'm sure he'll look better once he's shaved and changed his clothes.'

'He looks every inch a man. And he'd be perfect for you.'

Alice froze. 'I refuse to have this conversation with you again, Rita. And while we're at it, you can tell that receptionist of ours that I'm not having it with her either.'

Rita sniffed. 'Mary worries about you, as I do, and—'

'I'm not interested in men and both of you know that.'

'Well, you should be.' Rita folded her arms and her mouth clamped into a thin line. 'You're thirty years of age and—'

'Rita!' Alice interrupted her sharply. 'This is not a good time.'

'It's never a good time with you. You never talk about it.'

'Because there's nothing to talk about!' Alice took a deep breath. 'I appreciate your concern, really, but—'

'But you're married to your work and that's the way you're staying.' The older woman rose to her feet and Alice sighed.

'I'm happy, Rita.' Her voice softened slightly as she saw the worry in the older woman's face. 'Really I am. I like my life the way it is.'

'Empty, you mean.'

'Empty?' Alice laughed and stroked blonde hair away from her face. 'Rita, I'm so busy I don't have time to turn round. My life certainly isn't empty.'

Rita pursed her lips. 'You're talking about work and work isn't enough for anybody. A woman needs a social life. A man. Sex.'

Alice glanced pointedly at her watch. 'Was there anything else you wanted to talk about? I've got a surgery full of patients, Rita.'

And she was exhausted, hungry and thirsty and fed up with talking about subjects that didn't interest her.

'All right. I can take a hint. But the subject isn't closed.' Rita walked to the door. 'Actually, I did come to ask you something. Although he doesn't need your help, Gio wants two minutes to discuss the boy with you before he sends him out. Oh, and the police are here.'

Alice stood up and removed a bottle of water from the fridge in her consulting room. She couldn't do anything about the hunger, but at least she could drink. 'I don't have time for them right now.'

'If what Gio told me is correct, you're going to make time.' Suddenly Rita was all business. 'They can't go round behaving like that. And you need to lock the door behind you if you come in early in the morning. You might have been the only person in the building. You were careless. Up half the night with the little Bennett girl and not getting enough sleep as usual, no doubt.'

'Rita—'

'You'll tell me I'm nagging but I worry about you, that's all. I care about you.'

'I know you do.' Alice curled her hands into fists, uncomfortable with the conversation. Another person—*a different person to her*—would have swept across to Rita and given her a big hug, but Alice could no more do that than fly. Touching wasn't part of her nature. 'I know you care.'

'Good.' Rita gave a sniff. 'Now, drink your water before you die of dehydration and then go and see Gio. And this time take a closer look. You might like what you see.'

Alice walked back to her desk and poured water into a glass. 'All right, I'll speak to Gio then I'll see the police. Ask Mary to give them a coffee and put them in one of the empty rooms. Then see if she can placate the remaining patients. Tell them I'll be with them as soon as possible.' She paused to drink the water she'd poured and then set the glass on her desk. 'Goodness knows if I'll get through them all in time to do any house calls.'

'Gio is going to help you see the patients once he's discharged the boy. For goodness' sake, don't say no. It's like the first day of the summer sales in the waiting room. If he helps then we might all stand a chance of getting some lunch.'

'The letting agent is dropping the keys to his flat round here. He needs to get settled in. He needs to rest after the journey and shave the designer stubble—'

'Any fool can see he's a man with stamina and I don't see his appearance hampering his ability to see patients,' Rita observed, with impeccable logic. 'We're just ensuring that the surgery is going to be crammed for weeks to come.'

'Why's that?'

'Because he's too gorgeous for his own good and all the women in the practice are going to want to come and stare.'

Alice opened the door. 'What exactly is it about men that turns normally sane women into idiots?' she wondered out loud, and Rita grinned.

'Whoever said I was sane?'

With an exasperated shake of her head, Alice walked along the corridor and pushed open the door of the room they used for minor surgery. 'Dr Moretti, I'm so sorry, I've had a steady stream of patients and I lost track of the time.'

He turned to look at her and for a brief, unsettling moment Alice remembered Rita's comment about him being a walking fantasy. He was handsome, she conceded, in an intelligent, devilish and slightly dangerous way. She could see that some women would find him attractive. Fortunately she wasn't one of them.

'No problem.' His smile came easily. 'I've just finished here. I don't need anyone to hold my hand.'

'Shame,' Rita breathed, and Alice shot her a look designed to silence.

Gio ripped off his gloves and pushed the trolley away from him. 'I think he's safe to discharge. He wasn't knocked out and his consciousness isn't impaired. Fortunately he obviously drank less than his friends. I see no indication for an X-ray or a CT scan at the moment.

He can be discharged with a head injury form.' He turned to the boy, his expression serious. 'I advise you to stay off the alcohol for a few days. If you start vomiting, feel drowsy, confused, have any visual disturbances or experience persistent headache within the next forty-eight hours, you should go to the A and E department at the hospital. Either way, you need those stitches out in four days. Don't forget and don't think it's cool to leave them in.'

The boy gave a nod and slid off the couch, his face ashen. 'Yeah. I hear you. Thanks, Doc. Are the guys outside?'

'They're having a cosy chat with the police,' Rita told him sweetly, and the boy flushed and rubbed a hand over his face.

'Man, I'm sorry about that.' He shook his head and breathed out heavily. 'They were a bit the worse for wear. We were at an all-night beach party.' He glanced sideways at Alice, his expression sheepish. 'You OK?'

She nodded. 'I'm fine.' She was busy looking at the wound. She couldn't believe how neat the sutures were.

The boy left the room, escorted by Rita.

'You did an amazing job, thank you so much.' Alice closed the door behind them and turned to Gio. 'I never would have thought that was possible. That cut looked such a mess. So many ragged edges. I wouldn't have known where to start.'

But obviously he'd known exactly where to start. Despite appearances. If she hadn't seen the results of his handiwork with her own eyes, she would still have struggled to believe that he was a doctor.

When David had described his friend, she'd imagined

a smooth, slick Italian in a designer suit. Someone safe, conservative and conventional in appearance and attitude.

There was nothing safe or conservative about Gio.

He hovered on the wrong side of respectable. His faded T-shirt was stretched over shoulders that were both broad and muscular and a pair of equally faded jeans hugged his legs. His face was deeply tanned, his jaw dark with stubble and his eyes held a hard watchfulness that suggested no small degree of life experience.

She tried to imagine him dressed in a more conventional manner, and failed.

'He'll have a scar.' Gio tipped the remains of his equipment into the nearest sharps bin. 'But some of it will be hidden by his hair. I gather from Rita that you have a very long queue out there.'

Remembering the patients, exhaustion suddenly washed over her and she sucked in a breath, wondering for a moment how she was going to get through the rest of the day. 'I need to talk to the police and then get back to work. I'm sorry I don't have time to give you a proper tour. Hopefully I can do that tomorrow, before you officially start.'

'Forget the tour.' His eyes scanned her face. 'You look done in. The girl who made your coffee told me that you were up in the night, dealing with an asthma attack. You must be ready for a rest yourself. Let's split the rest of the patients.'

She gave a wan smile. 'I can't ask you to do that. You've been travelling all night.' It occurred to her that he was the one who ought to look tired. Instead, his gaze was sharp, assessing.

'You're not asking, I'm offering. In fact, I'm insisting. If you drop dead from overwork before this afternoon, who will show me round?'

His smile had a relaxed, easy charm and she found herself responding. 'Well, if you're sure. I'll ask Mary to send David's patients through to you. If you need any help just buzz me. Lift the receiver and press 3.'

CHAPTER THREE

'WHAT a day!' Seven hours later, Gio rubbed a hand over his aching shoulder and eyed the waiting room warily. Morning surgery had extended into the afternoon well-woman clinic, which had extended into evening surgery. Even now the telephone rang incessantly, two little boys were playing noisily in the play corner and a harassed-looking woman was standing at the reception desk, wiggling a pram in an attempt to soothe a screaming baby. 'I feel as though I have seen the entire population of Cornwall in one surgery. Is it always like this?'

'No, sometimes it's busy.' Mary, the receptionist, replaced the phone once again and gave him a cheerful smile as she flicked through the box of repeat prescriptions for the waiting mother. 'Don't worry, you get used to it after a while. I could try locking the door but it would only postpone the inevitable. They'd all be back tomorrow. There we are, Mrs York.' She handed over a prescription with a flourish and adjusted her glasses more comfortably on her nose. 'How are those twins of yours doing, Harriet? Behaving themselves?'

The young woman glanced towards the boys, her

face pale. 'They're fine.' Her tone had an edge to it as she pushed the prescription into her handbag. 'Thanks.'

The baby's howls intensified and Mary stood up, clucking. She was a plump, motherly woman with curling hair a soft shade of blonde and a smiling face. Gio could see that she was dying to get her hands on the baby. 'There, now. What a fuss. Libby York, what do you think you're doing to our eardrums and your poor mother's sanity?' She walked round the reception desk, glanced at the baby's mother for permission and then scooped the baby out of the pram and rested it on her shoulder, cooing and soothing. 'Is she sleeping for you, dear?' Despite the attention, the baby continued to bawl and howl and Harriet gritted her teeth.

'Not much. She—' The young woman broke off as the boys started to scrap over a toy. 'Stop it, you two!' Her tone was sharp. 'Dan! Robert! Come here, now! Oh, for heaven's sake...' She closed her eyes and swallowed hard.

The baby continued to scream and Gio caught Mary's eye and exchanged a look of mutual understanding. 'Let me have a try.' He took the baby from her, his touch firm and confident, his voice deep and soothing as he switched to Italian. The baby stopped yelling, hiccoughed a few times and then calmed and stared up at his face in fascination.

At least one woman still found him interesting in a dishevelled state, he thought with a flash of amusement as he recalled Alice's reaction to his appearance.

Mary gave a sigh of relief and turned to Harriet. 'There. That's better. She wanted a man's strength.' She put a hand on the young mother's arm. It was a comforting touch. 'It's hard when they're this age. I remember when mine were small, there were days when I thought I'd strangle them all. It gets easier. Before you know it they're grown.'

Harriet looked at her and blinked back tears. Then she covered her mouth with her hand and shook her head. 'Sorry—oh, I'm being so stupid!' Her hand dropped and she sniffed. 'It's just that I don't know what to do with them half the time. Or what to do with me. I'm so tired I can't think straight,' she muttered, glancing towards the baby who was now calm in Gio's arms. 'This one's keeping the whole family awake. It makes us all cranky and those two are so naughty I could—' She broke off and caught her lip between her teeth. 'Anyway, as you say, it's all part of them being small. There's going to come a time when I'll wish they were little again.'

With a forced smile and a nod of thanks, she leaned across and took the baby from Gio.

'How old is the baby?' There was something about the woman that was worrying him. He didn't know her, of course, which didn't help, but still…

'She'll be seven weeks tomorrow.' Harriet jiggled the baby in her arms in an attempt to keep her calm.

'It can be very hard. My sister had her third child two months ago,' Gio said, keeping his tone casual, 'and she's certainly struggling. If the baby keeps crying, bring her to see me. Maybe there's something we can do to help.'

'Dr Moretti has taken over from Dr Watts,' Mary explained, and Harriet nodded.

'OK. Thanks. I'd better be getting back home. She needs feeding.'

'I can make you comfortable in a room here,' Mary

offered, but the woman shook her head and walked towards the door, juggling pram and baby.

'I'd better get home. I've got beds to change and washing to put out.' She called to the boys, who ignored her. 'Come on!' They still ignored her and she gave a growl of exasperation and strapped the baby back in the pram. Libby immediately started crying again. 'Yes, I know, I know! I'm getting you home right now!' She glared at the twins. 'If you don't come now I'm leaving you both here.' Her voice rose slightly and she reached out and grabbed the nearest boy by the arm. 'Do as you're told.'

They left the surgery, boys arguing, baby crying. Mary stared after them, her fingers drumming a steady rhythm on the desk. 'I don't like the look of that.'

'No.' Gio was in full agreement. There had been something about the young mother that had tugged at him. 'She looked stretched out. At her limit.'

Mary looked at him. 'You think there's something wrong with the baby?'

'No. I think there's something wrong with the mother, but I didn't want to get into a conversation that personal with a woman I don't know in the reception area. A conversation like that requires sensitivity. One wrong word and she would have run.'

'Finally. A man who thinks before he speaks...' Mary gave a sigh of approval and glanced up as Alice walked out of her consulting room, juggling two empty coffee-cups and an armful of notes.

She looked even paler than she had that morning, Gio noted, but perhaps that was hardly surprising. She'd been working flat out all day with no break.

'Did I hear a baby screaming?' She deposited the notes on the desk.

'Libby York.' Mary turned her head and stared through the glass door into the street where Harriet was still struggling with the boys. As they disappeared round the corner, she turned back with a sigh. 'You were great, Dr Moretti. Any time you want to soothe my nerves with a short spurt of Italian, don't let me stop you.'

Gio gave an apologetic shrug. 'My English doesn't run to baby talk.'

Alice frowned, her mind focused on the job. 'Why was Harriet in here?'

'Picking up a repeat prescription for her husband.' Mary's mouth tightened and her eyes suddenly clouded with worry. 'I knew that girl when she was in primary school. The smile never left her face. Look at her now and her face is grim. As if she's holding it together by a thread. As if every moment is an effort. If you ask me, she's close to the edge.'

'She has three children under the age of six. Twin boys of five. It's the summer holidays so she has them at home all day.' Alice frowned slightly. Considered. 'That's hard work by anyone's standards. Her husband is a fisherman so he works pretty long hours. Her mother died a month before the baby was born and there's no other family on the scene that I'm aware of. On top of that her delivery was difficult and she had a significant post-partum haemorrhage. She had her postnatal check at the hospital with the consultant.'

She knew her patients well, Gio thought as he watched her sifting through the facts. She was making mental lists. Looking at the evidence in front of her.

'Yes.' Mary glanced at her. 'It might be that.'

'But you don't think so?'

'You want my opinion?' Mary pressed her lips together as the telephone rang yet again. 'I think she's depressed. And Dr Moretti agrees with me.'

'A new baby is hard work.'

'That's right. It is.' Mary reached out and picked up the receiver. 'Appointments line, good afternoon.' She listened and consulted the computer for an appointment slot while Alice ran a hand through her hair and turned to Gio.

'Did she seem depressed to you?'

'Hard to be sure. She seemed stressed and tired,' he conceded, wondering whether she gave all her patients this much thought and attention when they hadn't even asked for help. If so, it was no wonder she was tired and overworked.

'I'll talk to the Gina, the health visitor, and maybe I'll call round and see her at home.'

'You haven't got time to call and see everyone at home.' Mary replaced the receiver and rejoined the conversation. 'She was David's patient, which means she's now Dr Moretti's responsibility. Let him deal with it. Chances are she'll make an appointment with him in the next couple of days. If she doesn't, well, I'll just have to nudge her along.'

To Gio's surprise, Alice nodded. 'All right. But keep an eye on her, Mary.'

'Of course.'

Alice put the cups down and lifted a journal that was lying on the desk.

She had slim hands, he noticed. Delicate. Like the rest of her. It seemed unbelievable that someone so fragile-looking could handle such a punishing workload. She glanced up and caught him looking at her. 'If you want to know anything about this town or the people in it, ask Mary or Rita. They went to school together and they've lived here all their lives. They actually qualify as locals.' She dropped the journal back on the desk and looked at Mary. 'Did the letting agent drop off Dr Moretti's keys?'

'Ah—I was building up to that piece of news.' Mary pulled a face and adjusted her glasses. 'There's a slight problem with the let that David arranged.'

'What problem?'

Mary looked vague. 'They've had a misunderstanding in the office. Some junior girl didn't realise it was being reserved for Dr Moretti and gave it away to a bunch of holidaymakers.' She frowned and waved a hand. 'French, I think.'

Alice tapped her foot on the floor and her mouth tightened. 'Then they'll just have to find him something else. Fast.' She cast an apologetic glance at Gio. 'Sorry about this. You must be exhausted.'

Not as exhausted as she was, Gio mused, wondering whether she'd eaten at all during the day. Whether she ever stopped thinking about work. At some point, Rita had produced a sandwich and an excellent cup of coffee for him but that had been hours earlier and he was ready for something more substantial to eat. And a hot bath. His shoulder was aching again.

'Not that easy.' Mary checked the notes she'd made. 'Nothing is free until September. Schools are back by then. Demand falls a bit.'

'September?' Alice stared. 'But it's still only July.'

Gio studied Mary carefully. Something didn't feel quite right. She was clearly a caring, hospitable woman. Efficient, too. And yet she seemed totally unconcerned about his apparent lack of accommodation. 'You have an alternative plan?'

'Hotels,' Alice said firmly. 'We just need to ring round and see if—'

'No hotels,' Mary said immediately, sitting back in her chair and giving a helpless shrug. 'Full to the brim. We're having a good season, tourist-wise. Betty in the newsagent reckons it's been the best July since she took over from her mother in 1970.'

'Mary.' Alice's voice was exasperated. 'I don't care about the tourists and at the moment I don't care about Betty's sales figures, but I do care about Dr Moretti having somewhere to live while he's working here! You have to do something. And you have to do it right now.'

'I'm trying a few letting agents up the coast,' Mary murmured, peering over the top of her glasses, 'but I'm getting nowhere at the moment. Might need an interim plan. I know.' Her face brightened with inspiration. 'He can stay with you. Just until I find somewhere.'

There was a long silence and something flashed in Alice's eyes. Something dangerous. 'Mary.' There was an unspoken threat in her voice but Mary waved a hand airily.

'You're rattling around in that huge house in the middle of nowhere and it isn't safe at this time of year with all those weirdos on the beach and—'

'Mary!' This time her tone was sharp and she stepped closer to the desk and lowered her voice. 'Mary, don't you dare do this. Don't you *dare*.'

'Do what?'

'Interfere.' Alice gritted her teeth. 'He can't stay with me. That isn't a solution.'

'It's a perfect solution.' Mary smiled up at her innocently and Gio saw the frustration in Alice's face and wondered.

'You've gone too far this time,' she muttered. 'You're embarrassing me and you're embarrassing Dr Moretti.'

Not in the least embarrassed, Gio watched, intrigued. He wouldn't have been at all surprised if she was going to throw a punch. It was clear that she believed that Mary had in some way orchestrated the current problem.

Adding weight to his theory, the older woman looked over the top of her glasses, her gaze innocent. *Far too innocent.* 'It's the perfect solution while I look for somewhere else. Why not?'

'Well, because I…' Alice sucked in a breath and ran a hand over the back of her neck. 'You know I don't—'

'Well, now you do.' Mary beamed, refusing to back down. 'It's temporary, Alice. As a favour to the community. Can't have our new doctor sleeping rough in the gutter, can we? Are you ready to go, Rita?' She stood up as the practice nurse walked into reception. 'What a day. I'm going to pour myself a large glass of wine and put my feet up. Can we call in at Betty's on the way? I need to pick up a local paper. See you in the morning. Oh, and by the way…' She turned to Gio with a wink. 'I suggest you order a take-away for dinner. Our Dr Anderson is a whiz with patients but the kitchen isn't her forte.'

They left with a wave and Gio watched as Alice's hands clenched and unclenched by her sides.

He broke the tense silence. 'You look as though you're looking for someone to thump.'

She turned and blinked, almost as if she'd forgotten his existence. As if he wasn't part of her problem. 'Tell me something.' Her voice was tight. 'Is it really possible to admire and respect someone and yet want to strangle them at the same time?'

He thought of his sisters and nodded. 'Definitely.'

He noticed that she didn't use the word 'love' although it had taken him less than five minutes to detect the warmth and affection running between the three women.

'I want to be so *angry* with the pair of them.' Her hand sliced through the air and the movement encouraged wisps of her hair to drift over her eyes. 'But how can I when I know—' she broke off and let out a long breath, struggling for control. 'This isn't anything to do with you. What I mean is…' Her tone was suddenly tight and formal, her smile forced, 'you must think I'm incredibly rude, but that wasn't my intention. It's just that you've stepped into the middle of something that's been going on for a long time and—'

'And you don't like being set up with the first available guy who happens to walk through the door?'

Her blue eyes flew to his, startled. 'It's that obvious? Oh, this is so embarrassing.'

'Not embarrassing.' He watched as the colour flooded into her cheeks. 'But interesting. Why do your colleagues feel the need to interfere with your love life?'

She was a beautiful woman. He knew enough about men to know that a woman like her could have the male sex swarming around her without any assistance whatsoever.

She paced the length of the waiting room and back again, working off tension. 'Because people have a stereotypical view of life,' she said, her tone ringing with exasperation. 'If you're not with a man, you must want to be. Secretly you must long to be married and have eight children and a dog. And if you're not, you're viewed as some sort of freak.'

Gio winced. 'Eight is definitely too many.' He was pleased to see a glimmer of humour in her eyes.

'You think so?'

'Trust me.' He tried to coax the smile still wider. Suddenly he wanted to see her smile. Really smile. 'I am one of six and the queue for the bathroom was un-believable. And the battle at the meal table was nothing short of ugly.'

The smile was worth waiting for. Dimples winked at the side of her soft mouth and her eyes danced. Captivated by the dimples, Gio felt something clench inside him.

She was beautiful.

And very guarded. He saw something in the depths of her blue eyes that made him wonder about her past.

Still smiling, she gave a shake of her head. 'I know they mean well but they've gone too far this time. It's even worse than that time on the lifeboat.'

'The lifeboat?'

'Believe me, you don't want to know.' She sucked in a breath and raked slim fingers through her silky blonde hair. 'Let's look at this logically. I'm assuming Mary was telling the truth about your flat having fallen through—'

'You think she might have been lying?'

'Not lying, no. But she's manoeuvred it in some way. I don't know how yet, but when I find out she's going to be in trouble. Either way, at the moment, it looks as though you're going to have to stay with me. Aggh!' She tilted her head backwards and made a frustrated sound. 'And I'll never hear the last of it! Every morning they're going to be looking at me, working out whether I've fallen in love with you yet. Nudging. Making comments. I'll kill them.'

He couldn't keep the laughter out of his voice. 'Is that what you're afraid of? Do you think you're going to fall in love with me, Dr Anderson?'

She looked at him and the air snapped tight with tension. 'Don't be ridiculous!' Her voice was slightly husky. 'I don't believe in love.'

Could she feel it? Gio wondered. Could she feel what he was feeling?

'Then where is the problem?' He spread lean, bronzed hands and flashed her a smile. 'There is no risk of you falling in love with me. That makes me no more than a lodger.'

But a lodger with a definite interest.

'You don't know what they're like. Every moment of the day there will be little comments. Little asides. They'll drive us mad.'

'Or we could drive them mad. With a little thought and application, this could work in your favour.'

Her glance was suspicious. 'How?'

'Mary and Rita are determined to set you up, no?'

'Yes, but—'

'Clearly they believe that if they put a man under your nose, you will fall in love with him. So—I move in with you and when they see that you have no trouble at all resisting me, they will give up.'

She stared at him thoughtfully. 'You think that will work?'

'Why wouldn't it?'

'You don't know them. They don't give up easily.' The tension had passed and she was suddenly crisp and businesslike. 'And, to be honest, I don't know if I can share a house with someone. I've lived alone since I was eighteen.'

It sounded lonely to him. 'I can assure you that I'm house trained. I'm very clean and I pick up after myself.'

This time there was no answering smile. 'I'm used to having my own space.'

'Me, too,' Gio said smoothly. Was that what the problem was? She liked her independence? 'But Mary said that your house is large…'

'Yes.'

'Then we need hardly see each other.' In truth he'd made up his mind that he'd be seeing plenty of her but decided that the way to achieve that was a step at a time. He was fascinated by Alice Anderson. She was complex. Interesting. Unpredictable. And he knew instinctively that any show of interest on his part would be met with suspicion and rejection. If he looked relaxed and unconcerned about the whole situation, maybe she would, too. 'And think of it this way—' he was suddenly struck by inspiration '—it will give you a chance to brief me fully on the practice, the patients, everything I need to know.'

She looked suddenly thoughtful and he could see her mentally sifting through what he'd just said. 'Yes.' She gave a sharp nod. 'You're right that it will give us plenty of opportunity to talk about work. All right.' She took a deep breath, as if bracing herself. 'Let's lock up here and make a move. Where did you park?'

'At the top of the hill, in the public car park.'

'There are three spaces outside the surgery. You can

use one of those from now on.' She delved into her bag and removed a set of keys. 'I'll give you a lift to your car. Let's go.'

CHAPTER FOUR

STILL fuming about Mary and Rita, Alice jabbed the key into the ignition and gripped the steering-wheel.

She'd been thoroughly outmanoeuvred.

Why had she been foolish enough to let them arrange accommodation? Why hadn't she anticipated that they'd be up to their usual tricks? Because her mind didn't work like theirs, she thought savagely, that was why.

Vowing to tackle the two of them as soon as Gio wasn't around, Alice drove away from the car park, aware that his low black sports car was following close behind her.

Her mind on Mary and Rita, she changed gear with more anger than care and then winced at the hideous crunch. Reminding herself that her car wasn't up to a large degree of abuse, she forced herself to take a calming breath.

They'd set her up yet again, she knew they had. Rita and Mary. The two mother figures in her life. And they'd done it without even bothering to meet the man in question. Somehow they'd both decided that an attractive single guy was going to be perfect for her. It didn't matter that they'd never even met him, that they knew absolutely nothing about him. He was single and she was single and that was all it should take for the magic to kick in.

Anger spurted inside her and Alice thumped the steering-wheel with the heel of her hand and crunched the gears again. They were a pair of interfering old—old…

She really wanted to stay angry but how could she be when she knew that they were only doing it because they cared? When she remembered just how good they'd been to her since her very first day in the practice?

No, better to go along with their little plan and prove to them once and for all that love just didn't work for her. Gio Moretti was right. If she did this, maybe then they'd finally get the message about the way she wanted to live her life.

Yes, that was it. They obviously believed that Gio Moretti was the answer to any woman's prayers. When they realised that he wasn't the answer to hers, maybe they'd leave her alone. She'd live with him if only to prove that she wasn't interested. Since they considered him irresistible, her ability to resist him with no problem should prove something, shouldn't it?

Satisfied with her plan, she gave a swift nod and a smile as she flicked the indicator and took the narrow, winding road that led down to her house.

Her grip on the steering-wheel relaxed slightly. And living with him wouldn't be so bad. Gio seemed like a perfectly civilised guy. He was intelligent and well qualified. His experience in medicine was clearly very different to hers. She would certainly be able to learn from him.

And as for the logistics of the arrangement, she would put him in the guest room at the top of the house that had an *en suite* bathroom so she need never see him. He could come and go without bothering her. They need never have a conversation that didn't involve a patient. And when Mary and Rita saw how things were, they'd surely give up their quest to find her love.

Having satisfied herself that the situation wasn't irredeemable, she stepped on the brake, pulled in to allow another car to pass on the narrow road and drove the last stretch of road that curved down towards the sea.

The crowds of tourists dwindled and immediately she felt calmer.

This was her life. Her world.

The tide was out, the mudflats stretched in front of her and birds swooped and settled on the sandbanks. Behind her were towering cliffs of jagged rock that led out into the sea, and in front of her was the curving mouth of the river, winding lazily inland.

Cornwall.

Home.

Checking that he was still behind her, she touched the brake with her foot, turned right down the tiny track that led down to the water's edge and turned off the engine.

The throaty roar of the sports car behind her died and immediately peace washed over her. For a moment she was tempted to kick her shoes off and walk barefoot, but, as usual, time pressed against her wishes. She had a new lodger to show round and some reading that she needed to finish. And she was going to have to cook something for dinner.

With a shudder of distaste she stepped out of the car feeling hot, sticky and desperate for a cool shower. Wondering when the weather was finally going to break, she turned and watched as Gio slid out of his car and glanced around him. It was a long moment before he spoke.

'This place is amazing.' His hair gleamed glossy dark in the sunlight and the soft fabric of his T-shirt clung to his broad, powerful shoulders. There was a strength about him, an easy confidence that came with maturity, and Alice was suddenly gripped by a shimmer of something unfamiliar.

'Most people consider it to be lonely and isolated. They lecture me on the evils of burying myself somewhere so remote.'

'Do they?' He stood for a moment, legs planted firmly apart in a totally masculine stance, his gaze fixed on the view before him. 'I suppose that's fortunate. If everyone loved it here, it would cease to be so peaceful. You must see some very rare birds.'

'Over fifty different species.' Surprised by the observation, she leaned into her car to retrieve her bag, wondering whether he was genuinely interested in wildlife or whether he was just humouring her. Probably the latter, she decided. The man needed accommodation.

She slammed her car door without bothering to lock it and glanced at his face again. He looked serious enough.

He removed a suitcase from his boot. 'How long have you lived here?'

'Four years.' She delved in her bag for the keys and walked up the path. 'I found this house on my second day here. I was cycling along and there it was. Uninhabited, dilapidated and set apart from everything and everyone.' *Just like her.* She shook off the thought and wriggled the key into the lock. 'It took me a year to do it up sufficiently to live in it, another two years to get it to the state it's in now.'

He removed his sunglasses and glanced at her in surprise. 'You did the work yourself?'

She caught the look and smiled. 'Never judge by appearances, Dr Moretti. I have hidden muscles.' She pushed open the front door and stooped to pick up the post. 'I'll show you where you're sleeping and then meet you in the kitchen. I can fill you in on everything you need to know while we eat.'

She deposited the post, unopened, on the hall table and made a mental note to water the plants before she went to bed.

'It's beautiful.' His eyes scanned the wooden floors, which she'd sanded herself and then painted white, lifted to the filmy white curtains that framed large, picture windows and took in the touches of blue in the cushions and the artwork on the walls. He stepped forward to take a closer look at a large watercolour she had displayed in the hall. 'It's good. It has real passion. You can feel the power of the sea.' He frowned at the signature and turned to look at her. 'You paint?'

'Not any more.' She strode towards the stairs, eager to end the conversation. It was becoming too personal and she was always careful to avoid the personal. 'No time. Your room is at the top of the house and it has its own bathroom. It should be perfectly possible for us to lead totally separate lives.'

She said it to reassure herself as much to remind him and took the stairs two at a time and flung open a door. 'Here we are. You should be comfortable enough here and, anyway, it's only short term.' She broke off and he gave a smile.

'Of course.'

'Look, I don't mean to be rude and I'm thrilled that you're going to be working here, but I'm just not that great at sharing my living space with anyone, OK?' She shrugged awkwardly, wondering why she felt the need to explain herself. 'I'm selfish. I'm the first to admit it. I've lived on my own for too long to be anything else.'

And it was the way she preferred it. It was just a shame that Rita and Mary couldn't get the message.

He strode over to the huge windows and stared at the view. 'You're not being rude. If I lived here, I'd protect it, too.' He turned to face her. 'And I'm not intending to invade your personal space, Alice. You can relax.'

Relax?

His rich accent turned her name into something exotic and exciting and she gave a slight shiver. There would be no relaxing while he was staying with her.

'Then we won't have a problem.' She backed towards the door. 'Make yourself at home. I'm going to take a shower and change. Come down when you're ready. I'll be in the kitchen. Making supper.'

Her least favourite pastime. She gave a sigh of irritation as she left the room. She considered both cooking and eating to be a monumental waste of time but, with a guest in the house, she could hardly suggest that they skip a meal in favour of a bowl of cereal, which was her usual standby when she couldn't be bothered to cook.

Which meant opening the fridge and creating something out of virtually nothing. She just hoped that Gio Moretti wasn't too discerning when it came to his palate.

Her blue eyes narrowed and she gave a soft smile as she pushed open the door to her own bedroom and made for the shower, stripping off clothes as she walked and flinging them on the bed.

If the way to a man's heart was through his stomach, she was surprised that Mary and Rita had given their plan even the remotest chance of success.

It didn't take a genius to know that it was going to be hard for a man to harbour romantic notions about a woman who had just poisoned him.

When Gio strolled into the kitchen after a shower and a shave, she was grating cheese into a bowl with no apparent signs of either skill or enthusiasm. He watched with amusement and no small degree of interest and wondered who had designed the kitchen.

It was a cook's paradise. White slatted units and lots of glass reflected the light and a huge stainless-steel oven gleamed and winked, its spotless surface suggesting it had never been used. In fact, the whole kitchen looked as though it belonged in a show home and it took him less than five seconds of watching the usually competent Alice wrestle with a lump of cheese to understand why.

At the far end of the room French doors opened onto the pretty garden. Directly in front of the doors, positioned to make the most of the view, was a table covered in medical magazines, a few textbooks and several sheets of paper covered in neat handwriting.

He could picture her there, her face serious as she read her way through all the academic medical journals, checking the facts. He'd seen enough to know that Alice

Anderson was comfortable with facts. Possibly more comfortable with facts than she was with people.

He wondered why.

In his experience, there was usually a reason for the way people chose to live their lives.

'Cheese on toast all right with you?' She turned, still grating, her eyes fixed on his face. 'Oh…'

'Something is wrong?'

She blew a wisp of blonde hair out of her eyes. 'You look…different.'

He smiled and strolled towards her. 'More like a doctor?'

'Maybe. Ow.' She winced as the grater grazed her knuckles and adjusted her grip. 'I wasn't expecting guests, I'm afraid, so I haven't shopped. And I have to confess that I loathe cooking.' Her blonde hair was still damp from the shower and she'd changed into a pair of linen trousers and a pink top. She looked young and feminine and a long way from the brisk, competent professional he'd met earlier. The kitchen obviously flustered her and he found her slightly clumsy approach to cooking surprisingly appealing. In fact, he was fast discovering that there were many parts of Alice Anderson that he found appealing.

'Anything I can do?' Wondering if he should take over or whether that would damage her ego, he strolled over to her, lifted a piece of cheese and sniffed it. 'What is it?'

'The cheese?' She turned on the grill and watched for a moment as if not entirely confident that it would work. 'Goodness knows. The sort that comes wrapped in tight plastic. Cheddar or something, I suppose. Why?'

He tried not to wince at the vision of cheese tightly

wrapped in plastic. 'I'm Italian. We happen to love cheese. Mozzarella, fontina, ricotta, marscapone...'.

'This is just something I grabbed from the supermarket a few weeks ago. It was covered with blue bits but I chopped them off. I assumed they weren't supposed to be there. I don't think they were there when I bought it.' She dropped the grater and stared down at the pile of cheese with a distinct lack of enthusiasm. 'There should be some salad in the fridge, if you're interested.'

He opened her fridge and stared. It was virtually empty. Making a mental note to shop at the earliest convenient moment, he reached for a limp, sorry piece of lettuce and examined it thoughtfully. 'I'm not bothered about salad,' he murmured, and she glanced up, her face pink from the heat of the grill, her teeth gritted.

'Fine. Whatever. This is nearly ready.' She pulled out the grill pan and fanned her hand over the contents to stop it smoking. 'I'm not that great a cook but at least it's food, and that's all that matters. Good job I'm not really trying to seduce you, Dr Moretti.' She flashed him a wicked smile as she slid the contents of the grill pan onto two plates. 'If the way to a man's heart is through his stomach, I'm completely safe.'

She wasn't joking about her culinary skills. Gio stared down at the burnt edges of the toast and the patchy mix of melted and unmelted cheese and suddenly realised why she was so slim. It was a good job he was starving and willing to eat virtually anything. Suddenly he understood Mary's suggestion that they get a takeaway. 'Did you eat lunch today?'

She fished knives and forks out of a drawer and sat down at the table, pushing aside the piles of journals and books to make room for the plates. 'I can't remember. I might have had something at some point. So what's your opinion on Harriet?' She pushed cutlery across the table and poured some water. 'Do you think she is depressed?'

He wondered if she even realised that she was talking about work again.

Did she do it on purpose to avoid a conversation of a more personal nature?

He picked up a fork and tried to summon up some enthusiasm for the meal ahead. It was a challenge. For him a meal was supposed to be a total experience. An event. A time to indulge the palate and the senses simultaneously. Clearly, for Alice it was just a means of satisfying the gnawing in her stomach.

Glancing down at his plate, he wondered whether he was going to survive the experience of Alice's cooking or whether he was going to require medical attention.

She definitely needed educating about food.

'Is Harriet depressed? It's possible. I'll certainly follow it up.' He cautiously tasted the burnt offering on his plate and decided that it was the most unappetizing meal he'd eaten for a long time. 'Postnatal depression is a serious condition.'

'And often missed. She was fine after the twins but that's not necessarily significant, of course.' Alice finished her toasted cheese with brisk efficiency and no visible signs of enjoyment and put down her fork with an apologetic glance in his direction. 'Sorry to eat so quickly. I was starving. I don't think I managed to eat at all yesterday.'

'Are you serious?'

'Perfectly. We had a bit of a drama in the bay. The

lifeboat was called out to two children who'd managed to drift out to sea in their inflatable boat.' She broke off and sipped her drink. 'I spent my lunch-hour over with the crew, making sure they were all right. By the time I finished I had a queue of people in the surgery. I forgot to eat.'

To Gio, who had never forgotten to eat in his life, such a situation was incomprehensible. 'You need to seriously rethink your lifestyle.'

'You sound like Mary and Rita. I happen to like my lifestyle. It works for me.' With a fatalistic shrug she finished her water and stood up. 'So, Dr Moretti, what can I tell you about the practice to make your life easier? At this time of year we see a lot of tourists with the usual sorts of problems. Obviously, on top of the locals, it makes us busy, as you discovered today.'

All she thought about was work, he reflected, watching as she lifted a medical journal from the pile on the table and absently scanned the contents. She was driven. Obsessed. 'Do you do a minor accident clinic?'

'No.' She shook her head and dropped the journal back on the pile. 'David and I tried it two years ago but, to be honest, there were days when we were swamped and days when we were sitting around. We decided it was better just to fit them into surgery time. We have a very good relationship with the coastguard and the local paramedics. Sometimes they call on us, sometimes we call on them. We also have a good relationship with the local police.'

'The police?' His attention was caught by the gentle sway of her hips as she walked across the kitchen. Her movements were graceful and utterly feminine and from nowhere he felt a sharp tug of lust.

Gritting his teeth, he tried to talk sense into himself.
They were colleagues.
He'd known her for less than a day.

'Beach parties.' She lifted the kettle and filled it. 'At this time of year we have a lot of teenagers just hanging out on the beach. Usually the problem's just too much alcohol, as you saw this morning. Sometimes it's drugs.'

To hide the fact that he was studying her, Gio glanced out towards the sea and tried to imagine it crowded with hordes of teenagers. *Tried to drag his mind away from the tempting curve of her hips.* 'Looks peaceful to me. It's hard to imagine it otherwise.'

She rested those same hips against the work surface while she waited for the kettle to boil. 'They don't come down this far. They congregate on the beach beyond the harbour. The surf is good. Too good sometimes, and then we get a fair few surfing accidents, as you also noticed this morning. Coffee?'

Gio opened his mouth to say yes and then winced as he saw her reaching into a cupboard for a jar. 'You are using instant coffee?'

She pulled a face. 'I know. It's not my favourite either, but it's better than nothing and I've run out of fresh. One of the drawbacks of living out here is that both the supermarket and the nearest espresso machine are a car ride away.'

'Not any more.'

'Don't tell me.' She spooned coffee into a mug. 'You've brought your own espresso machine.'

'Of course. It was a key part of my luggage. Along with a large supply of the very best beans.'

She stilled, the spoon still in her hand. 'You're not serious?'

'Coffee is extremely serious,' he said dryly. 'If you expect me to work hard, I need my daily fix, and if today is anything to go by then I'm not going to have time to pop up the hill to that excellent bakery.'

She scooped her hair away from her face and there was longing in her eyes. 'You're planning to make fresh coffee every morning?'

'*Si.*' He wondered why she was even asking the question when it seemed entirely normal to him. 'It is the only way I can get through the day.'

The smile spread across her face. 'Now, if Mary had mentioned that, I would have cancelled your flat with the letting agent myself.' She licked her lips, put down the spoon, a hunger in her eyes. 'Does your fancy machine make enough for two cups?'

He decided that if it guaranteed him one of her smiles, he'd stand over the machine all morning. 'A decent cup of coffee to start your day will be part of my fee for invading your space,' he offered. Along with the cooking, but he decided to wait a while before breaking that to her in case she was offended. 'So tell me about Rita and Mary.' He wanted to know about their relationship with her. Why they felt the need to set her up.

He wanted to know everything there was to know about Alice Anderson.

'They've worked in the practice for ever. Twenty-five years at least. Can you imagine that?' She shook her head. 'It helps, of course, because they know everything about everyone. History is important, don't you think, Dr Moretti?'

He wondered about her history. He wondered what had made a beautiful woman like her choose to bury herself in her work and live apart from others. It felt wrong. Not the setting, he mused as he glanced out of the window. The setting was perfect. But in his opinion it was a setting designed to be shared with someone special.

Realising that she was waiting for an answer, he smiled, amused by her earnest expression. She was delightfully serious. 'I can see that history is important in general practice.'

'It gives you clues. Not knowing a patient's history is often like trying to solve a murder with no access to clues.' Her eyes narrowed. 'I suppose as a surgeon, it's different. It's more task orientated. You get the patient on the operating table and you solve the problem.'

'Not necessarily that simple.' He sat back in his chair, comfortable in her kitchen. *In her company.* The problems of the past year faded. 'In plastic surgery the patient's wishes, hopes, dreams are all an important part of the picture. Appearance can affect people's lives. As a society, we're shallow. We see and we judge. As a surgeon you have to take that into account. You need to understand what's needed and decided whether you can deliver.'

'You did face lifts? Nose jobs?'

He smiled. It was a common misconception and it didn't offend him. 'That wasn't my field of speciality,' he said quietly. 'I did paediatrics. Cleft palates, hare lips. In between running my clinic in Milan, I did volunteer work in developing countries. Children with unrepaired clefts lead very isolated lives. Often they can't go to school—they're ostracised from the community, no chance of employment…'

She was staring at him, a frown in her blue eyes as if she was reassessing him. 'I had no idea.' She picked up her coffee, but her focus was on him, not the mug in her hand. 'That's so interesting. And tough.'

'Tough, rewarding, frustrating.' He gave a shrug. 'All those things. Like every branch of medicine, I suppose. I also did a lot of training. Showing local doctors new techniques.' He waited for the dull ache of disappointment that always came when he was talking about the past, but there was nothing. Instead he felt more relaxed than he could ever recall feeling.

'It must have been hard for you to give it up.'

He shrugged and felt a twinge in his shoulder. 'Life sometimes forces change on us but sometimes it's a change we should have made ourselves if we only had the courage. I was ready for a change.'

He sensed that she was going to ask him more, delve deeper, and then she seemed to withdraw.

'Well, there's certainly variety in our practice. If you're good with babies, you can run the baby clinic. David used to do it.'

She was talking about work again, he mused. 'Immunisations, I assume?' Always, she avoided the personal. *Was she afraid of intimacy?*

'That and other things.' She sipped at her coffee. 'It's a really busy clinic. We expanded its remit a few months ago to encourage mothers to see us with their problems during the clinic rather than making appointments during normal surgery hours. It means that they don't have to make separate appointments for themselves and we reduce the number of toddlers running around the waiting room.' Her fingers tightened on the mug. 'I have to confess it isn't my forte.'

'I've seen enough of your work to know that you're an excellent doctor.' He watched as the colour touched her cheekbones.

'Oh, I can do the practical stuff.' She gave a shrug and turned her back on him, dumping her mug in the sink. 'It's everything that goes with it that I can't handle. All the emotional stuff. I'm terrible at that. How are you with worried mothers, Dr Moretti?' She turned and her blonde hair swung gently round her head.

Was she afraid of other people's emotions or her own? Pondering the question, he flashed her a wicked smile. 'Worried women are my speciality, Dr Anderson.'

She threw back her head and laughed. 'I'll just bet they are, Dr Moretti. I'll just bet they are.'

Alice woke to the delicious smells of freshly ground coffee, rolled over and then remembered Gio Moretti. Living here. In her house.

She sat upright, pushed the heavy cloud of sleep away and checked the clock. 6 a.m. He was obviously an early riser, like her.

Tempted by the smell and the prospect of a good cup of coffee to start her day, she padded into the shower, dressed quickly and followed her nose.

She pushed open the kitchen door, her mind automatically turning to work, and then stopped dead, taken aback by the sight of Gio half-naked in her kitchen.

'Oh!' She'd assumed he was up and dressed, instead of which he was wearing jeans again. This time with nothing else. His chest was bare and the muscles of his shoulders flexed as he reached for the coffee.

He was gorgeous.

The thought stopped her dead and she frowned, surprised at herself for noticing and more than a little irritated. And then she gave a dismissive shrug. So what? Despite what Rita and Mary obviously thought, she was neither blind nor brain dead. And it wasn't as if she hadn't experienced sexual attraction before. She had. The important thing was not to mistake it for 'love'.

He turned to reach for a cup and she saw the harsh, jagged scars running down his back. 'That looks painful.'

The minute she said the words she wished she hadn't. Was he sensitive about it? Perhaps she wasn't supposed to mention it. If he was the type of guy that spent all day staring in the mirror, then perhaps it bothered him.

'Not as painful as it used to. *Buongiorno.*' He flashed her a smile and handed her a cup, totally at ease in her kitchen. 'I wasn't expecting you up this early. I have to have coffee before I can face the shower.'

'I know the feeling.' Wondering how he got the scar, she took the cup with a nod of thanks and wandered over to the table, trying not to look in his direction.

She might not believe in love but she could see when a man was attractive and Gio Moretti was certainly attractive. When she'd said he could have her spare room, she hadn't imagined he'd be walking around her house half-naked. It was unsettling and more than a little distracting.

She sat down. Her body suddenly felt hot and uncomfortable and she slid a finger around the neck of her shirt and glanced at the sun outside. 'It's going to be another scorcher today.' Even though she made a point of not looking in his direction, she sensed his gaze on her.

'You're feeling hot, Alice?'

Something in his voice made her turn her head. Her eyes met hers and an unexpected jolt shook her body. 'It's warm in here, yes.' She caught her breath, broke the eye contact and picked up her coffee, but not before her brain had retained a clear image of a bronzed, muscular chest covered in curling dark hairs. He was all muscle and masculinity and her throat felt suddenly dry. She took a sip of coffee. 'This is delicious. Thank you.'

Still holding her cup, she stared out of the window and tried to erase the memory of his half-naked body. She wasn't used to having a man in her kitchen. It was all too informal. Too intimate.

Everything she avoided.

To take her mind off the problem she did what she always did. She thought about work.

'Rita has a baby clinic this afternoon,' she said brightly, watching as a heron rose from the smooth calm of the estuary that led to sea and flew off with a graceful sweep of its wings. 'Invariably she manages it by herself but sometimes she needs one of us to—'

'Alice, *cara*.' His voice came from behind her, deep and heavily accented. 'I need at least two cups of coffee before I can even think about work, let alone talk about it.' His hands came up and touched her shoulders and she stiffened. She wasn't used to being touched. No one touched her.

'I just thought you should know that—'

'This kitchen has the most beautiful view.' He kept his hands on her shoulders, his touch light and relaxed. 'Enjoy it. It's still early. Leave thoughts of work until later. Look at the mist. Enjoy the silence. It's perfect.'

She sat still, heart pounding, thoroughly unsettled. Usually her kitchen soothed her. Calmed her. But today she could feel the little spurts of tension darting through her shoulders.

It was just having someone else in the house, she told herself. Inevitably it altered her routine.

Abandoning her plan to read some journals while drinking her coffee as she usually did, she stood up and firmly extricated herself from his hold.

'I need to get going.' Annoyed with herself and even more annoyed with him, she walked across the room, taking her cup with her. 'I'll meet you at the surgery later.'

His eyes flickered to the clock on the wall. 'Alice, it's only 6.30.' His voice was a soft, accented drawl. 'And you haven't finished your coffee.'

'There's masses of paperwork to plough through.' She drank the coffee quickly and put the cup on the nearest worktop. 'Thank you. A great improvement on instant.'

His eyes were locked on her face. 'You haven't had breakfast.'

'I don't need breakfast.' What she needed most of all was space. Air to breathe. The safety of her usual routine. She backed out of the door, needing to escape. 'I'll see you later.'

Grabbing her bag and her jacket, she strode out of the house, fumbling for her keys as she let the door swing shut behind her.

Oh, bother and blast.

Instead of starting her day in a calm, organised frame

of mind, as she usually did, she felt unsettled and on edge and the reason why was perfectly obvious.

She didn't need a lodger and she certainly didn't need a lodger that she noticed, she thought to herself as she slid into the sanctuary of her car.

And she was *definitely* going to kill Mary when she saw her.

He made her nervous.

She claimed not to believe in love and yet there was chemistry between them. An elemental attraction that he'd felt from the first moment. And it was growing stronger by the minute.

Gio made himself a second cup of coffee and drank it seated at the little table overlooking the garden and the sea.

She was serious, academic and obviously totally unaccustomed to having a man in her life. He'd felt the sudden tension in her shoulders when he'd touched her. Felt her discomfort and her sudden anxiety.

He frowned and stretched his legs out in front of him.

In his family, touching was part of life. Everyone touched. Hugged. Held. It was what they did. But not everyone was the same, of course.

And, for whatever reason, he sensed that Alice wasn't used to being touched. *Wasn't comfortable being touched.*

The English were generally more reserved and emotionally distant, of course, so it could be that. He drained his coffee-cup. Or it could be something else. Something linked with the reason he was sitting here now instead of in a flat in another part of town.

Why had Mary seen the need to interfere?

Why did she think that Alice needed help finding a man in her life?

And, given his distaste for matchmaking attempts, why wasn't he running fast in the opposite direction?

Why did he suddenly feel comfortable and content?

The question didn't need much answering. Everything about Alice intrigued him. She was complex and unpredictable. She had a beautiful smile but it only appeared after a significant amount of coaxing. She was clever and clearly caring and yet she herself had humbly confessed that she wasn't good with emotions.

And she was uncomfortable with being touched.

Which was a shame, he thought to himself as he finished his coffee. Because he'd made up his mind that he was going to be touching her a lot. So she was going to have to start getting used to it.

CHAPTER FIVE

MARY sailed into the surgery just as Alice scooped the post from the mat. 'You're early.' There was disappointment in her expression, as if she'd expected something different. 'So—did you have a lovely evening?'

'Wonderful. Truly wonderful.' Alice dropped the post onto the reception desk to be sorted and gave a wistful sigh, deriving wicked satisfaction from the look of hope that lit Mary's face. 'I must do it more often.'

'Do what more often?'

'Go home early, of course.' Alice smiled sweetly. 'I caught up on so many things.'

Mary's shoulders sagged. 'Caught up on what? How was your lodger?'

'Who?' Alice adopted a blank expression and then waved a hand vaguely. 'Oh, you mean Dr Moretti? Fine, I think. I wouldn't really know. I hardly saw him.'

Mary dropped her bag with a thump and a scowl. 'You didn't spend the evening together?'

'Not at all. Why would we? He's my lodger, not my date.' Alice leaned forward and picked up the contents of her in tray. 'But he does make tremendous coffee. I suppose I have you to thank for that, given that you arranged it all.'

'You already drink too much coffee,' Mary scolded as they both walked towards the consulting rooms. She caught Alice's arm in a firm grip. 'Are you serious? You didn't spend any time with him at all?'

Alice shrugged her off. 'None.'

'If that's true, you're a sad case.' Her eyes narrowed. 'You're teasing me, aren't you?'

'All right, I'll tell you the truth.' Thoroughly enjoying herself now, Alice threw Mary a saucy wink as she pushed open the door to her room. 'I'm grateful to you, really I am. Even I can see that Gio Moretti is handsome. I don't suppose they come much handsomer. If I have to share my house with someone I'd so much rather it was someone decorative. I could hardly concentrate on my breakfast this morning because he was standing in my kitchen half-naked. *What* a body!' She gave an exaggerated sigh and pressed her palm against her heart. 'I'd have to be a fool not to be interested in a man like him, wouldn't you agree?'

'Alice—'

'And I'm certainly not a fool.' She dropped her bag behind her desk. 'Anyway, I just want you to know that we've been at it all night like rabbits and now I've definitely got him out of my system so you can safely find him somewhere else to live, you interfering old—'

'*Buongiorno.*'

The deep voice came from the doorway and Alice whirled round, her face turning pink with embarrassment. She caught the wicked humour in his dark eyes and cursed inwardly.

Why had he chosen that precise moment to walk down the corridor?

He lounged in her doorway, dressed in tailored trousers and a crisp cotton shirt that looked both expensive and stylish. The sleeves were rolled up to his elbows, revealing bronzed forearms dusted with dark hairs. The laughter in his eyes told her that he'd heard every word. 'You left without breakfast, Dr Anderson. And after such a long, taxing night…' He lingered over each syllable, his rich, Italian accent turning the words into something decadent and sinful '…you need to replenish your energy levels.'

Mary glanced between them, her expression lifting, and Alice suppressed a groan. Friendly banter. Teasing. All designed to give Mary totally the wrong idea. And she'd been the one to start it.

'Finally, someone else to scold you about not eating proper meals.' Mary put her hands on her hips and gave a satisfied nod. 'If Dr Moretti values his stomach lining, he'll take over the cooking.'

'I'm perfectly capable of cooking,' Alice snapped, sitting down at her desk and switching on her computer with a stab of her finger. 'It's just that I don't enjoy it very much and I have so many other more important things to do with my time.'

'Like work.' Mary looked at Gio. 'While you're at it, you might want to reform her on that count, too.' She walked out of the room, leaving Alice glaring after her.

'I've decided that David had the right idea after all. London is looking better all the time. In London, no one cares what the person next to them is doing. No one cares whether they eat breakfast, work or don't work.

And for sure, no one cares about the state of anyone else's love life.' She hit the return key on the keyboard with more force than was necessary, aware that Gio was watching her, a thoughtful expression in his dark eyes. His shoulders were still against the doorframe and he didn't seem in any hurry to go anywhere.

'She really cares about you.'

Alice stilled. He was right, of course. Mary did care about her. And she'd never had that before. Until she'd arrived in Smuggler's Cove, she'd never experienced interference as a result of caring.

'I know she does.' Alice bit her lip. 'I wish I could convince her that I'm fine on my own. That this is what I want. How I want to live my life.'

His gaze was steady. 'Sounds lonely to me, Dr Anderson. And perhaps a bit cowardly.'

'Cowardly?' She forgot about her computer and sat back in her chair, more than a little outraged. 'What's that supposed to mean?'

He walked further into the room, his eyes fixed on her face. 'People who avoid relationships are usually afraid of getting hurt.'

'Or perhaps they're just particularly well adjusted and evolved,' Alice returned sweetly. 'This is the twenty-first century and we no longer all believe that a man is necessary to validate and enhance our lives.'

'Is that so?' His gaze dropped to her mouth and she felt her heart stumble and kick in her chest.

With a frown of irritation she turned her head and concentrated on her computer screen. Why was he looking at her like that? Studying her? As if he was trying to see deep inside her mind? Her fingers drummed a rhythm on the desk. Well, that was a part of herself that she kept private. Like all the other parts.

She looked up, her expression cool and discouraging. 'We don't all have to agree on everything, Dr Moretti. Our differences are what make the world an interesting place to live. And now I'm sure you have patients to see and I know that I certainly do.' To make her point, she reached across her desk and pressed the buzzer to alert her first patient. 'Oh, and please don't give Mary and Rita the impression that we're living a cosy life together. They'll be unbearable.'

'But surely the point is to prove that we can be cosy and yet you can still resist me,' he reminded her in silky tones, and she stared at him, speechless. 'Isn't that the message you want them to receive? Unless, of course, you are having trouble resisting me.'

'Oh, please!' She gave an exclamation of impatience and looked up just as the patient knocked on the door. 'Let's just move on.'

'Yes, let's do that.' He kept his hand on the doorhandle, his eyes glinting darkly, 'but at least try and keep this authentic. For the record, you would not get me out of your system in one night, *cara mia.*'

Her mouth fell open and she searched in vain for a witty reply. And failed.

His smile widened and he wandered out of the room, leaving her fuming.

Alice took refuge in work and fortunately there was plenty of it.

Her first patient was a woman who was worried about a rash on her daughter's mouth.

'She had this itchy, red sore and then suddenly it turned into a blister and it's been oozing.' The mother pulled a face and hugged the child. 'Poor thing. It's really bothering her.'

Alice took one look at the thick, honey-coloured crust that had formed over the lesion and made an instant diagnosis. *Impetigo contagiosa,* she decided, caused by *Staphyloccocus aureus* and possibly group A beta-haemolytic streptococcus. This was one of the things she loved about medicine, she thought as she finished her examination and felt a rush of satisfaction. You were given clues. Signs. And you had to interpret them. Behind everything was a cause. It was just a question of finding it.

In this case she had no doubt. 'She has impetigo, Mrs Wood.' She turned back to her computer, selected a drug and pressed the print key. 'It's a very common skin condition, particularly in children. As it's only in one area I'm going to give you some cream to apply to the affected area. You need to wash the skin several times a day and remove the crusts. Then apply the cream. But make sure you wash your hands carefully because it's highly contagious.'

'Can she go back to nursery?'

Alice shook her head. 'Not until the lesions are cleared. Make sure you don't share towels.'

Mrs Wood sighed. 'That's more holiday I'll have to take, then. Being a working mother is a nightmare. I wonder why I bother sometimes.'

'It must be difficult.' Alice took the prescription from the printer and signed it. 'Here we are. Come back in a week if it isn't better.'

Mrs Wood left the room clutching her prescription and Alice moved on to the next patient. And the next.

She was reading a discharge letter from a surgeon when her door opened and Gio walked in, juggling two coffees and a large paper bag.

'I'm fulfilling my brief from Mary. Breakfast.' He flashed her a smile, kicked the door shut with his foot and placed everything on the desk in front of her. He ripped open the bag and waved a hand. 'Help yourself.'

She sat back in her chair and stared at him in exasperation. She never stopped for a break when she was seeing patients. It threw her concentration and just meant an even longer day. 'I've still got patients to see.'

'Actually, you haven't. At least, not at this exact moment. I checked with Mary.' He sat down in the chair next to her desk. 'Your last patient has cancelled so you've got a break. And so have I. Let's make the most of it.'

She stared at the selection of croissants and muffins. 'I'm not really hungry but now you're here we could quickly run through the referral strategy for—'

'Alice.' He leaned forward, a flash of humour in his dark eyes. 'If you're about to mention work, hold the thought.' He pushed the bag towards her. 'I refuse to discuss anything until I've seen you eat.'

The scent of warm, freshly baked cakes wafted under her nose. 'But I—'

'Didn't eat breakfast,' he reminded her calmly, 'and you've got the whole morning ahead of you. You can't get through that workload on one cup of black coffee, even though it was excellent.'

She sighed and her hand hovered over the bag. Eventually her fingers closed over a muffin. 'Fine. Thanks. If I eat this, will you leave me alone?'

'Possibly.' He waited until she'd taken a bite. 'Now we can talk about work. I'm interested in following up on Harriet. You mentioned that there's a baby clinic this afternoon. Is she likely to attend?'

'Possibly.' The muffin was still warm and tasted delicious. She wondered how she could have thought she wasn't hungry. She was starving. 'Rita would know whether she's down for immunisation. Or she may just come to have the baby weighed. Gina is around this morning, too. It would be worth talking to her. I've got a meeting with her at eleven-fifteen, to talk about our MMR rates.'

'I'll join you. Then I can discuss Harriet.'

'Fine.' Her gaze slid longingly at the remaining muffins. 'Can I have another?'

'Eat.' He pushed them towards her and she gave a guilty smile.

'I'll cook supper tonight in return.' She thought she saw a look of alarm cross his face but then decided she must have imagined it.

'There's no need, I thought we could—'

'I insist.' It was the least she could do, she thought, devouring the muffin and reached for another without even thinking. She loathed cooking, but there were times when it couldn't be avoided. 'Last night's supper of cheese on toast was hardly a gourmet treat. Tonight I'll do a curry.' She'd made one once before and it hadn't turned out too badly.

'Alice, why don't you let me—' He broke off and turned as the door opened and Rita walked in.

'Can you come to the waiting room? Betty needs advice.'

Alice brushed the crumbs from her lap and stood up. 'I'll come now. Nice breakfast. Thanks.'

Dropping the empty bag in the bin on his way past, Gio followed, wondering if she even realised that she'd eaten her way through three muffins.

It was almost eleven o'clock, and she'd been up since dawn and working on an empty stomach until he'd intervened.

Something definitely needed to be done about her lifestyle.

He gave a wry smile. Even more so if he was going to be living with her. After sampling her cheese on toast, he didn't dare imagine what her curry would be like, but he had a suspicion that the after-effects might require medication.

He walked into the reception area and watched while she walked over to the couple standing at the desk.

'Betty? What's happened?'

'Eating too quickly, that's what happened.' Betty scowled at her husband but there was worry in her eyes. 'Thought I'd cook him a nice bit of fish for breakfast, straight from the quay, but he wasn't looking what he was doing and now he's got a bone lodged in his throat. And, of course, it has to be right at peak season when the shop's clogged with people spending money and I can't trust that dizzy girl on her own behind the counter. If we have to go to A and E it will be hours and—'

'Betty.'

Gio watched, fascinated, as Alice put a hand on the woman's arm and interrupted her gently, her voice steady and confident. 'Calm down. I'm sure we'll manage to take the bone out here, but if not—' She broke off as the door opened again and another woman hurried in, her face disturbingly pale, a hand resting on her swollen stomach. 'Cathy? Has something happened?'

'Oh, Dr Anderson, I've had the most awful pains this morning. Ever since I hung out the washing. I didn't know whether I should just drive straight to the hospital but Mick has an interview later this morning and I didn't want to drag him there on a wild-goose chase. I know surgery has finished, but have you got a minute?'

Obviously not for both at the same time, Gio reflected with something close to amusement. No wonder Alice looked tired. She never stopped working. Surgery was finished and still the patients were crowding in. Had he really thought that he was in for a quiet summer?

He glanced towards the door, half expecting someone else to appear, but there was no one. 'Point me in the direction of a pair of Tilley's forceps and I'll deal with the fishbone,' he said calmly, and Alice gave a brief nod, her eyes lingering on Cathy's pale face.

'In your consulting room. Forceps are in the top cupboard above the sink. Thanks.'

Her lack of hesitation impressed him. She might be a workaholic but at least she didn't have trouble delegating, Gio mused as he introduced himself to the couple and ushered them into the consulting room.

'If you'll have a seat, Mr…?' He lifted an eyebrow and the woman gave a stiff smile.

'Norman. Giles and Betty Norman.' Her tone was crisp and more than a little chilly, but he smiled easily.

'You'll have to forgive me for not knowing who you are. This is only my second day here.'

Betty Norman gave a sniff. 'We run the newsagent across the harbour. If you were local, you'd know that. There have been Normans running the newsagent for five generations.' She looked at him suspiciously, her gaze bordering on the unfriendly. 'That's a foreign accent I'm hearing and you certainly don't look English.'

'That's because I'm Italian.' Gio adjusted the angle of the light. 'And I may be new to the village, Mrs Norman, but I'm not new to medicine so you need have no worries on that score.' He opened a cupboard and selected the equipment he was going to need. 'Mr Norman, I just need to shine a light in your mouth so that I can take a better look at the back of your throat.'

Betty dropped her handbag and folded her arms. 'Well, I just hope you can manage to get the wretched thing out. Some surgeries insist you go to A and E for something like this but we have a business to run. A and E is a sixty-minute round trip at the best of times and then there's the waiting. Dr Anderson is good at this sort of thing. Perhaps we ought to wait until she's finished with young Cathy.'

Aware that he was being tested, Gio bit back a smile, not remotely offended. 'I don't think that's a trip you're going to be making today, Mrs Norman,' he said smoothly, raising his head briefly from his examination to acknowledge her concerns. 'And I don't think you need to wait to see Dr Anderson. I can understand that you're wary of a new doctor but I can assure you that I'm more than up to the job. Why don't you let me try and then we'll see what happens?'

She stared at him, her shoulders tense and unyielding, her mouth pursed in readiness to voice further disapproval, and then he smiled at her and the tension seemed to ooze out of her and her mouth relaxed slightly into a smile of her own.

'Stupid of me to cook fish for breakfast,' she muttered weakly, and Gio returned to his examination.

'Cooking is never stupid, Mrs Norman,' he murmured as he depressed her husband's tongue to enable him to visualise the tonsil. 'And fish is the food of the gods, especially when it's eaten fresh from the sea. I see the bone quite clearly. Removing it should present no difficulty whatsoever.'

He reached for the forceps, adjusted the light and removed the fishbone with such speed and skill that his patient barely coughed.

'There.' He placed the offending bone on a piece of gauze. 'There's the culprit. The back of your throat has been slightly scratched, Mr Norman, so I'm going to give you an antibiotic and ask you to come back in a day for me to just check your throat. If necessary I will refer you to the ENT team at the hospital, but I don't think it will come to that.'

Mr Norman stared at the bone and glanced at his wife, an expression of relief on his face.

'Well—thank goodness.'

She picked up her handbag, all her icy reserve melted away. 'Thank the doctor, not goodness.' She gave Gio a nod of approval. 'Welcome to Smuggler's Cove. I think you're going to fit in well.'

'Thank you.' He smiled, his mind on Alice and her soft mouth. 'I think so, too.'

* * *

Alice watched from the doorway, clocked the killer smile, the Latin charm, and noted Betty's response with a sigh of relief and a flicker of exasperation. Why was it that the members of her sex were so predictable?

She'd briefly examined Cathy and what she'd seen had been enough to convince her that a trip to hospital was necessary for a more detailed check-up. Then she'd returned to the consulting room, prepared to help Gio, only to find that her help clearly wasn't required.

Not only had he removed the fishbone, which she knew could often be a tricky procedure, but had obviously succeeded in winning over the most difficult character in the village.

It amused her that even Betty Norman wasn't immune to a handsome Italian with a sexy smile and for a moment she found herself remembering David's comment about women going weak at the knees. Then she allowed herself a smile. *Not every woman.* Her knees were still functioning as expected, despite Mary's interference.

She could see he was handsome, and she was still walking with no problem.

Clearing her throat, she walked into the room. 'Everything OK?'

But she could see that everything was more than OK. Betty had melted like Cornish ice cream left out in the midday sun.

'Everything is fine.' Betty glanced at her watch, all smiles now. She patted her hair and straightened her blouse. 'I can be back behind the counter before that girl has a chance to make a mistake. Nice meeting you Dr...I didn't catch your name.'

'Moretti.' He extended a lean, bronzed hand. 'Gio Moretti.'

His voice was a warm, accented drawl and Betty flushed a deep shade of pink as she shook his hand. 'Well, thank you again. And welcome. If you need any help with anything, just call into the newsagent's.' She waved a hand, flustered now. 'I'd be more than happy to advise you on anything local.'

Gio smiled. 'I'll remember that.'

'By the way…' She turned to Alice. 'Edith doesn't seem herself at the moment. I can't put my finger on it but something isn't right. It may be nothing, but I thought you should know, given what happened to her last month.'

'I'll check on her.' Alice frowned. 'You think she might have fallen again?'

'That's what's worrying me.' Betty reached for her handbag. 'Iris Leek at number thirty-six has a key if you need to let yourself in. I tried ringing her yesterday for a chat, but I think she was away at her sister's.'

'I'll call round there this week,' Alice promised immediately. 'I was going to anyway.'

Betty smiled. 'Thank you, dear. You may not have been born here but you're a good girl and we're lucky to have you.' She turned to Gio with a girlish smile. 'And doubly lucky now, it seems.'

The couple left the surgery and Alice shook her head in disbelief. 'Well, you really charmed her. Congratulations. I've never seen Betty blush before. You've made a conquest.'

His gaze was swift and assessing. 'And that surprises you?'

'Well, let's put it this way—she's not known for her warmth to strangers unless they're spending money in her shop.'

'I thought she was a nice lady.' He switched off the light and tidied up the equipment he'd used. 'A bit cautious, but I suppose that's natural.'

'Welcome to Smuggler's Cove,' Alice said lightly. 'If you can't trace your family back for at least five generations, you're a stranger.'

'And how about you, Alice?' He paused and his dark gold eyes narrowed as they rested on her face. 'From her comments, you obviously aren't a local either. So far we've talked about work and nothing else. Tell me about yourself.'

His slow, seductive masculine tones slid over her taut nerves and soothed her. It was a voice designed to lull an unsuspecting woman into a sensual coma.

'Alice?'

Alice shook herself. She wasn't going to be thrown off her stride just because the man was movie-star handsome. She'd leave that to the rest of the female population of the village. 'There's nothing interesting to say about me. I'm very boring.'

'You mean you don't like talking about yourself.'

He was sharp, she had to give him that. 'I came here after I finished my GP rotation five years ago so, no, I don't qualify as a local,' she said crisply, delivering the facts as succinctly as possible. In her experience, the quickest way to stop someone asking questions was to answer a few. 'But I'm accepted because of the job I do.'

'And it's obviously a job you do very well. So where is home to you? Where are your family?'

Her blood went cold and all her muscles tightened. 'This is my home.'

There was a brief pause and when he spoke again his voice was gentle. 'Then you're lucky, because I can't think of a nicer place to live.' His eyes lingered on her face and then he strolled across the room to wash his hands. 'Do you often do night visits?'

Relieved that he'd changed the subject, some of the tension left her. 'Not since the new GP contract. Why?'

'Because I was told that the other night you were up with a child who had an asthma attack.'

'Chloe Bennett.' She frowned. 'How do you know that?'

He dried his hands. 'I was talking to the girl in the coffee-shop yesterday. Blonde. Nice smile.'

Alice resisted the temptation to roll her eyes. 'Katy Adams.' Obviously another conquest.

'Nice girl.'

Knowing Katy's reputation with men, Alice wondered if she should warn her new partner that he could be in mortal danger. She decided against it. A man who looked like him would have been fending off women from his cradle. He certainly wouldn't need any help from her.

'Chloe Bennett is a special case,' she explained briskly. 'Her mother has been working hard to control her asthma and give her some sort of normal life at school. It's been very difficult. She has my home number and I encourage her to use it when there's a problem, and that's what happened the night before last. I had to admit her in the end but not before she'd given me a few nasty moments.'

'I can't believe you give patients your home number.'

'Not every patient. But when the need is real…' She gave a shrug. 'It makes perfect sense from a management point of view. I'm the one with all the information. It means Chloe gets better care and her mother doesn't have to explain her history all the time.'

'You can't be there for everyone all the time. It isn't possible.'

'But continuity makes sense from a clinical point of view.' She frowned as she thought of it. 'In Chloe's case it means that a doctor unfamiliar with her case doesn't have to waste time taking details from a panicking parent when it's dark outside and the child can't breathe properly.'

'I can clearly see the benefits for your patients.' His eyes, dark and disturbingly intense, searched hers in a way that she found unsettling. 'But the benefits for you are less clear to me. It places an enormous demand on your time. On your life.'

'Yes, well, my job is important to me,' she said quickly, wondering whether there was anyone left in the world who felt the way she did about medicine. 'For me the job isn't about doing as little as possible and going home as early as possible. It's about involving yourself in the health of a community. About making a real difference to people's lives. I don't believe that a supermarket approach to health care is in anyone's interests.' She broke off and gave an awkward shrug, spots of colour touching her cheeks as she reflected on the fact that she was in danger of becoming carried away. 'Sorry. It's just something I feel strongly about. I don't expect you to understand. You probably think I'm totally mad.'

'On the contrary, I think your patients are very fortunate. But in all things there has to be compromise. How can you be awake to see patients—how can you be truly at your best—when you've been up half the night?' He strolled towards her and she felt her whole body tense in a response that she didn't understand.

She'd always considered herself to be taller than average but next to him she felt small. Even in heels she only reached his shoulder. Unable to help herself, she took a step backwards and then immediately wished she hadn't. 'You don't need to worry about me, Dr Moretti,' she said, keeping her tone cool and formal to compensate for her reaction. 'I'm not short of stamina and I really enjoy my life. And my patients certainly aren't suffering.'

'I'm sure they're not.' He gave a slow smile and raised an eyebrow. 'Does it make you feel safer, Alice?'

She took another step backwards. 'Does what make me feel safer?'

'Calling me Dr Moretti.' His expression was thoughtful. 'You do it whenever I get too close. Does it help give you the distance you need?'

She felt her heart pump harder. 'I don't know what you're talking about.'

'Was it a man?' He lifted a hand and tucked a strand of blonde hair behind her ear, his fingers lingering. 'Tell me, Alice. Was it a man who hurt you? Is that why you live alone and bury yourself in work? Is that why you don't believe in love?'

With a subtle movement that was entirely instinctive she moved her head away from his touch. 'You're obviously a romantic, Dr Moretti.'

'You're doing it again, *tesoro,*' he said softly, his hand

suspended in midair as he studied her face. 'Calling me Dr Moretti. It's Gio. And of course I'm romantic.'

'I'm sure you are.' She tilted her head, her smile mocking. 'All men are when it suits their purpose.'

He raised an eyebrow. 'You're suggesting that I use romance as some sort of seduction tool? You're a cynic, Alice, do you know that?'

Was it even worth defending herself? 'I'm a realist.' Her tone was cool. 'And you're clearly an extremely intelligent man. You should know better than to believe in all that woolly, emotional rubbish.'

'Ah, but you've overlooked one important fact about me.' His eyes gleamed dark and dangerous as he slid a hand under her chin and forced her to look at him. 'I'm Sicilian. We're a romantic race. It's in the blood. It has nothing to do with seduction and everything to do with a way of life. And a life is nothing without love in it.'

'Oh, please.' She rolled her eyes. 'I'm a scientist. I prefer to deal with the tangible. I happen to believe that love is a myth and the current divorce statistics would appear to support my view.'

'You think everything in this world can be explained given sufficient time in a laboratory?'

'Yes.' Her tone was cool and she brushed his hand away in a determined gesture. 'If it can't then it probably doesn't exist.'

'Is that right?' He looked at her as if he wanted to say something more but instead he smiled. 'So what do you do to relax around here? Restaurants? Watersports?'

For some reason her heart had set up a rhythmic pounding in her chest. 'I read a lot.'

'That sounds lonely, Dr Anderson,' he said softly. 'Especially for someone as young and beautiful as you.'

Taken aback and totally flustered, she raked a hand through her blonde hair and struggled for words. 'I—If you're flirting with me, Dr Moretti, it's only fair to warn you that you're wasting your time. I don't flirt. I don't play those sorts of games.'

'I wasn't flirting and I certainly wasn't playing games. I was stating a fact.' He said the words thoughtfully, his eyes narrowed as they scanned her face. 'You are beautiful. And very English. In Sicily, you would have to watch that pale skin.'

'Well, since I have no plans to visit Sicily, it isn't a problem that's likely to keep me awake at night.' Her head was buzzing and she felt completely on edge. There was something about him—something about the way he looked at her...

Deciding that the only way to end the conversation was to leave the room, she headed for the door.

'Wait. Don't run,' he said gently, his fingers covering hers before she could open the door.

His hand was hard. Strong. She turned, her heart pounding against her chest when she realised just how close he was.

'We have to meet Gina and—'

'What are you afraid of, Alice?'

'I'm not afraid. I'm just busy.' There was something in those dark eyes that brought a bubble of panic to her throat and her insides knotted with tension.

'You don't have to be guarded around me, Alice.' For a brief moment his fingers tightened on hers and then he let her go and took a step backwards, giving her the distance she craved. 'People interest me. There's often such a gulf between the person on the surface and the person underneath. It's rewarding to discover the real person.'

'Well, in my case there's nothing to discover, so don't waste your time.' She opened the door a crack. 'You're a good-looking guy, Dr Moretti, you don't need me to tell you that. I'm sure you can find no end of women willing to stroll on the beach with you, fall into bed, fall in love or do whatever it is you like to do in your spare time. You certainly don't need me. And now we need to meet Gina. She'll be waiting.'

CHAPTER SIX

GIO spent the rest of the day wondering about Alice. Wondering about her past.

She'd claimed that it hadn't been a man who'd forged her attitude to love, but it had to have been someone. In his experience, no one felt that strongly about relationships unless they'd been badly burned.

He tried to tell himself that it wasn't his business and that he wasn't interested. But he was interested. Very. And she filled his mind as he worked his way through a busy afternoon surgery.

The patients were a mix of locals and tourists and he handled them with ease and skill. Sore throats, arthritis, a diabetic who hadn't brought the right insulin on holiday and a nasty local reaction to an insect bite.

The locals lingered and asked questions. Where had he worked last? Had he bought a wife with him? Was he planning on staying long? The tourists were eager to leave the surgery and get on with their holiday.

Gio saw them all quickly and efficiently and handled the more intrusive questions as tactfully as possible, his mind distracted by thoughts of Alice. She was interesting, he mused as he checked glands and stared into throats. Interesting, beautiful and very serious.

Slightly prickly, wary, definitely putting up barriers. But underneath the front he sensed passion and vulnerability. He sensed that she was afraid.

He frowned slightly as he printed out a prescription for eye drops and handed it to his last patient.

There had been no mention of a social life in her description of relaxation. And David had definitely said that his partner had no time for anything other than work.

'You finished quickly today.' She walked into the room towards the end of the afternoon, just as his patient left. 'Any problems?'

'No. No problems so far.' He shook his head and leaned back in his chair. 'Should I have expected some?'

'People round here are congenitally nosy. You should have already realised that after twenty minutes in the company of the Normans this morning.' This time she stood near the door. Keeping a safe distance. 'This is a small, close-knit community and a new doctor is bound to attract a certain degree of attention. I bet they've been asking you no end of personal questions. Do you answer?'

'When it suits me. And when it doesn't...' he gave a shrug '...let's just say I was evasive. So, Dr Anderson, what next? I've asked about you but you haven't asked anything about me and you're probably the only one entitled to answers, given that we're working closely together.'

Their eyes met briefly and held for a long moment. Then she looked away. 'I've read your CV and that's all that matters. I'm not interested in the personal, Dr Moretti. Your life outside work is of no interest to me whatsoever. I really don't feel the need to know anything about you. You're doing your job. That's all I care about.'

Gio studied her in thoughtful silence. There was chemistry there. He'd felt it and he knew she'd felt it, too. Felt it and rejected it. Her face was shuttered. Closed. As if a protective shield had been drawn across her whole person.

Why?

'Make sure you have your key tonight because I have two house calls to make on the way home, so I'll be a bit late. Then I'm going to call at the supermarket and pick up the ingredients for a curry.' What exactly went into a curry? She knew she'd made it once before but she had no precise recollection of the recipe. 'How was the mother and baby clinic?'

'Fun. Interesting. But no Harriet.'

Alice frowned. 'Did you talk to Gina after our meeting?'

'At length. Interestingly enough, she's found it very hard to see Harriet. Every time she tries to arrange a visit Harriet makes an excuse, but she said that she'd sounded quite happy on the phone so she hasn't pushed. She thinks Harriet is just under a normal amount of strain for a new mother but she's promised to make another attempt at seeing her.'

'And what do you think?'

His gaze lifted to hers. 'After what I saw in the waiting room, I need to talk to her before I can answer that question.'

Alice grabbed her keys and popped her head into the nurse's room to say goodbye to Rita. 'I'm off. If Harriet comes to see you for anything in the next few days, make sure you encourage her to make an appointment with Dr Moretti.'

'I certainly will.' Rita returned a box of vaccines to the fridge and smiled. 'If you ask me, the man is a real find. Caring, warm and yet still incredibly masculine. You two have a nice evening together.'

'Don't you start. It isn't a date, Rita,' Alice said tightly. 'He's my lodger, thanks to Mary.'

Only somewhere along the way he'd forgotten his role. Lodgers weren't supposed to probe and delve and yet, from what she'd seen so far, Gio just couldn't help himself. Probing and delving seemed to be in his blood. Even with Harriet, he'd refused to take her insistence that she was fine at face value. Clearly he didn't intend to let the matter drop until he'd satisfied himself that she wasn't depressed.

Alice watched absently as Rita closed the fridge door. But, of course, at least where the patients were concerned, that was a good thing. It was his job to try and judge what was wrong with them. To pick up signs. Search for clues. To see past the obvious. She just didn't need him doing it with *her*.

'It's not Mary's fault the letting agency made a mess of things,' Rita said airily as she washed her hands. 'And if he were my lodger, I'd be thanking my lucky stars.'

'Well, you and I are different. And we both know that the letting agency wouldn't have made a mess of things without some significant help from certain people around here.' Alice put her hands on her hips and glared. 'And just for the record, in case you didn't get the message the first two hundred times, I don't need you to set me up with a man!'

'Don't you?' Rita dried her hands and dropped the paper towel in the bin. 'Strikes me you're not doing anything about it yourself.'

'Because, believe it or not, being with a man isn't compulsory!'

Reaching the point of explosion, Alice turned on her heel and strode out to her car before Rita had a chance to irritate her further. That day had been one long aggravation, she decided as she delved in her bag for her keys. All she wanted was to be left in peace to live her life the way she wanted to live it. What was so wrong with that?

Climbing into her car, she closed the door and shut her eyes.

Breathe, she told herself firmly, trying to calm herself down. Breathe. In and out. Relax.

Beside her, the door was pulled open. 'Alice, *tesoro,* are you all right?'

Her eyes opened. Gio was leaning into the car, his eyes concerned.

'I'm fine.' Gripping the wheel tightly, she wondered whether the sight of a GP screaming in a public place would attract attention. 'Or at least I will be fine when people stop interfering with my life and leave me alone. At least part of this is your fault.' She glared at him and his eyes narrowed.

'My fault?'

'Well, if you weren't single and good-looking, they wouldn't have been able to move you into my house.'

He rubbed a hand across his jaw and laughter flickered in his eyes. 'You want me to get married or rearrange my features?'

'No point. They'd just find some other poor individual to push my way.' Her tone gloomy, she slumped back in her seat and shook her head. 'Sorry, this really isn't your fault at all. It's just this place. Maybe David was right to get away. Right now I'd pay a lot to live among people who don't know who on earth I am and can't be bothered to find out. I must get going. I've got house calls to make on my way home.'

Unfortunately her car had other ideas. As she turned the key in the ignition the engine struggled and choked and then died.

'Oh, for crying out loud!' In a state of disbelief Alice glared at the car, as if fury alone should be enough to start it. 'What is happening to my life?'

Gio was still leaning on the open door. 'Do you often have problems with it?'

'Never before.' She tried the ignition again. 'My car is the only place I can get peace and quiet these days! The only place I can hide from people trying to pair me off with you! And now even that has died!'

'Shh.' He put a hand over her lips, his eyes amused. 'Calm down.'

'I can't calm down. I've got house calls to make and no transport.'

'I'm leaving now.' His tone was calm and reasonable as he gestured to the low, sleek sports car parked next to hers. 'We'll do the calls together.'

'But—'

'It makes perfect sense. It will help me orientate myself a little.'

'What's happening?' Mary hurried up, a worried expression on her face. 'Is it your car?'

'Yes.' Alice hissed the word through gritted teeth. 'It's my car.'

'Give me the keys and I'll get it taken care of,' Mary said immediately, holding out her hand. 'I'll call Paul at the garage. He's a genius with cars. In the meantime, you go with Dr Moretti.'

A nasty suspicion unfolded like a bud inside her. 'Mary…' Alice shook her head and decided she was becoming paranoid. No matter how much Mary wanted to push her towards Gio, she wasn't capable of tampering with a car. 'All right. Thanks.'

Accepting defeat, she climbed out of her car, handed the keys to Mary and slid into Gio's black sports car.

He pressed a button and the roof above her disappeared in a smooth movement.

She rolled her eyes. 'Show-off.'

He gave her a boyish grin, slid sunglasses over his eyes and reversed out of the parking space.

The last thing she saw as they pulled out of the surgery car park was the smug expression on Mary's face.

He drove up the hill, away from the harbour, with Alice giving directions.

'I'm embarrassed turning up at house calls in this car,' she mumbled as they reached the row of terraced houses where Edith lived. 'It's hardly subtle, is it? Everyone will think I've gone mad.'

'They will be envious and you will give them something interesting to talk about. Is this the lady that Betty was talking about earlier?' Gio brought the car to a halt and switched off the engine.

'Yes. Edith Carne.' Alice reached for her bag. 'She's

one of David's patients but she had a fall a few weeks ago and I just want to check on her because she lives on her own and she's not one to complain. You don't have to come with me. You're welcome to wait in the car. Who knows? Keep the glasses on and you might get lucky with some passing female.'

'But I am already lucky,' he said smoothly, leaning across to open the door for her, 'because you are in my car, *tesoro*.'

She caught the wicked twinkle in his dark eyes and pulled a face. 'Save the charm, Romeo. It's wasted on me.' She climbed out of the car and walked towards the house, her hair swinging around her shoulders, frustration still bubbling inside her.

'If she's David's patient, she's going to be mine,' Gio pointed out as he caught up with her, 'so this is as good a time as any to make her acquaintance. It's logical.'

It was logical, but still she would have rather he'd waited in the car. Having him tailing her flustered her and put her on edge. She needed space to calm herself. Normally she loved her work and found it absorbing and relaxing but today she felt restless and unsettled, as if the door to her tidy, ordered life had been flung wide open.

And it was all thanks to Mary and Rita, she thought angrily, and their interfering ways.

If she hadn't been living with the man, she could have easily avoided him. The surgery was so busy that often their paths didn't often cross during the day.

The evenings were a different matter.

Pushing aside feelings that she didn't understand, she rang the doorbell and waited. 'Her husband died three years ago,' she told Gio, 'and they were married for fifty-two years.'

He raised an eyebrow. 'And you don't believe in love?'

'There are lots of reasons why two people stay together.' She tilted her head back and stared up at the bedroom window through narrowed eyes. 'But love doesn't come into it, in my opinion. Why isn't she answering?'

'Does she have family?'

'No. But she has lots of friends in the village. She's lived here all her life.' Alice rang the bell again, an uneasy feeling spreading through her.

'Why did she fall last time? Does anyone know?'

'I don't think they found anything. The neighbour called an ambulance. She had a few cuts and bruises but nothing broken. But I know David was worried about her.' And now she was worried, too. Why wasn't Edith answering the door? She sighed and jammed her fingers through her hair. 'All right. I suppose I'll have to go next door and get the key, but I hate the thought of doing that.' Hated the thought of invading another person's privacy.

'Could she have gone out?' Gio stepped across the front lawn and glanced in through the front window. 'I can hear voices. A television maybe? But I can't see anyone.'

Alice was on the point of going next door to speak to the neighbour when the door opened.

'Oh, Edith.' She gave a smile of relief as she saw the old lady standing there. 'We were worried about you. We thought you might have fallen again. I wanted to check on how you're feeling.'

'Well, that's kind of you but I'm fine, dear.' Edith was wearing a dressing-gown even though it was late afternoon, and the expression on her face was bemused. 'No problems at all.'

Alice scanned Edith's face, noting that she looked extremely pale and tired. Something wasn't right.

'Can I come in for a minute, Edith? I'd really like to have a chat and check that everything's all right with you. And I need to introduce you to our new doctor.' She flapped a hand towards Gio. 'He's taken over from David. Come all the way from Sicily. Land of *canolli* and volcanoes that misbehave.'

'Sicily? Frank and I went there once. It was beautiful.' Edith's knuckles whitened on the edge of the door. 'I'm fine, Dr Anderson. I don't need to waste your time. There's plenty worse off than me.'

'Consider it a favour to me.' Gio's voice was deep and heavily accented. 'I am new to the area, Mrs Carne. I need inside information and I understand you've lived here all your life.'

'Well, I have, but—'

'Please—I would be so grateful.' He spread his hands, his warm smile irresistible to any female, and Edith looked into his dark eyes and capitulated.

'All right, but I'm fine. Completely fine.'

At least Gio used his charm on the old as well as the young, Alice thought as they followed Edith into the house. Wondering whether she was the only one who felt that something wasn't right, she glanced at Gio but his attention was focused on the old lady.

'This is a lovely room.' His eyes scanned the ancient, rose-coloured sofa and the photographs placed three deep on the window-sill. 'I can see that it is filled with happy memories.'

'I was born in this house.' Edith sat down, folded her hands in her lap and stared at the empty fireplace. 'My parents died in this house and Frank and I carried on living here. I've lived here all my life. I can see the sea from my kitchen window.'

'It's a beautiful position.' Gio leaned towards a photograph displayed on a table next to his right hand. 'This is you? Was it taken in the garden of this house?'

Edith gave a nod and a soft smile. 'With my parents. I was five years old.' She stared wistfully at the photo, her hands clasped in her lap. 'The garden was different then, of course. My Frank loved the garden. I used to joke that he loved his plants more than me.'

Gio lifted the photo and took a closer look. 'It must be lovely to walk in the garden that he planted.'

Alice shifted impatiently in her chair. What was he talking about? And why wasn't he asking Edith questions about her blood pressure and whether she'd felt dizzy lately? What was the relevance of the garden, for goodness' sake?

Edith was staring at him, a strange expression in her eyes. 'Very few people understand how personal a garden can be.'

'A garden tells you so much about a person,' Gio agreed, replacing the photo carefully on the table. 'And being there, you share in their vision.'

Edith twisted her hands in her lap. 'Just walking there makes me feel close to him.'

Alice frowned, wondering where the conversation was leading. True, Edith was much more relaxed than she'd been when they'd arrived and she had to admit that Gio had a way with people, but why were they talking about gardening? She wanted to establish some facts. She wanted to find out whether Edith had suffered another fall but Gio seemed to be going down an entirely different path.

She forced herself to sit quietly and breathed an in-audible sigh of relief when Gio eventually steered the talk round to the topic of Edith's health. It was so skill-fully done that it seemed like a natural direction for the conversation.

'I can barely remember the fall now,' Edith said dis-missively, 'it was so long ago.'

'A month, Edith,' Alice reminded her, and the old lady sniffed, all the tension suddenly returning to her slim frame.

'I was just clumsy. Not looking where I was going. Tripped over the carpet. It won't happen again—I'm being really careful.'

Alice glanced around the room. The carpet was fitted. There were no rugs. The carpet in the hall and on the stairs had been fitted, too. Her eyes clashed with Gio's and she knew that he'd noticed the same thing.

'Can I just check your pulse and blood pressure?' He opened his bag and removed the necessary equipment. 'Just routine.'

'I suppose so…'

Gio pushed up the sleeve of her dressing-gown and paused. 'That's a nasty bruise on your arm,' he com-mented as he wrapped the blood-pressure cuff around her arm. 'Did you knock yourself?'

Edith didn't look at him. 'Just being a bit careless walking through the doorway.'

Without further comment Gio checked her pulse, blood

pressure and pulse and then eased the stethoscope out of his ears. 'When you went into hospital after your fall, did anyone say that your blood pressure was on the low side?'

Edith shook her head. 'Not that I remember. They just sent me home and told me they'd set up another appointment in a few months. I'm fine. Really I am. But it was good of you to call in.' She stood up, the movement quite agitated. 'I'll come to the surgery if I need any help. Good of you to introduce yourself.'

Not giving them a chance to linger, she hurried them out of the front door and closed it.

'Well.' Standing on the doorstep, staring at a closed door, Alice blinked in amazement. 'What was all that about? She's normally the most hospitable woman in the community. From her reaction today, you would have thought we were planning to take her away and lock her up.'

'I think that's exactly what she thought.' Gio turned and walked down the path towards his car.

'What do you mean?' She caught up with him in a few strides. 'You're not making sense.'

He unlocked the car doors. 'I think your Mrs Carne has had more falls since David saw her. But she isn't ready to confess.' He slid into the car while Alice gaped at him from the pavement.

'But why?' It seemed simple to Alice. 'If she's falling then she should tell us and we'll try and solve it.'

The engine gave a throaty roar and he drummed long fingers on the steering-wheel while he waited for her to get into the passenger seat. 'Life isn't always that simple, is it?'

She climbed in next to him and fastened her seat belt. 'So why wouldn't she tell us?'

'General practice is very like detective work, don't you think?' He glanced towards her. 'In hospital you see only the patient. At home you have the advantage of seeing the patient in their own environment and that often contains clues about the person they are. About the way they live their lives.'

'And what clues did you see?'

'That her whole life is contained in that house. There were photographs of her parents, her as a child, her husband. There were cushions that she'd knitted on a sofa that I'm willing to bet belonged to her mother. The garden had been planted by her husband.'

Alice tried to grasp the relevance of what he was saying and failed. 'But that's all emotional stuff. What's that got to do with her illness?'

'Not everything about a patient can be explained by science alone, Alice.' He checked the rear-view mirror and pulled out. 'She doesn't want us to know she's falling because she's afraid we're going to insist she leaves her home. And she loves her home. Her home is everything to her. It contains all her memories. Take her from it and you erase part of her life. Probably the only part that matters.'

He was doing it again, Alice mused, delving deep. Refusing to accept people at face value.

She stared ahead as he drove off down the quiet road and back onto the main road. 'Take a left here,' she said absently, her mind still on their conversation. 'Aren't you making it complicated? I mean, if Edith is falling, we need to find the reason. It's that simple. The rest isn't really anything to do with us.'

'The rest is everything to do with us if it affects the patient. You're very afraid of emotions, aren't you, Alice?' His voice was soft and she gave a frown.

'We're not talking about me.'

'Of course we're not.' There was no missing the irony in his tone but she chose to ignore it.

'So now what do we do?'

'I want to check on a couple of things. Look at the correspondence that came out of her last appointment and speak to the doctor who saw her before I go crashing in with my diagnosis.'

'Which is?' The wind picked up a strand of hair and blew it across her face. 'You think you know why she's falling?'

'Not for sure, no. But certainly there are clues.' He eased the car round a tight corner, his strong hands firm on the wheel. 'Her heart rate is on the slow side and her blood pressure is low. What do you know about CSS?'

'Carotid sinus syndrome. I remember reading a UK study on it a few years ago.' Alice sifted through her memory and her brow cleared. 'They linked it to unexplained falls in the elderly. It can result in syncope— fainting. Are you saying that you think—?' She broke off and Gio gave a shrug that betrayed his Latin heritage.

'I don't know for sure, of course, but it's certainly worth considering. It's important that elderly patients who fall are given cardiovascular assessment. Do you think this happened in her case?'

'Not to my knowledge. We'll check the notes and, if not, we'll refer her immediately.' The wind teased her hair again and Alice slid a hand through the silky strands and tried to anchor them down. 'Well done. That was very smart of you. And all that stuff about her house and the way she was feeling…' She frowned, angry and disappointed with herself. 'I wouldn't have thought of that.'

'That's because you work only with facts and not emotions, but the truth is that the two work together. You can't dissociate them from each other, Alice. Emotions are a part of people's lives.' He gave her a quick glance, a slight smile touching his mouth, a challenge in his dark eyes. 'And she was definitely in love with her husband.'

She tipped her head back against the seat and rolled her eyes upwards. 'Don't let's go there again.'

'You heard the way she talked about him. You saw the look on her face. Do you really think she didn't love him?'

'Well, obviously you're going to miss someone if you've lived with them for over fifty years,' Alice said tetchily, 'and I'm sure they were best friends. I just don't believe in this special, indefinable, woolly emotion that supposedly binds two people together.'

'You don't believe in love at first sight?'

'Nor on second or third sight,' Alice said dryly, letting go of her hair and pointing a finger towards a turning. 'You need to take a right down there so that I can pick up some dinner.'

He followed her instructions and turned into the supermarket car park. 'Listen, about dinner. You cooked last night. Perhaps I ought to—'

'No need. I've got it. Back in five minutes.' She slammed the door and braced herself for her second least favourite pastime after cooking. Shopping for the ingredients.

* * *

Later, wondering whether his taste buds would ever recover, Gio drank yet another glass of water in an attempt to quench the fire burning in his mouth. 'Alice, tomorrow it's my turn to cook.'

'Why would you want to do that?'

Was it all right to be honest? He gave a wry smile and risked it. 'Because I want to live?'

Because he respected his stomach far too much to eat another one of her meals and because he needed to show her that there was more to eating than simply ingesting animal and plant material in any format.

She sighed and dropped her fork. 'All right, it tasted pretty awful but I'm not that great at curry. I think I might have got my tablespoons mixed up with my tea-spoons. Does it really matter?'

'When you're measuring chilli powder? Yes,' he replied dryly. 'And, anyway, I'm very happy to cook from now on. I love to cook. I'll do you something Italian. You'll enjoy it.'

She pushed her plate away, the contents only half-eaten. 'We eat to live, Gio, not the other way round. The body needs protein, carbohydrate, fats and all that jazz in order to function the way it should. It doesn't care how you throw them together.'

She was all fact, he thought to himself. All fact and science. As far as she was concerned, if it couldn't be explained by some fancy theory then it didn't exist.

It would be fun to show her just what could be achieved with food, he decided. And atmosphere.

At least she'd stopped jumping every time he walked into the room. It was time to make some changes. Time to push her out of her comfort zone.

He tapped his foot under the table, his mind working. Maybe it was time to show Dr Alice Anderson that there was more to life than scientific theory. That not every-thing could be proven.

Maybe it was time for her to question her firmly held beliefs. But before that he needed to deal with his indigestion.

'Let's go for a walk on the beach.'

She shook her head and dumped the remains of the totally inedible curry in the bin. 'I need to catch up on some reading. You go. Take a left at the bottom of the garden, along the cycle path for about two hundred metres and you reach the harbour. Go to the end and you drop straight down onto the beach. You can walk for miles if the tide is out. Once it comes in you have to scramble up the cliffs to the coast path.'

'I want you to come with me.' Not giving her a chance to shrink away from him, he reached out a hand and dragged her to her feet. 'The reading can wait.'

'I really need to…' Her hand wriggled in his as she tried to pull away, but he kept a tight hold and used his trump card. Work.

'I want to talk about some of David's patients.' He kept his expression serious. Tried to look suitably con-cerned. 'It's obvious to me that the only time we're going to have for discussion is during the evenings. And I have so many questions.'

He struggled to think of a few, just in case he needed to produce one.

'Oh.' She thought for a moment and then gave a shrug. 'Well, I suppose that makes sense, but we don't have to go out. We could do it here and—'

'Alice, we've been trappcd inside all day. We both need some air.' Letting go of her hand, he reached out and grabbed her jacket from the back of the door. 'Let's walk.'

'Have you come across a specific problem with a patient? Who is on your mind?'

He racked his brains to find someone to talk about, knowing that if he didn't start talking about work immediately, she'd vanish upstairs and spend the rest of the evening with her journals and textbooks, as she had the previous evening.

'I thought we could talk about the right way to approach Harriet.' He stepped through the back door and waited while she locked it. 'You know her after all.'

'Not that well. She was David's patient. Mary knows her, she might have some ideas.'

She slipped the keys into her pocket and they walked down to the cycle way. Although it was still only early evening, several cyclists sped past them, enjoying the summer weather and the wonderful views.

The tide was far out, leaving sandbanks exposed in the water.

'It's beautiful.' Gio stared at the islands of sand and Alice followed his gaze.

'Yes. And dangerous. The tide comes in so fast, it's lethal.' She stepped to one side to avoid another cyclist. 'There are warnings all over the harbour and the beach, but still some tourists insist on dicing with death. Still, it keeps the lifeboat busy.'

They reached the harbour and weaved a path through the crowds of tourists who were milling around, watching the boats and eating fish and chips on the edge of the quay.

Gio slipped a hand in his pocket. 'Ice cream, Dr Anderson?'

'I don't eat ice cream.' She was looking around her with a frown. 'Bother. We shouldn't have come this way.'

'Why not?'

'Because I've just seen at least half a dozen people who know me.'

'And what's wrong with that?' He strolled over to the nearest ice-cream shop and scanned the menu. Vanilla? Too boring. Strawberry? Too predictable.

'Because if I've seen them, then they've seen me.' She turned her head. 'With you.'

'Ah.' Cappuccino, he decided. 'And surely that's a good thing.'

'Why would fuelling town gossip possibly be a good thing?'

'Because you want to prove that you don't want a re-lationship.' He wandered into the shop and ordered two cones. 'In order to do that, you at least have to be seen to be mixing with members of the opposite sex. If you do that and still don't fall in love then eventually every-one will just give up trying. If you don't, they'll just keep fixing you up.'

She glared at him and he realised that the lady selling the ice creams was listening avidly.

'Perfect evening for a walk, Dr Anderson. We don't see you in here often enough. That will be three pounds forty, please.' The woman took the money with a smile and turned to Gio. 'You must be our new doctor. Betty told me all about you.'

'That's good. Saves me introducing myself.' Gio pocketed the change and picked up the ice creams with a nod of thanks and a few more words of small talk.

Outside he handed a cone to Alice.

'I said I didn't want one.'

'Just try it. One lick.'

'It's—'

'It's protein, Dr Anderson.' He winked at her and she raised an eyebrow.

'How do you work that out?'

'All that clotted cream.' He watched, noting with satisfaction the smile that teased the corners of her mouth. He was going to teach her to relax. To loosen up. To enjoy herself.

'It's a frozen lump of saturated fat designed to occlude arteries,' she said crisply, and he nodded.

'Very possibly. But it's also a mood lifter. An indulgence. A sensory experience. Smooth. Cold. Creamy. Try it.'

She stared at him. 'It's ice cream, Gio. Just ice cream.' She waved a hand dismissively and almost consigned the ice cream to the gutter. 'The body doesn't need ice cream in order to function efficiently.'

'The body may not *need* ice cream,' he conceded, 'but it's extremely grateful to receive it. Try it and find out. Go on—lick.'

With an exaggerated roll of her eyes she licked the cone. And licked again. 'All right, so it tastes good. But that's just because of the coffee. You know I love coffee.' The evening sunlight caught the gold in her hair and her blue eyes were alight with humour. 'It's my only vice.'

Looking at the way her mouth moved over the ice cream, he decided that before the summer was finished Alice would have expanded her repertoire of vices. And he was going to help her do it.

'Lick again and close your eyes,' he urged her, ignoring the fact that his own ice cream was in grave danger of melting.

She stared at him as if he were mad. 'Gio, I'm not closing my eyes with half the town watching! I have to work with these people long after you've gone! I need to retain my credibility. If I stand in the harbour with my eyes closed, licking ice cream, they'll never listen to me again.'

'Stop trying to be so perfect all the time. And stop worrying about other people.' She was delightfully prim, he thought, noticing the tiny freckles on her nose for the first time. He doubted she'd ever let her hair down in her life.

And he was absolutely crazy about her.

The knowledge knocked the breath from his lungs. 'Close your eyes, or I'll throw you in the harbour.' His voice was gruff. 'And that will seriously damage your credibility.'

How could he possibly be in love with a woman he'd only known for a couple of days?

'Oh, fine!' With an exaggerated movement she squeezed her eyes shut and he stepped closer, tempted by the slight pout of her lips.

Suppressing the desire to kiss her until her body melted like the ice cream in her hand, he reminded himself that it was too soon for her.

He was going to take it slowly. Take his time. *Coax her out of her shell.*

'Now lick again and tell me what you taste. Tell me what it makes you feel. What it reminds you of.'

Her lick was most definitely reluctant. 'Ice cream?' Receiving no response to her sarcasm, she licked again and he waited. And waited. But she said nothing.

'Don't you go straight back to your childhood?' He decided that he was going to have to prompt her. Clearly she'd never played this game before. 'Seaside holidays, relaxation? All the fun of being young?'

There was a long silence and then her eyes opened and for a brief moment he saw the real Alice. And what he saw shocked and silenced him. He saw pain and anguish. He saw hurt and disillusionment. But most of all he saw a child who was lost and vulnerable. Alone.

And then she blanked it.

'No, Dr Moretti.' Her voice had a strange, rasping quality, as if talking was suddenly difficult. 'I don't see that. And I'm not that keen on ice cream.' Without giving him time to reply, she tossed it in the nearest bin and made for the beach, virtually breaking into a run in her attempt to put distance between them.

CHAPTER SEVEN

AT THE bottom of the path, Alice slowed her pace and took several gulps of air. Her stomach churned and she felt light-headed and sick but most of all she felt angry with herself for losing control.

Oh, damn, damn damn.

How could she have let that happen? How could she have revealed so much? And because she had, *because she'd been so stupid,* he was going to come after her and demand an explanation. He was that sort of man. The sort of man who always looked beneath the surface. The sort of man who delved and dug until he had access to all parts of a person.

And she didn't want him delving. She didn't want him digging.

She bent down, removed her shoes and stepped onto the sand, intending to walk as far as possible, as fast as possible. *Even though she knew that even if she were to run, it wouldn't make any difference.* The problems were inside her and always would be, and she knew from experience that running couldn't change the past. Couldn't change the feelings that were part of her.

But she'd learned ways to handle them, she reminded

herself firmly as she breathed in deeply and unclenched her hands. Ways that worked for her. It was just a question of getting control back. Of being the person she'd become.

She stared at the sea, watching the yachts streak across the bay, the wind filling their brightly coloured sails. Breathing in the same strong sea breeze, she struggled to find the familiar feeling of calm, but it eluded her.

She was concentrating so hard on breathing that the feel of Gio's hand on her shoulder made her jump, even though she'd been expecting it.

Her instinct was to push him away, but that would draw attention that she didn't want. She could have run but that, she told herself, would just make it even harder later. It would just delay the inevitable conversation. So she decided to stay put and give him enough facts to satisfy him. Just enough and no more.

She turned to face him and dislodged his hand in the process. Immediately she wished she'd thought to wear sunglasses. Or a wide-brimmed hat. Anything to give her some protection from that searching, masculine gaze.

She felt exposed. Naked.

Wishing she'd decided to run, she hugged herself with her arms and looked away, gesturing towards the beach with a quick jerk of her head. 'You can walk along here for about an hour before the tide turns.' The words spilled out like girlish chatter. 'Then you have to climb up to the coast path if you don't want to get cut off.'

'Alice—'

'It's a nice walk and you always lose the crowds about ten minutes out of the harbour.' The wind picked up a strand of her hair and threw it across her face, but she ignored it. 'It will take you about an hour and a half to reach the headland.'

He stepped closer and his hands closed over her arms. 'Alice, don't!' He gave her a little shake. 'Don't shut me out like this. I said something to upset you and for that I'm sorry.'

'You don't need to be sorry. You haven't done anything wrong.' She tilted her head back and risked another glance at his face. And saw kindness. Kindness and sympathy. The combination untwisted something that had been knotted inside her for years and she very nearly let everything spill out. Very nearly told him exactly how she was feeling. But she stopped herself. Reminded herself of how she'd chosen to live her life. 'I just don't happen to like ice cream that much.'

'Alice...' He tried to hold her but she shrugged him off, swamped by feelings that she didn't want to feel.

'I'm sorry, but I need to walk.'

He muttered something in Italian and then switched to English. 'Alice, wait!' With his long stride, he caught up with her easily. 'We need to talk.' His Italian accent was stronger than ever, as if he was struggling with the language.

'We don't need to talk.' She walked briskly along the sand, her shoes in one hand, the other holding her hair out of her eyes. This far up the beach the sand was soft and warm, cushioning the steady rhythm of her feet and causing her to stumble occasionally. 'I don't want to talk! Not everyone wants to talk about everything, Gio.'

'Because you're afraid of your own emotions. Of being hurt. That's why you prefer facts.' He strode next to her, keeping pace. 'You've turned yourself into a machine, Alice, but emotions are the oil that makes the machine work. Human beings can't function without emotions.'

She walked faster in an attempt to escape the conversation. 'You don't need to get into my skin and understand me. And I don't need healing.'

'Most people need healing from something, Alice. It's—*Dios,* can you stop walking for a moment?' Reaching out, he grabbed her shoulders and turned her, his fingers firm on her flesh as he held her still. 'Stop running and have a conversation. Is that really so frightening?'

'You want facts? All right, I'll give you the facts. You and Edith obviously have lots of happy childhood memories. I don't.' Her heart thumped steadily against her chest as her past spilled into her present. 'It's as simple as that. Ice cream doesn't remind me of happy holidays, Gio. It reminds me of bribes. A way of persuading me to like my mother's latest boyfriend. A way of occupying me for ten minutes while my father spent romantic time with his latest girlfriend. Ice cream was a salve to the conscience while they told me I needed to live in a different place for a while because I was getting in the way of *"love".*' Her heart was beating, her palms were sweaty and feelings of panic bubbled up inside her. Feelings that she hadn't had for a very long time.

Gio sucked in a breath. 'This was your childhood?'

'Sometimes I was a ping-pong ball, occasionally I was a pawn but mostly I was just a nuisance.'

'And now?' He frowned and his grip on her arms tightened. 'Your parents are divorced?'

'Oh, several times. Not just the once.' She knew her tone was sarcastic and brittle but she couldn't do anything about it. Couldn't be bothered to hide it any more. Maybe if he understood the reasons for the way she was, he'd leave her alone. 'You know what they say—practice makes perfect. My parents had plenty of practice. They are quite expert at divorce.'

His eyes were steady on her face. Searching. 'And you?'

'Me? I survived.' She spread her hands. 'Here I am. In one piece.'

He shook his head. 'Not in one piece. Your belief in love has been shattered. They took that from you with their selfish behaviour.' He lifted a hand and touched her cheek. 'My beautiful Alice.'

Her breathing hitched in her throat and her shoulders stiffened. 'Don't feel sorry for me. I like my life. I don't need fairy-tales to be happy.' She tensed still further as he slid a hand over her cheek, his thumb stroking gently. 'What are you doing?'

'Offering you comfort. A hug goes a long way to making things better, don't you think?' His voice was soft. 'Touch is important.'

'I'm not used to being touched.' She stood rigid, not moving a muscle. 'I don't like being touched.'

'Then you need more practice. Everyone likes being touched, as long as it's in the right way.'

He was too close and it made her feel strange. His voice made her feel strange.

'Enough.' Shaken and flustered, she took a step backwards. Broke the contact. 'You just can't help it, can you? I've only known you for a short time but during that time I've seen how you always have to dig and delve into a person's life.'

'Because the answers to questions often lie below the surface.'

She scraped her hair out of her eyes. 'Well, I don't need you to delve and I don't want you to dig. There are no questions about my life that you need to answer. I'm not one of your patients with emotional needs.'

'Everyone has emotional needs, Alice.'

'Well, I don't. And I don't have to explain myself to you! And I don't need you to understand me. I didn't ask to take this walk and I didn't ask for your company. If you don't like the way I am then you can go back to the house.'

'I like the way you are, *cara mia.*' Without warning or hesitation, his hands cupped her face and he brought his mouth down on hers, his kiss warm and purposeful.

Alice stood there, frozen with shock while his mouth moved over hers, coaxing, tempting, growing more demanding, and suddenly a tiny, icy part of herself started to melt. The warmth started to spread and grew in intensity until she felt something explode inside her. Something delicious and exciting that she'd never felt before.

Feeling oddly disconnected, she tried to summon up logic and reason. *Any minute now she was going to pull away.* But his arms slid round her, his hold strong and powerful, and still his mouth plundered and stole the breath from her body. *She was going to punch him somewhere painful.* But his fingers stroked her cheek and his tongue teased and danced and coaxed a response that she'd never given to any man before.

In the end it was Gio who suspended the kiss. 'My Alice.' He lifted his head just enough to breathe the words against her mouth. 'They hurt you badly, *tesoro.*'

She felt dazed. Drugged. Unable to speak or think. She tried to open her eyes but her eyelids felt heavy, and as for her knees—hadn't David said something about knees?

'Dr Anderson!' A sharp young voice from directly behind her succeeded where logic had not. Her eyes opened and she pulled away, heart thumping, cheeks flaming.

'Henry?' Her voice cracked as she turned to acknowledge the ten-year-old boy behind her. Flustered and embarrassed, she stroked a hand over her cheeks in an attempt to calm herself down. 'What's the matter?'

Henry pointed, his expression frantic. 'They're cut off, Dr Anderson. The tide's turning.'

Beside her, Gio ran a hand over the back of his neck and she had the satisfaction of seeing that he was no more composed than she was.

For a brief, intense moment their eyes held and then she turned her attention back to Henry, trying desperately to concentrate on what he was saying.

And it was obviously something important. He was hopping on the spot, his expression frantic, his arms waving wildly towards the sea.

'Who is cut off from what?' She winced inwardly as she listened to herself. Since when had she been unable to form words properly? To focus on a problem in hand?

'The twins. They were playing.'

'Twins?' Alice shielded her eyes from the evening sun and stared out across the beach, her eyes drawn to two tiny figures playing on a small, raised patch of sand. All around them the sea licked and swirled, closing off their route back to the beach. They were on a sand spit and the tide was turning. 'Oh, no…'

Finally she understood what Henry had been trying to tell her and she slid her hand in her pocket and reached for her mobile phone even as she started to run towards the water. 'I'll call the coastguard. Where's their mother, Henry? Have you seen Harriet?' She was dialling as she spoke, her finger shaking as she punched in the numbers, aware that Gio was beside her, stripping off as he ran.

The boy shook his head, breathless. 'They were on their own, I think.'

Alice spoke to the coastguard, her communication brief and succinct, and then broke the connection and glanced around her. They couldn't possibly have been on their own. They were five years old. Harriet was a good mother. She wouldn't have left them.

And then she saw her, carrying the baby and weighed down by paraphernalia, walking along the beach and calling for the twins. Searching. She hadn't seen them. Hadn't seen the danger. And Alice could hear the frantic worry in her voice as she called.

'You go to Harriet, I'll get the twins,' Gio ordered, running towards the sea, his long, muscular legs closing the distance.

The tide was still far out but she knew how fast it came in, how quickly those tempting little sand spits disappeared under volumes of seawater.

She ran with him, aware that Henry was keeping up with them. 'Henry, go to the cliff and get us a line.' She barked out the instruction, her throat dry with fear, her heart pounding. 'You know the line with the lifebuoy.' She knew the dangers of entering the water without a buoyancy aid. 'Gio, wait. You have to wait. You can't just go in there.'

For a moment the kiss was forgotten. The ice cream was forgotten. Nothing mattered except the urgency of the moment. Two little boys in mortal danger. *The weight of responsibility.*

'In a few more minutes those children will be out of reach.'

Alice grabbed his arm as they ran. Tried to slow him. Tried to talk sense into him. The sand was rock hard now as they approached the water's edge and then finally she felt the damp lick of the sea against her toes and stopped. 'You're not going into that water without a line. Do you know how many people drown in these waters, trying to save others?' Her eyes skimmed his body, noticed the hard, well-formed muscles. He had the body of an athlete and at the moment it was clad only in a pair of black boxer shorts.

'Stop giving me facts, Alice.' His expression was grim. 'They're five years old,' he said roughly, 'and they're not going to stand like sensible children on that spit of sand and wait to be rescued. What do you want me to do? Watch while they drown? Watch while they die?' Concern thickened his accent and she shook her head.

'No, but—'

'Get me a buoyancy aid and go to Harriet,' he urged as he stepped into the water. He caught her arm briefly, his eyes on her face. 'And remember emotions when you talk to her, Alice. It isn't always about facts.'

He released her and Alice swallowed and cast a frantic glance up the coast. She knew the lifeboat would come from that direction. Or maybe the coastguard would send the helicopter. Either way, she knew they needed to hurry.

From the moment he plunged into the water she could see that Gio was a strong swimmer, but she knew that the tides in this part of the bay were lethal and she knew that it would only take minutes for the water level to rise. Soon the spit of sand that was providing the twins with sanctuary would vanish from under their feet.

She could hear them screaming and crying and closed her eyes briefly. And then she heard Harriet's cry of horror.

'Oh, my God—my babies.' The young mother covered her mouth with her hand, her breathing so rapid that Alice was afraid she might faint.

'Harriet—try and stay calm.' *What a stupid, useless thing to say to a mother whose two children were in danger of drowning.* She took refuge in facts, as she always did. 'We've called the coastguard and Dr Moretti is going to swim out to them. Henry Fox is getting the buoyancy aid.'

'Neither of them can swim,' Harriet gasped, her eyes wild with panic, and Alice remembered what Gio had said about remembering emotions.

She swallowed and felt helpless. She just wasn't in tune with other people's emotions. She wasn't comfortable. What would Gio say? Certainly not that the ability to swim wouldn't save the twins in the lethal waters of Smuggler's Cove.

'They don't need to swim because the coastguard is going to be here in a moment,' she said finally, jabbing her fingers into her hair and wishing she was better with words. She just didn't know the right things to say. And then she remembered what Gio had said about touch. Hesitantly she stepped closer to Harriet and slipped an arm round her shoulders.

Instantly Harriet turned towards her and clung. 'Oh, Dr Anderson, this is all my fault. I'm a useless mother. Terrible.'

Caught in the full flood of Harriet's emotion, Alice froze and wished for a moment that she'd been the one to go in the water. She would have been much better at dealing with tides than with an emotional torrent.

'You're a brilliant mother, Harriet,' she said firmly. 'The twins are beautifully mannered, tidy, the baby is fed—'

'But that isn't really what being a mother is,' Harriet sniffed, still clinging to Alice. 'A childminder can do any of those things. Being a mother is noticing what your child really needs. It's the fun stuff. The interaction. And I'm so tired, I just can't do any of it. They wanted to go to the beach so I took them, but I was too tired to actually play with them so I sat feeding the baby and then I just lost sight of them and they wandered off.'

Alice watched as Gio climbed onto another sand spit. Between him and the twins was one more strip of water. Treacherous water.

And then she heard the clack, clack, clack of an approaching helicopter and breathed a sigh of relief. Gio didn't even need to cross the water now. The coastguard could—

'No! Oh, no, don't try and get in the water,' Harriet shrieked, moving away from Alice and running towards the water's edge. 'Oh, Dr Anderson, my Dan is trying to get into the water.'

Gio saw it too and shouted something to the boys before diving into the sea to cross the last strip of water. He used a powerful front crawl but even so Alice could see that he was being dragged sideways by the fast current.

It was only after he pulled himself safely onto the strip of sand that Alice realised that her fingernails had cut into her palms.

She saw him lift one of the twins and take the other by the hand, holding them firmly while the coastguard helicopter hovered in position above them.

The sand was gradually disappearing as the tide swirled and reclaimed the land, and a crowd of onlookers had gathered on the beach and were watching the drama unfold.

Alice bit her lip hard. The helicopter crew would rescue them all. Of course they would.

Still with her arm round Harriet, she watched as the winchman was lowered down to the sand to collect the first child.

The baby was screaming in Harriet's arms but she just jiggled it vaguely, all her attention focused on her twins.

'Let me take her.' Alice reached across and took the baby and Harriet walked into the sea, yearning to get to the boys. 'Hold it, Harriet.' With a soft curse Alice held the baby with one arm and used the other to grab Harriet and hold her back. 'Just wait. They're fine now. Nothing's going to happen to them.' Providing the coastguard managed to pick up the second child and Gio before the tide finally closed over the rapidly vanishing sand spit.

Discovering new depths of tension within herself, Alice watched helplessly as the winchman guided the first child safely into the helicopter and then went down for the second.

By now Gio's feet were underwater and he was

holding the child high in his arms, safely away from the dangerous lick of the sea.

The helicopter held its position, the crowd on the beach grew and there was a communal sigh of relief as the winchman picked up the second child, attached the harness and then guided him safely into the helicopter.

'Oh, thank God!' Harriet burst into tears, her hands over her face. 'Now what?' She turned to Alice. 'Where are they taking them?'

'They'll check them over just in case they need medical help,' Alice told her, her eyes fixed on Gio who was now up to mid-thigh in swirling water. She raked fingers through her hair and clamped her teeth on her lower lip to prevent herself from crying out a warning. What was the point of crying out a warning when the guy could see perfectly well for himself what was happening?

'Will they take them to the hospital?' Harriet was staring up at the helicopter but Alice had her gaze fixed firmly on Gio.

There was no way he'd be able to swim safely now. The water was too deep and the current was just too fierce.

The crowd on the beach must have realised it too because a sudden silence fell as they waited for the helicopter to lower the winchman for a third time.

And finally Harriet saw...

'He's risking his life.' She said the words in hushed tones, as if she'd only just realised what was truly happening. 'Oh, my God, he's risking his life for my babies. And now he's going to—'

'No, he isn't.' Alice snapped the words, refusing to allow her to voice what everyone was thinking. 'He's going to be fine, Harriet,' she said, as much to convince herself as the woman standing next to her in a serious state of anxiety. 'They're lowering the winchman again.'

What was the Italian for *you stupid, brave idiot?* she wondered as she watched Gio exchange a few words with the winchman and then laugh as the harness was attached. They rose up in the air, swinging slightly as they approached the hovering helicopter.

Alice closed her eyes briefly as he vanished inside. For a moment she just felt like sinking onto the sand and staying there until the panic subsided. Then her mobile phone rang. She answered it immediately. It was Gio.

'Twins seem fine but they're taking them to hospital for a quick check.' His voice crackled. 'Tell Harriet I'll bring them home. It isn't safe for her to drive in a state of anxiety and shock and by the time she gets up to the house, picks up the car and drives to the hospital, I'll be home with them.'

Deciding that it wasn't the right moment to yell at him, she simply acknowledged what he'd said and ended the call. 'They seem fine but they're going to take them to the hospital for a check. Dr Moretti will bring them home, Harriet,' she said quietly. 'Let's go back to your house now and make a cup of tea. I don't know about you, but I need one.'

Gio arrived back at the house three hours later. Three long hours during which she'd had all too much time to think about *that kiss* and the fact that she'd told him far more about herself than she'd intended.

Annoyed with herself, confused, Alice abandoned all pretence of reading a medical journal and was pacing backwards and forwards in the kitchen, staring at the clock, when she finally heard the doorbell. She closed her eyes and breathed a sigh of relief.

She opened the door and lifted an eyebrow, trying to regain some of her old self. Trying to react the way she would have reacted before *that kiss*. 'Forgot your key?'

He was wearing a set of theatre scrubs and he looked broad-shouldered and more handsome than a man had a right to look. She sneaked a look at his firm mouth and immediately felt a sizzle in her veins.

'Careless, I know. I went swimming and I must have them in my trousers.' He strolled past her with a lazy grin and pushed the door closed behind him. Suddenly her hallway seemed small.

'Talking of swimming...' she took a step backwards and kept her tone light '...you certainly go to extreme lengths to pull the women, Dr Moretti. Plunging into the jaws of death and acting like a hero. Does it work for you?'

He paused, his eyes on hers, his expression thoughtful. 'I don't know. Let's find out, shall we?' Without warning, he reached out a hand and jerked her against him, his mouth hovering a mere breath from hers. 'We have unfinished business, Dr Anderson.'

He kissed her hard and she felt her knees go weak but she didn't have the chance to think about the implications of that fact because something hot and dangerous exploded in her body. She wound her arms round his neck for support. *Just for support.*

He gave a low groan and dug his fingers into her hair, tilting her head, changing the angle, helping himself to her mouth.

'You taste good, *cara mia,*' he muttered, trailing kisses

over her jaw and then back to her mouth. He kissed her thoroughly. Skilfully. And then lifted his head, his breathing less than steady. 'I'm addicted to your mouth. It was one of the first things I noticed about you.'

Her head swam dizzily and she tried to focus, but before she could even remember how to regain control he lowered his head again.

With a soft gasp, she tried to speak. 'Stop…' His lips had found a sensitive spot on her neck and she was finding it impossible to think straight. With a determined effort, she pushed at his chest. 'We have to stop this.'

'Why?' His mouth returned to hers, teasing and seducing. 'Why stop something that feels so good?'

Her head was swimming and she couldn't concentrate. 'Because I don't do this.'

'Then it's good to try something new.' He lifted his head, his smile surprisingly gentle. 'Courage, *tesoro*.'

Her fingers were curled into the hard muscle of his shoulders and she remembered the strength he'd shown in the water.

'Talking of courage, you could have drowned out there.'

His eyes searched hers. Questioning. 'You're telling me you were worried, Dr Anderson?' He lifted a hand and gently brushed her cheek. 'Better not let Mary hear you say that. She'll be buying a hat to wear at our wedding.'

'Oh, for goodness' sake.' She knew he was teasing but all the same the words flustered her and she pulled away, trying not to look at his mouth. Trying not to think about the way he kissed. About the fact that she wanted him to go on kissing her. 'What took you so long, anyway? I was beginning to think you'd gone back to Italy.'

'I hurried the twins through A and E, we got a ride home with one of the paramedics and then I dropped them home.'

'And that took three hours? Did you drive via Scotland?'

'You really were worried. Careful, Alice.' His voice was soft, his gaze searching. 'You're showing emotion.'

She flushed and walked past him to the kitchen. 'Given the distance between here and the hospital, with which I'm entirely familiar, I was expecting you back ages ago. And you didn't answer your mobile.'

'I was with Harriet.' He followed her and went straight to the espresso machine. 'She had a nasty shock and she was blaming herself terribly for what happened. She needed TLC.'

And he would have given her the comfort she needed, because he was that sort of man. He was good with people's emotions, she thought to herself. Unlike her.

'I stayed with her for the first two hours,' she muttered, raking fingers through her hair, feeling totally inadequate, 'but she just kept pacing and saying she was a terrible mother. And I didn't know what to say. I'm hopeless at giving emotional comfort. If she'd cut her finger or developed a rash, I would have been fine. But there was nothing to see. She was just hysterical and miserable. I did my best, but it wasn't good enough. I was useless.'

He glanced over his shoulder, his eyes gentle. 'That's not true. You're not hopeless or useless. Just a little afraid, I think. Emotions can be scary things. Not so easily explained as some other things. You'll get better with practice. She's calmer now.' Reaching across the work surface, Gio opened a packet of coffee-beans and tipped them into a grinder. 'And she definitely has postnatal depression.'

Alice stared. 'You're sure?'

'Certain.'

'So what did you do?'

'I listened.' He flicked a switch, paused while the beans were ground and then gave a shrug. 'Sometimes that's all a person needs, although, in Harriet's case, I think she does need something more. Tomorrow she is coming to see me and we are going to put together a plan of action. I think her condition merits drug treatment but, more importantly, we need to get her emotional support. Her husband isn't around much and she needs help. She needs to feel that people love and care for her. She needs to know that people mind how she's feeling. She doesn't have family to do that, so we need to find her the support from elsewhere.'

Alice watched him. He moved around the kitchen the same way he did everything. With strength and confidence. 'You really believe that family holds all the answers, don't you?'

'Yes, I do.' He emptied the grinder and turned to look at her. 'But I realise that you may find that hard to understand, given your experience of family life. You haven't ever seen a decent example, so why would you agree with me?'

She stiffened. 'Look, I wish I'd never mentioned it to you. It isn't important.'

'It's stopped you believing in love, so it's important.'

'I don't want to talk about it.'

'That's just because you're not used to talking about

it. A bit like kissing. You'll be fine once you've had more practice.'

The mere mention of kissing made her body heat. 'I don't want more practice! I hate talking about it!'

'Because it stirs up emotions and you're afraid of emotions. Plenty of people have problems in their past, but it doesn't have to affect the future. Only if you let it. Family is perhaps the most important thing in the world, after good health.' His voice was calm as he started making the coffee, his movements steady and methodical. It seemed to her as she watched that making coffee was almost a form of relaxation for him.

'Is that how it happens in Italy? I mean Sicily?' She corrected herself quickly and saw him smile.

'In Sicily, family is sacred.' He watched as coffee trickled into the cup, dark and fragrant. 'We believe in love, Alice. We believe in a love that is special, unique and lasts for a lifetime. I'm surrounded by generations of my family and extended family who have been in love for ever. Come with me to Sicily and I will prove it to you.'

He was teasing, of course. He had to be teasing. 'Don't be ridiculous.'

'You have been to Sicily?' She shook her head and took the coffee he handed to her.

'No.'

His smile was lazy and impossibly attractive. 'It is a land designed to make people believe in romance and passion. We have the glittering sea to seduce, and the fires of Etna to flame the coldest heart.' He spoke in a soft, accented drawl and she rolled her eyes to hide how strongly his words affected her.

'Drop the sweet talk. It's wasted on me, Dr Moretti. Romance is just a seduction tool.'

And she'd had three long hours to think about seduction.

Three long hours to think about the kiss on the beach.

And the way he'd plunged into the water after two small children in trouble.

And now she also had to think about the way he'd spent his evening with a vulnerable, lonely mother with postnatal depression.

Bother.

She was really starting to like the man. And notice things about him. Things that other women probably noticed immediately. Like his easy, slightly teasing smile and the thick, dark lashes that gave his eyes a sleepy look. A dangerous look. The way, when he talked to a woman, he gave her his whole attention. His rich, sexy accent and the smooth, confident way that he dealt with every problem. And the way he shouldered those problems without walking away.

It was just the kiss, she told herself crossly as she drank her coffee. The kiss had made her loopy. Up until then she really hadn't looked at him in *that way*.

'Did you pick up my clothes?' He strolled over to her and she found herself staring at his shoulders. He had good shoulders.

'Sorry?'

'My clothes.' He lifted an eyebrow, his eyes scanning her face. 'Did you pick them up from the beach?'

'Oh.' She pulled herself together and dragged her eyes away from the tangle of dark hairs at the base of his throat. 'Yes. Yes, I did. I put them on the chair in your room.'

Heat curled low in her pelvis and spread through her limbs. Sexual awareness, she told herself. The attraction of female to male. Without it, the human race would have died out. It was a perfectly normal chemical reaction. *It's just that it wasn't normal for her.* She tried to shut the feeling down. Tried to control it. But it was on the loose.

'Thanks.' He was watching her. 'It would have been hard to explain that to Mary if some helpful bystander had delivered them to the surgery tomorrow.'

She folded her arms across her chest in a defensive gesture. 'It would have made Mary's day.'

'So would this, I suspect.' He lowered his head and kissed her again, his mouth lingering on hers.

This time she didn't even think about resisting. She just closed her eyes and let herself feel. Allowed the heat to spread through her starving body. Her nerves sang and hummed and when he finally lifted his head she felt only disappointment.

It was amazing how quickly a person could adapt to being touched, she thought dizzily.

'I—We…' She lifted a hand to her lips and then let it drop back to her side, suddenly self-conscious. 'You've got to stop doing that.' But even she knew the words were a lie and he gave a smile as he walked towards the door.

'I'm going to keep doing it, *cara mia.*' He turned in the doorway. Paused. His eyes burned into hers. 'So you're just going to have to get used to it.'

CHAPTER EIGHT

GIO looked at Harriet and felt his heart twist. She looked so utterly miserable.

'Crazy, isn't it?' Her voice was little more than a whisper. 'I have this beautiful, perfect baby and I'm not even enjoying having her. I snap at the twins and yesterday I was so miserable I didn't even notice that they'd wandered off.'

'Don't be so hard on yourself and never underestimate a child's capacity for mischief,' Gio said calmly. 'They are young and adventurous, as small boys should be.'

'But I can't cope with them. I'm just so tired.' Her eyes filled. 'I snap at Geoff and he says that suddenly he's married to a witch, and I really can't face sex...' She blushed, her expression embarrassed. 'Sorry, I didn't mean to say that. Geoff would kill me if he thought I was talking about our sex life in the village.'

'This isn't the village,' Gio said gently. 'It's my consulting room and I'm a doctor. And it's important that you tell me everything you are feeling so that I can make an informed judgement on how to help you.'

Her eyes filled and she clamped a hand over her mouth, struggling for control. 'I'm sorry to be so pathetic, it's just that I'm so tired. I'll be fine when I've had some sleep—the trouble is I don't get any. I'm so tired I ought to go out like a light but I can't sleep at all and I'm totally on edge all the time. I'm an absolutely *terrible* mother. And do you know the worst thing?' Giving up her attempts at control, she burst into heartbreaking sobs. Gio reached across his desk for a box of tissues, his eyes never leaving her face.

'Tell me.'

'I'm so useless I don't even know what my own baby wants.' Wrenching a tissue from the box, she blew her nose hard. 'She's my third child and I find myself sitting there, staring at her while she's crying, totally unable to move. And I worry about everything. I worry I'm going to go to her cot in the morning and find she's died in the night, I worry that she's going to catch something awful and I won't notice—'

Gio put his hand over hers. 'You're describing symptoms of anxiety, Harriet, and I think—'

'You think that I'm basically a completely terrible mother and a hideously pathetic blubbery female.' She blew her nose again and he shook his head and tightened his grip on her hand.

'On the contrary, I think you are a wonderful mother.' He hesitated, choosing his words carefully. 'But I think it's possible that you could be suffering from depression.'

She frowned. Dropped the tissue into her bag. 'I'm just tired.'

'I don't think so.' He kept his hand on hers and she clamped her lower lip between her teeth, trying not to cry.

'I can't be depressed. Oh, God, I just need to pull myself together.'

'Depression is an illness. It isn't about pulling your-self together.'

Her eyes filled again and she reached for another tissue. 'Do you mean depressed as in postnatal depression?'

'Yes, that's exactly what I think.'

Tears trickled down her face. 'So maybe this isn't just about me being useless?'

'You're not useless. In fact, I think the opposite.' He shook his head, a look of admiration on his face. 'How you are coping with three children under the age of six and postnatal depression, I just don't know.'

'I'm not coping.'

'Yes, you are. Just not as well as you'd like. And you're not enjoying yourself.' Gio let go of her hand and turned back to his desk, reaching for a pad of paper. 'But that's going to change, Harriet. We're going to sort this out for you.'

She blew her nose. 'My husband will just tell me to pull myself together and snap out of it.'

'He won't say that,' Gio scribbled on a pad, 'because I'm going to talk to him. Many people are ignorant about the true nature of postnatal depression, he isn't alone in that. Once I explain everything to him, he will give you the support you need. I've spoken to Gina, the health visitor, and done some research. This is a group that I think you might find helpful.' He handed her the piece of paper and she looked at it.

'It's only in the next village.'

Gio nodded. 'Will you be able to get there?'

'Oh, yes. I can drive.' She stared at the name. 'Do I have to phone?'

'I've done it. They're expecting you at their next

meeting, which happens to be tomorrow afternoon. You can take the twins and the baby, there'll be someone there to help.'

Harriet looked at him. 'Do I need drugs?'

'I'd like to try talking therapy first and I want to see you regularly. If you don't start to feel better then drug treatment might be appropriate. Let's see how we go.'

Harriet slipped the paper into her bag and gave a feeble smile. 'I feel a bit better already, just knowing that this isn't all my fault.'

'None of it is your fault.' Gio rose to his feet and walked her to the door. 'Go to the meeting and let me know how you get on.'

Alice parked her newly fixed car outside her house and stared at the low black sports car that meant that Gio was already back from his house calls.

Bother. She'd been hoping that he'd work late.

It had been almost a week since the episode on the beach. A week during which she'd virtually lived in the surgery in order to put some distance between her and Gio. A week during which she'd drunk endless cups of black coffee and eaten nothing but sandwiches at her desk. A week during which she'd been cranky and thoroughly unsettled. It was as if her neat, tidy life had been thrown into the air and had landed in a different pattern. And she didn't know how to put it back together.

What she did know was that it was Gio's fault for kissing her.

And Mary's fault for arranging for him to lodge with her.

Pushing open the front door, she was stopped by the smell.

'Well, well. The wanderer returns. I was beginning to think you'd taken root in the surgery.' Gio emerged from the kitchen and her heart stumbled and jerked. A pair of old, faded jeans hugged his hard thighs and his black shirt was open at the neck. 'If you hadn't returned home at a decent hour, I was coming to find you.'

Even dressed so casually he looked handsome and— she searched for the word—exotic?

'I had work to do. And now I'm tired.' She had to escape. Had to get her mind back together. 'I'm going straight up to bed, if you don't mind.'

'Alice.' His tone was gentle and there was humour in his eyes. 'It's not even eight o'clock, *tesoro*. If you are going to try and avoid me, you're going to have to think of a better excuse than that. You've kept your distance for a week. It's long enough, I think.'

Something in his tone stung. He made her feel like a coward. 'Why would I try and avoid you?'

'Because I make you uncomfortable. I make you talk when you'd rather be silent and I make you feel when you'd rather stay numb.'

'I don't—'

'And because I kissed you and made you want something that you've made a point of denying yourself for years.'

'I don't—'

'At least eat with me.' He held out a hand. 'And if after that you want to go to bed, I'll let you go.'

She kept her hands by her sides. 'You've cooked?'

'I like cooking. I've made a Sicilian speciality. It's

too much for one person and, anyway, I need your opinion.' His hand remained outstretched and there was challenge in his dark eyes.

Muttering under her breath about bullying Italian men, she took his hand and felt his strong fingers close firmly over hers.

Instead of leading her into the kitchen, he took her into the dining room. The dining room at the back of the house that she never used. The dining room that was now transformed.

All the clutter was gone and tiny candles flickered on every available surface. The smells of a warm summer evening drifted in through the open French doors.

The atmosphere was intimate. Romantic.

Something flickered inside her. Panic? She turned to him with a shake of her head. 'No, Gio. This isn't what I do, I—'

He covered her lips with his fingers. 'Relax, *tesoro*. It's just dinner. Food is always more enjoyable when the atmosphere is good, and the atmosphere in this room is perfect. Go and take a shower and change. Dinner is in fifteen minutes.'

She stared after him as he strolled back to the kitchen. The guy just couldn't help himself. He'd obviously decided that she needed rescuing from her past and he thought he was the one to do it. The one to show her that romance existed.

She stared at the candles and rolled her eyes. Well, if he thought that a few lumps of burning wax were going to make her fall in love, he was doomed to disappointment.

Telling herself that she was only doing it because she was hot and uncomfortable, she showered and changed into a simple white strap top and a green silk skirt that hugged her hips softly and then fell to mid-thigh.

Staring at her reflection in the mirror, she contemplated make-up and decided against it. She didn't want to look as though she was making an effort. She didn't want him getting the wrong idea.

With that thought on her mind, she walked back into the dining room and came straight to the point.

'I know that some women would just drop to their knees and beg for a man who does all this.' She waved a hand around the room. 'But I'm not one of them. Really. I'm happy with a sandwich eaten under a halogen light bulb. So if you're trying to make me fall in love with you, you're wasting your time. I just thought we ought to get that straight right now, before you go to enormous effort.'

'I'm not trying to make you fall in love with me. True love can't be forced,' he said softly as he pulled the cork out of a bottle of wine, 'and it can't be commanded. True love is a gift, *cara mia*. Freely given by both parties.'

'It's a figment of the imagination. A serious hallucination,' she returned, her tone sharper than she'd intended. 'A justification for wild, impulsive and totally irrational behaviour, usually between two people who are old enough to know better.'

'That isn't love.' He pushed her towards the chair that faced the window. 'From what you've told me, you haven't seen an example of love. But you will do. I intend to show you.'

She rolled her eyes and watched while he filled her glass. 'What are you? My fairy godmother?'

His smile broadened. 'Do I look like a fairy to you?'

She swallowed hard and dragged her eyes away from the laughter in his. No. He looked like a thoroughly gorgeous man. And he was standing in her dining room about to serve her dinner.

'All right.' She gave a shrug that she hoped looked suitably casual. 'I'm hungry. Let's agree to disagree and just eat.'

The food was delicious.

Never in her life had she ever tasted anything so sublime. And through it all Gio topped up her wineglass and kept up a neutral conversation. He was intelligent and entertaining and she forgot her plan to eat as fast as possible and then escape to her room. Instead she ate, savouring every mouthful, and sipped her wine. And all the time she listened as he talked.

He talked about growing up on Sicily and about his life as a surgeon in Milan. He talked about the differences in medicine between the two cultures.

'So...' She reached for more bread. 'Are you going to tell me why you had to give up surgery as a career? Or am I the only one who has to spill about my past?'

'It's not a secret.' He lounged across the table from her, his face bronzed and handsome in the flickering candlelight. 'I was working in Africa. We were attacked by rebels hoping to steal drugs and equipment that they could sell on.' He gave a shrug and lifted his glass. 'Unfortunately the damage was such that I can't operate for any length of time.'

She winced. 'I'm sorry, I shouldn't have asked.'

'It's part of my life and talking about it doesn't make it worse. In a way I was lucky. I took some time off and went home to my family.' He continued to talk, telling her about his sisters and his brother, his parents, his grandparents and numerous aunts, uncles and cousins.

'You were lucky.' She put her glass down on the table. 'Having such good family.'

'Yes, I was.' He passed her more bread. 'Luckier than you.'

'She took me to the park once—my mother.' She stared at her plate, the memory rising into her brain so clearly that her hands curled into fists and her shoulders tensed. 'She was meeting her lover and I was the excuse that enabled her to leave the house without my dad suspecting anything. Although I doubt he would have cared because he was seeing someone, too. Only she didn't know that.'

She looked up, waiting for him to display shock or distaste, but Gio sat still, his eyes on her face. Listening. It occurred to her that he was an excellent listener.

She shrugged. 'Anyway, I was playing on the climbing frame. They were sitting on the seat. Kissing. Wrapped up in each other.' She licked dry lips. 'I remember watching two other children and envying them. Their mothers were both hovering at the bottom of the climbing frame, hands outstretched. They said things like "be careful" and "watch where you put your feet" and "that's too high, come down now". My mother didn't even glance in my direction.' She broke off and ran a hand over the back of her neck, the tension rising inside her. 'Not even when I fell. And in the ambulance she was furious with me and accused me of sabotaging her relationship on purpose.'

Gio reached across the table and took her hand. But still he didn't speak. Just listened, his eyes holding hers.

She chewed her lip and flashed him a smile. 'Anyway, he was husband number two and life just carried on from there, really. She went through two more— Oh, sorry.' She gave a cynical smile that was loaded with pain. 'I should say she "fell in love" twice more before I was finally old enough to leave home.'

'And your sister?'

Alice rubbed her fingers over her forehead. 'She's on her second marriage. She had high hopes of doing everything differently to our parents. She still believed that true love existed. I think she's finally discovering that it doesn't. I've never told anyone any of this before. Not even Rita and Mary. They know I'm not in touch with my parents, but that's all they know.'

It had grown dark while she was talking and through the open doors she could hear the sounds of the night, see the flutter of insects drawn by the flickering candlelight.

Finally Gio spoke. 'It's not surprising that you don't believe that love exists. It's hard to believe in something that you've never seen. You have a logical, scientific brain, Alice. You take a problem-solving approach to life. Love is not easily defined or explained and that makes it easy to dismiss.'

She swallowed. How was it that he seemed to understand her so well? And why had she just told him so much? She looked suspiciously at her wineglass but it was still half-full and her head was clear. She waited for regret to flood through her but instead she felt strangely peaceful for the first time. 'If love really existed then the divorce rate wouldn't be so high.'

'Or maybe love just isn't that easy to find, and that

makes it even more precious. Maybe the divorce rate is testament to the fact that love is so special that people are willing to take a risk in order to find it.'

She shook her head. 'What people feel is sexual chemistry and, if they're lucky, friendship. But there isn't a whole separate emotion called love that binds people together.'

'Because you haven't seen it yet.' He studied her face. 'True love is selfless and yet the emotion you saw was greedy and selfish. They allowed you to fall and they weren't there to catch you.'

Instinctively she knew he wasn't just talking about the incident on the climbing frame.

She lifted her glass. 'So, if you believe in love, Dr Moretti, why aren't you married with eight children?' Her eyes challenged him over the rim of her glass and he smiled.

'Because you don't choose when to love. Or even who to love. You can't just go out and find it in the way that you can find friendship or sex. Love chooses you. And chooses the time. For some people it's early in life. For others…' he gave a shrug that showed his Latin heritage '…it's later.'

She frowned. 'So you're waiting for Signorina Right to just bang on your door?' Her tone had a hint of sarcasm and he smiled.

'No. She gave me a key.' Something in his gaze made her heart stop.

Surely he wasn't saying…

He couldn't be suggesting…

She put her glass down. 'Gio—'

'Go to bed, *tesoro*,' he said softly. 'The other thing

about love is that it can't be controlled. Not the emotion and not the timing. It happens when it happens.'

She stared at him. 'But—'

He rose to his feet and smiled. 'Sleep well, Alice.'

Gio left via the back door, knowing that if he didn't leave the house, he'd join her in her bedroom.

It had taken every ounce of willpower to let her walk away from him.

But he knew instinctively that they'd taken enough steps forward for one night. She'd talked—really talked—perhaps for the first time in her life and he could tell that she was starting to relax around him.

Which was how he wanted it to be.

They'd come a long way in a short time.

He breathed in the warm, evening air and strolled down towards the sea, enjoying the comfort of the semi-darkness.

It felt strange, he thought to himself as he walked, to have fallen in love with a woman who didn't even believe that love existed.

After that night, the evenings developed a pattern and, almost a month after he'd arrived in the surgery, Alice sat staring out of the window of her consulting room, wondering what Gio would be cooking for dinner.

It was so unlike her to dream about food, but since he'd taken over the cooking she found herself looking forward to the evenings.

Sometimes they ate in the dining room, sometimes they ate in her garden and once he'd made a picnic and they'd taken it down to the beach.

Thinking, dreaming, she missed the tap on the door.

It was friendship, she decided, and she liked it.

She could really talk to him and he was an excellent listener. And she enjoyed working with him. He was an excellent doctor.

And, of course, there was sexual chemistry. She wasn't so naïve that she couldn't recognise it. She'd even experienced it before, to a lesser degree, with a man she'd dated a few times at university. Not love, but a chemical reaction between a man and a woman. And it was there, between her and Gio.

But since the incident on the beach, he hadn't kissed her again.

Hadn't made any attempt to touch her.

The door behind her opened. 'Alice?'

Why hadn't he touched her since?

'Dr Anderson?'

Finally she heard her name, and turned to find Mary standing in the doorway. 'Are you on our planet?'

'Just thinking.'

'Dreaming, you mean.' Mary looked at her curiously and then handed her a set of notes. 'You've got one extra. The little Jarrett boy has a high temperature. I don't like the look of him so I squeezed him in.'

'That's fine, Mary.' She took the notes. 'Thanks.'

She pulled herself together, saw Tom Jarrett and then walked through to Reception with the notes just as Gio emerged from his consulting room, with his hand on Edith Carne's shoulder.

He was so tactile, Alice thought to herself, observing the way he guided the woman up the corridor, his head tilted towards her as he listened.

Touching came entirely naturally to him, whereas she—

'The cardiology referral was a good idea,' he said to
her as he strolled back from reception and saw her
watching him. 'They're treating Edith and it appears that
they've found the cause of her falls.'

'You mean, you found the cause. She never would
have—'

A series of loud screams from Reception interrupted
her and she exchanged a quick glance with Gio before
hurrying to the reception area just as a mother came
struggled through the door, carrying a sobbing child. He
was screaming and crying and holding his foot.

Alice stepped towards them. 'What's happened?'

'I don't know. We were on the beach and then suddenly he just started screaming for no reason.' The
mother was breathless from her sprint from the beach
and the child continued to howl noisily. 'His foot is
really red and it's swelling up.'

Gio picked up the foot and examined it. 'Erythema.
Oedema. A sting of some sort?'

Alice tilted her head and looked. 'Weaver fish,' she
said immediately, and glanced towards Mary. 'Get me
hot water, please. Fast.'

Mary nodded and Gio frowned. 'What?'

'If you're expecting the Italian translation you're going to be waiting a long time,' Alice drawled, her fingers
gentle as she examined the child's foot, 'but basically
weaver fish are found in sandy shallows around the
beaches down here. It has venomous spines on its dorsal
fin and that protrudes out of the sand. If you tread on it,
you get stung.'

The mother shook her head. 'I didn't see anything on the sand.'

'It's a good idea to keep something on your feet when you're walking in the shallows at low water,' Alice advised, taking the bucket of water that Mary handed her with a nod of thanks. 'All right, sweetheart, we're going to put your foot in this water and that will help the pain.'

She tested the water quickly to check that it wasn't so hot that it would burn the child and then tried to guide the child's foot into the water. He jerked his leg away and his screams intensified.

'We really have to get this into hot water.' Alice looked at the mother. 'Heat inactivates the venom. After a few minutes in here, the pain will be better. Trust me.'

'Alex, please...' the mother begged, and tried to reason with her son. 'You need to put your foot in the bucket for Mummy. Please, darling, do it for Mummy.'

Alex continued to yell and bawl and wriggle and Gio rubbed a hand over his roughened jaw and crouched down. 'We play a game,' he said firmly, sounding more Italian than ever. He produced a penny from his pocket, held it up and then promptly made it disappear.

Briefly, Alex stopped crying and stared. 'Where?'

Gio looked baffled. 'I don't know. Perhaps if you put your foot in the bucket, it will reappear. Like magic. Let's try it, shall we?'

Alex sniffed, hesitated and then tentatively dipped his foot in the water. 'It's hot.'

'It has to be hot,' Alice said quickly, guiding his foot into the water. 'It will take the pain away.'

She watched gratefully as Gio distracted Alex, producing the coin from behind the child's ear and then from his own ear.

Alex watched, transfixed, and Gio treated him to ten minutes of magic, during which time the child's misery lessened along with the pain.

'Oh, thank goodness,' the mother said, as Alex finally started smiling. 'That was awful. And I had no idea. I've never even heard of a weaver fish.'

'They're not uncommon. There were five hundred cases along the North Devon and Cornwall coast last year,' Alice muttered as she dried her hands on the towel that Mary had thought to provide. 'Keep his foot in the bucket for another ten minutes at least and give him some paracetamol and antihistamine when you get home. He should be fine but if he isn't, give us a call.'

'Thank you so much.' The mother looked at her gratefully. 'What would I have done if you'd been shut?'

'Actually, lots of the cafés and surf shops around here keep a bucket just for this purpose so it's worth re-membering that. But the best advice is to avoid walking near the low-water mark in bare feet.'

Alice walked over to the reception desk and Gio followed.

'Weaver fish? What is this weaver fish?' He spoke slowly, as if he wasn't sure he was pronouncing it correctly.

'Nobody knows exactly what is in weaver fish venom but it contains a mixture of biogenous amines and they've identified 5-hydroxytryptamine, epinephrine, norepinephrine and histamine.' She angled her head. 'Alex was probably stung by *Echiichthys vipera*—the lesser weaver fish.'

Gio lifted a brow. 'Implying that there is a greater weaver fish?'

She nodded. '*Trachinus draco*. There are case reports of people being stung. Often fisherman. We've seen one in this practice. It was a few years ago, but we sent him up to the hospital to be treated. The symptoms are severe pain, vomiting, oedema, syncope—in his case, the symptoms lasted for a long time.'

He smiled at her and she frowned, her heart beating faster as she looked into his eyes.

'What? Why are you looking at me like that?'

'Because I love it when you give me facts.' He leaned closer to her, his eyes dancing. 'You are delightfully serious, Dr Anderson, do you know that? And I find you incredibly sexy.'

'Gio, for goodness' sake.' Her eyes slid towards Mary, who was filling out a form with the mother. But she couldn't drench the flame of desire that burned through her body.

And he saw that flame.

'We're finished here.' Gio's voice was low and determined. 'Let's go home, Dr Anderson.'

'But—'

'It's home, or it's your consulting room with the door locked. Take your pick.'

She chose home.

CHAPTER NINE

THEY barely made it through the front door.

The tension that had been building for weeks reached breaking point as she fumbled with her key in the lock, aware that he was right behind her, his hand resting on the small of her back.

Gio's fingers closed over hers and guided. Turned the key. And then he was nudging her inside and shouldering the door closed.

For a moment they both stood, breathing heavily, poised on the edge of something dangerous.

And then they cracked. Both moved at the same time, mouths greedy, hands seeking.

'I need you naked.' He ripped at Alice's shirt, sending buttons flying across the floor, and she reciprocated, fumbling with his buttons while her breath came in tiny pants.

'Me, too. Me, too.' And all the time a tiny voice in her head was telling her that she didn't do this sort of thing.

She ignored it and slipped his shirt from his shoulders, revelling in the feel of warm male flesh under her hands. 'You have a perfect body, Dr Moretti.'

He gave a groan and slid his hands up her back, his

eyes feasting on the swell of her breasts under her simple lacy bra. He spoke softly in Italian and then scooped her into his arms and carried her up the stairs to her bedroom.

'I don't understand a word you're saying, but I suppose it might be better that way. I like it.' With a tiny laugh she buried her head in his neck, breathed in the tantalising scent of aroused male and then murmured in protest as he lowered her onto the bed. 'I want you to carry on holding me. Don't let me go.'

'No chance.' With a swift movement he removed his trousers and came down on top of her, his hands sliding into her hair, his mouth descending to hers. 'And this from the girl who hated being touched.'

He was touching her now. Everywhere. His hands seeking, seducing, soothing all at the same time.

'That was before—' She arched under him, burning to get closer still to his hard, male body while his hands explored ever curve of hers. 'Before...'

'Before?' His hand slid over her breast and she realised in a daze that she hadn't even felt him remove her bra.

'Before you.' The flick of his tongue over her nipple brought a gasp to her throat and she curled a leg around him, the ache in her pelvis intensifying to unbearable proportions. 'Before I met you.' The touch of his mouth was skilful and sinful in equal measures and she closed her eyes and felt the erotic pull deep in her stomach.

'You're beautiful.' His mouth trailed lower and his fingers dragged at her tiny panties, sliding them downwards, leaving her naked.

She slid a hand over the hard planes of his chest, felt his touch grow more intimate. His fingers moved over her, then his mouth, and she offered herself freely, wondering what had happened to her inhibitions.

Drowning in sensation, she shifted and gasped and finally he rose over her and she reached for him, desperate.

'Now.' Her eyes were fevered and her lips were parted. 'I need you now. Now.'

And he gathered her against him and took her, his possessive thrust bringing a gasp to her lips and a flush to her cheeks. For a moment he stilled, his eyes locked on hers, his breathing unsteady. And then he lowered his head and his mouth covered hers in a kiss that was hot and demanding, his powerful body moving against hers in a rhythm that created sensations so exquisitely perfect that she cried out in desperation.

Her skin was damp from the heat and her fingers raked his back as the sensation built and threatened to devour her whole.

She toppled fast, falling into a dark void of ecstasy, and immediately he slowed the pace, changing the rhythm from desperate to measured, always the one in control.

With a low moan she opened her eyes and slid her arms round his neck. 'What are you doing?'

'Making love to you.' He spoke the words against her lips, the hot brand of his mouth sending her senses tumbling in every direction. 'And I don't ever want to stop.'

She didn't want him to stop either and she arched her back and moved her hips until she felt the change in him. Felt his muscles quiver and his skin grow slick, heard the rasp of his breath and the increase in masculine thrust.

And then she felt nothing more because he drove them both forward until they reached oblivion and fell,

tumbling and gasping into a whirlpool of sexual excitement that sucked them both under.

She lay there, eyes closed, struggling for breath and
sanity. His weight should have bothered her, but it didn't.

And she was relieved that he didn't seem able to
move either.

Eventually he lifted his head and nuzzled her neck
gently, his movements slow and languid. 'Are we still
alive?' With a fractured groan he rolled onto his back,
taking her with him. 'You need to wear more clothes
around the house. I find it hard to resist you when
you're naked.'

Her eyes were still closed. 'It's your fault that I'm
naked.'

'It is?' He stroked her hair away from her face and
something about the way he was touching her made her
open her eyes. And she saw.

'Gio—'

'I love you, Alice.'

Her heart jerked. Jumped. Kick-started by pure, blind
panic. 'No need to get all mushy on me, Dr Moretti. You
already scored.'

'That's why I'm saying it now. If I'd said it when we
were making love then you would have thought it was
just the heat of the moment. If I said it over dinner with
candles and wine, you would have said it was the romance of the moment. So I'm saying it now. After we've
made love. Because that's what we just did.'

'I don't need to hear this.' She tried to wriggle away
from him but he held her easily, his powerful body trapping hers.

'Yes, you do. The problem is that you're not used to

hearing it. But that's going to change because I'm going to be saying it to you a lot. A few weeks ago you weren't used to talking or touching but you do both those now.'

'This is different.' Her heart was pounding. 'It was just sex, Gio. Great sex, admittedly, but nothing more.'

His mouth trailed over her breast and she groaned and tried to push him away. 'Stop. You're not playing fair.'

'I'm in love with you. And I'm just reminding you how you feel about me.' He lifted his head, a wicked smile in his eyes, and she ran a hand over her shoulder, trying not to lick her lips. He had an incredible body and every female part of her craved him.

But that was natural, she reminded herself. 'It's sexual attraction,' she said hoarsely, trying to concentrate despite the skilled movement of his mouth and hands. 'If sexual attraction didn't exist then the human race would have died out long ago. It isn't love.' She gave a low moan as his fingers teased her intimately. 'Gio…'

'Not love?' He rolled onto his back and positioned her above him. 'Fine, Dr Anderson. Then let's have sex. At the moment I don't care what you call it as long as you stop talking.'

A week later, Alice walked into work with a smile on her face and a bounce in her step.

And she knew why, of course.

It was her relationship with Gio. And she was totally clear about her feelings. Friendship and sex. It was turning out to be a good combination. In a month or so he'd probably be leaving and that would be fine. Maybe they'd stay in touch. Maybe they wouldn't. Either way, she felt fine about it. She felt fine about everything.

And the fact that he always said 'I love you' and she didn't just didn't seem to matter any more. It didn't change the way things were between them.

The truth was, they were having fun.

Mary caught her as she walked into her consulting room. 'You're looking happy.'

'I am happy.' She dropped her bag behind the desk and turned on her computer. 'I'm enjoying my life.'

'You weren't smiling this much a month ago.'

A month ago Gio hadn't been in her life.

She frowned slightly at the thought and then dismissed it. What was wrong with enjoying a friendship?

'Professor Burrows from the haematology department at the hospital rang.' Mary handed her a piece of paper. 'He wants you to call him back on this number before ten o'clock. And I've slotted in Mrs Bruce because she's in a state. She had a scan at the hospital and they think the baby has a cleft palate. She's crying in Reception.'

Alice looked up in concern. 'Oh, poor thing. Send her straight in.' She flicked on her computer while Mary watched, her eyes searching.

'It's Gio, isn't it?'

'What is?'

'The reason you're smiling. So relaxed. You're in love with him, Alice.'

'I'm not in love.' Alice lifted her head and smiled sweetly. 'And the reason I know that is because there's no such thing. But I'm willing to admit that I like him a lot. I respect and admire him as a doctor. He's a nice man.'

And he was great in bed.

Mary looked at her thoughtfully. 'A nice man? Good, I'm glad you like him.'

Alice felt slightly smug as she buzzed for her first patient. Really, in her opinion, it all went to prove that love just didn't exist. In many ways Gio was perfect. He was intelligent and sharp and yet still managed to be kind and thoughtful. He was a terrific listener, a great conversationalist and a spectacular lover. What more could a girl want in a man?

The answer was nothing. But still she didn't feel anything that could be described as love. And when he left to return to Italy, as he inevitably would, she'd miss him but she wouldn't pine.

Which just went to prove that she'd been right all along.

There was a tap on the door and she looked up as Mrs Bruce entered, her face pale and her eyes tired.

'I'm sorry to bother you, Dr Anderson,' she began, but Alice immediately shook her head.

'Don't apologise. I understand you had a scan.'

Mrs Bruce sank into the chair and started to sob quietly. 'And they think the baby has a cleft palate.' The tears poured down her cheeks and she fumbled in her bag for a tissue. 'There was so much I wanted to ask. I had all these questions...' Her voice cracked. 'But the girl couldn't answer any of them and now I have to wait to see some consultant or other and I can't even remember his name.' The sobs became gulps. 'They don't know what it's like. The waiting.'

'It will be Mr Phillips, the consultant plastic surgeon, I expect.' Alice reached for her phone and pressed the button that connected her to Gio's room. 'Dr Moretti?

If you could come into my room for one moment when you've finished with your patient, I'd be grateful.'

Then she replaced the receiver and stood up. 'You poor thing.' She slipped an arm around the woman's shoulders and gave her a hug without even thinking about it. 'You've had a terrible shock. But there's plenty that can be done, trust me. There's an excellent cleft lip and palate team at the hospital. They serve the whole region and I promise that you won't leave this surgery until you know more about what to expect, even if I have to ring the consultant myself.'

Mrs Bruce blew her nose hard and shook her head. 'She isn't even born yet,' she said in a wavering voice, 'and already I'm worried that she's going to be teased and bullied at school. You know what kids are like. They're cruel. And appearance is everything.'

Alice gave her another squeeze and then looked up as Gio walked into the room.

'Dr Moretti—this is Mrs Bruce. The hospital have told her that her baby has a cleft palate and she's terribly upset, which is totally understandable. They don't seem to have given her much information so I thought you might be able to help reassure her about a few things. Answer some questions for her.'

'It's just a shock, you know?' Mrs Bruce clung to Alice's arm like a lifeline and Gio nodded as he pulled out another chair and sat down next to her.

'First let me tell you that I trained as a plastic surgeon,' he said quietly, 'and I specialised in the repair of cleft lips and palates so I know a lot about it.'

Mrs Bruce crumpled the tissue in her hand. 'Why are you a GP, then?'

Gio pulled a face and spread his hands. 'Unfortunately life does not always turn out the way we intend. I had an accident which meant I could no longer operate for long periods. So I changed direction in my career.'

'So you've operated on children with this? Can you make them look normal?'

'In the hands of a skilled surgeon the results can be excellent but, of course, there are no guarantees and there are many factors involved. A cleft lip can range in severity from a slight notch in the red part of the upper lip...' he gestured with his finger '...to a complete separation of the lip, extending into the nose. The aim of surgery is to close the separation in the first operation and to achieve symmetry, but that isn't always possible.'

He was good, Alice thought to herself as she sat quietly, listening along with the mother. Really good.

Mrs Bruce sniffed. 'Will they do it straight away when she's born?'

'They usually wait until the baby is ten weeks old. The repair of a cleft palate requires more extensive surgery and is usually done when the child is between nine and eighteen months old so that it is better able to tolerate the procedure.'

'Is it a huge operation?'

'In some children a cleft palate may involve only a tiny portion at the back of the roof of the mouth or it might be a complete separation that extends from front to back.' Gio reached for a pad and a pen that was lying on Alice's desk. 'It will make more sense if I draw you a picture.'

Mrs Bruce watched as his pen flew over the page, demonstrating the defect and the repair. 'How will she be able to suck if her mouth is—?' She broke off and gave a sniff. 'If her mouth looks like that?'

'There are special bottles that will help her feed.' Gio put the pad down on the desk. 'Looking after the child with a cleft lip and palate has to be a team approach, Mrs Bruce. She may need help with feeding, with speech and other aspects of her development. The surgeon is really only one member of the team. You will have plenty of support, be assured of that.'

Alice sat patiently while Gio talked, reassuring the mother, answering questions and explaining as best he could.

Finally, when she seemed calmer, he reached for the pad again and scribbled a number on a piece of paper. 'If you have other worries, things you think of later and wish you'd asked, you can call me,' he said gently, handing her the piece of paper.

She stared at it. 'You're giving me your phone number?'

He nodded. 'Use it, if you have questions. If the hospital tells you something you don't understand. Or you can always make an appointment, of course.'

'Thank you.' Mrs Bruce gave him a shaky smile and then turned to Alice and squeezed her hand. 'And thank you, too, Dr Anderson.'

'We'll tackle the problem together, Mrs Bruce,' Alice said firmly. 'She'll be managed by the hospital, but never forget that you're still our patient.' She watched Mrs Bruce—a much happier Mrs Bruce—leave the room and then turned to Gio. 'Thanks for that. I didn't have a clue what to say to her. And I don't know much about cleft palates. Will the baby have long-term problems?'

Gio pulled a face. 'Possibly many. They can be very prone to recurrent middle-ear infections, which can lead to scarring of the ossicular chain in the middle ear, and that can damage hearing or even cause deafness.'

'Why are they susceptible to ear infections?'

'In cleft babies, the muscle sling across the palate is incomplete, divided by the cleft, so they can't pull on the eustachian tube,' he explained. 'Also, scar formation following the postnatal correction of cleft lip and palate can lead to abnormal soft tissue, bone and dental growth. There has been some research looking at the possibilities of operating *in utero* in the hope of achieving healing without scarring.'

This was his area. His speciality. And she was fascinated. 'What else?'

'Sometimes there is a gap in the bone, known as the alveolar defect. Then the maxillary facial surgeon will do an alveolar bone graft.'

There was something in his face that made her reach out and touch his arm. 'Do you miss it, Gio?'

'Sometimes.' He gave a lopsided smile. 'Not always.'

'Well, you were great with her. I knew you would be.'

'You were good with her, too.' He shot her a curious look. 'Do you even realise how much you've changed.'

'Changed? How have I changed?' She went back to her chair and hit a button on her computer.

'You were touching a patient and you were doing it instinctively. You were offering physical comfort and emotional support.'

Alice frowned. 'Well, she was upset.'

'Yes.' Gio's voice was soft. 'She was. And you coped well with it. Emotions, Alice. Emotions.'

'What exactly are you implying?'

'That you're getting used to touching and being touched.' He strolled to the door. 'All I have to do now is persuade you to admit that you love me. Tomorrow I'm taking you out to dinner. Prepare yourself.'

'That's nice.' Her breath caught at the look in his eyes. She didn't love him. *She had absolutely nothing to worry about because she didn't love him.* 'Where are we going?'

'My favourite place to eat in the whole world.'

'Oh.' She felt a flicker of surprise. Knowing Gio's tastes for the spectacular, she was surprised that there was anywhere locally that would satisfy him. Perhaps he'd discovered somewhere new. 'I'll look forward to it.'

It took a considerable amount of planning and a certain amount of deviousness on his part, but finally he had it all arranged.

He was gambling everything on a hunch.

The hunch that she loved him but wasn't even aware of it herself.

She'd lived her whole life convinced that love didn't exist, so persuading her to change her mind at this stage wouldn't be easy.

Words alone had failed and so had sexual intimacy, so for days he'd racked his brains for another way of proving to her that love existed. That she could let herself feel what he already knew that she felt.

And finally he'd come up with a plan.

A plan that had involved a considerable number of other people.

And now all he could do was wait. Wait and hope.

* * *

Alice had just finished morning surgery the following day when Gio strolled into the room.

'Fancy a quick lunch?' His tone was casual and she gave a nod, surprised by how eager she was to leave work and spend time with him.

'Why not?' It was just because she enjoyed his company and was making the most of it while he was here. What was wrong with that?

She followed him out of the surgery, expecting him to turn and walk up the street to the coffee-shop. Instead, he turned left, round the back of the building and towards the surgery car park.

'You're taking the car?' She frowned. 'Where are we going?'

'Wait and see.' He held the door of his car open and she slipped into the passenger seat, a question in her eyes.

'We can't go far. We have to be back for two o'clock.'

He covered his eyes with a pair of sunglasses and gave her a smile. 'Stop thinking about work for five minutes.'

It was on the tip of her tongue to tell him that she hardly thought about work at all these days, but something stopped her. If she made a comment like that, he'd read something into it that wasn't there.

Wondering where he could possibly be taking her and thinking that he was acting very strangely, Alice sat back in her seat and pondered some of the problems that she'd seen that morning. And found she couldn't concentrate on any of them.

It was Gio's fault, she thought crossly. Going out for lunch with him was too distracting. She should have said no.

The wind played with her hair and she caught it and swept it out of her eyes. And noticed where they were.

'This is the airport.' She glanced behind her to check that she wasn't mistaken. 'Gio, this is the road to the airport. Why are we going to the airport?'

He kept driving, his hands steady on the wheel. 'Because I want to.'

'You want to eat plastic sandwiches in an airport?'

'You used to live on plastic sandwiches before you met me,' he reminded her in an amused voice, and she laughed.

'Maybe I did. But you've given me a taste for pasta. Gio, what is going on?' They'd arrived at the small airport and everything seemed to be happening around her.

Before she could catch her breath and form any more questions, she was standing on the runway, at the foot of a set of steps that led into the body of an aircraft.

'Go on. We don't want to miss our slot.' Gio walked up behind her, carrying two cases and she stared at them.

'What are those?'

'Our luggage.'

'I don't have any luggage. I was just coming out for a sandwich.' She brushed the hair out of her eyes, frustrated by the lack of answers she was receiving to her questions. 'Gio, what is going on?'

'I'm taking you to my favourite place to eat.'

'That's this evening. It's only one o'clock in the afternoon.' She watched as a man appeared behind them and took the cases onto the plane. 'Who's he? What's he doing with those?'

'He's putting them on the plane.' Gio took her arm. 'We're leaving at one o'clock because it takes a long time to get there, and we're going by plane because it's the best way to reach Sicily.'

'Sicily?' Her voice skidded and squeaked. 'You're taking me to *Sicily?*'

'You'll love it.'

Had he gone totally mad? 'I'm sure I'll love it and maybe I'll go there one day, but not on a Thursday afternoon when I have a well-woman clinic and a late surgery!' She looked over her shoulder, ready to make a dash back to the car, but he closed a hand over her arm and urged her onto the steps.

'Forget work, *tesoro*. It's all taken care of. David and Trisha are taking over for five days.'

'David?' With him so close behind her, she was forced to climb two more steps. 'What's he got to do with this? He's in London.'

'Not any more. He's currently back in your surgery, preparing for your well-woman clinic.' He brushed her hair away from her face and dropped a gentle kiss on her mouth. 'When did you last have a holiday, Alice?'

'I haven't felt the need for a holiday. I like my life.' She took another step upwards, her expression exasperated. 'Or, rather, I liked my life the way it was before everyone started interfering!'

He urged her up another step. 'I'll do you a deal— if, after this weekend, you want to go back to your old life, I'll let you. No arguments.'

'But I can't just—'

He nudged her forwards. 'Yes, you can.'

'You're kidnapping me in broad daylight!'

'That's right. I am.' His broad shoulders blocked her

exit and she made a frustrated sound in her throat and turned and stomped up the remaining steps.

This was totally ridiculous!

It was—

She stopped dead, her eyes widening as she saw the cabin. It was unlike any plane she'd ever seen before. Two soft creamy leather sofas faced each other across a richly carpeted aisle. A table covered in crisply laundered linen was laid for lunch, the silver cutlery glinting in the light.

Her mouth dropped.

'This isn't a plane. It's a living room.' Glancing over her shoulder, she realised that she'd been so distracted by the fact he was planning to take her away, she hadn't been paying attention. 'We didn't come through the airport the normal way.'

'This is a private plane.' He pushed her forward and nodded to the uniformed flight attendant who was smiling and waiting for them to board.

'Private plane?' Not knowing what else to do, she walked towards the sofas, feeling bemused and more than a little faint. 'Whose private plane?'

He sat down next to her. 'My brother, Marco, has made quite a success of his olive oil business.' Gio's tone was smooth as he leaned across to fasten her seat belt before placing another kiss on her cheek. 'It has certain compensations for the rest of his family. And now, *tesoro,* relax and prepare to be spoiled.'

She wished he'd stop touching her.

She couldn't think or concentrate when he touched her and she had a feeling that she was really, really going to need to concentrate.

CHAPTER TEN

THE moment the plane landed, Alice knew it was possible to fall in love. With a country, at least.

And as they drove away from the airport and along the coast, the heat of the sun warmed her skin and lifted her spirits. It was summer in Cornwall, of course, but somehow it didn't feel the same.

As she relaxed in her seat and watched the country fly past, all she knew was that that she'd never seen a sky more blue or a sea that looked more inviting. As they drove, the coast was a golden blur of orange and lemon orchards and she wanted to beg Gio to stop the car, just so that she could pick the fruit from the tree.

As if sensing the change in her, he reached across and rested a hand on her leg, his other hand steady on the wheel. 'It is beautiful, no?'

'Wonderful.' She turned to look at him. 'Where are we going?'

'Always you ask questions.' With a lazy smile in her direction, he returned his hand to the wheel. 'We are going to dinner, *tesoro*. Just as I promised we would.'

The warmth of the sun and the tantalising glimpses of breathtaking coastline and ancient historical sights distracted her from delving more deeply, and it was early evening when Gio pulled off the main road, drove down a dusty lane and into a large courtyard.

Alice was captivated. 'Is this where we're staying? It's beautiful. Is it a hotel?'

'It has been in my family for at least five generations,' Gio said, opening the boot and removing the cases. 'It's home.'

'Home?' The smile faded and she felt nerves flicker in the pit of her stomach. 'You're taking me to meet your parents.'

'Not just my parents, *tesoro*.' He slammed the boot shut and strolled over to her, sliding a hand into her hair and tilting her head. 'My whole family. Everyone lives in this area. We congregate here. We exchange news. We show interest in each other's lives. We offer support when it's needed and praise when it's deserved and quite often when it isn't. But most of all we offer unconditional love. It's what we do.'

'But I—'

'Hush.' He rested a finger on her lips to prevent her from speaking. 'You don't believe in love, Alice Anderson, because you've never seen it. But after this weekend you will no longer be able to use that excuse. Welcome to Sicily. Welcome to my home.'

She looked a little lost, he thought to himself, seated among his noisy, ebullient family. A little wary. As if she had no idea how to act surrounded by a large group of people who so clearly adored each other.

As his mother piled the table high with Sicilian delicacies, his father recounted the tale of his latest medical drama in his severely restricted English and Gio saw Alice smile. And respond.

She was shy, he noticed. Unsure how to behave in a large group. But they drew her into the conversation in the way that his family always welcomed any guest at their table. The language was a mix of Italian and English. English when they addressed her directly and could find the words, Italian when the levels of excitement bubbled over and they restarted to their native tongue with much hand waving and voice raising, which would have sent a lesser person running for cover. His grandmother spoke only a Sicilian dialect and his younger sister, Lucia, acted as interpreter, her dark eyes sparkling as she was given the opportunity to show off her English in public.

And gradually Alice started to relax. After eating virtually nothing, he saw her finally lift her fork. He intercepted his mother's look of approval and understanding.

And knew that he'd been right to bring her.

The buzz of conversation still ringing in her ears, Alice followed Gio out into the semi-darkness. 'Where are we going?'

'I don't actually live in the house any more.' He took her hand and led her towards a track that wound through a citrus orchard towards the sea. 'Years ago my brother and I built a small villa at the bottom of the orchard. The idea was to let it to tourists but then we decided we wanted to keep it. He's long since moved to something more extravagant but I keep this place as a bolthole. I love my family but even I need space from them.'

'I thought they were lovely.' She couldn't keep the envy out of her voice and suddenly she stopped walking and just stood and stared. Tiny lights illuminated the path that ran all the way to the beach. The air was warm and she could smell the fruit trees and hear the lap of the sea against the sand. 'This whole place is amazing. I just can't imagine it.'

'Can't imagine what?'

'Growing up here. With those people.' She took her hand away from his and reached out to pick a lemon from the nearest tree. It fell into her hand, complete with leaves and stalk, and she stared at it, fascinated. 'It's no wonder you believe in love, Dr Moretti. I think it would be possible to believe in just about anything if you lived here.'

He stepped towards her. Took her face in his hands. 'And do you believe in it, Alice? You met my family this evening. My parents have been together for almost forty years, my grandparents for sixty-two years. I believe that my great-grandparents were married for sixty-five years, although no one can be sure because no one can actually remember a time when they weren't together.' His thumb stroked her cheek. 'What did you see tonight, Alice? Was it convenience? Friendship? Any of those reasons you once gave me for people choosing to spend their lives together?'

Her heart was thumping in her chest and she shook her head slowly. 'No. It was love.' Her voice cracked as she said the words. 'I saw love.'

'Finally.' Gio closed his eyes briefly and murmured something in Italian. 'Let's go—I want to show you how I feel about you.'

* * *

It was tender and loving, slow and drawn out, with none of the fevered desperation of their previous encounters. Flesh slid against flesh, hard male against soft female, whispers and muttered words the only communication between them.

The bedroom of the villa opened directly onto the beach and she could hear the sounds of the sea, feel the night air as it flowed into the room and cooled them.

Long hours passed. Hours during which they feasted and savoured, each reluctant to allow the other to sleep.

And finally, when her body was so languid and sated that she couldn't imagine ever wanting to move again, he rolled onto his side and looked into her eyes.

'I love you, Alice.' His voice was quiet in the semi-darkness. 'I want you to be with me always. For ever. I want you to marry me, *tesoro*.'

'No, Gio.' The word made her shiver and she would have backed away but he held her tightly.

'Tonight you admitted that love exists.'

'For some other people maybe.' She whispered the words, almost as if she was afraid to speak them too loudly. 'But not for me.'

'Why not for you?'

'Because I don't—I can't—'

'Because when you were a child, your mother let you fall.' He lifted a hand and stroked the hair away from her face. 'She let you fall and now you don't trust anyone to be there to catch you. Isn't that right, Alice?'

'It isn't—'

'But you have to learn to trust. For the first time in your life you have to learn.' His mouth hovered a mere breath away from hers. 'You can fall, Alice. You can fall, *tesoro,* and I'll be standing here ready to catch you. Always. That's what love is. It's a promise.'

Tears filled her eyes. 'You make it sound so perfect and simple.'

'Because it is both perfect and simple.'

'No.' She shook her head and let the tears fall. 'That is what my mother thought. Every time she was with a man she had these same feelings and she thought they were love. But they turned out to be something entirely different. Something brittle and destructive. My father was the same. And I have their genes. I believe that *you* can love, but I don't believe the same of myself. I can't do it. I'm not capable of it.'

'You are still afraid.' He brushed the tears away with his thumb. 'You think that you are still that little girl on the climbing frame, but you're not. Over the past few weeks I've watched you and I've seen you learning to touch and be touched. I've seen you becoming comfortable with other people's emotions. All we need to do now is make you comfortable with your own.'

'It won't work, Gio. I'm sorry.'

Their bags were packed and Gio was up at the house having a final meeting with his brother about family business. She hovered in the courtyard, enjoying the peace and tranquillity of the setting.

After four days of lying on the beach and swimming in the pool, she should have felt relaxed and refreshed. Instead, she felt tense and miserable. And the last thing she wanted was to go home.

From the courtyard of the main house she stared down through the citrus orchard to the sea and then glanced behind her, her eyes on the summit of Mount Etna, which dominated the skyline.

'We will miss you when you've gone. You must come again soon, Alice.' Gio's mother walked up behind her and gave her a warm hug.

'Thank you for making me feel so welcome.' The stiffness inside her subsided and she hugged the older woman back, envying Gio his family.

'Anyone who has taught my Gio to smile again will always be welcome here.'

Alice pulled away slightly. 'He always smiles.'

'Not since the accident. He was frustrated. Sad. Grieving for the abilities that he'd lost. His ability to help all those poor little children. You have shown him that a new life is possible. That change can be good. You have given him a great deal. But that is what love is all about. Giving.'

Alice swallowed. 'I haven't—I don't—'

'You will come and see us again soon. You must promise me that.'

'Well, I...' she licked her lips, 'Gio will probably want to bring some other girl—'

His mother frowned. 'I doubt it.' Her voice was quiet. 'You are the first girl he has ever brought home, Alice.'

The first girl?

Alice stared at her and the other woman smiled.

'He has had girlfriends, yes, of course. He is an attractive, healthy young man so that is natural. But love...' She gave a fatalistic shrug. 'That only happens to a man once in a lifetime, and for my Giovanni it is now. Don't take too long to realise that you feel the same way, Alice. To lose something so precious would be nothing short of a tragedy.'

With that she turned and walked back across the courtyard into the house, leaving Alice staring after her.

Gio stood on the beach and stared out to sea, unable to drag himself away. Disappointment sat in his gut like a lead weight that he couldn't shift.

He'd relied on this place, *his home,* to provide the key he needed. To unlock that one remaining part of Alice that was still hidden away. But his plan had failed.

Maybe he'd just underestimated the depth of the damage that her parents had done to her.

Or maybe he was wrong to think that she loved him. Maybe she didn't love him at all.

'Gio?' Her voice sounded tentative, as if she wasn't sure of her welcome, and he turned with a smile. It cost him in terms of effort but he was determined that she shouldn't feel bad. None of this was her fault. None of it.

He glanced at his watch. 'You're right—we should be leaving. Are you ready?'

'No. No, I'm not, actually.' She stepped away from him, a slender figure clothed in a blue dress that dipped at the neck and floated past her knees. Her feet were bare and she was wearing a flower in her hair.

The transformation was complete, he thought to himself sadly. A few weeks ago her wardrobe had all been about work. Practical skirts and comfortable shoes. Neat tops with tailored jackets.

Now she looked relaxed and feminine. Like the exquisitely beautiful woman that she was.

'Well, you have five more minutes before we have to

leave.' He prompted her gently. 'If there are still things you need to fetch, you'd better fetch them fast.'

'There's nothing I need to fetch.' In four days on the beach her pale skin had taken on a soft golden tone and her blonde hair fell silky smooth to her shoulders. 'But there are things that I need to say.'

'Alice—'

'No, I really need to be allowed to speak.' She stood on tiptoe and covered his lips with her fingers, the way he'd done to her so many times. 'I didn't realise. I didn't realise that giving up surgery had meant so much to you. You hid that well.'

He tensed. 'I—'

'It's nice to know that other people hide things, too. That it isn't just me. It makes me realise that everyone has things inside them that they don't necessarily want to share.' She let her fingers drop from his mouth. 'It doesn't stop you from moving forward. It's nice to know that, even though you didn't smile for a while, you're smiling again now. And it's nice to know that I'm the only woman that you've ever brought home.'

'You've been speaking to my mother.'

'Yes.' She glanced down at her feet. Curled her toes into the sand. 'And I want it to stay that way. I want to be the first and last woman that you ever bring here. I should probably tell you that I'm seriously in love with your mother. And your sisters and brother, grandparents, uncles and aunts.'

'You are?' Hope flickered inside him, and the tiny flicker grew as she lifted her head and looked at him, her blue eyes clear and honest.

'You're right that I'm afraid. I'm afraid that everything that's in my past might get in the way of our future. I'm afraid that I might mess everything up.' She swallowed and took a deep breath, her hands clasped in front of her. 'I'm afraid of so many things. But love only happens once in a lifetime and it's taken me this long to find it so I can't let my fear stand in my way.' She held out her hand and lifted her chin. 'I'm ready to climb, Gio, if you promise that you'll be there to catch me. I'm ready to marry you, if you'll still have me.'

He took her hand, closed his eyes briefly and pulled her hard against him. 'I love you and I will always love you, even when you're ninety and you're still trying to talk to me about work when all I want to do is lie in the sun and look at my lemon trees.'

She looked up at him, eyes shining, and he felt his heart tumble. 'I have another confession to make—I haven't actually been thinking about work as much lately.'

'Is that so, Dr Anderson?' His expression was suddenly serious. 'And that's something that we haven't even discussed. What we do about work. Where we are going to live.' Did she want to stay in Cornwall? Was she thinking of moving to Italy?

She shrugged her shoulders. 'It doesn't matter.'

He couldn't hide his surprise. 'Well, I—'

'What matters is us,' she said quietly, her hand still in his. 'You've shown me that. I love you, Gio, and I always will. I believe in love now. A love that can last. This place makes me believe that. You make me believe it.'

For the first time in his adult life words wouldn't come, so he bent his head and kissed her.

THE SICILIAN'S
SURPRISE
LOVE-CHILD

CAROL MARINELLI

For my great friend, Frances Housden.
Love you, Cuzzy.
C xxx

CHAPTER ONE

'AURORA WILL BE shadowing me today.'

Nico Caruso did not look up from his computer as Marianna, his PA, walked into his opulent Rome office. Instead he frowned.

'Aurora Messina from the Sicilian hotel,' Marianna elaborated, clearly assuming from Nico's frown that Aurora's was a name he did not know.

Oh, but he did.

Aurora Messina. Aged twenty-four—six years younger than him.

Aurora Eloise Messina, with her velvet brown eyes and thick dark hair that was not quite raven, though too dark to be called chestnut. Ah, yes... Aurora, with her olive skin that went pink in the sun.

'Don't you remember me, Nico?'

There was a tease in that familiar rasp to her throaty voice, and she brought with her the scent of home. The white crochet dress that she wore must have been hung out on the washing line, for it had caught not just the hot Sicilian sun but also the breeze from the ocean and the sweet scent of jasmine from her parents' garden.

'How rude of you to forget me,' Aurora continued, 'given that you have slept in my bed so many times.'

Marianna sucked in her breath at Aurora's cheeky

implication, but Nico didn't miss a beat with his dry reply, 'Ah, but never with *you* in it.'

'True...' Aurora conceded with a smile.

She had trained herself not to blush when Nico was near, but it was a struggle not to now. The stunning view of Rome panning out behind him went almost unnoticed and the lavish, expensive surroundings barely registered, for Nico, on this Monday morning, was proving more than enough for her senses to take in.

His thick black hair had been cut with skill and his strong jaw, with that slight dent in the centre, was so clean-shaven that she was actually anticipating the brief brush that would come when they shared a light cheek-to-cheek kiss.

Aurora came around the desk to greet him properly.

Of course she did.

After all, the two of them went way back.

But when Nico raised his hand to halt her approach, when his black eyes warned her not to come any closer, Aurora stepped back as if she'd been slapped.

She knew she was bolshie, and often came across as too forward, but after a lot of soul-searching as to how best to face him, she had decided to greet him as she would any old friend.

But Nico had halted her and that had hurt Aurora.

She tried not to let it show.

'Take a seat,' he told her, and then turned to his PA. 'Marianna, let's get started. We have a lot to get through.'

'First, though...' Aurora said. And instead of taking a seat, as instructed, she removed a large leather bag from her shoulder, took out a bottle of tomato sauce, and placed it on his immaculate, highly polished walnut desk. And then she took out another bottle.

'Homemade *passata* from my mother,' Aurora said, 'and here is some *limoncello* from my father.'

Nico glanced over to Marianna, who was trying to keep the shock from her expression as Aurora turned his gleaming desk into a market stall. And then his black gaze returned to Aurora.

'I don't need these,' Nico said, and gave a dismissive wave of his hand. 'You can take them back with you.'

'No!'

He had rejected her greeting. And now this!

Nico was not doing as he should. He was not saying that he missed the taste of that homemade sauce, and nor was he inviting her to join him in sharing the feast that the sauce would create.

He was not playing by the endless ingrained codes of home.

But then, she reminded herself, Nico never had.

For if that were the case then Aurora would be his wife.

Aurora Eloise Caruso.

As a teenager she had practised writing that name in her journals and saying it out loud. Now her cheeks flushed, just a little, as she tried to keep the note of anger from her voice. 'You know very well that my family would never let me visit you without gifts.'

'This is *work*—not a visit,' Nico snapped. 'You are here for five days to train for the opening of a new hotel; it is not a social occasion. Now, get these things off my desk.'

Nico knew he was being harsh, but he *had* to set the tone—and not just with Aurora.

The Silibri contingent had been in Rome for just eighteen hours and already he was fed up with the lot of them.

Francesca, who was to be Regional Manager, had brought, of all things, a salami, and left it for him at the reception desk. Did she assume that Nico could not get salami in Rome?

And Pino, who would be chief concierge at the new hotel, had somehow found his private number. Nico guessed he had got it from Aurora. He had given it to her once.

Once...

Nico refused to think of that time now.

The fact was, on their arrival yesterday evening Pino had called and asked Nico where they should go for dinner and what time he would be joining them!

Nico had rather sternly declined to do so.

The village of Silibri had come to Rome, and it seemed determined to bring him several slices of home.

Except Nico had been trying to run from home since he was sixteen.

Was it guilt or duty that always pulled him back?

He truly did not know.

'Get these off my desk, Aurora,' he repeated. It was a warning.

'But I don't want them.' She shook her head. 'I have shoes to buy, and I need the space in my suitcase.' She fixed him with narrowed eyes. 'Assuming I'm allowed to shop during non-work hours?'

He almost smiled at her sarcastic tone, but did not.

A smile.

A kiss.

When combined with Aurora, Nico knew full well the trouble they made...

So he met her glare with one of his own and hoped she'd hear the message in his veiled words. 'When you're not working, Aurora, I don't care what you do.'

'Good.'

'For now...' Nico flicked his hand at the desk. '...
can we get rid of these and start work? We're already
running behind.'

'I'll take them.'

Marianna was rarely flustered as she was now. Aurora had that effect on people.

'And I'll get the swatches for the meeting...'

'Swatches?' Nico checked.

'It's decision day for the Silibri uniforms.'

'What decision?' Nico inhaled deeply and tried not
to show his irritation. *Really?* Since when did he get
involved in orders for uniforms?

'They don't like the green,' Marianna said.

'But it's the same as in all my hotels. I want continuity—'

Nico halted himself, deciding that he would save it
for the meeting. He nodded to Marianna, who gathered the bottles and, with Nico's desk back to its usual
order, headed out.

He was surprised when Aurora did not follow, and
instead took a seat. 'I thought you were supposed to be
shadowing Marianna?'

Aurora could hear the irritation beneath the silk of
his low tone and she spoke hurriedly. 'I wanted a moment alone to apologise for being indiscreet. I was making a little joke about the times when you used to stay
at our house.'

She grimaced then, because despite her best efforts
that hadn't come out right. There really wasn't anything to make a joke about. Her father had used to find
the young Nico asleep in the park after a beating from
his father and had insisted he come and sleep at their

home. Aurora would be moved to a made-up bed at the foot of her parents' and Nico would be given her room.

'Apology accepted,' Nico said, and got back to his spreadsheets.

He was still angry, though, Aurora knew, and she was cross with herself too, for she had been so determined to be serene when she saw him.

Nico did not make her feel serene.

'Anyway...' Aurora continued, and under the desk she gave his knee a playful little tap with her foot. 'We were never in bed together—you took my virginity on the couch!'

Her breath hitched as he caught her ankle with his hand and gripped it tight for a second. She wished—how she wished—that he would run that hand up her calf, but he scolded her instead.

'I didn't *take* it, Aurora. You very willingly gave it to me.' He pointedly removed her foot and released his grip. 'You *pleaded* with me, in fact.' He turned back to the computer. 'It's forgotten now.'

Liar.

For Nico, sex was necessary and frequent—if a touch emotionless. And it was always a smooth and controlled affair, taking place in his suite at the hotel, never at his home.

It did not compare to the panting, hot, sweaty coupling that had taken place with Aurora.

Nothing could ever compare.

'Forgotten?' Aurora checked.

'It happened just the once and it was a long time ago.'

'Four years, Nico.'

Yes, it had been four years since that night, and Nico had been paying for it ever since.

That one slip had cost him millions.

Tens of millions, in fact.

Though the cost of a new hotel had been preferable to another night under the Messina roof.

He did not glance up as she stood and walked to the window.

This was hell.

Nico was aware he had treated her terribly.

He should never have slept with her.

They had been supposed to marry. Of course they had never had a say in it, but as they'd grown up it had become a given. Her *nonna*'s house had been left to her father, Bruno, and he had kept it for them to reside in after their wedding day.

Nico had been able to think of nothing worse. Stuck in that damned village, living opposite the in-laws and working all day on the vines.

Aurora had taken it well when he'd told her they would never marry. She had laughed and said something along the lines of *Thank God for that.*

It had been the sun that had made her eyes sparkle, Nico told himself. She had been sixteen then, and a skinny, slip of a girl. He hadn't seen her for a few years after that.

Oh, but when he had…

He glanced over to where she stood, looking out towards the Vatican City, and though he wanted to turn back to his computer screen he could not resist a double-take.

There was nothing, Nico thought, more beautiful than a beautiful Sicilian woman.

She was dark-eyed and dark-haired, with voluptuous curves that had never seen a gym let alone a scalpel or silicone. Beneath her full bust in the white crochet dress there was a thin strap of leather, tied in a bow.

He could think of no other woman who might look so sexy in such a dress, but she certainly did. He wanted to pull on that bow…he wanted to bare her breasts and pull her onto his knee. To kiss that mouth and properly welcome her to Rome.

His eyes drifted down to her shoes, which were neutral. Her legs, though, were not—their olive skin was bare and her calves were toned. His gaze followed the line of her long limbs until it rested where he knew he would find dark silken curls; he knew, too, the grip of those thighs.

She was fire. And he must do all he could not to let it catch him. For what Nico craved in his life was order.

Aurora could feel his eyes on her and she liked the vague, unsettled feeling that tightened low in her stomach and brought a hot and heavy sensation between her legs.

She had seen him since that fateful night—of course she had. But since the morning after they had never been alone.

Now, for a few precious moments, they were.

Aurora had practised this moment in her head and in the mirror so many times, and had sworn to rein herself in. But what had she gone and done?

Teased and cajoled and tried to draw a reaction from this cold immutable man, who had ruined her for anyone else.

Yet she could not bring herself to regret losing her virginity to him. Aurora would never regret that.

She attempted a more bland conversation. 'I like Rome…'

'Good.'

'Though I *love* it in the early morning. I went exploring this morning…'

Nico looked back to his computer screen.

'I felt as if I had the city all to myself. Well, not quite...'

She thought of the cafés and markets opening, and the street cleaners she had encountered on her early-morning walk—the walk during which she had promised herself that when she saw Nico later she would be serene and controlled. Sophisticated. Like the slender beauties he dated, whom she read about while bile churned in her stomach.

'Tonight we're all going on a bus tour...' She halted, thinking how touristy and gauche she must sound to him. 'Are you excited about the Silibri opening?' she asked, because that seemed safe.

'I will be glad when it's done.'

Glad when he would be able to hand it over to his executive and the managers. When it would be up and running and no longer at this intense stage.

Right now, though, the tension was all in his office.

It was a relief when Marianna appeared and, with Aurora observing, they began to go through his schedule.

Nico was to meet with the Silibri hotel staff in fifteen minutes, and after that his day was back-to-back meetings with accountants, financiers and lawyers—and, no, Nico said, he would not be staying at the hotel that night.

'You have a breakfast meeting at seven and the helicopter is booked for nine...' Marianna frowned at this slight anomaly. 'Usually you stay here if you're flying out.'

'I'll be residing at home tonight,' Nico said. 'Now, can we check my Silibri schedule? I want to see my father's doctor as soon as I arrive.'

'You're going home…?' Aurora blinked. 'Why are you going home when we are all *here*?'

'Again…' Nico sighed. 'You are here for staff training.'

He looked to Marianna and was grateful when she stepped in.

'Signor Caruso and I run through his schedule each morning, Aurora. This is not a meeting, and nor is it a discussion; it is to ensure that everything is in order and that we are both clear on timings.'

'Of course…' Aurora attempted, but there were a million questions in her eyes about why he was leaving Rome so soon after they had arrived.

Nico answered none of them.

Instead, having gone through his impossibly busy week, they headed out of his office, with Nico holding the door for both the women.

'After you,' Nico said.

He wished his good manners were not quite so ingrained, and that he did not have to hold open the door, for the scent of her reached him again. The chemistry that flared between them was undeniable, and the want was still there.

Nico, though, was first to walk into the boardroom.

The Silibri contingent were there, waiting, and they greeted him warmly.

Too warmly.

'Hey, Nico!'

And there were *more* gifts set out on the table.

Amongst other things, Francesca had brought homemade *biscotti* to go with the coffee being served. Only Vincenzo, his marketing manager, sat rigid, clearly taken back by the party-like atmosphere in the room.

He smoothed his auburn hair nervously and cast a

slightly aghast look at Nico. Bizarrely, for the briefest of seconds, Nico wanted to tell Vincenzo to relax. Did he not know how things worked in Sicily? Did he not know that humour and conversation were an art form there, especially in Silibri?

Of course not. Vincenzo had been brought in from the Florence branch.

'Let's get started,' Nico said.

It would hopefully be a quick meeting.

Aurora was to be assistant manager of marketing. It was not something she had studied for, but she knew the area well and loved taking photos—and she had ideas. Many of them.

Nico hadn't actually got her the job; she did not need him to succeed.

Well, maybe a bit...

For without him there would be no hotel.

Vincenzo was speaking of the excitement locally, and said there were a few interviews nationally, for various tourism shows and breakfast television and the like.

'I shall handle those,' Vincenzo said.

'You can take turns with Aurora,' Nico interjected.

'But I have had media training,' Vincenzo pointed out. 'Aurora can be a touch...forceful, and we want to extend a gentle invitation.'

'Vincenzo,' Nico said. 'I wasn't offering a suggestion, I was *telling* you to take turns with Aurora.'

He was not doing her any favours. Vincenzo was vain and self-serving—and, though he was brilliant at his job, it was as clear as day to Nico that Aurora, with her passion, her low throaty laugh, with her sheer love of Silibri, would be more enticing for potential guests.

'Next,' Nico said, and nodded to Francesca.

'The fittings for the uniforms have been delayed.'

'Then get them done,' Nico said, even while knowing it wasn't going to be as easy as that.

'I have tried, but the staff have issues with the colour.'

'And the fabric...' It was the first time Aurora had spoken. 'The wool is too heavy and the green makes us look like...' She snapped her fingers. 'That Englishman's Merry Men.'

Nico had to think for a moment. But then he always had to think when Aurora was around—she brought him no peace.

He thought of the dark green uniforms that looked so elegant against the old Roman and sophisticated Florentine buildings, and worked well in both England and France, and then he joined the dots she had led him to with her mention of 'the Englishman's Merry Men'.

'You mean Robin Hood?'

'Who?' Aurora frowned, and then she gave him a tiny smile to say of *course* she knew who he meant and was teasing him.

Their minds jostled, and she could see he was fighting not to return her smile. She was still looking at Nico's full mouth, with a smile on her own, when Vincenzo cleared his throat and spoke up.

'We think that Silibri should have a more casual feel.'

'It's a five-star hotel.' Nico gave a shake of his head. 'I do *not* want my staff looking casual.'

'Of course not,' Vincenzo agreed. 'But there is a stunning French navy linen, and teamed with crisp white shirts...'

'We would look like sailors,' Aurora sulked.

Nico pressed the bridge of his nose between finger and thumb. What the hell had he been thinking? What had possessed him to venture into Silibri? He should have sold the land there and been done with it...

Yet as he sat there he recalled Aurora's emphatic *no* when he had suggested that the night after—

Damn, no matter how he tried to avoid it, all roads led to that night.

Nico forced himself back to the moment: What in God's name was he doing, sitting here discussing fabric? It was *his* hotel and it had been four years in the making.

The trouble with the Silibri venture was that the staff considered it to be *their* hotel too. They were all *so* involved and took it all *so* personally.

'What about the same green as the other hotels, but in linen?' Francesca suggested.

Aurora shook her head.

'That just takes us back to the Merry Men,'

'So what do *you* suggest, Aurora?' Nico threw down his pen in exasperation.

Of course she had an immediate answer. 'Persian Orange.'

From her seemingly bottomless bag she produced several swatches of fabric and proceeded to pass them around. It was a linen blend that wouldn't crease, she assured them, and with one look Nico knew she was right.

'It is the colour of the temple ruins and the monastery just before sunset,' Aurora said. 'And you know how beautiful Silibri looks at that time of night. Mother Nature chose her colours wisely.'

'It is a bold colour,' Vincenzo objected. 'A touch too bold, perhaps?'

'I don't agree that it is too bold; it is, in fact, quite plain,' Aurora refuted, then cocked her head to the side.

Nico watched as her knowing eyes weighed up Vincenzo.

'Are you worried that it might clash with your red hair?'

'Of course not...' Vincenzo was flustered and smoothed said red hair down.

'Because,' Aurora continued, 'we could have bespoke shades on the same theme, with Persian Orange being the main one.'

'*Bespoke* shades...?' Vincenzo checked.

And Nico watched silently as his marketing manager warmed to his new assistant's idea, and watched, too, Aurora's small, self-satisfied smile as of course she got her way.

Heaven help Vincenzo, Nico thought, trying to manage her. Because Aurora could not be managed nor contained.

She was as Sicilian as Mount Etna, as volatile as the volcano it was famous for, and she could not be beguiled or easily charmed. She was perceptive and assiduous and...

And he refused to give in to her ways.

'I'll consider it,' Nico said.

'Consider it?' Aurora checked. 'But what is there to consider when it's perfect?'

'There is plenty to consider,' Nico snapped. 'Next.'

It had been scheduled as a thirty-minute meeting but in the end it took sixty-three—and of course it did not end there.

As Marianna disappeared for a quick restroom break, and Nico attempted to stalk off, Aurora caught up with him. 'I wonder if we could speak? I have an idea.'

'It has all been said in the meeting.'

'This isn't about the uniforms. I have another idea for the Silibri hotel.'

'Then speak with Vincenzo, your manager.'

'Why would I share my idea with *him*?'

'Because I don't generally deal with assistants.'

Aurora felt his cool, snobbish dismissal and told him so. 'It is spring, Nico, and the sun is shining—yet you are so cold that when I stand near you I shiver.'

'Then get a coat! Aurora, let me make something very clear—and this is a conversation that you can re-peat to all your colleagues. You are here for a week of training to find out how *I* like things done and how *I* want my hotel to operate. You're *not* here for little chats and suggestions, and catch-ups and drinks. I did *not* build a hotel in Silibri to expand my social life.'

Nico wanted this conversation to be over.

'You are shadowing Marianna for the rest of the day?' he checked.

'*Sì?*'

'Then what are you doing standing in mine?'

CHAPTER TWO

DAMN YOU, NICO!

How much clearer could he have made it that he did not want her near him? He could not have been more horrible had he tried.

As Nico stalked off Aurora wanted to be done with her feelings for him. To shed them. To discard them. To stamp her foot on them and kick them to the kerb. She was tired of them and bone-weary from this unrequited love.

'Aurora.' Marianna had found her. 'We need to talk. Or rather, you need to listen.'

'I already know what you're going to say.'

But she was told anyway.

A little more decorum and a lot less sass, or she would be shadowing the bottle-washer for the rest of the week.

And while Aurora understood what was being said, she just did not know how to squeeze herself into the box demanded of her. Or how *not* to be herself when she was near Nico.

'Hello, husband,' she had used to greet him teasingly when, as a young girl, she had opened the door to him.

He would shake his head and roll his eyes at the precocious child who constantly fought for his smile and attention. 'Your father says he wants some firewood chopped,' Nico would respond.

Yet, as much as he'd dismiss her, she would still sit and watch him chop firewood, and her heart would bleed when he took off his top and she saw a new bruise or a gash on his back.

How could Geo do that to him?

How could anyone hate Nico so?

Then he would look over, and sometimes he would smile rather than scowl at his devoted audience. And her day would be made.

Nico hadn't broken her heart when he had first left Silibri—after all, she had only been ten then—though for a while she had cried herself to sleep at night.

No, the heartbreak had occurred on one of his rare trips home, when Aurora had been sixteen.

Her heart had sung, just at knowing he was home, and then one afternoon he had spoken at length with her father behind closed doors. She had assumed they were drinking the grappa her father had saved for this very day.

And then Nico had come out and asked if she'd like to take a walk. She had quickly washed her face and hands and scrubbed her nails, so her hands would look pretty for the ring. And she had brushed her teeth for she had wanted to taste fresh for her first kiss.

They had walked down the hill and around the old monastery, but instead of heading to the ancient temple ruins, Aurora's favourite place, Nico had suggested they take the steps down the cliff to the beach.

'Our fathers are very old fashioned...' Nico had said as they walked on the deserted sands.

'Yes!' Aurora had beamed, for she had known he had just been speaking with hers.

'They try to make decisions for us.'

She'd felt the first prickle of warning that this conversation might not be going as she had long hoped. 'They do,' she had rather carefully agreed.

'Aurora, I stopped allowing my father to dictate to me a long time ago.'

'I know he is difficult. I know you hate him. But—'

'Aurora,' he broke in. 'I can't see myself ever marrying. I don't want to have a family. I want freedom...'

It had been the worst moment of her life.

'Aurora!'

Marianna's voice broke in on her painful reminiscence.

'Are you even listening to what I'm saying?'

'Of course,' Aurora said. She hadn't been listening, but she could guess very well what Marianna had said. 'Don't worry, I...' She gave a slow nod, took a deep breath and made a vow—not just to Marianna but also to herself. 'I will not embarrass myself again.'

Aurora was done with Nico Caruso.

For eight years she had loved him in secret.

A whole third of her life!

Well, no more.

It was time to snuff out the torch she carried.

She would be calm and distant and professional if she ever saw him again.

'I didn't mean you to take it like that...' Marianna gave her first kind smile. 'Nico is a wonderful boss, but he's no one's friend. Just remember that when you're working together.'

'I will.'

'Come on—the driver is waiting.'

'The driver?'

'So I can go and pack for Signor Caruso's trip. Oh,

and I must organise his driver for the morning, now he's no longer staying at the hotel…'

Aurora just wanted the day to be over. She wanted to go back to her hotel room, throw herself on the bed and cry…and then emerge better and stronger and step into the future without him.

Instead, she had to step into his home.

It was beautiful, of course.

Nico lived in the Parioli district, and his residence was just a short drive from the hotel. It was elegant and tasteful and her heels rang out on the marble floors.

There was a huge gleaming kitchen, where Marianna deposited the *limoncello* and *passata* in rather empty cupboards. Then they went back to the main corridor, with its cathedral-high ceilings and a grand staircase which she climbed reluctantly—for surely Nico's bedroom was not the best place to attempt to get over him?

The master bedroom had French windows and a balcony and looked out to Villa Borghese Park. And, had it not been Nico's bedroom that she stood in, Aurora might have been tempted to step out onto the balcony and drink in the view. Instead she looked at the vast bed, dressed in white with dark cushions, and imagined Nico beneath the crisp linen.

His bedroom daunted and overwhelmed her, although Marianna was clearly very used to it and quickly pulled out a suit carrier and a case and started to select shirts and suits.

'Aurora, could you please sort out underwear?'

Joy!

It was agony—sheer agony— Once, a long time ago, she had slipped her hand inside similar black silk boxers and felt his velvet skin…

Oh, it killed her to be in his bedroom, and to remember how it had been between them, but she tried hard to keep her vow and focus on work.

'Should I pack these?' Aurora asked, holding up a pair of black lounge pants. To her surprise, Marianna laughed.

'No, I bought those just in case he has to go into hospital or something.'

'Oh…'

'You have to think of all eventualities if you're a PA.'

Except Aurora didn't want to be one. 'Marianna, why am I shadowing you today? I'm enjoying it, of course, but I thought I would stay with the marketing team.'

Marianna put the suit she was holding down on the bed before answering. 'Well, I don't always travel with Signor Caruso and, given that he'll presumably be spending some considerable time in Silibri, I thought it might be prudent to train someone to assist me when he's there. I have someone in each of his hotels with whom I liaise. I spoke with Francesca and she suggested you.'

'*I* would be Nico's PA?'

'No. But I want someone in the Silibri hotel that I can liaise with directly regarding him.'

'Does Nico know about this?'

'No, it's just something Francesca and I have discussed. I would not trouble Signor Caruso unless I considered it viable…' She gave a thin smile, which told Aurora that she was already having her doubts as to her suitability for the role.

Aurora had doubts of her own.

Getting closer to Nico wasn't going to snuff out the torch. Instead it would fan the eternal flame that burned for him. So Aurora said the bravest thing she could. 'It

is very nice of you to consider me—but, no.' Aurora
shook her head. 'I don't think that role would be for me.'

Tonight, when she was back in the hotel, she would
cry one final time over him, Aurora decided.

There would be no bus tour.

She was a little tired of being with her friends. They
saw each other every day and they were all so much
older than she.

No, tonight she would recall with shame her own
behaviour earlier with Nico and then she would weep
into the pillow. And then...

Well, it was time she moved on—time she started
dating.

Time to flirt.

To be twenty-four and single in Rome.

She might even download the dating app that Chi-
Chi and Antonietta had told her about!

*To hell with you, Nico Caruso, because I want to
be with a man who wants me. I am finally out of your
shadow.*

And she was soon to be out of Marianna's.

'Where's Aurora?' Nico asked late in the day.

'Oh, she's with the marketing team,' Marianna said
and then glanced at the time. 'Though they'll all be off
on their bus tour now.'

Nico gave a small eye-roll, though not with any mal-
ice. It was more in amusement that Pino had called and
invited him to join them.

Again he had declined.

'Do you know?' Marianna said. 'I have never met
a more enthusiastic lot of people. With their energy
and exuberance I'm sure the new hotel is going to be
amazing.'

'If you like Persian Orange,' Nico said, and he pushed over the uniform order he had signed off on. Persian Orange! With bespoke tones of Butterscotch and Burnt Caramel for those who felt the shade might not suit their colouring.

Nico had a headache from looking at so much orange.

And he had another question. 'Why was Aurora shadowing you today? I thought her role was in marketing.'

'Correct,' Marianna agreed. 'But presumably you will be spending a lot of time in Silibri...?'

'Not once the hotel is up and running.'

'You are always between hotels. I have Teresa in Florence, Amelie in France... Francesca thought that Aurora might be suitable—'

'No.' Nico said it too fast, and with too much force, and he attempted a quick recovery. 'Look, I'm sure Aurora will be excellent in her marketing role, but I don't think she would work out as—'

'It's fine,' Marianna cut in. 'Aurora said the same.'

'She did?'

Why did that feel like a punch to his guts rather than spread relief? And why did the thought of working closely with Aurora unsettle him so?

Nico grabbed his jacket and took the elevator down to head for home.

He did not need to ponder further to know the answer: there was *way* too much history between them.

CHAPTER THREE

The night that neither can forget...

'YOU CAN TELL Nico that I'm not leaving my home.'

Just hearing Nico's father say his name had Aurora's heart both soaring and shattering anew.

It was a regular occurrence in Silibri. Nico Caruso's name was mentioned often.

'Since when did I have a direct line to your son, Geo?' Determined not to give herself away, Aurora responded light-heartedly as she plumped the old man's cushions behind him. 'I haven't spoken to Nico in ages.'

'He's sending his helicopter to take me to Rome.'

Aurora's cushion plumping was paused for a moment.

Geo got confused at times, and was also known to exaggerate, but even by Geo's standards this was too far-fetched to be believed.

'Who told you that?' Aurora asked as he rested back in his chair and she straightened up.

'The doctor did.'

'Oh? And is this the same doctor who told you that your drinking would kill you?' Aurora checked.

Geo gave a reluctant smile.

'The same doctor who said that you couldn't manage here alone and needed to be in a nursing home?' she continued. 'Because I thought you told me that that doctor could not be believed.'

'Perhaps,' Geo conceded, 'but he was telling the truth this time—Nico is sending a helicopter to fetch me.'

Wildfires had been ravaging the south coast of Sicily and steadily working their way towards their small village for more than a week. They had been told to get out—of course they had—but, like Geo, her father had refused.

She didn't doubt that Nico wanted his father away from the fires, but a private helicopter was *way* beyond a boy from Silibri—even a successful one!

Geo's lies were becoming more and more extreme. A few weeks ago, when Aurora had dropped off his shopping, he had told her that she had just missed seeing Maria. Maria, Geo's wife and Nico's mother, had died the year Aurora had been born—some twenty years ago.

Last week he had said that Nico owned three hotels across Europe. When Aurora had refused to believe him, Geo had corrected himself: Nico owned *four*!

'He stole from me!' Geo said now, and cursed. 'He took what was mine.'

'You tell tall tales, Geo,' Aurora said gently.

'Well, he can stick his nursing home in Rome. I hate him. Why would I want to live closer to him?'

Aurora knew that father and son did not get on. She knew it very well.

But, though she loathed Geo's treatment of Nico, she could not walk past the old man's house and not drop in. It was worth it if it made things a little easier on Nico to know that his father was being cared for.

'Now,' Aurora said. 'Is there anything else that you need me to do?'

'Take some money from my dresser and run down to the store.'

'I'm not getting you whisky, Geo,' Aurora told him.

'Why not? We're all going to die in these fires!'

Aurora beamed. 'Then you will meet your maker sober.'

'Take the money and get me my whisky.'

'Don't.'

The very deep voice caused Aurora's stomach to flip over, but even before she turned to face its direction she knew its source.

'Nico…' she said. 'You're here?'

'Yes.'

He wore suit trousers and a white shirt—which somehow, despite the ash floating in the air, looked fresh. His hair was black and clean, unlike hers, which felt heavy after a day spent sweeping leaves outside Geo's home and trying to get his house as safe as possible.

Oh, *why* couldn't he have arrived in a couple of hours, when she was all washed and dressed up for Antonietta's party?

But, really, what did it matter? Nico would never look at her in *that* way.

'How did you get here?' Aurora asked. 'The road from the airport is closed.'

'I came by helicopter,' Nico said.

'Told you,' Geo declared to Aurora, but then he addressed his son. 'I'm not going anywhere and you're not welcome here. Get out!'

Here we go, Aurora thought, and sure enough, within two minutes of Nico arriving, Geo was shouting and waving his stick at his son.

'Get out!' he raged.

'Pa…'

'Out!' Geo shouted. 'I want you gone. You bring nothing but trouble. You're not welcome in my home. You're a thief and a liar and you ruined me.'

It was Aurora who calmed things down. 'I'll take Nico outside and show him what has been done to prepare for the fire,' she suggested.

They stepped out of the small house, but there was no reprieve—Geo's words followed them out into the oppressive heat, where the air was smoky.

'He won't leave willingly,' she said.

'I know he won't.' Nico sighed.

He had his chopper waiting, and a care facility in Rome ready to receive Geo, but even as Nico had asked Marianna to put the arrangements in place he had known it was futile.

'You could carry him out,' Aurora suggested.

'I could,' Nico agreed, 'but then he would die on my shoulders just to spite me. What about you?'

'Me?'

'Yes, why are *you* staying, Aurora?'

'Because we have to protect the village.'

'And what can you do against the might of a wildfire?' Nico asked.

All five-foot-three of her. She was tiny—a stick.

Except she wasn't a stick any more.

They had avoided each other as much as possible since that awkward walk four years ago, and he had watched her blossom from a distance. The child he had rejected was now all woman. The cheeky, precocious brat who had hung on his every word was a forthright, assertive woman who, to Nico's cold surprise, completely turned him on.

Not that he showed it. For one thing had not changed.

Nico did not want a family and he did not want the responsibility of another heart.

'Aurora, you can't do anything to stop the fire.'

'I can feed the firefighters,' Aurora responded. 'Anyway, Pa says the village is safe.'

'Aurora...' Nico kept his voice even, but fear licked at his throat at the thought of her staying here.

The village was not safe. Far from it. Nico had, after all, just viewed the fires from the sky, and heard the worrying comments from his pilot, who was ex-military. Bruno, Aurora's father, was probably regretting his foolish decision and just putting on a brave face.

'Leave.'

'No.'

He persisted. 'Come with me now and get out.'

'I already told you—no.'

'I could insist...' Nico said, and it angered him when she snorted.

Did she not get that the village was going to go up in smoke and that the fire would destroy all in its path?

'I could just put you over my shoulder—the same way I am tempted to do with my father.'

'And then what, Nico? What will you do with me in Rome?'

He gritted his teeth.

'My father would not object,' she said. 'In fact, all the villagers would come out and cheer if you carried me off.' She gave him a smile that did not quite meet her eyes. 'But then you would surely return me, Nico, and that would *not* go down very well.'

No, Nico thought, it would not. 'Don't you *ever* think of leaving?' he asked.

'Why would I?' Aurora shrugged. '*La famiglia* is everything to me. Give me good food and family and my day is complete. What more could I want?'

'You should deepen your voice, Aurora,' Nico said, 'when you impersonate your father.'

'But I wasn't impersonating him.'

'No? You've heard it so often you believe it to be your own thought.'

'Why do you have to criticise?'

'I'm not.'

'Oh, but you are.'

Nico took a breath. Aurora was correct. He *was* criticising—and he had no right to. Especially when she did so much for his father.

He addressed that issue. 'You still haven't sent me your bank account details so that I can pay you for the time spent with my father.'

'I don't count it as work.'

No, she saw it as duty. Nico knew that.

Even though he had not married her, she had taken on the role of caring for his family.

'Aurora…'

'I don't have time for this, Nico. I want to move the firewood away from your father's home. I thought my brother had done it…'

'Give me a moment,' Nico said.

Walking away from the house, he took out his phone and made a call to his pilot.

He could get out.

Perhaps he even *should* get out.

As he and the pilot both agreed, it would be a waste of vital resources to have a pilot and helicopter sitting idle, just in case Geo changed his mind.

But Nico could not leave his father to his fate alone.

And neither could he leave Aurora behind.

He looked over to her, lifting logs, doing all she could to keep the old man safe.

'Right,' he said walking towards her. She was filthy from the effort and he watched the streaks of ash grow as she wiped her forehead. 'Leave the firewood to me. What else needs to be done?'

'Aren't you leaving?'

'No.'

Their conversation was interrupted with the arrival of Aurora's father. 'Nico!'

Bruno greeted him warmly, as he always did—and that consistently surprised Nico. The fact that he had refused to marry his daughter should have caused great offence, yet Bruno had confounded Nico's expectations and still treated him as a future son-in-law.

'You will stay with us,' Bruno said.

'No, no...' Nico attempted, for he did *not* want to be under the same roof as Aurora.

Or rather, he wanted to be under the same roof *alone* with Aurora. He wanted to strip her off in the shower and soap those breasts that now had sweat dripping between them.

He was trying to hold a conversation with Bruno even as filthy visions of the man's daughter flashed in his mind. What was *wrong* with him?

'So you're too good for us now?' Bruno demanded.

They all spoke from the same script, Nico thought as he dragged his mind from Aurora's breasts. To refuse Bruno's hospitality would be an insult, and although in his professional life Nico did not care who he offended, he attempted to do things differently here.

Like it or not, while his father was alive, he still needed these people.

More, though, he wanted to do the right thing.

'You can have Aurora's bed.'

'No. Absolutely not!' Nico would not hear of it.

'She will be out tonight, at Antonietta's birthday party.'

'Aurora should be at home,' Nico said. 'With the threat to the village I thought the roads would be closed.'

'The main one is, but some are open between the villages, and the threat has been here for weeks,' Bruno said. 'Life goes on, and Antonietta's father is the fire chief. The firefighters are camping on his grounds so it is the safest place for her to be.'

Nico wasn't so sure of that—and it had nothing to do with the fire!

'I could be on lookout,' Nico said, but Bruno shook his head.

'It is Pino's turn tonight. I did it last night. You shall stay with us.'

'Well, thank you for your offer, 'Nico said, 'but I shall stay only if I sleep on the sofa.'

'Up to you.' Bruno shrugged.

Before dinner Nico checked in on his father, who had drifted off into a drunken stupor. Aurora was already there, and rolling him onto his side, making sure Geo would not choke should he become unwell during the night.

'I told the store not to supply him with whisky,' Nico said to her.

'There is home delivery now.' Aurora shrugged. 'Even your father has worked out the Internet. And there's always Pino stopping by, or Francesca. You can't stop him.'

'I send money, but then I wonder...'

'If you didn't send it he would drink cheap wine instead,' Aurora pointed out. 'Come on, it's time to get back. Supper will soon be ready.'

'I need to speak with the doctor first.'

The news from the doctor was the same.

Geo needed to stop drinking and he needed a more comprehensive level of care—except there was no staff to provide it in Silibri.

'I have spoken to the agency,' Nico said to him. 'And I am looking to purchase the house across the street. That way—'

'You could purchase ten houses,' the doctor interrupted. 'No one wants to live here. The village is dying faster than your father.'

Why did Aurora choose to remain here?

Nico thought of long-ago evenings at the Messina dinner table. She would talk of her photography, and how she would pester the manager at the winery to change the labels on his wine. To rename, rebrand. She had passion and dreams—but they had been smothered by this village, like the smoke that blanketed the valley now.

'Come and sit down,' Bruno said as Nico walked into the Messina home. 'Good food and family and my day is complete. Come now, Aurora.'

But Aurora did not join them at the table.

'No, Pa, there will be food at the party and I have to get ready.'

'And will there be firemen at this party?' Bruno checked. And though he spoke to Aurora, he looked over to Nico.

'I think they are a little too busy fighting fires.' Aurora smiled sweetly as she left the room.

Nico's gut tightened.

'Aurora has a thing for one of the firefighters,' Bruno

said, and rolled his eyes. '*Per favore, mangia, mangia*, Nico. Come on—eat.'

The pasta, though delectable, tasted like ash in Nico's mouth.

Worse still, he could hear the pipes groan as Aurora turned on the shower...

It was bliss to have the hot day and all the grime slide off her skin and to feel the dirt and grease being stripped from her hair. This morning she had risen before six, and had worked every minute since, and yet though she ached, Aurora was not tired.

She looked down at her skin, brown as nutmeg, and saw her fleshy stomach and full breasts and all too solid legs.

She was too much.

Too much skin and bum and boobs.

Too much attitude.

Although as it had turned out for Nico she was not enough. Never enough for him.

How, Aurora pondered as the water drenched her, could Nico manage to turn her on even from the kitchen table?

Last week she had kissed a firefighter, and all she had felt was the tickle of his beard, and all she had tasted was the garlic on his breath, and all she had smelled was the smoke in his hair.

There was something so *clean* about Nico.

Even if his morals were filthy.

Oh, yes, she had heard the gossip about his many women!

But there was still something so clean about him— the tang of his scent and the neatness of his nails that made her shiver on the inside.

She stepped out of the shower and wrapped a towel around her body that was burning inside like the mountains that were aflame all around them.

She headed into her pink bedroom. It was too childish—she knew that—but then she should be gone by now.

Aurora thought now that she would either be the village spinster or perhaps she would marry one day.

But she would never know the bliss of Nico.

Never.

Ever.

And that made angry tears moisten her eyes.

Her nipples felt as if the surface skin had been roughened as she stuffed her breasts into her bra. And as she wrestled her dark hair into some semblance of style there was suddenly the snap of a chain, and her *collana*, the cross and chain she had worn for ever, fell to the floor.

It felt like a sign.

She felt dangerous and reckless and everything she should not be.

Oh, what was the point of being a good Italian girl when the perfect Italian boy didn't want you?

And so she went to the special book on her shelf, out of which she had cut the middle and in which hid the forbidden Pill.

The Pointless Pill, she called it, for she could not imagine sex with anyone other than Nico.

Tonight she would drink wine and try kissing that firefighter again—and maybe this time when his hand went to her breasts she would not brush him off.

To hell with you, Nico Caruso. I shall get over you.

She put blusher on her cheeks and lengthened her

lashes with mascara before sliding glossy pink onto her lips.

She dabbed perfume on her neck and wrists and then strapped on high heels. And she knew that she was not dressing for the fireman tonight, but for the one minute when she would pass Nico on her way out.

She wanted him to ache with regret.

Instead Nico ached with need when, mid-meal, Aurora teetered out in heels and a silver dress.

Nico tried not to look up.

'Go and change, Aurora,' Bruno warned.

'Why? I would just have to put my dress and shoes in a bag and change in the street,' Aurora said cheekily. 'Because I *am* wearing my silver dress tonight, whatever you say.'

Nico could not help but smile. Aurora did not hide, or lie, she just was who she was.

The taxi tooted. The one taxi that ferried people between villages.

He had to ignore the effect of her and the feeling, a lot like fear, that rose when he thought of her out on those fiery mountains tonight.

As she bent and kissed her father, her mother, her brother, he found he had to stop himself from running a tense hand down his jaw and neck as he awaited the torture to come.

Torture for them both.

If she did not extend to him the traditional farewell it would give rise to comments. Her omission would be noted and it would be awkward indeed.

He sat at the head of the table, and as she bent she put her hand on its surface to make as little contact with Nico as she could.

His cheek was cool when her lips brushed it. His scent she tried to obliterate by not breathing in. But because her brother leaned forward to ladle out more pasta she had to move quickly and put out a hand on Nico's shoulder.

It was solid and warm.

One cheek to go.

Both were holding their breath.

Their desire was like the cattails and the bulrushes, waiting to be snapped open and for a million seeds to fly out and expand.

'Be safe,' he told her, in a voice that was somewhat gruff.

She gave the tiniest unreadable smile, and in it was a glint of danger as she straightened up.

'I'm not your problem, Nico.'

She was, Nico knew, looking for trouble tonight.

Hell.

CHAPTER FOUR

Later on the night that neither can forget...

'WE SHOULD HAVE got out.'

Aurora turned and looked at Antonietta as the three friends sat on the hillside, watching the ominous glow.

'We'll make it,' Chi-Chi said. 'There is soon to be a storm.'

'And with storms come lightning,' Antonietta pointed out. 'I wish I had left. I wish I had taken off to...' She thought for a moment. 'Paris.'

'But you don't speak French,' Aurora said.

'I'm learning it.' Antonietta shrugged, and then was silent for another moment before continuing. 'Pa says we shall have a proper party after the fires. I'm getting engaged.'

Chi-Chi let out a squeal and jumped up in excitement.

'To Sylvester,' Antonietta added, and she looked to Aurora, who had to fight not to pull a face.

For Antonietta and Sylvester were second cousins, and Aurora was sure this was a match to keep money within the family rather than for love.

'Are you happy?' Aurora asked carefully.

Antonietta was silent for a very long time, and then she shrugged an odd response. *'C'est la vie!'*

Aurora didn't really know what that meant, but she could hear the weary resignation in her friend's voice and it troubled her.

'I hear your Nico is back,' Antonietta said.

'He is not *my* Nico,' Aurora said.

'No,' Chi-Chi agreed, and made a scoffing noise. 'You should forget about him,' she said. And then she nudged her as a fire truck turned into the hillside, bringing weary firefighters for a break, some food, and maybe a kiss…

But Antonietta caught Aurora's arm. 'If Nico is back, then what are you doing here?'

'He doesn't want me,' Aurora said.

But Antonietta, though only newly twenty-one, had an old head on her young shoulders.

'Go home,' Antonietta said. 'Fix what you can, while you still can. I heard my father speaking to his men about the direction of the fire…'

And hearing the solemn note in Antonietta's voice, and watching the weary firefighters approach, Aurora no longer wanted to be out in the valley tonight.

This… Nico thought as he sat at the table with Aurora's parents playing cards. *This would have been my life.*

Hard work out on the vines by day, and a tired body at night.

Except no amount of labour would be enough to tire his mind.

Yet, on the plus side, he would be sitting with Aurora in the now vacant house across the road, rather than looking at Bruno's hairy arms as he shuffled the cards.

Just because Nico did not want to be married to Aurora, and just because Nico did not want to stay, it did not mean there was not desire. It did not mean he did not care.

And he *loathed* the thought of her out there tonight.

'I'm going to check on my father,' Nico said.

He found Geo deeply asleep, and as he came out Nico felt the hot winds lick his face. He looked at the glowing mountains, and the approaching fire spreading towards them, and in the distance he could see lightning strikes.

They were sitting ducks, Nico thought as he went back into the Messina house.

'Bruno, can I borrow your car and go and get Aurora? The fire is moving fast…'

But Aurora's work-shy brother had just taken it, Bruno said. 'And anyway, Aurora will not thank you if you interfere with her plans for tonight. I've told you she is in the safest place. They're not going to let the chief firefighter's house burn.'

Dio! Nico wanted to shout. *Do you really think the fire will give them a choice?*

'If it gets much closer,' Bruno continued, 'Aurora knows to come home and we will head to the beach.'

He wanted to shake Bruno and ask, *Is it not better that we all die together?* But then, he did not want to worry her mother.

'Grab a cushion from Aurora's room,' Bruno said, 'You know where it is.'

Oh, he knew.

The scent of Aurora lingered in the air. He looked down and saw her gold cross on the floorboards. He picked it up and held it in his palm for a moment.

He caught sight of the book on her chest of drawers and he was intrigued, because he knew that poetry was not her thing. Even before he opened it Nico almost knew what he would see.

The little packet of pills, half of them gone, had been left for him to see, Nico was sure.

He replaced the book in her top drawer.

Message received, Aurora. Loud and clear.

And tonight it was killing him.

The sofa was soft.

Nico was not.

He heard the taxi drop some people off in the street, followed by some chatter—but not Aurora's throaty voice.

The taxi service stopped at midnight.

It was ten past midnight now.

He thumped the cushion and put it over his head to block out the sound of Bruno's snores.

Signora Messina must have had enough, because she shouted for her husband to be quiet and for a short while silence reigned. Except for the drone of the firebombers, filling up in the ocean and then heading back to the hills.

Then, deep in the night, he heard the baker's truck rattle past and stop. He knew that truck was the last chance to get home, for he had taken it many times— except in his case Nico would often leave Silibri in it, heading to the next village.

Anything to get away.

He ached from his calves to his groin to hear Aurora's footsteps. From the small of his back to his chest, need gripped him tightly and fear for her choked him.

And then the door opened quietly, and Nico breathed a sigh of relief when he heard the pad of bare feet and guessed that she was carrying her shoes.

Aurora tiptoed past him.

She couldn't really see him on the sofa—it was more she could feel that he was there.

She was so sick of Nico and his effect on her that it was all she could do not to spit in his direction.

Instead, she crept into the bathroom and stared at her streaked mascara and wild hair for a moment before she brushed her teeth.

She couldn't even kiss anyone else.

The fireman was quite attractive.

Big and bearded, he was the type of man who would get on with her father. He lived in the next village and had said he was more than happy to come and meet her family, if that was what it took to get to know Aurora some more.

He was perfectly nice—but he was not Nico.

In every dream, in every thought, it was Nico she kissed, Nico who was her first, and she did not know how to change the grooves in which her mind was stuck.

Nico's hands on her body.

Nico's mouth on hers.

She washed her face, stripped off her clothes and pulled on a baggy old T-shirt that had seen better days.

But instead of heading to her bedroom it was the kitchen to which she headed, her choice fully made.

Nico *would* be her first.

He heard the fridge door open and water being poured, but feigned sleep as she stood over him.

'I know you're awake,' Aurora said.

'How come you're back?'

She didn't answer.

'What have you been doing?'

'I don't answer to you,' Aurora said, and then shrugged. 'I was just sitting on the hillside, talking…'

'With?'

'You forfeited any right to ask, Nico.'

'With?' he asked again.

'Chi-Chi and Antonietta.'

'And your firefighter?'

'He wants me. You don't.'

'So why are you here?'

'I don't want him. I want you.'

Nico could hear her despair and he took her hand, pulled her a little towards him, indicating for her to sit down.

'Aurora,' he said. 'Me not wanting to marry has nothing to do with you.'

'I would say it has *everything* to do with me, given our fathers agreed—'

'Since when did I *ever* do as my father wished?' Nico interrupted.

'You rejected me.'

'You were *sixteen*—and if you want to take offence that I was not attracted to some teenager who I looked at as a sister, then that is your choice.'

Aurora swallowed. She had never thought of it like that.

'You think of me as a sister?'

'I did.'

And now he did not.

'Do you think of me the same way now? Or as a friend?' she asked.

'We can never be friends Aurora.'

Some might take that as an insult, Aurora thought, but it was true. She did not want to do the things she wanted to do to Nico with her friends.

'What have you been doing?' he asked again.

'Trying to fit in—but as always I didn't.'

'What do you mean?'

'Chi-Chi is desperate to marry and Antonietta…' She hesitated, and then told Nico what he might not know, as it was very recent news. 'She is soon to be engaged to Sylvester.'

'But isn't he her cousin?'

'Second cousin, I think,' Aurora said, and watched as Nico pulled a slight face. 'I don't think she's happy about it.'

'I can't say I blame her.'

Nico sighed. If Aurora was fire, then Antonietta was ice, and did not show her feelings. If Aurora thought Antonietta unhappy, then she was.

'So,' Aurora continued. 'There is Chi-Chi wanting a husband, Antonietta not wanting one, and as for me...' She took a breath and told him, 'I am twenty and only last week had my first kiss.'

'Just a kiss?' Nico asked, and she nodded.

'I hated it,' she admitted.

Nico wasn't sure he believed her. 'You need to hide your Pill better, Aurora.'

'You were snooping?'

'And you think your parents don't?' said Nico.

'Usually I'm more careful. I was in a rush tonight.'

'So, if you have just had your first kiss, and hated it, why are you on the Pill?'

'If you build it they will come,' Aurora said. 'Or hopefully *I* will.'

He laughed.

So did she.

Oh, they laughed—and it was such a moment, such a shared flash of bliss, to see cold, immutable Nico lie there and laugh, that she did what she knew she should not and moved her hand to his cheek.

His hand went to remove it, but instead it held hers there.

'It's me who doesn't fit in, Aurora. I don't want relationships. I don't want responsibilities.'

'And you probably don't want someone who can't kiss.'

'Aurora, trust me—you can kiss.'

'Can I try it on you?'

'No.'

'I repulse you so much?'

'You know you don't.'

'Then why not let me kiss you?'

'I'm not your practice board.'

'So I go back to my firefighter...' Aurora said, and felt his hands grip her fingers tighter.

'One kiss.'

He said it with authority, but the undercurrent suggested they both hoped he was lying.

How to kiss him? Aurora pondered. How best to claim her one kiss?

'What are you doing?' Nico asked.

'I want to see you,' Aurora said, and she climbed up so she sat on his stomach, and it made her insides melt that he helped her *and* that he smiled.

She had not looked at her firefighter. In fact she had closed her eyes—though not in bliss.

Now she looked.

His face was still beautiful in the dark: the shadows in the hollows of his cheeks, the dent in his strong jaw, and those delectable lips, and those black eyes watching her.

'You know how to kiss, Aurora,' he told her, and she lowered her head to his.

She felt the softness of his mouth, and his pleasurably rough jaw, and she lingered there for a moment, lightly kissing his full lips.

He had *such* a nice mouth.

She gave that nice mouth playful kisses that teased, that were almost friendly—but not chaste. It was like a little warm-up…like poking a big, sleeping bear.

She could feel his naked torso between her legs and the warmth of his belly on her sex as she practised her kiss on him.

'Taste me with your tongue,' he told her, and she saw that Nico's eyes were now closed.

'I'm too shy.'

That elicited another laugh from them both. It was nice to laugh as their mouths mingled, to share in each other's breath—and then his hand came behind her head and Aurora received her first proper kiss, for with one sweep of his tongue he discounted all the others.

Finally, she closed her eyes.

Then, as he sucked her tongue and pressed her head into his, she knew she was right to be there, for her body was on fire for him.

He tasted of *limoncello* and water and skill. He gave her a taste of the passion beneath that aloof exterior and he made her crave him.

She rose on her haunches and his other hand came to her waist as he kissed her more deeply, tangling with her in indecent ways. His hand slipped down to her buttocks—and he pulled his head away.

'*Dio*, Aurora, where are your knickers?'

'I don't wear them to bed.' She smiled. 'It's too hot.'

His hands were on her ripe flesh and she could feel his fingers digging hard into her. And then she recognised the reluctance in him and felt regret as he removed them.

'Do you wear *your* underwear to bed?' she asked.

She slid back and sat on his thighs. It was a very provocative move, for in doing so she slid her naked sex over the hardest part of him. She pulled back the cotton blanket and saw beneath his black silk boxers and the clear evidence of his desire for her.

'Oh, Nico...'

She touched him without fear or hesitation, freeing him from the restraint that had kept their actions decent. She explored him with her eyes and her hands and knew she had never seen anything more beautiful in her life.

'Aurora...' he warned, and removed her hand, or soon he wouldn't be able to control himself any more.

But she did not stop, and when her hand returned he did not halt it.

'Make it stop, Nico,' she begged.

'Make what stop?'

'This *fire.*'

'Go to bed,' he told her, pushing at her hips and attempting to lift her from his thighs.

But she dug in. 'No.'

'Okay,' he compromised. 'I'll make you come, and then you are to go to bed.'

His arrogant tone only turned her on even more, and she relished the opportunity to discover what he could make her body feel.

Oh, he brought bliss with his fingers. He was not gentle, and she stifled a cry as he slipped his fingers inside her. She moved with his hand for a moment, but then sobbed in frustration. 'It's not your hand I want...'

'Let go,' he told her as he stroked her more insistently, increasing the speed and pressure of his fingers according to the responses of her body.

When she climaxed, Nico decided, he would allow himself to join her, and then they could both get some sleep.

'We might be going to die tonight, Nico,' she told him. 'Don't let me die a virgin.'

She looked down at him and felt a shiver rippling inside her as he almost smiled.

But *was* it a smile?

Aurora did not know, for it was a look she had never before seen. It was a kind of grim smile that made her stomach flip, and his voice, when it came, was deeper than thunder, with a low warning edge.

'Get on the floor,' he told her.

'No,' she said. For that would mean separating their bodies and she did not want to give him even a second to change his mind.

That grim smile remained as his hand left her sex and moved to his own. 'Take off your top,' he told her. 'I want to know every inch of you.'

With anticipation bubbling inside her, and delight that she was finally getting her way, she pulled her T-shirt over her head.

Aurora put her hands on his chest and lifted herself a little. She looked down as he held himself in one hand and ran the glistening tip against her most sensitive flesh.

'Don't make a noise,' he warned as he nudged against her, except she was too tight for his thick length.

He could feel her thighs shaking as she knelt up. 'Get on the floor,' he said again, for he could better control things there.

'Please, Nico, *now*!'

He was just a little way inside her, and he took her hips in his large palms. He'd meant to do it more gently, but she was damp with perspiration, and so was he, and as he pushed her down their bodies slid together and he pulled her down harder than he'd intended and seared into her virgin flesh.

It was the most painful, exquisite, blissful moment

of her life and she did not make a sound. It was Nico who let out a breathless cry as he took her virginity.

'Shh...' Aurora said, though the sound stroked through her as they locked together. She stayed still, so still, because it was agony, but it was delicious too, and she felt his hands very gently on her hips, steadying her.

'Come here,' he told her, but did not move an inch. 'Let me kiss you.'

Now he made her moan, for his kiss was her first taste of the true Nico—utterly tender and all man. His kiss and his tongue took all the hurt away as his hands stroked her hips—not to move her, just to feel her—and he made her whimper. And as the hurt receded desire took its place and she started to move according to the demands of her own body.

She wanted to linger on his lips, to savour this side of Nico, but her body wouldn't allow it, for she could not kiss him softly *and* move as she wished to at the same time.

Nico took over, holding her hips and bringing her in line with his building rhythm, lifting his hips to thrust into her.

'Nico...' she said, in a voice that was fighting not to scream. 'Nico...'

He wasn't putting out the fire in her—it was spreading and consuming her, and she did not recognise the approaching bliss, but sought it all the same.

And then he let out that breathless shout again and lifted himself.

Feeling Nico swell and then the rush of his relief fill her, caused Aurora to shatter into a thousand tiny pieces. And Nico, *her* Nico, pressed his hand over her mouth as her world went black and her orgasm coursed through her.

It was the most intense moment she had ever known and he guided her through it.

Aurora started kissing his palm. Kissing and tasting his salty skin. His hand slid behind her head and he pulled her back to his kiss.

They came down from their high together and slowly. Back to the world they had left for a while. Back to the sound of the choppers and her father's snores.

He held her for a while, but he was concerned about the pace and direction of the fire, and soon he went to the window and checked the solid red glow on the hillside.

And then he looked back to the sofa, where Aurora lay…

Aurora knew she must return to her bed.

'Come on,' Nico said, and took her hand.

He helped her up, and as Aurora stood on shaky legs she fought the sting of tears. How could he be so close one moment and then pack her off to bed like a child the next?

He picked up her T-shirt and led her through to the small kitchen. He turned on the light and she looked down and saw blood, and the evidence of their coupling.

'I can't have a shower—they'll hear the pipes.'

'I know,' Nico said.

Instead he turned on the water at the sink and began to wash her, slowly and carefully.

Tenderly.

It was the second best moment of her life.

Then he put the T-shirt over her head. She did not get another kiss, but he held her for a moment and then released her.

Aurora returned to her pink bedroom and lay in a bed in which she no longer felt she belonged.

CHAPTER FIVE

AURORA AWOKE VERY EARLY, as she always did, in her own bed, but to a world that felt different.

She gave no thought to the wildfires.

For days she had been obsessed by them, but now her first thoughts were of Nico and what had happened between them.

There was no regret—in fact it was bliss to recall. But there was a tremble of fear. For she had not thought she could love him more, or want him more, than she had this time yesterday.

But she did.

Only then did she register the sound of rain—a light patter against her window. Aurora climbed out of bed and peered out. There was steam from the heat, and black smoke in the sky, and a steady fine drizzle of rain.

Aurora pulled on a dress and sandals, and as she slipped out of the house she stole just one look at Nico, crashed out on the couch.

Nico was not feigning sleep this time, but he woke at the sound of the door closing softly and then the steady, welcome patter of rain.

He was not one to examine his emotions—more often he shut them down—but for a moment he lay there, trying to label how he felt.

It wasn't so much regret that had him closing his eyes tight, for in all his twenty-six years those hours last night had been the best of his life.

It was guilt.

Guilt because although everything had changed between them nothing had changed about what he wanted from his life. He did not want love and he certainly didn't want marriage.

Nico had lost control in the small hours and he was not used to losing control.

He always used condoms.

Always.

Yet last night he had not given them so much as a thought.

Had her brother come home, or if her parents had got up and caught them, they would be heading over to the priest right now to arrange a wedding.

Instead he dressed, and headed out to where he knew he would find her.

It was muggy and humid, and no doubt the water would evaporate long before it got to the fires, but the rain would certainly help because the mountains had been tinder-dry.

Down through the village he headed, towards the cliffs overlooking the ocean.

He found her walking through the temple ruins, clearly deep in thought, because she jumped a little when she saw him, evidently not having heard his approach.

'Are you okay?' Nico asked.

'Of course,' Aurora said.

She knew she must look a sight, with her damp dress and hair, but there was nothing she could do about that.

Nico's shirt was damp too, and his black hair was

wet from the rain. She guessed this was what he would look like coming out of the shower, and thought of the shower they hadn't been able to have last night.

'Do you have any regrets?' Nico asked.

'About last night?' Aurora checked. 'None.'

She wouldn't change it even if she could. The things Aurora would change would be the now and the future without him.

'Do you?'

'In part,' Nico admitted, 'because I loathe mixed messages and—'

'I get the message, Nico,' Aurora halted him. 'I heard it loud and clear—you don't want to marry me and—'

'I don't want to marry, *period*,' Nico said. 'I don't ever want a relationship.'

And therein lay the difference between them, thought Aurora. How did he so easily separate sex from a relationship? For she felt as if she was in a relationship with Nico. Right now, as they walked through the ruins, she felt the closest she ever had to another soul.

'Aurora, you don't want to be married to me.'

Yes, Aurora did. But for dignity's sake she had to sound as if she wasn't imploding when she spoke, and so she took a breath.

'No, I don't,' she said. 'I don't want to be married to a man whose skin crawls at the thought of being here. I don't want to be married to a man who keeps his hand on my shoulder but his eyes on the pretty—'

'What are you *talking* about?'

Aurora just shrugged, and then asked him a question. 'When are you leaving?'

'I'll see what's happening with the fires,' Nico said, 'but I expect I shall leave today.'

Even the heavens were against her, Aurora decided,

because as he said it the drizzle turned into heavy rain.
Yes, he would be leaving today.

'Aurora, did you think last night might change
things?'

'No.'

She had been under no illusion that having sex with
Nico would change anything for him. There had been
a kernel of hope, though…

And Nico crushed it.

'I'll never marry, Aurora.'

'I shall,' she said, and she said it harshly.

Her words punished Nico, but determinedly he did
not let it show. 'You have your own life to live and you
have no obligation to me.'

'I know.'

'So, please, if you are going to help care for my father, at least give me your bank details.'

'I don't want your dirty money.'

'*Dirty* money?'

'Oh, come on, Nico, don't take me for a fool. Since
when did a boy from Silibri leave school at sixteen and
go on to own hotels and his own helicopter?'

'You really are good at assuming the worst, aren't
you, Aurora?'

'What else is there to think?' She stopped walking
then and looked at him. 'Nico, be careful.'

'Of what?'

'Whatever it is you're mixed up in.'

'You think I'm in the mafia?' Nico said. 'Or moving
drugs?' He *loathed* that she thought that of him. 'I'm
not involved in anything like that.'

'Come off it, Nico,' Aurora said, and tried to walk
off. 'Don't lie to me.'

He caught her arm. 'I'm not,' Nico said, he was

angry. 'Please don't take me for some corrupt mafia gangster.'

'I don't,' Aurora said. 'Or I'm trying not to.'

'Aurora, ask and I'll tell you—but only you.'

She stood in the rain and it *still* felt like a relationship. She should walk away now, not draw herself in closer to a man who would never want her completely.

She asked, 'How?'

'You know when I left here that I went to my grandfather's?'

Aurora nodded. 'On your mother's side?'

'*Sì.* They are very modest people, who never cared much for my father. They thought my mother had made a poor choice, but she ran off and married him anyway. My grandfather suggested that I cut all ties with my father, but I could not. I got a job there and I sent half my wage home to him. I knew that he was not well and could no longer work the vines—'

'He could have,' Aurora interrupted. 'He chose not to.'

'Perhaps,' Nico conceded. 'Anyway, I made my own way. I worked in a bar, and then I took a loan, and then I bought a small stake in the bar and put in more hours.'

'That does *not* buy you a five-star hotel in Rome and three others.'

'I don't *own* four hotels, Aurora. I have stakes in them.'

She shook her head, disbelieving. No, a Sicilian woman could not be beguiled.

'What I *do* own,' Nico said, 'is land.'

He looked to the misty grey waters and the cliffs shining from the rain.

'This will go no further?' he checked.

'Of course.'

'Even when you sit on the hill drinking wine with Antonietta?'

'She won't be hearing about last night, Nico.'

'This might be a more difficult secret to keep.'

He smiled at her slight eyebrow-raise, and the fact was he *wanted* to tell her. Nico wanted her take on the decision he was about to make.

'My father married my mother not for love, but for what he thought he would get.'

'Which was...?'

He led her out of the temple ruins and they walked towards the old monastery.

'My grandfather owned the land we stand on—right to the edge of the temple ruins. When my mother died, he said the only good that could come out of it was that my father would never get his hands on it. He left it to me. That is why my father says I stole from him.'

'Why did he want it?' Aurora said.

She did not doubt it was beautiful—and, yes, the view was divine—but as far as she could see it was worthless, and she told him so.

'Houses sit empty here for years. My father goes on about the house he had for—' She swallowed, not wanting to say 'us' when no such thing existed. 'He could not even give it away.' She looked around again. Yes, it was her playground and, yes, she loved it, but... 'There's just the carcass of the old monastery and those steps down to the beach.'

'It's *gold*, Aurora. And my father would have sold it to developers. We would be standing now in a concrete jungle, with tourists being bussed in from the airport every day.'

Aurora could not picture it, though she tried to. 'It

would be good for the village, though, to have people coming through...'

'In some ways it would—but that is not what my grandfather wanted and I agreed with him. He thought the monastery should be restored, but that would mean bringing stone up from the quarries...' He halted. The cost and logistics were appalling. 'Believe me, I have been tempted to just sell it—'

'No!' Aurora cried, and it was emphatic. 'He left it to you!'

'Yes.' Nico nodded. 'But I didn't even know he owned it until a short while before he died.'

'Yet you spoke of his plans for it?'

'I thought they were just nostalgic ramblings about his hometown,' Nico admitted. 'And my father certainly never told me about it—though when I found out I understood better why he hates me so. He married my mother to get his hands on it.'

Aurora looked at the land she loved and knew so well, but she looked with different eyes now. It was Nico's.

'What will you do with it?'

'I don't have to do anything. It's a huge asset and I can keep building on that.'

'Or sell it to developers?'

'No,' Nico said, for he had ruled that option out long ago, even if at times he'd been tempted. And then he said what had long been on his mind. 'I could restore the monastery.'

'And make it into what?'

'A very exclusive, very luxurious hotel.'

Aurora swallowed.

'Just a few suites...'

'But how would that make a profit?'

'I would charge a fortune to stay in my Silibri hotel, and I believe I would get it.'

Aurora heard the steely resolve in his voice and blinked, because businessman Nico was someone she did not know.

She spoke then. 'It would bring people back to Silibri...'

'It would,' Nico said, and then he made sure he crushed that last kernel of hope. 'But not me. At least not permanently.'

'I get it, Nico.'

She did.

Nico would not be returning to Silibri to live.

He looked at the ruins, and then he looked to the shell of an old stone cottage, and vowed it would be the first thing that was restored. Yes, he would be back to see his father, but there would be no reason to spend another night in the Messina house.

Nico would not do that to Aurora.

And finally, after years of indecision over the land, his decision was made.

He would not marry Aurora.

But he would take care of her this way.

CHAPTER SIX

Rome

THE LAST TEAR.

It spilled out as she began to pull herself together.

Enough.

She swore there and then that it would be the last tear she shed over Nico Caruso.

Aurora wiped it from her cheek and crumpled the sodden tissue in disgust.

Alone in her hotel room, with the others on the bus tour, she was bent double with the strength of her tears as she relived that night and the morning after.

Well, she had relived it for the last time and she had embarrassed herself enough over him.

It really was time to move on.

So, instead of peeling another tissue from the box she topped up her lip-gloss over swollen lips and tried to repair the damage her crying binge had caused to her eyes.

She would not sit in her hotel room and mourn him—or rather mourn the fantasy of him—for a moment longer.

It was springtime in Rome.

She downloaded that dating app and scrolled through

it, but when she tried to write her profile she gave in and thought, *Baby steps, Aurora.*

She headed down to the bar, more than a little nervous about walking in alone.

And just as she was doing her best to get over Nico, who did she see walking towards her?

A scowling Nico, who, from his expression, wasn't expecting to see her either.

'Aurora.' He gave a swift nod.

'Buona sera.' It took everything she had to greet him with a smile.

'Buona sera. I thought you were on a bus trip?'

'No.' She did not elaborate 'I'm going to have a drink at the bar.'

'Alone?' Nico frowned.

'Not for long hopefully!' She smiled at her own little joke. 'I'll see you tomorrow.' Then she corrected herself. 'Oh, no, I won't. You're heading home in the morning.'

'Here is my home, Aurora.'

'Ah, but home is where the heart is, Nico. You know that.'

'I do,' he agreed. 'And I shall say it again—here is my home.'

He ordered his head to give her a nod and his legs to turn and walk off, but neither obeyed. And then, even as his common sense was screaming at him to walk away, he spoke. 'And, given you are in my hometown, let me get you a drink.'

He'd done it again.

Just when she was determined to move on from him he pulled her back to him.

Well, not this time, Aurora told herself. Yes, she would have a drink with him, but she would not be making a fool of herself again.

He was her boss and she would hold on to that fact.

The bar was busy and he put a hand on her upper arm to guide her through. Staff jumped into action and they were taken to a quiet corner table.

'It's so busy I thought I'd have to drink at the bar,' Aurora said. Although that was possibly the reason he had joined her. 'It's lucky we got a table.' That sounded naïve. 'I mean, I'm glad no one was asked to move to make way for the boss.'

'It would be poor form to do that to my guests, which is why this table is reserved solely for me.'

He watched as her lips pursed and wondered what he could possibly have said to upset her, for it looked as if she was tempted to get up and walk out.

Aurora was.

His private table did not impress her. In fact she felt a little insulted as she wondered how many other women had sat in this very seat. How many hands had he held across this very table?' And then she halted herself, for Nico was the last person she could imagine being affectionate.

They ordered their drinks—a spritzer for Aurora and a red wine for Nico—and then sat in tense silence as they waited for them to arrive.

'Aren't you going to ask me how your father is?' Aurora asked.

'I spoke with him two hours ago and I see his doctor tomorrow.'

'My mother is taking in his meals while I'm away. In case you were wondering.'

Nico said nothing and Aurora took a deep breath, trying to keep her exasperation in. Reminding herself that Nico did not want to hear anything about home...

She was supposed to be keeping things professional,

Aurora told herself. Except his father was fading. Did Nico properly know that?

'Look, Nico, I know that after all he did to you, you must hate him, but I think—'

'I don't,' Nico interrupted. 'I love him very much.'

For Aurora the sky turned purple, the floor was now sand and the people in the bar were green.

Everything she knew was gone.

'I have to accept, though, that he does not want my love. Still, tomorrow I will try again, and I will be told to get lost again.'

Their drinks were brought to them and even after Aurora had taken a sip of hers the revelation had not sunk in.

'You *love* him?'

'Always.'

His response was made in a voice she had never heard. One she did not know how to describe, for it was both decided and resigned.

'So, no,' Nico continued, 'I will *not* ask you how my father is, because I am in touch with his doctor every day. I know he is failing. I have sent him the lifting chair that you texted me about. And I have a chef in Palermo currently trying to recreate some dinner he keeps speaking about. One that his mother once made. I hope that it will prompt him to eat.'

'Nico...'

She did not know what to say. Oh, the hell of loving someone who beat you! The hell of loving someone who goaded and taunted you.

'He seems a little happier,' she said, and saw his disbelieving look. But she spoke the truth. 'He seems calmer,' she told him. 'Although I have a confession, Nico. I was a very bad carer and bought him some

whisky last week. We watched a television show together and we laughed...'

'Thank you,' Nico said.

Aurora resisted reaching over and taking his hand.
Nico did not like affection, but she ached to give it to
him. She attempted to keep some distance, as she told
him the painful truth. 'He's nearing the end.'

'I know he is.'

Aurora felt selfish for her assumption that Nico was
going home just to avoid her. She sensed he had closed
the subject, and so, after a moment's pensive silence
between them, she looked around the lavish bar.

'Pino will be upset he missed this,' Aurora said. 'He
wanted to buy you a drink and a meal.'

'He wanted me to go on the bus tour.'

That made Aurora laugh.

'I'm meeting them all for breakfast tomorrow, before I fly off.'

'I wasn't told.'

'There's an invitation being delivered to your rooms
at turndown,' Nico said. 'And before you tell me that I
should not be so formal with old friends, I will explain
again that this trip is not about friends visiting Rome.
It is work—and I take my work very seriously.'

'I know,' Aurora said. 'And so do your staff. But
aside from that fact, we *are* friends visiting Rome.'

He said nothing.

'Well, *they* are your friends,' she amended, for Nico
had once told Aurora that they could never be friends.
'Whether you want them to be or not.'

Nico's eyes shuttered, and he wished that it was
enough to obliterate the knives of her words—for she
was right. Pino *et al* were his friends.

More than friends.

It takes a village...

And it was true that the people of Silibri had raised him.

He had sat in the park as a terrified child and Bruno Messina had insisted he come back to their home to sleep.

And he had been so hungry at times, too proud to beg, but the emptier his cupboards the more frequent the invitations.

'Hey, Nico!' Pino would say. 'I need some work done in my yard.'

And that had meant supper...

'Nico,' Francesca would say. 'I have made too many *biscotti*. Take them before they go stale.'

Tomorrow, at breakfast, he would take off his jacket and he would smile and laugh with them. Somehow, before the hotel opened and it was all down to business, he would thank the people who had always been there.

'Don't you ever wonder about home?' Aurora asked.

'I hear enough of what's going on,' Nico said. He didn't like invasive gossip and exaggerated stories, but then he looked at Aurora. 'Yes.'

They shared a small smile.

'How's Chi-Chi?' he asked.

'Still looking for a husband.'

'Do you ever hear from Antonietta?'

'Occasionally.' Aurora nodded, but then she shook her head. 'Not as much as I would like. I miss her a lot.'

'You were close,' he agreed.

'Yes.'

'I *would* like to know what happened at The Wedding that Never Was.'

'You heard about that?' Aurora checked.

'Everyone who has a drop of Sicilian blood probably did!'

Aurora gave a small smile and took a sip of her drink, but she didn't lean forward in glee and share the details with him. He knew Aurora hurt for her friend.

'We just sat there in the church...waiting,' she told him. 'Waiting and waiting for the bride to arrive.'

'Did you have any clue that Antonietta wasn't going to show up?'

'No.'

'Aurora...?' he checked.

'It's the truth, Nico. I guessed she wasn't happy, but I knew no more than I told you that night—'

Whoops! They were trying not to refer to that.

'I was surprised and a bit hurt that she didn't ask me to be her bridesmaid. And I knew she wasn't thrilled at the idea of marrying Sylvester, but her father is so forceful. Both families are.'

'And so you sat in the church and you waited...?' Nico prompted.

'Yes. A car arrived, and then word spread that it was not the bride—just Antonietta's father. The priest spoke to him outside.'

'And...?'

'A fight broke out in the church. It was terrible, Nico. As soon as I worked out what was happening I left and got a ride up to her parents' house, but Antonietta was already on the *cuccette* to France.'

'She took the train out?'

Aurora nodded. 'I miss her very much, but she will never be back. She wrote and told me, but I knew it already—for how *can* she come back? Her name is mud all through the village and beyond. Not with her friends, but she has a very large family.'

Nico would have liked to tell her that time would

heal things, but he knew only too well how people could hold a grudge.

'Anyway,' Aurora said, 'I've decided that I'm going to go and see her.'

'In France?'

She nodded. 'As soon as I've saved up enough and have some leave owing I'm going to book my flight.'

He wanted to point out that she'd already have enough money if she would just let him pay her for his father's care. Nico really wanted her to have that holiday with her friend in France, but he'd have to work out a way to give it to her. Without offending her, of course. Or misleading her.

'Do you want another drink?' Nico offered. 'Or perhaps we could get dinner.'

'You told me to step out of your shadow, Nico,' Aurora said. 'You told me that I was here for work. We've caught up on family and friends, so let's just keep it about business.' Aurora was proud of herself for that, at least.

'Okay. Tell me about this idea you have.'

'I thought you didn't deal with assistants?' Aurora sneered, reminding herself of how appalling his treatment of her today had been. 'I'm going to speak with Vincenzo tomorrow. I will give *him* my idea and watch as he gets promoted.'

He smiled.

It was the most dangerous thing, for she could feel her resolve melting like the ice cubes at the bottom of her glass.

'Tell *me*, Aurora.'

'No.' But she was so excited that she couldn't *not* share it. 'Okay—I think we should offer a very exclusive package for weddings at the temple ruins.'

'I don't own that land.'

'But you own the land that surrounds it, and without that access it's very difficult to get to.'

'Yes, but there might be tourists about, or—'

'Nico, it will be the same as a beach wedding. Of course there might be tourists or people walking there. And,' she went on, 'I know that whatever we come up with it might have to change later—there might one day be ten hotels in Silibri—'

'Not like mine.' Nico gave an adamant shake of his head.

The monastery had been a hellish restoration, and no developer in their right mind would have gone to the lengths he had. That aside, there was nowhere else with the views from the old monastery, nowhere with such access.

'Aurora, it would be...' He was about to put up obstacles, and there were many, but she was right. He knew that, for of course *he* had considered it. 'It would be brilliant—'

'But only in the right hands,' Aurora said. 'Only with the right manager.'

'We have a functions manager.'

'I'd want to make weddings at the temple separate. Exclusive,' Aurora said. 'And I want that role.'

'You have no experience,' Nico pointed out. 'You have been in the hospitality industry for four weeks. Before that—'

'I was a cleaner—and a very good one,' Aurora said. 'Is your father's house not spotless?'

'It is.'

Aurora had just combined three of his least favourite topics—his father, the fact that she was his father's unpaid help, and weddings.

'And I have contacts,' she said. 'I know everyone…'

'Aurora…' He kept his voice even. 'It's a good idea—an excellent one. But let's get the hotel up and running first.'

She could not wait, though. 'Nico, we could have wedding gowns for hire, for couples who want to be spontaneous. I *want* this to happen. I *want* that role and I will tell you why. I *know* what the temple looks like in the early morning, and in summer and in winter. I *know* how it looks when the moon is low at night…' To prove it she took out her phone and moved her chair round the table so she sat next to him. 'Look!'

With the scent of her close, with her bare arm next to his suited one, with her voice so close he could *feel* its vibration, Nico decided it was safer indeed to look at the images on her phone.

And they really were breathtaking.

'Since I could walk I have explored those ruins almost daily. For years I have—'

It was she who halted now, for she could not reveal to Nico that it was there she had envisaged their wedding. Not in the tiny little village church, but there at the temple ruins.

It had been a pointless dream—she had known even then—for her parents would never have agreed to her marrying anywhere other than in church.

She felt his arm against hers and the heat from his thigh—or was it from hers? They were sitting so close to each other, and it had happened so naturally, but she felt terribly aware of that fact.

She moved herself and her chair to a far safer location.

Opposite him.

'At least think about it,' Aurora said. 'And think of

me...' She paused and their eyes met across the table. 'I mean, consider me for the role.'

'Of course,' Nico said, and still his eyes held hers. 'And I *do* think of you, Aurora.'

She did not know what to say to that. She felt the pull of him, but it was all too late, she decided. She had put him behind her.

She tore her eyes from his gaze and looked down to her glass, which was empty.

'Another one?' Nico said.

'I had better get on,' Aurora said. She stood and put her bag over her shoulder. 'Thank you for the drink, Nico. It was good to catch up.'

He walked her out and towards the elevators, and she could feel the thick energy between them. She dreaded that he might kiss her—but only because it would take a stronger woman than her to say no.

'You had better go,' Aurora said. 'You have an early start. I know because I booked your driver.'

'I *should* go,' Nico agreed.

In fact, Aurora was the very reason he wasn't staying at the hotel that night—to avoid just such a situation as this. And yet even with all his exit strategies planned here they stood, face to face.

'I will see you at breakfast before I leave?'

'I await my invitation,' Aurora said.

'It will be on your pillow.'

She wanted *him* on her pillow—and far more dangerous than her want, which was perpetually there, was the clear arrival of his.

Nico's hand came to her cheek and he smoothed a stray lock of hair. It wasn't only Aurora's resolve that was fading.

She floored him.

Always.

The sexual attraction between them was undeniable, for sure. But there was also this banter between them—this life they both knew and this world they had shared. And Nico, despite doing everything he could to avoid it, now did not want the night to end.

His hand remained, cupping her ear, and his fingers were in her hair.

She could remember that hand, pressed over her mouth as she came, and she fought not to kiss it, not to flirt.

She won the former battle but failed on the latter.

'I packed your underwear,' Aurora said in a provocative tone—and there went the express train of her mouth again, saying things it should not and being too familiar.

Not that Nico seemed to mind, for he was stroking her earlobe and his eyes were telling of his desire.

And the guard she had fought to keep up was dissolving, for she did not know how to be anyone other than the person she was. The person who was in love with him.

He brought out the Aurora in her.

'Aurora…' Nico said, and she heard in the sound of him saying her name a summons to bed.

She ached to turn her head just a fraction and kiss the palm that held her cheek, to give in to the bliss of him just one last time. To have Nico make love to her in Rome.

He was leaving in the morning and would return only after she had left. This was their only chance, and Aurora did not know how to resist him.

Her neck fought not to arch and her mouth not to part to kiss his palm.

But then her guardian angels dashed in.

They flew from their clouds, or wherever they'd been hiding, and there was no time for them to apologise for their absence. They hauled her back from the brink.

'Goodnight, Nico.'

Well done, Aurora!

Though it wasn't actually Aurora who had halted things, for she was *desperate* for his kiss. No, it was a force greater than she that had somehow gathered and dragged those words from her mouth.

'It's been a long day,' she added, then gave him a smile and walked off.

It would be a long, lonely night.

But at least she would awake with her pride.

CHAPTER SEVEN

Tuesday:
Room Service breakfast
RSVP'd Marianna to decline Nico's kind invita-
tion to breakfast, explaining I had already made
plans.
Social Media Training.
Room Service dinner.
Read for a little while
Cried.

Wednesday:
Breakfast in restaurant.
Forgot about Nico!
Bought a red dress during lunch break.
Worked the day on Reception and was shouted at.
Went to the hotel's hair salon and drank cham-
pagne while hair was done!
Read some more.
Hate him.

Thursday:
Woke early
Coffee at sunrise in a café opposite the hotel.
Grateful that I didn't sleep with him again...
Not really...

THERE WAS SOMETHING so special about Rome early in the morning. The gleaming cobbled streets, fresh from the street cleaners, the lack of people, the abundance of all things beautiful.

Everywhere she looked there was more to see.

The disgusting gargoyles with their erections and horrible tongues.

The timeless beauty of the Spanish Steps.

And there it was. The Trevi Fountain, standing resplendent.

Almost alone, Aurora gazed into the water and saw there were just a few coins, so it must have recently been cleaned out. Then she looked up to Triton and his horses and then back down to the water.

All she had to do was throw in a coin to assure her return to Rome.

Never.

Aurora wanted to return to her simple life.

She *almost* meant it.

She would find her fireman, or a man who worked the vines, and she would love him completely, and he would love her in return.

And she would not hanker for Rome.

Nor for sitting in a bar with Nico and the sheer exhilaration of being near him.

And she would not regret that abrupt goodnight. She would be proud of her resolve. For instead of kissing his palm, and going where that would have led, she had called a halt and said goodnight.

Good, Aurora!

And she would say this to her daughter, if God gave her one.

I knew a wicked man once. A man who made my heart both bleed and sing at the same time...a man who made me succumb to my wildest urges. A man who made me believe we had been together in another life, for even if I did not know him completely I recognised him in my soul.

But I walked away, dear daughter. I did not let him use me again and again. And I don't regret it. No, not even for a moment.

So why was she suddenly crying and scrabbling in her purse for a coin? Throwing it into the water with her eyes closed as she wished with all her heart for her time again…?

Because she would *always* regret Rome and the decision to walk away from the man she would love until her last breath.

She couldn't tell that to her daughter…

Her wings were unfurling in colours she had never envisaged, and no matter how hard she tried she could not stuff them back in.

Aurora tossed in the coin.

Let me return to you, Nico. Let me in. Make love to me in Rome.

She was ashamed of her coin-toss in a way it would be too complicated to explain to someone else, or even to herself, but Aurora also felt better for it. And her mood lifted.

Today she was to work in the Club Lounge, which the very best of the guests frequented, and she had been told to dress to impress.

Back in the hotel, her curls fell into perfect shape as she ran her fingers through them, and she took out the make-up she had bought and applied it.

A little blusher, but not too much.

Eyeliner. Her new best friend.

Mascara.

And a slick of very subtle lipstick.

Should she wear the red dress, even though Nico would never see her in it?

Aurora couldn't make up her mind.

But first she put on a new bra and panties in the most stunning coral.

They would clash, if she wore the red dress, but who cared? No one was going to see.

Aurora wore the red dress.

She found the Club Lounge rather fascinating.

There was breakfast, and then pastries mid-morning, and even champagne cocktails just before midday for a couple who, Aurora found out, had just got engaged.

'Complimente!' Aurora smiled as she placed the drinks down.

She was pleased for them—excited for them as she spied the way they held hands even as they sipped their drinks.

But she was sad for herself.

They knew love.

She looked out at the panoramic view of Rome that the Club Lounge afforded and wondered why all she could think of was Silibri and the temple ruins, and the little house her *nonna* had lived in, and had anyone watered the jasmine? Was Nico there now, strolling around confidently because there was no chance of bumping into her?

'Aurora!'

Realising that she had been daydreaming, and had missed what Marianna had said, Aurora snapped to attention. 'I'm sorry. I was miles away.'

Many miles away, in fact—all the way to Silibri.

'I asked if you'd mind going to Nico's. There's some maintenance being done on the balcony. You might be there for a couple of hours. I don't like to ask just anyone, and you *were* there the other day.'

'Of course,' Aurora responded politely, for what else could she say?

'You look nice,' Marianna commented.

'I was worried it was too much for work.'

'Not here, it's not,' Marianna said. 'Every day is like a wedding! Your hair is nice too.'

All her early life Aurora's mother had trimmed her hair, and later Aurora had done it herself. For her confirmation and on special occasions she had gone to an aunt who, until yesterday, Aurora had believed to be a hairdresser.

Oh, no, she wasn't.

Luigi was a hairdresser!

And a therapist.

And an ego-boost.

All rolled into one delicious package.

Aurora had left the hotel salon feeling like a rock star.

Her dark locks felt like silk, and looked as if every strand had been polished by hand. Her hair now fell in a glossy, snaky curtain, several inches shorter than it had been when she had walked through the heavy brass doors.

The cost?

Astronomical.

Almost a week's pay, gobbled up in two luxurious hours.

Actually, *two* weeks' pay had been spent, if she included the dress, but when in Rome...

It was a short trip to Nico's, and the driver gave her his number to call when the maintenance was done.

Soon she would be alone in his stunning villa... But

not quite, for there were two men in overalls who were waiting for her to arrive.

'Buongiorno!' Aurora greeted them warmly as she disarmed the security system and let them in. And as she led them up the grand stairs she learned a little more about Nico's home.

It was a heritage building, they said, and the balcony inspection was just routine.

There was nothing routine about Nico, Aurora thought.

His bedroom was exactly as it had been the last time she had seen it, with not a thing out of place.

Except for Aurora!

She was a little unsure of *her* place.

In Silibri, she would have put on coffee for the men, and then gone to chat with them as they worked.

But of course she was not at home, so she hovered in the main bedroom as the men inspected the balcony.

It took mere minutes.

'Completato,' the older man said.

'You're finished?'

'Sì.'

It really had been a routine check.

Aurora saw them out and then went back upstairs and locked the French doors. She took out her phone to call the driver to come and take her back to the hotel.

Except she didn't make the call.

Instead she stood in his bedroom for what was undoubtedly the last time. The coffered ceiling was a work of art, and she looked at the intricate engravings and wondered if Nico lay on the vast bed pondering how such art had been crafted and by whom.

Or did he lie with the drapes open at night and look out to Rome and Villa Borghese Park? Aurora wondered.

Or was he too busy when he was in bed?

Of all the regrets she had—and there were many where Nico was concerned—her biggest regret was Monday night.

Despite her promise to be aloof and professional, despite her promise to herself to get over him, it was the closest they had ever been.

Two people sharing a drink and conversation.

He had told her he loved his father, and that had been a revelation in itself. And he had been about to kiss her, Aurora was sure.

And take her to bed too.

Her body and her heart had wanted him to, yet foolish pride and her determination to put him behind her had told her no.

She wasn't snooping, Aurora told herself as she wandered around the stunning room. Of course she wasn't.

She was merely checking that everything was in order for Nico's return, just as his PA surely would.

She walked to his bedside and saw the small shelf of books that was beside it. Leafing her way through them, she frowned when she saw they were all books on productivity and increasing focus.

'Nico, how do you relax with this?' she asked out loud.

And then Aurora smiled and reached into her bag—not for her phone, but for the sexy romance she was currently reading. She would slip it into his reading pile, and even if he didn't want *her* she would spice up one of his nights, somehow!

But she hadn't finished reading it herself yet.

Well, she almost had. It wouldn't take her long to do so, and Marianna wasn't expecting her back for a couple of hours...

Putting her bag on the floor, she sat down on the edge of his bed—and, truly, that was how Aurora meant to remain. Except as she read unthinkingly she slipped off her high heels.

Nico would have told her to make herself at home, she told herself as she lifted her legs onto the bed and lay back on plump pillows. Of course he would. Well, if he'd behaved as he should then he would. How many times had he rested his head in her pink bedroom, after all?

It was the most peaceful hour she had found in Rome. There, in his bed.

Now and then she would glance up and look out to the lush green park, and then back to her book she'd go, letting out a contented sigh at the end.

It would be Nico who would read it next!

After she'd leant over and placed the book on his shelf, between his boring other ones, she lay back with a smile, imagining Nico's expression when he found it.

Imagining him.

Imagining *them*.

It was something she knew all too well in her head…

'Aurora!'

It was clearly her day for being caught daydreaming.

His voice startled her and her eyes snapped open. She realised she had dozed off. 'You're back!'

'Clearly.'

In fact Nico wasn't surprised to find her here. Marianna had mentioned that Aurora was at the house, sorting out the maintenance guys.

For the first time in living memory Nico had 'popped home' in the middle of a working day.

And there, in a blood-red dress, with her snaky black curls and bare feet, lay Aurora, asleep on his bed.

He was turned on even before he called her name.

'I wasn't asleep,' she said.

'Then what are you doing?' he asked.

'Daydreaming,' Aurora said, for to her it was the most normal thing in the world to do.

She wasn't flustered. She didn't rush to sit up, and nor did she apologise; instead she looked him right in the eyes.

'About...?' Nico asked, when he knew full well he should be telling her off, or just getting the hell out. For there was seduction in the look she gave him, and he had sustained it with his low reply.

'My husband,' Aurora said. 'My future one.'

'Really?'

'Yes.'

'And what is he like?'

'He has a beard,' Aurora said.

'A beard?'

'*Sì.*' She nodded. 'And when he comes home to surprise me at lunchtime, he laughs when he finds me reading in bed and the house unkempt.'

'Where has he been?' Nico asked, arrogantly assuming she was speaking of him, and of the life they might have lived had he stayed in the village. 'Out working on the vines?'

'No.' Aurora shook her shiny new curls. 'He's a firefighter.'

'I seem to remember you left a firefighter to come home to me,' Nico pointed out, and he could not keep the slight snap of possession from his voice.

'That was for sex, Nico. I'm talking about my *husband*.'

'The one who laughs when he finds you in bed?'

'Not at first,' she said. 'I think he pretends to be cross.'

He stood so still, fighting not to be provoked.

Except a vital part of him was extremely provoked, and he felt her eyes drift there.

'He spanks me,' Aurora said, and with a smirk moved her eyes back up to his.

'That's your fantasy, is it, Aurora?' Nico drawled, trying to sound bored. 'Some bearded man lumbers home and gives you a spanking?'

'Perhaps...' She shrugged. 'What is *your* future wife like?'

'I told you once, but I will tell you again—I will never marry.'

'But if you did, what would she be like?' Aurora persisted. 'Come on, Nico, it's just a game.'

Nico did not and would not play games—not that it perturbed Aurora, for with only her eyes she dragged in the most unwilling participant.

'Tell me about your future wife.'

'She's quiet,' Nico said. 'Undemanding.'

'How nice.'

'I never come home in the middle of the day to find her asleep.'

'She sounds rather boring.'

'I think *demure* would be a better word.'

'No,' Aurora said, and shook her head. 'She bores you so much that I bet you don't even bother coming home in the middle of the day just for sex.'

'Exactly!' Nico said. And it was a most dangerous admission, because it exposed him. With one word he had revealed to Aurora his craving for her. 'I don't come off the phone hard after speaking to her. She gives me no drama, leaves no chaos in my brain. And when I'm working she respects that fact and leaves me alone.'

'Good for her,' Aurora sneered.

She pulled her knees up—not in a deliberately provocative move, more to relieve the ache low in her belly and thighs.

His quick gaze caught a damp patch on her coral silk panties. He didn't know if he had imagined it, but once the idea was in his head he could not rid himself of it.

He should not be playing this game—glimpsing how they might have been. Or rather, he had already played it out in his mind. He should certainly not be sharing that vision with Aurora.

Yet Nico did.

He dragged his eyes from her silk-lined sex and back to her face as he told her some more about his perfect wife.

'There aren't fifty missed calls, demanding to know where I am; there's no, *"Nico, we didn't make love this morning..."*'

He did a lower version of her raspy voice, but it was certainly Aurora that he impersonated, and now they were heading into dangerous territory indeed.

'In fact, when I come home late she doesn't even ask where I've been. She *accepts* that I've been working.'.

'She's *so* understanding!' Aurora cooed.

'Yes,' Nico said. 'She is.'

'And do you make slow, boring love to her?'

'There is nothing boring about me in bed, Aurora. But, yes, I make *very* slow love to her.'

She had to remind herself to breathe. 'Does she fake it and let out a little whimper to signal that she's done?'

'No, she *screams* my name.'

Those shaky curls shook as she refuted him. 'I don't think so.'

He crossed the room and decided to lose the stunning view of Rome. He had something infinitely better to look at.

'Not only that,' Nico said. 'She even closes the drapes.'

He did so, and it was unthinkable that he was closing out the busy day he'd had planned.

Not quite unthinkable—because with Aurora he knew this was how life would be. Chaos and tangled limbs. Making up and kisses and heaving tears. Drama from which he had run as a young man as though there was a wolf on his heels.

The heavy drapes blocked out the light, denying him the sight of her body, so he turned on the bedside light and looked down at her.

'Get into bed.'

'But you forgot to switch off your phone, darling,' Aurora said, in the voice of his fabled wife.

Nico wagged a finger to chastise her for the poor imitation. 'She would not ask me to.'

'That is true,' Aurora conceded, for Nico's perfect demure wife would not ask him to do any such thing. And yet she fixed him with a glare. 'But every game has its rules.'

And for the first time—and *only* for Aurora—he turned off his phone, while silently vowing his perfect revenge: she *would* scream out his name.

His eyes roamed her body and made her flood with warmth and shiver at the same time.

'Get undressed and into bed before I turn off the light.'

'Don't turn off the light,' Aurora said, for she wanted to see him.

'But I come home in the *dark*, dear wife.'

She swallowed, and reminded herself of the game they were playing.

It was a little hard to get undressed, sitting on the

bed, and Nico did not help with the zip at the back of her dress. He watched her struggle.

She got the zipper undone and wriggled the dress down instead of up. Took it off by lifting up her bottom and sliding it down her legs.

Aurora could feel that her face was flushed, but not for a second was she embarrassed. Instead she was turned on by his scrutiny, turned on by his silent observation. And wondering how she could even have cared that her underwear might clash when it mattered not.

Again, her hands went behind her back and she unhooked her bra. She heard his ragged breath as, without support, her breasts fell heavy.

Her nipples hurt because they were so erect, and she glanced over and saw his hands that had been clenched by his sides were now undoing his belt.

'Wait,' she choked. 'I want to see you undress too.'

Oh, what was this game they were playing? For they had not so much as kissed, and she was not even in bed—they had not even *started*—but her thighs wanted to squeeze together and her throat was closing with the tension.

She slid down her panties and went to move back the sheets, impatient to get into bed, impatient for his touch. But he growled a word.

'*Fermare.*'

Stop.

Halt.

Do not cover your body just yet, Nico said with that one word. *Do not remove it from my gaze.*

For on that torrid night, so many years ago, he had not gazed and he had not lingered.

Now he took in the gleaming olive skin and the delicious softness of her stomach, the dark brown nipples that were like searchlights for him and the dark shadow where her shapely thighs met.

He fought not to take her this very second.

He fought not to unzip himself as he parted her legs and take her there and then.

He admired his own control as he removed his jacket.

But it was not quite perfect control, because he could not seem to stop the thrill of anticipation that made his breath shorten.

For it might be daylight on the other side of the curtains, but this was their one night as husband and wife.

And so he dropped his jacket to the floor, and with the same carelessness and impatience discarded his socks and shoes. And then he took off his shirt and felt her eyes reclaim his skin.

Oh, Nico.

She had missed that chest so. It was broad and had a smattering of hair. His long arms were so toned that he *could* have been out working the vines.

Her breath hitched as she watched him remove the last of his clothes.

'You could have had me on Monday night,' Nico said.

'I know.' Her voice was so low and thick that she almost turned around to see who stood behind her, but of course it came from her.

'Why didn't you?' he asked. For that was a side of Aurora that he wanted to know.

'Things were different then,' Aurora said.

Then she had been trying to get over him—then she had been denying the throbbing of her body and the beckoning of his soul to hers and telling herself she did not have to succumb.

But she did not have to tell Nico all that. She did not have to tell him that this very morning she had thrown a coin in the Trevi Fountain and asked to be made love to by Nico in Rome.

She hastily amended that wish.

For now she did not want to be made love to by Nico, she told herself. She wanted powerful sex with him, the way she had known it before.

Aurora was too afraid to know his love and then attempt life without it.

'Please…' she said.

Please come to bed. Please let me know again that flat stomach and those muscular thighs. Let me be taken by you again.

He got into bed.

'Hello, husband,' she said.

And this time when she said it Nico did not roll his eyes.

He turned off the light and lay beside her. 'Are you awake?' he said to the dark.

'I'm awake,' she said, and rolled to face him.

Have me now. Take me now, her eyes told him as they lay facing each other on their sides. *Give me your untamed passion again.*

Instead he spoke. 'Life is peaceful with my wife—calm and without demands.'

Except his heart battered his chest as if he had run home from the hotel and his body was primed.

They faced each other and embraced the war that raged between them.

Her silent screams were for all of him, for Nico's refusal to give anything other than the inches that now nudged her thigh. Aurora wanted his fire and his untamed passion, and she provoked and pushed for the same.

But instead he gave her a taste of slow love.

Just this one time, Nico said to himself. He would give in once and kiss her as he should have on her first time. Not hot, raw sex on a sofa, but deep, slow kisses in his bed.

And while Nico told himself he was giving Aurora the experience she had deserved back then, he was aware enough to know that he wanted it for himself too.

'I should have been more tender then...'

Four years on from *that* night he answered the question she had asked the following morning, and told Aurora his regrets.

'No,' she whispered. 'It was perfect just as it was.'

She was actually scared to know him as tender, but *that* was the kiss he now gave her. A slow kiss that sent her mind dizzy with little arrows of affection delivered by his velvet lips.

His clean, male sent made her ache for more—more of his body, more of his mouth—but she lingered a while in this bliss.

He kissed her slowly. His hand was warm on the back of her head and she almost fought him with her mouth, fought for him to kiss her harder.

Because a taste of his slow love was now a terrifying prospect. The game they had been playing was just a little too much for her heart to recover from.

He removed his mouth from hers.

She did not want him to stop. His mouth, tender like this, made her tremble, and his tongue, his lips caressing hers, demanded her pleasure. She let herself revel in it.

'I should have seduced you,' Nico said.

'You did,' Aurora breathed as she recalled that even with walls between them on that hot, sultry night, desire had coursed through her, just as it was rolling through her now. 'You are.'

He slipped in his tongue and she tasted him again. He devoured her with his mouth and her hands shot to his head, just to feel his hair, just to hold his face so that she never had to separate from this bliss.

Their mouths touched and she found out how powerful his slow kiss could be. For she was not here in his dark bedroom in Rome, and she was not even thinking of that night in Silibri. She was in a place that was reserved on this earth just for them. A place that could be found whenever their mouths met.

He dragged his lips from hers, and then Aurora discovered that there were kisses she still did not know.

He took his hands from her head and turned her with a silent command, so she lay on her back as his mouth met her neck. And the slight suction he made on that sensitive flesh made her gasp.

'Take me, Nico.'

She did not want to linger in this bliss. She did not want to know the tender pleasure of this Nico, for it would surely be safer not to know.

He licked her nipple, making generous wet circles. And she bit on her lip as he blew cool air there. Then moaned as he sucked hard. She felt her hips rise and his hand slip down.

'I want you so badly, Aurora.'

'Take me, then…' she pleaded again.

'I was too rough that night.'

'No, no…' she sobbed. 'You weren't.'

'I should have been gentler for your first time.'

He kissed her stomach. She had always thought it too fat, yet she found she adored her own ripe flesh when it was loved by his mouth.

'I should have tasted you…' He moved down the bed

so that his head was between her legs. 'I should have cooled you with my mouth.'

'Cooled me?' she checked, for she could never have been cooled. And certainly not by what he did now.

'Oh...'

His tongue made deep, slow strokes and he nibbled at places she did not think it right for him to do so, but her hands knotted in his hair and she let him show her bliss.

Nico was turned on by the humming noises she made, but she refused to call out his name. He could feel the tension building in her and the grip of her thighs on his head.

He sucked and he probed with his tongue and though sometimes he licked slowly he did not let up for a second.

He was relentless.

'I—I'm...' she gasped.

He knew.

For how could he not know when her tension was unleashed and she held on to a scream? How could he not know when he was drinking from her pulsing, tender place?

He pulled himself up over her.

Now he would take her—fast. Now this torture would be done. Aurora pleaded with him in her mind, and she knew she should never have made that wish at the Trevi Fountain.

To know his love even just once more would hurt later.

But when he slid into her...when he crushed her with his weight, and when she anticipated his rapid thrusts... she wrapped her legs round him, to join in and bring them both to the delicious end.

And yet his hands removed her legs and now he took

her arms and held them above her head on the pillows as he moved onto his forearms.

'Slow, boring love…' he said.

Aurora heard the creak of the bed and the way his breathing sounded as he strove to hold on to his release.

'Am I boring you Aurora?'

'No…' She no longer knew the rules of the game. For she was burning and melting at the same time.

He released her hands from the trap of his arms. Her fingers pressed into his shoulders and she wanted to dig her nails in, but she did not. Instead, her hands disobeyed her mind and slipped around the sides of his torso, lovingly stroking him, feeling the bliss of his smooth back and sliding her hands over the slight sheen of his skin, exploring the muscles. And then she met his taut buttocks.

Now her head lifted and she offered Nico a devoted kiss.

Better that than sob his name.

Better that then tell him how much she loved him.

She would not give in.

And soon Nico would have no choice but to give in himself, because he was moving faster now, thrusting without any measure of control.

'I want you,' he told her, and he took her faster.

'Nico,' Aurora said, 'I can't do this over and over.'

'You can.'

'I can't pretend I don't want you.'

'Keep wanting me,' he told her.

'I'm scared to keep wanting you,' she admitted.

'*Never* stop wanting me,' he told her.

And those ragged words felt like permission simply to give in.

She collided with the stars, with the darkness, with

the fantasy of husband and wife, with the rush and power of the orgasm *he* had made. She had not known such intensity lived in her and it felt as if she'd been tasered.

'Nico!' She thought she screamed his name, but her throat was so tight it came out as a hoarse cry.

Nico let out his own breathless shout as he drove into her for the final time.

And then they kissed—a breathless panting kiss that sedated her in her post-coital bliss.

He rolled off her and she lay in the dark bedroom, naked and uncovered, for the sheet had long since gone.

And now she found out what he had meant. For she was cooling now. The air on her damp body felt calming, and she could hear his breath evening out as hers did the same.

No, his slow love was not boring.

For even as she lay cooling she knew that at any given moment she would want him again.

Like this.

In his bedroom.

Night after night after night.

Did he regret it already? Aurora pondered as he lay quietly beside her.

Possibly *she* did, for she was replaying his words.

Keep on wanting me.

CHAPTER EIGHT

KEEP ON WANTING ME.

Aurora lay there repeating his words in her head.

Was that to be her destiny?

To keep on wanting him? To keep on being available to him?

That sated feeling was fading, and as Nico reached across her for his phone the doubts and the hopelessness kicked back in.

'Nico, why did you come back to Rome early?'

'Work finished sooner than I expected and I had a good visit with my father, for once.'

Couldn't he just say he had come back so he might see her?

'Can't you give me even the smallest victory, Nico?'

He couldn't.

Instead he sat on the edge of the bed and checked his damned phone.

What was she supposed to do? Get showered and dressed and head back to work?

Sit in her hotel room biting her nails and wondering if Nico would take her out on her last night in Rome?

She was far too easy where Nico was concerned. The sum total of their dating history was having a drink together.

'Nico,' she said. 'Tonight, I would like—'

'Aurora, stop.'

Just stop.

He looked at the endless missed calls and the frantic texts, and knew that if he had been able to choose he really would have preferred to be alone for this moment.

'Pronto?' he said into his phone.

Aurora heard for the first time a slight shake in his strong voice as Nico asked when. And if anyone had been with him. And if his father had been in pain when he passed.

She started to cry.

When he'd ended the call Nico did not speak. Aurora went up on her knees and pressed herself into his back, wrapping her arms around him and crying and kissing his neck. Not in a sensual way. This time she was the tender one. But though she held him, it was Aurora who shed the tears.

Nico did not know how to.

'Your mother took him lunch,' Nico said. 'Then called for the doctor to come quickly. It was peaceful, the doctor said.'

She moved around him so she sat facing him, on his lap, her legs wrapped around his body. She tried to read his face, to measure his pain, but it was blank.

'I shouldn't have come away this week,' Aurora cried. 'I knew he was weak...'

Her tears were genuine, for she had both loved and hated the old bastard. Loved his wit and his humour and his proud ways. Hated that his hands had put bruises on her beautiful Nico, and she detested the insults that had been hurled from his mouth.

'I need to get back,' Nico said.

He prised himself out of her arms, but they sprang back.

'Soon.'

'Now,' Nico said, and stood so she slid off his lap.

He went towards the bathroom and she followed, but he closed the bathroom door in her face.

She stood there with the thick wood between them. *Geo was dead.*

Panic thudded in her chest.

She opened the drapes, and although Rome looked the same, as she turned naked from the French windows the bedroom did not. There were rumpled sheets and discarded clothes and the scent of sex in the air.

Aurora saw the chaos she'd brought to him.

He had returned to this.

She dressed. It seemed wrong to be pulling on a red dress when Geo was dead, but she had a black one back at the hotel she could change into.

Aurora wanted to help, and so she thought about what Marianna would do—she would pack, of course, except Nico had not even unpacked.

'What are you doing?' he asked as he came out of the bathroom with a towel around his waist to the sight of Aurora going through his wardrobe.

'Finding a black suit...'

'I can manage.'

'And a black tie...'

'Aurora, go back to work—get on with your job.'

'Work?' She swung around and looked at him aghast. 'How selfish of you! Do you really think we can all carry on working now? We have lost someone too.'

'Cut me some slack, Aurora. I'm not thinking straight.'

He was hanging on by his fingernails even as she turned away in that red dress with tears streaming down her face. It dizzied his mind.

Where the hell was the calm wife from their game? The one who'd pour him a drink and leave him to spend these first moments on earth without his father alone.

Where was the demure woman who would accept his silence and lack of outward grief?

He would like to take Aurora back to bed, right now. To close the drapes and to weep.

'Oh, Nico...'

She was crying again and, frankly, he would have liked to join her.

'Aurora, go back to the hotel. I am going to make some phone calls and then I will be flying back to Si-libri.'

'I'll go and pack.' Aurora nodded. Now her phone was ringing. She saw that it was Pino, but did not answer. 'They will all have heard and be wondering what to do.' She looked from her phone to Nico. 'Shall I meet you back at the hotel?'

'Sorry?' He really was not thinking straight. 'Why?'

'Nico, we will be returning to Silibri with you, of course.'

'Aurora, what you guys do is up to you—but I need to get back now.'

'So do we scramble to get a flight and the *cuccette* while you fly in your big plush helicopter alone?'

He sighed, defeated. 'Of course not.'

His driver offered condolences, and in the hotel lobby stood Marianna, looking grim. There too were the Si-libri contingent, all dressed in black.

'No one is better prepared for death than a Sicilian,' Aurora commented.

Even in grief she could still make him smile.

'Royalty travel with black outfits too,' Nico pointed out.

'Not always,' Aurora said, and Nico gave a soft laugh.

She disappeared and returned fifteen minutes later, showered and changed, wearing no make up, and he could tell there had been a fresh batch of tears.

Those stunning locks had been washed and her hair was now pulled back in a severe low bun. Her dress was black, as were her shoes, and those gorgeous legs were encased in black stockings.

Yes, these Sicilians were more prepared for death than the Queen of England. And none of them had ever been in a helicopter, which meant there were a lot of shouts and nervous laughter as they took off.

The Silibri contingent had been to Rome but now they were returning.

And they were bringing their Nico home.

CHAPTER NINE

'CONDOGLIANZE...'

One by one they took his hand and kissed his cheeks, but all Nico wanted was for this day to be over and then never to have to return to the place that had brought him so much grief.

As the last member of his family, Nico stood alone. There was just this line-up to get through, he told himself. And then his duty would be almost done.

There was to be a small gathering back at the house and then he could return to Rome.

'Le mie più sentite condoglianze,' Pino said.

'Thank you for all you did for him,' Nico said.

Aurora was just a couple of people down the line. Soon her hand would find his.

'Condoglianze,' Francesca said. 'Nico, he is at peace.'

'I know—thank you.'

Where was his own peace, though? Nico thought, for his head felt like a warzone.

'Nico...' Aurora said.

There was his peace.

A small moment of it in the chaos of a turbulent day.

Her hand took his and he closed his fingers around hers, causing her to look down at their hands rather than up at his face.

'*Condoglianze,*' she said.

'*Grazie,*' he responded, but he did not let her hand go.

She leant forward and kissed his cheek and it was as cool as marble against hers. She kissed the other and then looked at his beautiful mouth, now so pale.

'He thought a lot of you,' Nico told her.

I did it all for you, Nico. I know what Geo did, and I did not respect him for that. But he is...was...your father. Though it was hard at times, I always tried to respect that. I took care of Geo as I would have had you been my husband.

She did not say that, of course. 'I thought a lot of him too,' was her gentle response.

'Thanks for all your help with the arrangements.'

'Of course,' Aurora said.

It was, for Aurora, as simple as that. Of course she would be there for him.

Marianna, who had thought she knew everything there was to know about Nico's life, did not quite know how things were done down here.

Aurora had sat in the house during the vigil, as the villagers came, stayed and went.

That was not the role of a PA.

And Aurora had sat with Nico when he had asked the priest not to speak too much of a Geo having had a loving marriage to Maria, or to go on about his loving son.

'You did love him, though, Nico,' she had said.

And that was not the role of a PA.

But she did not know her own role with Nico. She did not know what part she played in his life. She had been Geo's carer, and at times she had been Nico's lover, but what was she now? His employee?

Still, Aurora had worked hard for this funeral. And she took care of things as a wife would when the mourners moved back to Geo's house. She oversaw the proceedings like a hawk.

The coffee needed to be served more seamlessly, she told Chi-Chi, who was trying to chat up a guy. And the people over there had not been offered food for a while.

Aurora dealt with it all. She was constantly watching, swooping when needed, and then returning to be beside her master.

She looked across the room and could see that Nico was struggling to speak with Pino and his wife Rosa.

'Stay tonight,' Pino said. 'Come and eat with us.'

'Yes, Nico,' Rosa said. 'Don't go back to Rome tonight.'

Aurora, who had been speaking to her father, saw the strain drawing Nico's features taut. She caught his eye and moved to his side.

'We were just saying to Nico he can stay with us tonight,' Rosa explained as Aurora joined the conversation.

'My father has offered the same,' Aurora said. 'But Nico has to get back to Rome.'

'When will you be in Silibri again?' Pino asked him. 'We'll see.'

Aurora felt the cannelloni she had just eaten curdle in her stomach at Nico's vague reply. Nico truly answered to no one.

And then, one by one and two by two, the mourners were gone.

There is no sadder place than a house after a funeral when everyone has gone home, she thought.

Just Nico and Aurora remained. They were alone again. But she was suddenly scared that it was for the very last time. That the next time she saw him it would only be about work.

The cups and glasses and plates were all washed and put away. None of the endless food that had been made and brought was left in the kitchen—Nico had asked his guests to take the leftovers with them.

'You could stay at the hotel if you don't want to stay here,' Aurora suggested as she plumped the cushions in Geo's empty chair and missed the grumpy old man. 'I know it's not open yet, but there are suites...'

'I would rather go home.'

And that made her breath hitch—because *here* was home. Could he not see that?

'When do you think you will be back?' Aurora could not stop herself from asking, hoping that although he had been vague with Pino he might not be with her.

'I don't know,' Nico said.

He had an army of people who would take care of the small paperwork trail Geo had left. And the house...? He would send someone to shut it up properly, and work out what to do with it later.

Right now he wanted to get back to the cool order of his life in Rome.

He turned his mind to answer her question. 'I'll be back for the hotel opening.'

'But that is four months away,' Aurora pointed out, and dread clenched like a fist as she realised Nico was really putting Silibri—and her—behind him.

'Yes.'

'Will you sell the house?'

'Probably.' *Just stop with the questions*, he wanted to tell her, for his head was pounding. 'Yes.'

'But wouldn't it be nice to have a home here? Like you do in Rome?'

'This was never my home, Aurora.'

'I don't mean the house. I mean Silibri...'

'I do too,' Nico said.

He did not have family here. There was no guilt or duty to bring him back to the village. Just work.

And he would soon pass that on. He would get the hotel up and running and then sell it, he decided. Finally he would be done with Silibri.

He would not keep her hanging.

'Aurora, the hotel will be up and running in no time. I will pass on the management of it and then...'

He shared his business decisions with no one, and yet Aurora did not fit into the category of 'no one', so he told her what his grieving mind had decided.

'And then I shall sell it.'

It was too painful for him to be here now. He had done his best for the village, and now his father was gone.

'There is no reason for me to return to Silibri,' Nico said. 'I have not one decent memory of this place.'

Aurora gasped.

Not one? What about that time on the sofa, Nico? Does the night you took my virginity not even rate?

Hawks had talons, and Aurora felt hers then.

She wanted to slap his face, to deliver to him some of the pain he had flung at her. But she was not a violent person. She had never understood how Geo could lay a hand on someone he loved, and she would not lower herself to do it now.

'Not one decent memory?' Aurora checked.

Nico closed his eyes and wished that she had slapped him, for it would have been so much easier to end this on a row. To throw up his arms and feel justified in walking away.

But instead her velvet brown eyes tried to meet his. 'How many more ways can you hurt me, Nico?'

'Aurora…' He already regretted those words. He could both see and hear the hurt they had caused, for her voice was raw and her face was bleached white. 'I should not have said—'

'No,' she interjected. 'Don't bother apologising, or rephrasing, or trying to find another way to say what you really mean. I *finally* get the message, Nico. It's the same one you have been giving me for eight years now. You. Don't. Want. Me.'

If he refuted that, Nico knew that they would end up in bed.

Again.

Or rather they would have sex on the floor, because he could not stand the thought of sex in his father's bed.

Or perhaps they would go to one of the empty suites at the hotel and he would bury himself in her there.

He thought all that even as he stood with her sad vocalisation of his feelings for her ringing in his ears.

And when he did not refute Aurora got her answer from his silence.

Aurora regretted so many things, but somehow— *somehow*—she must not live to regret the moment she left. She must not break down within his sight.

Instead, she was as brave as she could be. 'Live well, Nico,' she said, and kissed his cold, pale cheeks. 'I wish you nothing but good things.'

And finally she let herself out of the house and let Nico out of her life.

CHAPTER TEN

Four months later

'NICO JUST LANDED.'

Aurora, who stood in the cool of Reception, nodded to Francesca. 'Everything is ready.'

The press were here for the official opening of the hotel, and the guests mainly consisted of Nico's wealthy contacts and a few select people from the travel industry, who would be dining in the restaurant and staying in the sumptuous suites on this very exciting day for Silibri.

The real guests would start arriving next week.

Nico had made it clear—via correspondence rather than in person—that he did not want their luxury stay to be encroached upon by the opening celebration.

Nico had stayed well away from Silibri—had not been back since the funeral. And Aurora had never been more nervous in her life to see him—though that had nothing to do with work.

Work was the one thing in her life that was going very well.

The hotel was stunning: each suite had a sumptuous view, either of the ocean or of the ancient temple ruins. Many of the suites had their own private pool, and all had a balustrade balcony made from the same stone as the temple.

It was sheer opulent luxury, and it would change the village economy entirely.

Guests would soon be strolling through the long empty streets. Cafés that had closed and lain empty for years had been renovated and would be opening again—not just for the hotel patrons, but for the fleet of staff who would work at the hotel, as well as their families.

Life was returning to Silibri.

And soon Aurora would have no choice but to leave.

She was pregnant.

In the first few weeks after Nico had left Aurora had been too angry and confused to consider the possibility that she might be pregnant. She had been grieving for Geo, as well as mourning the loss of Nico from her life.

She had buried herself in work and it had been her saviour. She hadn't just worked alongside Vincenzo, but off her own bat had made a gorgeous library of the photos she had taken of the renovations, which now had its own section on the hotel's website.

Her first inkling that something was amiss had come when the new uniforms had arrived. Aurora had at first assumed there had been a mix-up and that she had tried on someone else's.

The jacket had not done up across her generous bust.

The skirt had felt too snug on her hips.

Aurora had checked the label and seen that indeed it *was* her uniform—and then realisation had started to hit.

Stupido!

That had been her first thought as she had frantically tried to remember when her last period had been.

Stupido!

It had been her second thought too—but aimed at both of them. Because Nico hadn't used protection and neither had he asked if she was on the Pill.

And she hadn't told him that she wasn't.

There had been no thought on that balmy afternoon—just his mouth and his hands and his touch and the heaven to which he had taken her.

Aurora had sent the uniform back and today she wore one a full size bigger—already it was too tight.

She could not stand to think of Nico's reaction. He would consider that she had set out to get pregnant deliberately, Aurora was sure. That she was trying to trap him into marriage. It was an old-fashioned village and marriage was still a foregone conclusion for lovers who found themselves in the family way.

Family.

She gave a wry laugh at that.

Nico did not want one.

'Aurora?'

Vincenzo was going through the list of questions that might come their way as they took their separate groups around the hotel. He, of course, had Nico and all the bigwigs, and she had the local dignitaries. It didn't trouble Aurora, for it was an hour that she would not have to spend avoiding Nico's eyes.

'Right, I'm going to the oratory,' Vincenzo said. 'Good luck today. Any questions you can't handle, just refer them to me—though remember I have to leave by eight.'

Vincenzo was appearing on breakfast television tomorrow and could not stop mentioning it.

'Of course I'll remember. You look very smart,' Aurora added, for in his butterscotch suit indeed he did.

'Thank you,' Vincenzo said, smoothing his auburn hair. 'So do you.'

She wore her hair up and had subtle make-up on, but it had taken some considerable effort to conceal her new curves.

Aurora had let out the waistband of her skirt herself, and her breasts were practically strapped down. She was bursting out of everything and was just a day away from telling her family the news—once Nico had safely flown out.

Today, though, he had flown in.

Should she tell him?

It was the question that she both woke and fell asleep to, and then asked herself a thousand times during the hours in between.

And as Nico and his entourage crossed the foyer she asked it again.

Should she tell the man who did not want her—the man who was attempting to cut all ties with her and the village—that she was having his baby?

Or rather, did she tell the man who wanted her only in bed and not by his side that she was pregnant? The same man who had told her as they made love to keep on wanting him.

Oh, she still wanted him—for even from this distance the sight of him jolted her senses and turned her on.

He wore a dark suit, presumably stitched by his usual master tailor, but to Aurora's skilled eye it was looking a touch loose on him.

Nico had lost weight.

Not a lot, but enough that she wanted to race to the chef, scream for pasta and force-feed him. It was the Sicilian way.

But she restrained herself.

In fact, for once, Aurora was a picture of restraint.

'It is good to see you.' She smiled, and shook his hand. And this time, as Nico moved in to kiss her in the way old friends would, it was she who put up her hand to halt him. 'I believe Vincenzo has your people gathered in the oratory.'

'How are you, Aurora?'

'Very well.'

She looked incredible.

Nico knew she had been working frantically, but she looked as if she had spent all these weeks lying on a recliner by the pool in the hot Sicilian sun. The Persian Orange of her uniform was indeed perfect, and brought out the little flecks of gold in her dark eyes. Her lips were plump and shaped in a mild smile.

He tried to gauge her level of hurt, and he checked for hostility in those amazing eyes, but saw none.

For there was none.

She loved him—and that, sadly, was that.

'Aurora,' he said as she went to move off. He spoke with his people and then nodded to Francesca, who took the group through to the oratory. 'I need to see you.'

'Of course.' She fixed on a smile. 'What do you need?'

'Not here,' Nico said. 'Not now.'

Nico truly loathed his treatment of her on the day his father had been laid to rest. He regretted with every fibre of his being the way they had parted.

Her dignity.

His silence.

And he had missed her so. That throaty laugh, that raw passion for everything she did.

How to tell her of the mess in his head?

Where did he begin to explain to Aurora that if he were capable of love absolutely it would be with her?

'Your schedule is very full,' Aurora pointed out.

She did not want to be alone with him; she did not want to fall into his arms, to yearn for his kiss. To sob out that she was pregnant and then witness his dark reaction.

Aurora would tell him from a distance, she decided, then and there, because she felt like putty whenever he was near.

But Nico did not give up.

'Later tonight?' Nico said. 'I shall be done around ten.'

'But I finish at eight,' Aurora said, and tried to inject regret into her voice. 'Perhaps we could schedule a meeting for the morning?'

'I don't want a work meeting.'

No, he wanted sex. Aurora was very sure of that.

Nico was staying in the Temple Suite tonight, and no doubt he did not want to spend the night alone.

Damn you, Nico!

She corrected herself: she was not putty—more, she was a puppet on Nico's string. He thought he could bed her at will. And the real trouble was that he could.

Perhaps she wouldn't even *have* to tell him. She was feeling so hormonal right now that to be alone with Nico meant she would fall into his arms. He would just have to strip off her skirt and he would know. Or his hands would remove her bra and the heavy breasts that were now crushed against her chest would spring full into his hands…

Now he saw anger in her face. It flashed in her eyes and it formed in two red dots on her cheeks. But her smile remained.

'I want to speak to you Aurora,' Nico said.

But it would have to wait, for Vincenzo was making an approach.

'Ah, Signor Caruso!' Vincenzo said. *'Benvenuto!'*

'Welcome?' Nico checked. 'What do you mean, *welcome*? It's *my* damned hotel?'

'What's eating him?' Vincenzo asked as Nico stalked off.

Aurora knew she now had to tell a lie, and she watched Vincenzo's face fall as she spoke. But that lie would keep her sane.

It kept her sane even when Nico joined not the bigwigs' group, but the local dignitaries as Aurora gave them her tour—fully thirty minutes behind Vincenzo's schedule.

First she took them outside to the main pool, where the ruins of a Roman bath had been carefully brought back to life.

'Most of the suites,' Aurora explained, 'have their own private pool, but this is the central one. Though it is positioned so that it can't be viewed from the main building.'

'Why is that?' a reporter asked.

'For private functions,' Aurora said. 'It looks incredible when lit at night, and with the calibre of guests we expect to host we would not want to risk them being photographed.'

'Can a couple book just this area just for themselves?'

'Of course,' Nico answered, when Aurora could not.

She could feel the sun beating on her head, and Nico's eyes on her, and the air felt so thick she could barely drag it in.

Oh, how she wanted to discard the jacket and skirt!

To peel off her clothes and take his hand as he led her into the cool, inviting water.

'Let's head inside,' Aurora said, and deliberately avoided his eyes. 'This was once the oratory, where the monks would gather to pray and meditate,' she explained as they came in from the glittering pool into the huge, cool, dark building. 'The new stone is from the same quarry as the original monastery, and this whole wall...' she touched it lovingly '...is original. Now it's going to be a place for meditation and spa treatments. A place to hide from the world and restore oneself in peace and tranquillity.'

It was truly stunning. All those painstaking hours and millions of euros had been worth it, Nico knew.

Even his father had known. During their last visit, on the last morning of his life, Geo had admitted that he would have sold it to developers.

'But I like what you have done,' he had told Nico. And today Nico held on to those words as Aurora walked them around.

He could *never* palm this hotel off on his managers or sell it.

Yes, he had said that on the day of his father's funeral, and for a while he had thought he would, but as the grief had settled Nico knew he could never just hand it over.

It was his life's work.

'Now...' Aurora smiled as she led them up some stone stairs and across a long cloister. 'I shall take you into my favourite suite.'

'The Honeymoon Suite?' one of the crowd joked.

'No,' Aurora replied.

How could that be her favourite when she would

never know a honeymoon? The truth was she avoided the Honeymoon Suite as best she could.

'This is the Temple Suite,' Aurora told her audience. 'And I'm sure you will soon see why.'

She pushed open the heavy wooden door and as they took one step inside they all gasped—except for Aurora and Nico.

Even the sun had joined the party, and it seemed to split apart the stones of the old temple ruins in this most stunning view. It actually brought tears to Aurora's eyes as she stood and looked out.

'I had seen the temple ruins from every angle I thought possible,' Aurora explained. 'I grew up in Silibri and they were my playground. But some weeks ago I put on a hard hat and was shown the view from here. I admit I cried when I saw the temple from this height and distance. I believe this was the view that the monastery was built to capture. It is a slice of heaven, is it not?'

And it was—except that Nico was watching Aurora, and the way her eyes shone with tears. He could feel her love for this incredible space.

He wished—oh, how he wished—they were here alone.

They would be tonight.

She led them through the suite and onto the huge balcony and was grateful for the gentle breeze to cool her warm cheeks. Yes, she had trained herself not to blush around Nico, but it seemed she could not train herself out of desiring him. The easiest thing in the world, Aurora thought, would be to say yes to Nico.

'Dinner on this balcony would be amazing,' Nico said, as if reading her thoughts.

'Absolutely, it would be,' Aurora agreed.

'I don't think anyone would close the drapes on this.'

Please don't, her heart said in response to his words. *Please don't banter with me and take me back to that day in Rome. Please don't seduce me in this room that I love so much when I know you will only break my heart later...my heart that is trying so hard to mend itself.*

As the crowd moved off, Nico held back and waited for her attention.

'About ten?' he checked.

Aurora swallowed but gave no response.

'You have the key?'

No, she wanted to say, *you have the key. The permanent key. And you turn it, and you open me, and then you close me again. And I cannot be placed on lockdown for even one day more.*

No, she was not yet ready to tell him about the baby.

'I'd better get on,' she told him.

It had been a rewarding though exhausting day.

Aurora had slipped away in the evening, as Nico wined and dined his guests, though he himself barely ate a thing.

Tonight—after this—he would sit on that balcony and he would wine and dine Aurora. And with the temple ruins as their backdrop, he would say what he had come to say.

Nico escaped the celebrations just after ten.

So certain of her love was he that at first it didn't faze him that Aurora was not there.

He ordered champagne and a spritzer. He ordered the freshest pasta, with a light basil and tomato sauce, and for dessert her favourite—Tiramisu. And he asked for the tray to be decorated with wild flowers, picked just before sunset.

All the things he knew she loved.

And he waited.

And then he texted her.

And then he drank the champagne as he called her cell phone but got no answer.

The flowers and the food came, but the meal he had chosen with her in mind went cold beneath the cloches.

Nico put on the television in his room with its most stunning view—just to check the news and be sure that wildfire had not ravaged the village again, nor had there been an accident on the winding roads. For surely Aurora would come if she could...

He woke on the plush sofa to the sound of her laughter and a rare hangover.

The sound of her low, throaty laugh had him looking around the vast suite—and then staring, bemused, at the television.

Aurora looked amazing, with her hair freshly styled, wearing more make-up than usual, and in that gorgeous Persian Orange uniform.

'The Temple Suite,' she said to the interviewer, 'is more than luxury. It is a place where you can retreat, where you can heal, where you can rest and ponder your life choices.'

And it was then that he saw, tucked into the wilting wild flowers, a letter addressed to him. It was clear as he read it that Aurora had intended him to receive it last night.

Nico,
I have told Vincenzo that you want me to do the breakfast television interview. I've lied, but better that than be your plaything again.
The concierge can arrange an intimate massage in your suite or, if you do not want Pino

knowing your business, you can call Rubina's and ask Madame to send someone to help you create another unsatisfactory memory of your time in Silibri.

Sorry to disappoint, but my pride got in the way.
Aurora x

And then she laughed again.
At least the Aurora on breakfast television did.

CHAPTER ELEVEN

'*WHAT IS THIS?*'

Back in Rome, Nico wasn't certain he had read things right and was immediately on the phone.

Aurora had resigned.

Aurora Eloise Messina. Now aged twenty-five. With a passion for the hotel like no other and a hunger to succeed, had left.

It made no sense.

He knew full well that she was furious with him. And after the stunt she had pulled Nico had been furious too and had stayed well back.

But his anger was fading now—so much so that whenever he re-read that note he almost smiled.

'Why did she resign?' he asked.

'She was headhunted.'

Vincenzo sounded taken aback that the rather absent owner of the business was immediately on the phone to him the moment the email went out.

'By whom?'

'Aurora would not say. Apparently she was tired of her ideas being dismissed.'

They had *not* been dismissed. Had she turned up for dinner that night then she would have known that.

Nico called her. 'What's all this?'

'*Scusi?*' Aurora asked.

She was sitting in her little pink bedroom as she awaited a taxi to take her to the station.

Her parents had not taken the news of their daughter's pregnancy well at all—especially as Aurora refused to name the father. A terrible row had ensued.

Nico had been right: her parents *did* snoop, and they had gone through her phone and found the dating app she had downloaded in Rome.

And now she had Nico on the phone.

It was too much for her nerves today.

'Why have you resigned without speaking first with me?' he demanded.

'Nico, I resigned and I have left. I don't have to answer to you when you are no longer my boss.'

'All right, then. Forget that I was once your boss and tell *me*. Why did you resign?'

'So from what standpoint are we talking, Nico? As friends?' Aurora's voice was incredulous and angry, though she struggled to keep the hurt from it. 'Because we are *not* friends, Nico. You yourself told me we could never be.'

'Aurora—'

'Or are we speaking as lovers?' she interrupted. 'But that can't be because you have so many—surely you don't expect them all to give you career updates?'

'Aurora!'

She would not let him in. 'Or are we in a *relationship*, Nico? Oh, but that's right—no. Because you don't want one. You told me—'

'And *you* told me you would never leave Silibri.'

'I was sixteen years old when I said that. Tell me, Nico, is that the only reason you decided not to marry me?'

Silence.

As always, his silence killed her.

She wanted to curl up on her bed and weep into the phone.

Tell him. Tell him about the baby. Tell him that you have never felt so lonely nor so scared.

No!

And Aurora knew why she did not.

'I have to go, Nico. The taxi will come soon.'

It wasn't a lie.

She went downstairs. Her case stood at the front door and her parents sat at the table, looking at the photos the estate agent had taken of her *nonna*'s home.

The home meant for her and Nico.

'The part I don't understand,' Aurora said now, as she stood by the window, still awaiting her taxi, 'is why you would have been happy for me to live there, with a husband who did not love me and did not want me, but you would rather sell that house than give your pregnant daughter a home for her child.'

But they just wanted the problem to go away. By withdrawing their support her parents were assuming that Aurora would be forced to give her baby away.

'Aurora is career-minded,' her mother would declare in the village shop as she chatted to her friends. 'And she's making better money than Nico Caruso paid...'

And then, a few months later, Aurora would return to the village, minus the family shame, and pick up where she'd left off.

That was the unspoken plan in her parents' heads, but deep down they knew Aurora.

She would not be giving her baby away.

'You've bought shame to this family, Aurora,' her mother said. 'How do we hold our heads high when you don't even know who the father is?'

Aurora gave a soft mirthless laugh, for though her mother spoke in anger, it was half true all the same: Aurora *didn't* know who Nico was. Not really.

An ex?

That would mean they had actually been a couple at some point.

A family friend?

Sort of.

Her boss.

Not any more.

'We trusted you to go to Rome,' her mother said, her voice thick with tears. 'We trusted you to behave.'

'It wasn't a school trip, Mamma.'

'Less of your cheek,' Bruno stood. 'While you're under my roof—'

'But I'm *not* under your roof any more,' Aurora said as the taxi finally pulled up outside. 'You've asked me to leave, remember?'

'Because you don't even know the father's name.' Mamma's lips pulled in disgust, as they had when Aurora had first revealed the news that she was expecting a baby.

Tell them. Tell them who the father is. Tell them that you love Nico, your baby's father, with all your heart.

No!

And again Aurora knew why.

There would be shocked gasps, then shouts of anger, but eventually it would be all smiles and delight.

Because Nico would do the right thing by their daughter.

And Nico would.

You could take the man out of Silibri, but you could not take Silibri out of the man.

Oh, Nico might snub some of the village codes, but the basic ones were ingrained.

He would marry her for the sake of their child.

Aurora knew that down to her bones.

Beyond her bones, she felt it in her womb, and she felt it in the place low between her ribs—a little knot that tightened when she imagined their wedding.

Only not the way she had once envisaged it.

Now she saw the villagers' smiles, and heard their cheers, and she could even see the large bouquet she carried to cover her surprise pregnancy—but only for the photos.

Everyone would know about the baby and how delighted the villagers would be. Nico Caruso was putting down roots—back where he had always belonged. And she and Nico would wave and smile and kiss for the cameras, and that night they would lie in bed and have sex because—well, it would be their wedding night.

She could almost feel his resentment as he thrust into her. For Aurora Eloise Caruso had got exactly what Aurora Eloise Messina had always wanted.

Even if Nico never had.

So, no!

She would tell no one the truth.

CHAPTER TWELVE

As the train pulled into Stazione Roma Termini, the main train station in Rome, Aurora felt none of the excitement as she had the last time she'd arrived here.

Then she had been with colleagues, looking forward to training at a luxury Rome hotel. Then she had felt as if her career was on course.

Then she had been looking forward to seeing Nico. Now...

Aurora did not know.

Yet she had chosen to come to Rome.

Was it in the hope of seeing him?

No, for she dreaded that.

Or had she come with the intention of telling Nico that he was to be a father?

No.

One day she would tell him, but she dreaded that too.

It was more that her world felt safer when Nico was near.

She had arranged accommodation at a very basic hostel, but she would be spending only her nights there. Every day was to be devoted to trying to find work.

But it seemed most restaurants weren't hiring. At least not a visibly pregnant waitress.

And it was the same for cleaning work too.

Every day, on her way to interviews, Aurora passed Nico's grand hotel. And every day, after yet another slew of rejections, she grew more and more tempted simply to land unannounced at his door and demand to see him. To hand over the problem to Nico to deal with.

It was *his* baby after all.

Yet she could not bear the thought of his disappointment, or the way he would reluctantly carry out his duty.

She *would* find accommodation and work and she *would* be in a better position when she told him the truth.

Her family's reaction had hurt Aurora deeply, and if the people who loved her could cast her aside it left her with little hope for Nico's reaction to the news.

But then hope arrived, in the shape of a family of two young children, a stressed mother, and a father who travelled extensively for work. They lived in the Prati district, which was close to Parioli, where Nico resided.

'I need someone for nanny duties and some light cleaning,' Louanna explained. 'Our last nanny left us with no notice...'

'I won't let you down.'

It was a gorgeous old house, and Aurora had her own summerhouse at the bottom of the garden. Louanna was kind, and told her she had all the essentials Aurora's baby would need.

But then she added, 'You will have *three* little ones to care for...'

Aurora knew she would care for ten if it meant she had a home and could provide for her baby. For the first time since she had found out she was pregnant, she felt in control.

But then Louanna's husband returned, and the whole mood in the house changed.

'A pregnant nanny?' he said rudely to his wife. 'What the *hell*...?'

'Shh...' said Louanna as she closed the study door on them. 'Aurora is wonderful and she's a great help to me with Nadia and Antonio.'

As Christmas approached, and Rome grew cold and wet, being in the house was like living in tornado season, Aurora mused. She was watching the news at the moment, holed up in the little summerhouse at the bottom of the beautiful garden, but she kept casting anxious glances towards the house.

Soon the husband would travel again, and peace would prevail, but it was like watching dark clouds gather whenever he came home.

Aurora thought perhaps she had heartburn. Certainly the doctor had suggested that she did, but the burning high in her stomach seemed to coincide with the husband's arrival home and amplified when she saw bruises on Louanna's fragile arms.

'What happened?' Aurora asked.

'I bumped into the door.'

'And the door was shaped like fingers?' Aurora checked, in her usual forthright fashion. 'Louanna, you have to leave him.'

'Where will I go?' Louanna begged. 'Where will *you* go, Aurora? Your baby is due in two weeks.'

'Don't stay for me,' Aurora said.

Yet her heart was twisting in fear at the thought of being out on the streets so close to her due date.

'He is a good man...' Louanna was defensive. 'He just has a lot of stress at work.'

Nico had a lot of stress at work, Aurora thought, and he would never have carried on like that. She had never hidden her smile or her sass from him.

Call Nico, her mind said.

But then she caught sight of her reflection, her ripe body and troubled eyes, and she knew she did not want to land on him like this.

Not like this.

But soon the tornado had left again, and with the husband away on business the last few days of her pregnancy were among the nicest she had known.

She went to church with Louanna and the children, to watch the nativity play that Nadia was in, and it brought tears to Aurora's eyes. Louanna took the kindest care of her, and Aurora felt so spoiled when she woke to breakfast in bed one morning.

But the storm clouds were gathering again, for tomorrow Louanna's husband would be home.

That night Louanna made the supper. The children were sweet, and seemed to understand that Aurora was tired, and asked over and over again about her baby.

'I hope it's a girl,' Nadia said as Aurora lay on the sofa, scrolling through baby names on Louanna's laptop.

'I hope it's a boy,' said Antonio.

'What do *you* want, Aurora?' Louanna asked.

'I want this baby out of me,' she admitted. 'I'll take what comes, but I am ready for my baby to be born.'

'Have you chosen a name yet?'

'No,' Aurora admitted. 'I still have no clue. Maybe Nico…' She wasn't going to call her baby that, but it was such a relief to say his name out loud. 'Nicole, if it's a girl, but I love the name Nico.'

Nico.

Nico.

Nico.

She would say it at the end of every breath if she could.

Oh, when would these feelings end? she asked of herself, and foolishly looked him up on the computer.

Nico's world had clearly carried on very nicely without her. The woman with him just last month was blonde and pretty and petite. Then there was a beautiful redhead, who seemed to be getting him through the Christmas festivities.

Nico.

Louanna put the children to bed, and when she came down she gave Aurora a gentle talking-to.

'Do you know who the father is?'

She had asked before and Aurora had been evasive.

'Yes.' She was too tired to lie, but she would not name him. 'And I believe he would support me and would insist that we marry.' She looked over to Louanna. 'But I would rather be alone than live in an unhappy marriage.'

Louanna started to cry.

They spoke for a long while, and then Aurora headed down to her little summerhouse.

Deep in the night she lay restless and unable to sleep. She tossed and turned, and then got up and paced when it dawned on her that the ache in her back was not perhaps just from being heavily pregnant.

Aurora headed into the main house and made a drink. She looked out at the cold, pink morning sky and admitted to herself the very real reason she had not contacted Nico.

He might marry her, but he would never love her.

She would be his Silibri wife.

His mountain wife.

Living in the hills and tucked away.

Made love to when he returned to survey his grand hotel and then put on hold when he returned to Rome.

Or Florence.

Or England or France.

She wasn't sophisticated enough to hold his arm and smile serenely as he conversed. Neither was she calm enough to stand holding the baby and wave him off with a smile. Nor was she discreet enough to turn a blind eye to his philandering ways.

And there *would* be philandering ways, Aurora was quite sure of that.

She had no experience, save for Nico. No tricks to keep him amused. Just her.

And being almost nine months pregnant, and already rejected as his bride, wasn't a brilliant combination to inspire confidence.

Aurora would not be able to stand being a small part of his life—to live in the background. She was pure Sicilian and lava ran in her veins. She burnt at the thought of Nico with someone else—and, no, she would *not* stand back in dignified silence.

She moaned in horror at the thought of it.

'Aurora?' Louanna stood at the kitchen door. 'Are you okay?'

'No...'

She was scared and she was pregnant and she loved Nico so much that it hurt.

It hurt.

'I can't do this,' she admitted.

'You *are* doing this, Aurora,' Louanna said. 'Your baby is on its way.'

Aurora had changed her mind. 'I'm not ready.'

But the baby was.

She was in labour—without the man she had loved all her life by her side.

That was the hard truth, wrung from her soul as she bore down and gritted her teeth and knew she would rather be alone that accept his crumbs.

No matter if those crumbs might be solid gold and would provide for her baby and keep her in style.

'I hate him!' she shouted as she gripped her thighs in the delivery suite and bore down.

'Stop shouting and push,' the doctor said.

But Aurora ignored medical advice and carried on with her rant. 'He wants his freedom—he can have it!' she declared loudly. 'I'll survive better without him.'

Aurora did not pick up on the midwife's smile, but she got her support.

'Yes, you will! Come on, Aurora—use that anger to push!'

She was furious, and it felt so good to be angry as she pushed her baby out. 'I've *got* this,' she declared.

'You have, Aurora,' the midwife said. 'Come on—another big push.'

She was raging, and fury gave her strength, and she pushed with all her might...

And then fury left as love came rushing in—the purest love as she glimpsed her son.

He was long, and he had a lot of thick black hair, and huge navy eyes, and a dent in his chin as if an angel had stamped it there. His huge mouth let out husky and indignant cries.

She reached out for him with a love so fierce it pierced her soul. For the baby was the perfect blend of her and Nico. She laughed as she kissed him, for after one look not a person in her family or in the village would need to ask who his father was.

'He's beautiful!' she cried. 'He's perfect. My baby!'

Her baby—and also a real tiny person, who cried and seemed soothed when she held him. His eyes seemed to recognise her, for he held her gaze and fell quiet.

She had never fathomed that love for her son would be so immediate and so intense.

He was worth all the pain and fear and Aurora knew she could take care of him.

Louanna and the children came to visit her on the ward.

'Oh, Aurora…' Louanna said as she held the tiny little boy. 'He is perfection. Have you thought of a name?'

'Gabriel,' Aurora said. 'God-given strength.'

'Have you told your family?'

'Not yet.' They could wait.

'What about—?'

'I just want to get used to being a mother,' Aurora cut in. 'I want some time with my baby and to know what I'm doing. I want my confidence back.'

And Gabriel brought extra blessings! A little post-partum haemorrhage on the day Aurora was due to go home meant a trip to the operating theatre and staying in hospital for a few extra days.

Which meant that Christmas was over and Louanna's husband had gone by the time she brought her baby home.

It was a golden time.

The first two weeks passed by in a blur and she lived on Gabe's schedule.

He was such a sweet, quiet baby, and even when the husband came home Aurora did not notice as she was holed up in the summerhouse, getting to know her tiny baby.

When snow filled the garden and painted everything white, he went to South Africa for a couple of months.

Louanna was happy.

Aurora could not believe her luck to have found this gorgeous family that was allowing her to provide a home for her baby.

When Gabe—as he had become known—was eight weeks old, she walked little Nadia to school in the slushy snow, pushing the pram as Antonio skipped by its side, and then waving off the little girl.

'Today,' she said to Antonio as they walked home, 'we will make lasagne.'

'Can I roll the pasta?'

'You can,' Aurora said. 'But you have to roll it thin and not get bored like last time.'

Cooking always helped Aurora to think. And soon Gabe was asleep in his little bassinette and Antonio was helping to mix the dough.

She felt as if a fog was lifting. Not that she had returned to her old self, because along with Gabe a new Aurora had been born.

And on her next day off she would call Nico!

It came to her like a flash, and was followed by another rapid thought.

No, she would call Nico tomorrow. And if he wanted to meet her she would be free the next day to meet him—*with* Gabe.

She would not be asking Louanna to watch her son. Nico could get used to the idea, just as *she* had had to.

'You look happy,' Louanna commented.

'I am,' Aurora said, and then looked up to see her employer's pinched face. 'Are *you* okay?'

'Of course I am.' Louanna smiled. 'My husband just called—he's coming home a few days early.'

'Oh, when?' Aurora's voice was as strained as Louanna's smile.

'Tonight.'

'Then it's just as well I've made plenty to eat,' Aurora said.

He came through the door all smiles, and Aurora decided she must have imagined his dark moods, for he was pleasant to everyone.

Perhaps pregnancy had made her tired and more sensitive, Aurora thought as she put little Nadia and Antonio to bed and then came downstairs, to where Louanna was serving up the lasagne that Aurora had prepared.

'Eat with us,' he insisted.

'No, really.' Aurora smiled. 'I'm going to take my supper down to the summerhouse and settle Gabe. Have a nice evening.'

She wasn't avoiding him. The truth was that Aurora wanted to work out what she would say when she spoke to Nico.

'Nico,' she practised aloud, 'there's something I have not told you...' Or, 'Nico, this will come as a surprise...'

She fell asleep, still undecided how to break it to him, and woke to Gabe's cries at two a.m.

'Hey...' she said as she gave him his bottle.

Aurora loved these middle-of-the-night feeds—the contented noises her baby made; the way his fat little hands held hers as she fed him. There was no time more precious to be holding her son as when the world was so peaceful and quiet.

Except tonight the world was not so peaceful and quiet—there was a light on in the main house. Louanna and her husband must be up.

Aurora's heartburn returned as she lowered little Gabe into his bassinette and he slipped back to sleep.

She should just go to bed, Aurora told herself. It was no business of hers.

But as she listened Aurora changed her mind, and wondered if she should call the police.

Which would have been the sensible choice.

Except Aurora was bolshie and passionate, and she did not know how to look away…

CHAPTER THIRTEEN

Rome

THE GLORIOUS SIGHT of the city at night, from the vantage point of his helicopter, did not lift Nico's spirits and there was no sense of relief to be home.

With wealth, Nico decided, came too much cream.

Here in Rome the chefs had been drilled as to his preference for plain food, but it hadn't translated so well at the Silibri site. There the chefs had seemed determined to impress, but they had failed. Oh, the food had been spectacular, but for the first time Nico had heartburn.

Or was it more a sense of unease as he disembarked from his helicopter and saw his regular driver waiting for him?

'I thought you were on leave?' Nico said.

His driver and his housekeeper were married, and Nico had expected a stand-in driver to greet him.

'My leave starts tomorrow,'

Nico glanced at the time. 'It already *is* tomorrow.'

'Perhaps, but better a familiar face to greet you than a stranger. How was the trip?' his driver asked.

'Fine,' Nico responded. 'It went well.'

By all accounts it had been amazing. The new hotel

was sumptuous, and naturally he had his choice of suite there, so when he visited Silibri there would be no awkward stays with neighbours. He had visited the cemetery and knew his father was finally at peace. The hotel was thriving, with the rich and famous and even royalty reserving their spaces. It was wonderful to see the village come alive again.

Yet there was no Aurora.

And without her, without even the slightest chance of bumping into her, Silibri had felt more than ever like a ghost town.

He wished his driver all the best for his vacation and then let himself into his immaculate house. He left his case in the hall and went straight upstairs.

He stripped and showered. Got into bed. Though tired, he was restless. It was months since he and Aurora had last spoken, yet their last meeting still replayed in his head as if it were yesterday.

Why the hell couldn't he move on?

Aurora had. As he had wanted her to do for so long.

He needed distraction, so he climbed out of bed to select a book. He was more than aware that he had lost focus of late.

And then he frowned when he saw a book he didn't recognise on the shelf by his bed.

He laughed as he flicked through it—but then the laugh caught in his throat, because he had never shared his laughter with her.

Not really…

He turned off the light and lay there, thinking of a home that was far away, and the home he now lay in, and the world he had made for himself in Rome.

His driver had been right.

Better a familiar face to greet you than a stranger.

Aurora had always been the familiar face when he went to Silibri. Aurora had been the one he had tried to avoid yet nevertheless had found himself seeking out, and she had *always* made things better.

But now when he went to Silibri it was as if she had been erased.

Bruno hardly mentioned her, and her mother spoke only about Aurora's fancy new career that rendered her too busy to come back just yet. 'Maybe soon...'

And then Nico's eyes opened in the dark.

Hadn't he heard those same frustrating words growing up? Known the code of silence when Pino's daughter had suddenly left school and gone to take care of her aunt in Palermo.

She had returned a few months later, pale and gaunt and with the saddest eyes.

But not Aurora, surely?

Nico sat up.

She would tell him if she was pregnant.

Wouldn't she?

He went over and over that last conversation and within it he found not a clue.

Over and over he replayed it.

Not one clue.

Until the very end.

'The taxi will be here soon.'

Bruno had a car. Why would he not take his daughter to the station on the day she left home?

There was only one reason Nico could see.

His heart was jumping in his chest and he wanted to reach for his phone and call her. But it was the middle of the night. And anyway, she might not answer. Or even if she did she might not reveal anything.

Tomorrow.

Tomorrow he would have Marianna find out just where Aurora had relocated to and then he would call her.

He just had to get through this night.

Rome was not so beautiful this early morning. It was still dark, and also it was freezing cold. She only had with her a few hastily grabbed necessities for Gabe.

But she had her baby, Aurora told herself, and he was unharmed and safe and she cradled him close.

What to do?

She had always wondered why Nico had chosen to sleep in a park rather than in her family home, and now she knew—pride.

But she had a son.

Their son.

And Gabe deserved better than to be outside on a freezing cold morning.

She had never wanted to call Nico like this. She had wanted to be calm and together when she told him. But that choice had been taken from her now.

What if his number had changed or he had blocked her? Or what if he had taken her advice and started turning off his phone at night?

For once she was grateful that he had not.

'Aurora?'

Something inside her jolted. Her name must be on the phone he carried with him. He knew it was her.

'Nico, I am sorry to call—'

'*Never* be sorry for calling me.'

He sounded so calm and so steady and so *nice* compared to the hell she had just left.

'Where are you?' he asked.

'Sitting on a bench in the Prati district.' She gave him the specifics.

'I am ten minutes away,' Nico said, for the streets would be empty.

Make that eight minutes, because he dressed so hastily and continued speaking to her as he climbed in his car. 'What's happened?'

'I don't want to talk about it.'

'Okay.'

Sometimes she was grateful for the sparseness of his words, and grateful too that he did not fill every silence.

Aurora took a deep breath. 'Nico, there is something I have to tell you before you get here. It's not just me. I have my baby with me...'

'Okay.'

No questions.

Not even one.

And then she saw an expensive black car slow down and come to a stop. She found she could not bear to see the disappointment in his face, so as he got out and came towards her she looked down at Gabe.

'He's here,' she told her son.

'Aurora.'

She looked up, and standing there, in a heavy black coat and with snow in his hair, was Nico.

And Rome, early in the morning, was suddenly beautiful again.

'You haven't shaved.'

'Would you have preferred to sit a while longer on that freezing bench while I did?'

'No,' she admitted, and was surprised that he smiled.

She opened her mouth to speak again, but did not know what to say.

Nico spoke first. 'Not here,' he said. 'Not now.'

Instead, he took off his coat and wrapped it around both her and little Gabe and led them to the car.

'My car is just here—let's get you both inside.'

Both.

He said it so easily, but the word felt as if it pierced his brain, for there were two of them now.

Nico didn't quite know what he meant by that, but as he drove back to his home it played over and over...

There were two of them now.

The gates opened on their approach, as they had the first time she'd arrived. How had she ever thought his home intimidating? Aurora wondered as she stepped inside. It felt so delicious that she closed her eyes for a moment and breathed in the scent of Nico's home.

'What do you need for...?' He hesitated. 'Is it a boy or a girl?'

'A boy,' Aurora said. 'Gabe.' She swallowed. 'Well, he's Gabriel, but he's become Gabe.'

'What does Gabe need?'

'Everything,' Aurora said, her eyes filling with tears. 'I just have this bag...' It was enough to get him through the next six hours at best.

'I will call Marianna,' Nico said, and Aurora guessed that was often his solution to irksome things. 'What happened, Aurora?'

'I already told you,' she said, taking a seat on one of his plump couches. But instead of sinking into it she perched on the edge. 'I don't want to discuss it.'

'Perhaps...but you have a bruise on your cheek.'

'He didn't mean to do that.'

She looked up and saw Nico's face stretched into a grim smile.

She *knew* that look.

For she had seen it the night they had first made love. She had seen it when he had lifted her hips from his body and told her to go to bed, and she had said no.

It was the look he gave as his patience slipped away. It was the look he gave just before that steely control dissolved.

'Okay,' she said hurriedly. 'I'll tell you.'

And so she told him—about the job she had taken, and how wonderful Louanna and the children had been.

And then she watched his jaw quilt in tension when she told Nico about the husband.

'Things were fine when he was not there, but then...' Aurora said. 'I was desperate, Nico, and so I stayed.'

She saw that black smile which was not really a smile return to his face. Whatever she had said had clearly displeased him, so she moved on swiftly.

'This morning, at about two, I was putting Gabe back in his crib after feeding. I live in the summerhouse...'

'In winter?'

'It's heated. I was so happy there. Anyway, I saw a light, I saw them fighting—or rather I saw him hit her—and I...' She swallowed. 'I intervened.'

Silence from Nico.

'I couldn't just do nothing.'

'So you ran across the garden—I assume it is snowing there too—and stepped into a house where there was a raging man... Did he hit you?'

'No—no! I was trying to get him off his wife and he pushed me, and then he told me I was not welcome in his home and that I'd caused too many problems with his wife. Then he pushed me again and I fell.' She shook her head. 'I don't want to talk about it any more.'

'Fair enough,' Nico said. 'It will be exhausting enough going over things again with the *polizia*.'

'I'm not speaking to the *polizia*,' Aurora said urgently.

'So you want me to go round there and kill him?'

'Nico, it's a bruise.'

'Get it photographed while it's visible, and tell the police the details while they're fresh in your mind. Or,' Nico repeated, 'I will go round there now and I kill him.'

'Oh, grow up!' she sneered. 'What's that going to solve?'

'Plenty for me.' Nico shrugged. 'So what's it to be?'

'Nico, I don't want to cause trouble. I just want to forget—'

'You will *never* forget,' Nico interrupted. 'And nor will Louanna and the children,' he added. 'I know that for a fact. Ignoring and denying and sweeping things under the carpet does not improve the situation one iota. It needs to be faced.'

'Leave it, Nico, please.'

He did not.

Sometimes she forgot that Nico was just as Sicilian as her.

Nico's stunning apartment became busy with two uniformed police officers, who took a detailed statement. It was exhausting, but there was relief at the end, when Aurora asked if Louanna would be safe.

Nico answered for the police. 'She will be fine. Right now she is tucked up at my hotel with the children.'

When the police had gone, Aurora turned to him. 'You didn't have to do that.'

'It was my pleasure,' Nico said. 'I will ensure she is looked after and I will have my lawyers help her.' He saw her bemused frown. 'Louanna gave you a home when you needed one, and—' He stopped whatever he had been about to say. 'Go to bed,' he told her.

'I can't. Gabe is asleep,' she said. 'I don't like to bring him into bed with me in case I smother him.'

Yet she was tired—terribly so. All the adrenaline that had fired her seemed to have left en masse.

'I could maybe take a drawer and put him in it. Or if you have a box...'

'Or I could hold him.'

It was Aurora who was silent now.

'Surely that's better than a box?' Nico said.

'I sleep better when he is next to me.'

'Let me hold him, Aurora.'

She handed Gabe to him and he took the baby awkwardly and held him in one arm.

'You have to support his head.'

'I am.'

'And if he wakes there are two bottles left. I should put them in the fridge...'

'Go to bed, Aurora.'

'Which bed?'

She flushed as she asked the question—and then Nico took her breath away.

'The one he was made in.'

Such a direct answer—and it told her that Nico did not doubt for a second that the baby was his.

It was actually a relief to close the bedroom door and be alone.

Nico knows.

How he felt about being a father was another matter entirely, but she felt a sagging of relief that he finally knew.

The bed was unmade, Aurora saw. Of course it was—he would have been asleep when she called.

Her book was on the floor beside the bed, and it made her smile that he must have read it—or at least found it.

The shower was bliss—and so, too, was it bliss to put on not a crisp clean shirt, but the one he must have taken off last night that smelled of him.

She slipped between sheets that held his cologne and the male scent of him—and then the door opened and he stood there, holding a cup in one hand and their son in the other.

'Sweet milk,' he said. 'Do you want something to eat?'

'No, milk is fine.'

'I've called Marianna. She is getting some essentials and will sort out a nanny.'

'I don't need a nanny.'

'Well, *I* do,' Nico said.

'Ah, yes, you have a very busy social life.' She fixed him with her eyes. 'What with balls and trips to the theatre...'

'That was in the run-up to Christmas,' Nico said, though he knew full well what Aurora was getting at. Those had been high-profile functions he had attended, and there were photos everywhere. 'It has been a busy couple of months.'

'I saw,' Aurora said, and attempted to slice him in two with her eyes.

Nico held her gaze. He did not blink and then he spoke. 'One thing, Aurora...' He just could not let go of what she had said for a single moment longer. 'You were *never* desperate.'

'So had I arrived here eight months pregnant, with fat ankles—?'

'You know the answer,' he interrupted. 'You were *never* desperate.'

No, because she had the golden ticket—his baby. And, whether he wanted her or not, Nico would see to his duty—and she would have done anything to avoid that.

'Yes, Nico, I was.'

He closed the bedroom door and headed through to the lounge. He looked into navy blue eyes, and saw the groove in Gabe's chin that mirrored his, and then went back to gazing into those sumptuous eyes.

'Your mother,' Nico said to his son, 'is the most difficult woman on the face of this earth.'

And then he fell in love—because an eight-week-old could win a heart with a smile.

'You did *not* inherit that smile from me,' Nico said.

He had both of them now.

Two hearts that he had to take care of.

Two lives that twined and twisted into his.

When he had never even wanted one.

Aurora slept for a couple of hours and then woke to the sight of a crib by the bed.

And the weight of Nico's arm over her.

He was on top of the bed, not in it, and he was asleep.

She wriggled out from under his arm and sat up on the edge of the bed. She peered into the crib at her son, and for that moment all was right in her world.

'He wanted you,' Nico said sleepily. 'I couldn't get him to settle in the crib, but the moment I carried it in here he fell asleep.'

'I didn't hear you come in.'

'You were out of it. Come back to bed. Sleep when he does.'

'No, I'm awake now,' Aurora said. 'And I'm hungry.'

But the deeper truth was she was nervous beside Nico. Nervous of the conversation to come and not sure how she was going to react to his weary, inevitable proposal.

There would be questions first, and accusations, but something told her that a proposal of marriage would come at the end of them.

Happy now? his eyes would say.

No—for she had never wanted to force him into doing his duty like this.

'I'm going to make something to eat…' Aurora said.

'There's a meal being delivered in an hour.'

'A meal being delivered…?' She frowned.

'I often have the hotel chefs prepare my dinner.'

'Well, I just want some bread,' Aurora said. 'Do you have that in your fancy house?'

'I'm not sure,' he admitted. 'I don't do the shopping. Marianna brought a lot of stuff over for Gabe…'

'What did you tell her?'

'Nothing,' Nico said. 'I just told her to arrange a nanny and that I needed stuff for an eight-week-old baby.'

'And she didn't ask any questions?' Aurora looked over at him, and felt a delicious teasing in his vague answers.

'She asked if you were breastfeeding.'

'What did you say?'

'I said that I believed not.'

'I wasn't able to,' she said.

'Well, there's plenty of formula and bottles, and there's an emergency nanny on her way. There is a separate wing in the house, and she shall have Gabe with her at night.'

'No.'

'Aurora, even aside from the bruise, you look terrible.'

'Thank you for being so tender in your assessment of me.'

'You are exhausted.'

She was... Not from the birth—the fog had lifted from that. And not from the night feeds, nor the drama of Louanna and her husband.

It was from eight years of chasing his love and running from his love and then chasing it again.

'You look tired too,' she observed.

'Because you're exhausting, Aurora,' he said, and then he smiled.

The nanny arrived a little while later, and as Nico went to the entrance hall to let her in Aurora sat there, feeling on the back foot, still dressed in his shirt because her clothes were being washed. She braced herself for someone brisk and efficient, as all the people Nico hired in Rome seemed to be.

Instead she was a... Well, all Aurora could think of was a vast Italian *nonna*, who hugged Aurora as if she had raised her and was besotted as soon as she saw Gabe.

'He looks just like his daddy!'

'That's the assumption we're working on,' Nico said, to the nanny's bemusement, but it made Aurora laugh.

And as the nanny got to know Gabe, so he wouldn't get a fright when he woke in the night and saw her, Aurora and Nico ate dinner. A gorgeous *osso bucco* in a wine and herb sauce. There was even bread! Well, there were rolls...

And as they sat at his gleaming dining table, and dinner was served by staff from the hotel, Aurora's stomach growled as wine was poured.

Nico must have sensed her discomfort and dismissed the staff back to the hotel. *'Grazie,'* he said.

'But dessert…' one of the waiters said.

'We can manage.'

Manage.

That was what he would do, Aurora thought. Nico would manage this situation as best he could.

'I'm sorry to have landed on you,' Aurora said.

'I'm glad you called.'

'Please, Nico, don't be polite.'

'Okay,' he said. 'I won't be polite. Are you wearing underwear?'

She gave a shocked laugh, but then her smile faded as she felt his eyes on her.

And then Nico was serious. 'I *am* glad that you called.'

'Truly?'

'Yes. I just wish that it had been sooner.'

'And what would you have done?'

'I'd have done better than a summerhouse in winter.'

'Please don't…' She was starting to cry. 'I did my best, Nico. I got us into this…' She looked at him. 'You think I trapped you.'

'Did I say that?'

'Nico, I wasn't on the Pill.'

'And I didn't use a condom.'

'But you *thought* I was on the Pill.'

'Aurora, I am arrogant, yes, but not arrogant enough to expect you to remain on contraception for me because of one night four years ago.'

Oh.

'If you had actually told me that day that you were

ovulating I don't think I'd have even heard. I was going
to have you—'

'Oh!' She said it out loud this time.

Actually, she was surprised he knew such a word—
but then the witch in her head flew in and reminded her
that Nico knew *all* about female anatomy.

'We made love and we made a baby,' Nico said.

'Yes.'

'I came back from Silibri early because it stunk
without you,' he told her. 'Thank goodness I had that
last morning with my father, but I flew home early.
Marianna said you were at the house, for the balcony...'
He looked right at her. 'I came in and I knew you were
still there. I followed my desire up the stairs and we
seduced each other—the way we do and the way we
always have. We took each other beyond the edge and,
no, I was *not* thinking of pills, or condoms, or anything other than getting inside you. So, no, you did
not trap me.'

'Thank you,' she said.

'And another thing,' Nico said. 'My intention is not to
lay a finger on you until we have talked this out, however, please go on the Pill—because there will be times,
like this current one, where I want you on the floor.'

'I am on the Pill,' Aurora said.

Thank goodness, she thought, because she was
squirming with how turned on she was.

'Why?'

'Because whatever our feelings are, or are not, we
do always seem to end up in bed.'

'We do,' Nico agreed, and took a long drink of red
wine. He held it for a moment in his mouth, then swallowed it down. 'But not now, because we have a lot to
sort out.'

'I'm not ready to sort it all out.'

Tears were filling her eyes again. She did not want his practical solutions, she wanted his adoration—his relief that she was back in his life. Aurora wanted his love.

'Please, Nico, I'm not ready to thrash things out with you.'

'Then eat.'

She nodded.

'But I mean it, Aurora. No sex till we're sorted.'

'Good!'

She took a mouthful of her own wine and swallowed that lie.

For the first time in her life Aurora left dirty plates at the table. She was simply too drained and exhausted as she searched out the nanny. Her room was miles away!

'He's a delight,' the nanny said as Aurora took over bathing Gabe. 'Why don't I warm him a bottle?'

'Thank you,' Aurora said.

It was nice to sit in a chair and feed him, with this kindly woman watching on. She had missed her *mamma* so much these last few months.

'I hope you're settled in okay?' Aurora said.

'And you.' The nanny smiled. 'And little Gabe. It's our first night here for all of us.'

'True.' Aurora gave a tired laugh.

'Your cheek…?'

'It wasn't Nico,' Aurora said, in an effort to clear the air. 'He would never, ever do something like that.'

'I know,' the nanny agreed. 'Or I would not have taken the job.'

'I worked for someone who did, though,' Aurora said.

Oh, heavens, she was like a leaky tap all of a sudden,

but it dawned on her how much tension she had lived
with these past months. All the energy spent watching
the gathering storms.

Poor Louanna, Aurora thought. And Antonio and
little Nadia.

She looked down at Gabe, whose eyes were heavy
and sleepy. He gave her a soft smile, at the very edge of
his lips and looked at her with his trusting eyes.

Poor Nico.

It hit her then, fully, just how appalling it must be to
be beaten by someone you love—someone you should
be able to trust.

It was no wonder Nico did not want anything more
to do with love.

'Go to bed,' the nanny said when she saw Aurora's
tears. 'I'll take care of little Gabe.'

Nico and the nanny were right, Aurora thought as she
kissed her son goodnight. She needed a night to sleep
properly, knowing her baby was safe.

There was a surprise in the bedroom.

And not just that Nico had straightened up the bed.
He stood there in his black lounge pants.

Aurora laughed. 'I thought they were in case you
had to go to hospital.'

'Marianna talks too much,' Nico said. 'But, yes,
these are for emergencies—and you, Aurora, are always that.'

She did not know quite what he meant, but he'd said
it almost fondly.

Nico knew what he meant. She brought drama and
tension into Nico's life every time he saw her. She made
the blood race through his veins and sent warnings
screaming into his brain.

And always he fought to keep a cool head and control. The one time he hadn't, or rather the few times he hadn't…

But he must not think of sex now—he just did not want Aurora out of his sight.

At first they lay in a silence that was neither easy nor companionable; it was just silence as they both burrowed deeply into their own thoughts.

It was Aurora who broke it. 'I don't like leaving Gabe's night feeds to the nanny.'

'Well, try not to disturb me when you get up to go to him.'

She laughed in the darkness, and it scared her how right it felt to be in his bed.

'Did it hurt?' Nico asked. 'The birth?'

'Agony!' Aurora said.

'You didn't tell your parents I was the father?'

'No.'

'Why not?'

'I don't want to answer that, Nico.'

'Okay.'

'I don't want to talk any more.'

'Then don't.'

Aurora liked it that he did not push her to respond, and that he'd accepted her refusal to answer. She liked the feeling of being next to him in the darkness, even if he might not really want her there.

And so they slept—albeit restlessly.

Aurora rolled into him and rested her head on his chest, and then she found her fingers wanting to explore the dips in his ribs, and the hair on his stomach, but before she caved in and did, Aurora rolled away.

And at midnight Nico woke up hard and pressed against her, so he turned onto his back and tried to think boring, unsexy thoughts.

It was a joke that they'd pretended either of them would sleep. Nico wanted sex. And the woman he wanted to have sex with lay beside him. He could feel her desire in the thick air between them.

Yet sex could only muddy the waters.

He could tell that she was awake next to him.

'Nico?' she said. 'We have to talk…'

She said it as if *he* was the one who was reluctant—as if *he* was the one who had shut down the conversation two hours ago.

Life with Aurora!

But he didn't bother pointing it out, for indeed it *was* time to talk, to work things out. Here in the dark.

'What do you want to happen, Aurora?'

'I don't know.'

'You must have thought about it or at least considered it.'

'I'm confused,' she admitted, and when he took her hand, she squeezed his back.

'Then let's talk it out.'

'From what I can see I have two options.'

'Options are good—so tell me.'

'I want to tell you…' She just did not know how.

But as she lay in the darkness she found a way, and she spoke to him as she had to Louanna the night before Gabe had been born.

'I wanted to tell—' She had been about to say, *to tell you*, but held it in. 'From the moment I found out I was pregnant I wanted to tell the baby's father. After all, there is no doubt that Gabe is his. And I believe he would support the baby.'

'Of course he would,' Nico answered carefully. He would give the world to get her real thoughts, and if taking himself out of the equation helped, then that was fine with him.

'But I worry,' Aurora said, 'that he might suggest the other option.'

Nico was silent.

'Marriage,' she said. 'You see, he turned me down once, and I would always feel I had forced him into it.'

'Okay...'

It was a gentle *okay*. It gave no indication as to his thoughts. More an acknowledgment that he had heard her.

'I think,' Aurora said, 'that he will want the second option—even if he doesn't *really* want it. He's a good man, and very respected by my family. They would certainly expect him to marry me.'

'And you don't want that?'

'No. I think I would prefer option one.'

'Okay...?'

It was the same response as before, but it contained a question.

'You see,' Aurora ventured, 'I think he might regret that day.'

'Well, I don't think he does.'

'I mean, he never wanted to marry...'

Silence from Nico.

'But now he will try to do the right thing by me. I would hate that. I think our marriage would be a terrible mistake.' She struggled to voice the picture that danced in her mind. 'He would come to Silibri and see us now and then...perhaps at weekends...and then return to his life. I would have a husband and Gabe a father and we would have respect in the village, and he would have his life in Roma. His stunning apartment and...' She did not finish.

'And?' Nico pushed.

'Other women.'

Her breath was held tight in her lungs as he seemed to consider it.

'You'd be okay with that?' Nico checked.

And because it was dark she could not see his smile. And because she was so focussed on the awful scenario that danced in her mind she did not hear the tiny tease in his words.

She missed, completely, the fact that Nico had made a joke.

'Of course not,' she snapped.

'Do you love him, Aurora?'

'Too much.'

'Do you believe he loves you?'

'If he does it is a very occasional love—not enough to endure a lifetime. Which is why I prefer option one.'

'You will *always* have option one, where he supports both you and the baby, but what of option two?' Nico persisted. 'What if he wants marriage and a family now? What if he has changed his mind?'

'Perhaps he is just saying that to humour me. You see, I know for a fact he would prefer a quiet wife who would stay in the background...'

'You know that for a *fact*?'

'Yes!' Aurora said. 'Because he told me so himself. And I'm not so good at being the type of wife he prefers. I could try to be her, though...'

'Why would you try to be someone you're not?'

'Because if he makes the effort for me, then I should do the same for him.'

'Would he want you to change?'

'He wants serene, he wants elegant, and he wants

calm and peace.' She turned and looked at him in the darkness. 'I could try to be all of that.'

'You won't last five minutes, Aurora.'

'Watch me, Nico.'

He did.

Nico watched her sleep.

CHAPTER FOURTEEN

Gabe!

Aurora woke in an empty bed and no baby.

No Nico.

Yes, she had the nanny, but panic had her dashing down the grand stairs and through the long entrance hall—and then coming to a halt at the door of the kitchen.

Nico sat on a bar stool holding her baby—or rather, *their* baby. He was wearing suit trousers, socks and shoes, but he was naked from the hips up and unshaven.

Half executive, half temptation.

'I overslept,' Aurora said. 'I never oversleep.'

'It's only seven.'

'That's late for me. Usually I'm up at six…sometimes five…' She was gabbling. But she had to keep speaking about inane things because the sight of him, the delicious sight of him, was too much for this hour.

'Gabe needs to be fed,' Aurora said, holding out her hands for him to hand over their son.

'I just fed him,' Nico said. 'And that is why I am not wearing a shirt. He vomited on me. The nanny is sorting me out another one.'

'Oh.' Aurora didn't know what to say to that, but

again held her hands out for her son. 'Well, he needs to be changed.'

'He's already been changed,' Nico said.

'Did you do that too?'

'No.' Nico shook his head. 'I left that to the nanny.'

He smiled, and it was so rare that he did, that when he did she felt as if she wore skates and the marble floor was ice, for she wanted to glide over to Nico.

Her outstretched hands were now for *him*, Aurora realised, so she dropped them to her sides.

'He's handsome,' Nico said, looking down at his son.

'Very.'

'I would expect his father must be too,' Nico said, slipping into the banter they had shared last night.

'Not really.' Aurora wrinkled her nose and teased him, but could not erase her smile. She tried to, but it just kept shining through.

And then it dawned on her how terrible she must look, in his crumpled shirt and with a bruise on her cheek. Surely his perfect wife would be in active wear at this hour, all glowing from her morning yoga—or from having just gone down on him.

Aurora preferred the thought of the latter, even if she had never done it before...

'I'd better go,' Nico said.

'Where?' Aurora asked.

'Where do you think?'

'Can't work wait, Nico? Surely we have a lot to discuss and—' She halted herself, for she had sworn at least to try and be the perfect wife. 'What time will you be...?' She swallowed. His perfect wife would not ask when he would be back. 'I'm going to cook today.'

'I have a housekeeper for that.'

Although then he realised that she and her husband had both just gone on leave.

'Or I have chefs down the road,' Nico said. 'And, anyway, you need to shop.'

'Why?'

'Because you need new clothes. And a haircut.' He picked up her hand. 'And a manicure, my dear elegant wife.'

She had never in her life had a manicure.

'I don't have time for that. I have a son to take care of.'

'And a husband to please...?' Then he stopped teasing her. 'You have taken care of our son alone for the last two months, so today is for you. Go to the boutiques at the hotel and then to the salon. I shall let them know to expect you.'

'Nico, I can't—'

'You never have to say that again, Aurora.'

But he was not saying it with the tender care she needed this morning. He was not holding her in his arms and telling her the nightmare of her world without him was over.

Instead, he was basically telling her that the money was taken care of.

Which was nice, of course. But it wasn't even the icing on the cake. It was like a sugar ball that rotted your teeth and stuck in your throat.

She could not bear to spend the day without him—without knowing what went on in his head and what his reaction was to the fears she had shared last night.

'I could come and see you on your lunchbreak?' she suggested.

'Aurora, I don't *have* a lunchbreak.'

'Is that only for peasants?' she sneered.

'Yep.'

'Well, I might bring Gabe up to your office…'

'No.' He shook his head. 'You need a day off to take care of yourself. Anyway, I'm too busy today.' He glanced at the time. 'I really had better go…'

Finally he handed her Gabe, and looked right into her eyes. For a second she thought he might kiss her, but it was a fleeting second, for he'd already pulled back.

'You need to shave,' Aurora said.

'Funny, that, because suddenly I don't have time.'

The nanny came in then, with another shirt. He dressed hastily and left.

Oh, what had she done…?

She looked at the baby bottle on the kitchen bench, at the dinner plates and wine glasses still on the dinner table from last night, and she thought of her dishevelled appearance and all the chaos she had brought into his supremely ordered life.

Nico was a man who liked order and calm.

Well, he would get it, Aurora decided. He would come home tonight to the fabled perfect wife.

Nico would get the woman he truly wanted.

'Aurora!'

Luigi greeted her like a long-lost friend. 'Marianna called and said you were coming in! It is so wonderful to see you again.'

'I look terrible,' Aurora grumbled as she sat in a chair in the luxurious salon. She looked so sallow in the mirror that she barely recognised herself.

'What happened to your cheek? You poor thing!'

'I got in the way of an angry man and his wife,' Aurora admitted.

'Well, Luigi is going to wave his magic wand and make you all better.'

'Can you make me elegant, Luigi?'

'Of course. I can do anything.'

Make him love me, Aurora thought as she handed herself over to Luigi and his minions.

It was *not* a little job.

She received a facial and, of all things, eyelash extensions. And a manicure. And a pedicure. All this before he even got to work on her make-up and hair.

And they chatted.

'What should I wear?'

'In the boutique next door,' Luigi told her, 'there is a grey chiffon dress… Oh, my, Aurora, it is so elegant.'

'Grey?'

'I shall call them now and have them bring it round for you to view it.'

It was very lovely—but very grey.

'Do you have it in red?'

'Aurora…' Luigi warned her.

Oh, that was right—she was to stand in the corner, fade into the background and pour his martini.

She would wear the grey.

And pearl drops for earrings, but please not these rather demure mid-height heels.

'They are very…' Aurora sat in the beauty chair as the boutique owner touted his wares and she slipped the shoes on her feet. 'Plain.'

'They are perfect, Aurora,' Luigi assured her as he finally got to work on her hair.

And Gabe was not left out.

He was a rich baby now, and he had a pretty powder-blue suit to look the part. And little powder-blue booties and a white silk bib.

She was getting good at this, Aurora thought as she arrived home at four, with her new eyelashes and nails, and lashings of make-up, and her hair in a gorgeous chignon.

'Oh, *bella*!' the nanny said. 'Look at you!'

'Thank you.' Aurora took the compliment with a smile. 'I'm going to get my new dress on soon and...' She looked around. 'Where is the housekeeper?'

'I don't know.'

'But what about dinner?' Aurora asked, and went down the hall and looked at the gleaming table, still littered with last night's plates. 'And the table needs to be dressed. I didn't even make the bed.'

She looked urgently to the nanny, who gave her the nicest smile.

'I don't do housework,' she said.

'Of course not.' Aurora said. 'But—'

'In any way shape or form.'

'Good...good...' Aurora said.

It was no problem.

And, despite having to get through a lot of domestic duties, she would *not* be ringing the hotel for their dinner. That would be ridiculous when Aurora loved to cook.

And so she made the bed, and tidied the room, and life felt much as it had when she had been a cleaner in Silibri.

Except now she wore a gorgeous dress and had pretty eyes and nails. She cleared the plates and set the table, and went down to his cellar and chose some wine— which was easy for a girl who had grown up surrounded by vines.

But time was creeping on.

She put on an apron and found luck was on her

side—because the *passata* she had bought Nico a year ago was still in the cupboard. And *passata* only got better with age!

One day she might take a course, so she would better be able to create the fancy dishes that Nico must like, but for now she would cook the way she knew how.

But there was no meat in his massive bare fridge. And by the time she got back from the butcher it was getting really late.

However, the pasta was made and had been cut into ribbons, and the sauce was bubbling away as she bathed Gabe and then dressed him.

'Look at you...' Aurora smiled at her chubby baby. His black hair was damp from the bath and he wore a pale blue sleepsuit and a gummy smile. 'Daddy will be back soon...'

Her voice trailed off. For Nico had left this morning, just after seven, and it was now dark—and he had not so much as texted, let alone called.

With her perfect baby lying on the bed, Aurora took off her apron and changed into the plain grey shoes and smoothed the elegant grey dress. She topped up her lipstick and then carried Gabe downstairs, taking dainty steps just in case Nico arrived.

The scent of *passata* filled the house, the aroma of herbs and the garlic making her stomach growl. Everything was in perfect order. The pasta just needed a couple of moments in boiling water and dinner would be ready.

When he came home.

'Perhaps I should text and see where he is,' Aurora said to little Gabe, but he stared back at her with huge navy eyes that were turning black, like his father's, and she remembered that Nico's perfect wife would not do such a thing.

She would *accept* that he was working when he was late.

Gabe started to rub his eyes and grizzle.

'He's tired,' the nanny said.

'He's okay,' Aurora insisted.

She wanted Nico to come home to a stunning Aurora and a gleaming, smiling baby.

'Why don't I put him down to sleep?' the nanny asked a full hour later. Gabe clearly wanted to lay down his head and he had been sick on his lovely pale blue suit. 'You can have your nice meal and relax...'

'No!' Aurora said, for she wanted to sleep beside her baby.

But then she remembered the new rules that she was enforcing. A calm house, a serene and smiling Aurora...

How it ached to hand Gabe over—and then, for the first time in eight weeks, she was alone.

Eight weeks and nine months—for she had loved Gabe even when he'd lived inside her.

And Aurora loved fiercely.

She could feel snakes of anger rising in her chest as she sat there in the lounge, tapping her grey-shod foot as the night wore on. Finally she caved, and called him—but of course his phone was off.

So she called the hotel, and was eventually put through to a weary-sounding Marianna.

'Signor Caruso is not here, Aurora.'

'What time did he leave work?'

'He hasn't been in today.'

Her new shoes hurt, so she took them off. Her new eyelashes itched as she took the *passata* off the stove and then decided she was starving and cooked the pasta.

He could reheat his own.

The louse.

She had told him of her love, and she had shared her dark fears. And his response?

Silence.

Always, always silence from Nico, when she needed his thoughts the most.

Argh!

She threw the spaghetti at the wall—and not to check if it might stick! She threw it in frustration, in despair and in pain—because she wanted this to stop.

For this love for Nico to fade.

For the depth of her soul, where he resided, to be excised, so that she could move on with her life with her head held high.

It was nearly midnight as she sat at the dinner table and wept—because *this* was her life. Loving a man who did not so much as call.

Perhaps he was out with his lover. Breaking it off with her because, sorry, he'd just found out he was a father...

Maybe they were making love now.

Break-up sex.

Which would lead to make-up sex when he weakened and grew bored with his Silibrian mountain girl.

'I hate you, Nico Caruso!' she wept.

'Of course you do.'

And there he was, standing in the doorway, looking a whole lot more crumpled than he had that morning but still with plenty of dash.

'Where *were* you?' Aurora demanded as she stood up. 'Marianna said you have not been in work today.'

'When you calm down I will tell you.'

'Don't tell me to calm down. You have a son now—

you have responsibilities—' She could have bitten off her tongue, and yet she could not stop, and now huge angry tears were spilling out. 'You stay out to this time of night like an alley cat! It is not a good example to set for your son.' She let out the hurt that was really on her mind. 'I told you I loved you, Nico. I gave you all my fears and you gave me nothing back. I will never forgive you for that!'

'Never?' he checked.

'Never, *ever*!'

She could feel her hair, uncoiled and spilling over her face, and she knew her make-up was smeared just when she wanted to be so calm and serene.

'Never!'

She jabbed a finger at his chest, but he caught it and pulled her into him, and kissed her hard, his mouth smothering hers.

She pulled her face back. 'Don't you dare kiss me to keep me quiet,' she said, but she made only a half-hearted effort to push him off. 'Anyway, you still haven't shaved. You will cut my face to ribbons...'

'You wanted a man with a beard, Aurora.'

'Perhaps—but I want a man who is devoted. I want a man who does not tell me he's in the office—'

His reply was to haul her over his shoulder.

'You wanted a man to come home to a house in chaos and laugh and then spank you.'

'Nico, no!' She was wriggling, and she did not know what was happening, but then he let her down, slowly against his chest.

He did not let her go; he held her tightly in his arms. 'Good, because I could never spank a woman—let alone the woman I love.'

She missed the moment. It was just so impossible that her mind brushed it off.

'Oh, the woman you love? Did you say that to your redhead? Did you say that to your blonde?'

Nico had the audacity to laugh.

'It's not funny, Nico—how *could* you?'

'As it turned out, I couldn't.' He was the accusing one now. 'You've not only messed with my head but with my prowess, Aurora.'

'Liar.'

'It's true,' Nico said. 'There's been no one since you.' And then he amended that a touch. 'The *second* time around.'

That should have made her rage, but then she saw the intense look in his eyes, and she realised that in the midst of all this he had told her he loved her—that in these past agonising months there had been no one but her.

'Don't tell me you love me unless you mean it,' she begged.

'I do mean it.'

He was breathing hard and he put his hands gently on her cheeks. His thumbs wiped away her tears and he made her look at him.

'I love you, Aurora, and you were wrong last night. This is not an occasional love—it's an endless love. Over and over I told myself that I didn't want it, but it turns out that I do.'

'Why would you not want love?' Aurora asked.

She thought she had already worked out the answer, but she needed to hear it from Nico.

'I never knew how good it could be,' Nico said. 'I thought life would be better lived for the most part alone.'

For look what love had done to him.

'I thought it was better to stay back,' he explained. 'But of course I couldn't. I always wondered if it was guilt or duty that pulled me back to Silibri—I could not decide between the two. But it was neither. It was love—my love for *you*.'

And then came that almost grim smile. The one she was getting to know. The one that meant Nico might lose his head at any given time.

It was a gesture she could read and it was a little more that she knew about this remote man.

A shiver that ran through her as she thought how much more there was to know, and that soon he would ravish her.

He lifted her onto the granite bench, so she was at eye level with him. She looked deep into his black eyes...

One day she would count those thick dark lashes, Aurora decided. One day, when she could hold off for a moment, she would count every last one.

But there was no holding back for Nico.

There should be sparks between them, Aurora thought as his mouth moved to claim hers. He was kissing her so hard it was as if he had been starving for her—as if the air in her mouth was the air he needed to breathe.

It wasn't elegant sex.

Nor was it serene.

She kissed him back—not just his mouth but his face, his eyes, his neck. She gave up trying to undo his shirt and moved down to his belt, but Nico had already taken care of that.

She looked down and saw him, huge and aroused. His impatient hands were tearing at her sophisticated underwear as he berated her for wearing knickers when he had to have her *now*.

'Is it too soon after...?'

He was trying to slow down even as he tore the last items off...even as he confirmed that she was ready with his fingers. He was trying to be measured and controlled and...well, a responsible new father.

'It's not soon enough,' she moaned. 'Are *we* sorted, though?'

She meant the Nico loving her thing—for it was all too new and too much to fully take in.

'We're sorted,' he told her.

And then he slipped slowly inside her, stretching her and filling her as only Nico could.

And then his hands were everywhere, shredding the flimsy dress, baring her breasts as he had wanted to on that first day in Rome.

He was the man she had first made love to—he was Nico unleashed and untamed—and he was everything Aurora needed tonight.

She *wanted* the fierce possession of his kiss, and she *wanted* the full power of Nico Caruso.

And he gave it.

Over and over and over.

She felt as hot in his hands as she had when the mountains had been ablaze in Sicily that night. And she felt as safe as she had been on that cold morning in Rome when she'd looked up into his eyes.

'I've kept on wanting you,' she told him as he thrust into her and dug his fingers into her hips.

He turned the blood in her veins into champagne and he took her body to places that would have otherwise remained unseen and unknown.

'Aurora!' he said, and his voice sounded like a car skidding and careering on gravel.

Aurora felt just as out of control until she heard the delicious sound of Nico calling her name.

'Nico...'

She wrapped her legs tight around him and buried her face in his neck, inhaling the scent of Nico aroused. It was the scent she craved from the man she adored and she wanted to linger there a moment, to imprint that scent combined with the delicious feel of Nico unleashed upon her, but then she felt a lurch inside her and the swell of him within.

He *summoned* an orgasm from her. He simply demanded it—this very instant.

The tears and frustrations of the day seemed to gather and tighten, pulling her into a frenzied peak, and Aurora sobbed in frustration—for she simply did not know what to do with all the love she had for this man.

Except give it to him.

So much for elegance.

Nico helped Aurora down from the bench and then zipped himself up. He pocketed her bra and knickers to save the nanny finding them.

And then he surveyed the chaos.

There was spaghetti on the wall, and he felt the *thump, thump* of his swelling heart as he looked in the pot on the stove and smelt the herbs and the garlic, and saw the remains of the perfect dinner she had prepared for them.

No, not exactly elegant. But he warmed it up, and she grated pecorino cheese, and then they ate standing up. Like two filthy beggars, they shared what was left in the pot.

'Your father was right,' Nico said.

'I'm not talking to my father,' Aurora said.

'But he was right about one thing,' Nico said, as he wiped a little bit of *passata* from her chin. '"Good food and family and my day is complete. What more could I want?"'

'You should raise your voice a little when impersonating my father,' Aurora said.

'But I wasn't impersonating him.'

CHAPTER FIFTEEN

HE TOOK HER TO BED.

And he did not close the drapes.

They just lay there, sated and spent, with her head on his chest, his fingers playing idly with her hair, and the steady *thump, thump* of their hearts.

Aurora still had many questions, and she could not stop herself asking the important one. 'Nico, where have you been all day?' She looked up at him with urgent eyes. 'And until so late in the night.'

She simply *had* to know.

'Where do you think I've been, Aurora?'

'You don't want to know my thoughts. In them you have been to many places.'

'Okay—where do you think a man goes when the love of his life shows up?'

She went pale in his arms.

'I went to Silibri to speak with your father.'

'You have told him that Gabe is yours?'

'Of course I have.'

Nico was quiet for a moment, for it had taken great restraint not to tear into Bruno and his wife for their treatment of Aurora. He could not stand to think of all they had put their daughter through when she had needed them the most.

But they would soon be family, and he had chosen to remember that.

'What did he say?'

'He huffed and puffed,' Nico said.

'And Mamma?'

He could hear the anguish in Aurora's voice.

'She asked how you were and then she started crying. She asked me what Gabe looked like.'

'Yet all she had to do to find out was pick up the phone.'

'Of course,' Nico said. 'But they spoke of your dating app...'

Aurora did not laugh.

'It was confusing for them,' he said gently. 'And then your father got out a bottle of—'

'Limoncello.' Aurora finished his sentence for him.

'I always wondered why he did not stop speaking to me after I refused to marry you,' Nico admitted.

'And me,' Aurora agreed. 'I thought your name would be mud in our house, but he kept insisting you join us.'

'He said he would believe that I had not offended you unless I married someone else. But if I did then all bets would be off.' He smiled as Aurora laughed. 'He knew,' Nico said. 'He knew, that night when you headed out to the party, that I was churning inside.'

'I would hope he does not know what occurred on the sofa.'

'Of course not—or I would be dead. And anyway, a nice girl like you would never...' He looked over and smiled.

'Aurora, he brought out the Grappa he had been saving for this moment.'

'You told him you were marrying me?'

'No,' Nico said. 'I told him that I wanted, more than anything, to marry his daughter. And then I told him we had stuff to sort out first.'

'Nico, don't make a mistake,' Aurora said. 'I am strong.'

'I know you are.'

'And if you marry me then you will get the full force of my love.'

'Aurora,' he said, very definitely, 'you will get the full force of mine.'

'All I want, Nico, is the full force of your love.'

It was all she had ever wanted, and she felt as if it had been fully received—but those worms of doubt had started wriggling, and then, from the other side of this vast house, she heard a tiny wail.

Was it Gabe he was here for?

'I have to go to him,' Aurora said.

'I know,' Nico agreed.

Even though there was the nanny he had had checked and re-checked a hundred times over. She was the very best nanny, and she would love both mother and infant, but she did not do housework.

In any way shape or form.

'Gabe...' Aurora walked into the comfy lounge, where her son was being winded midway through his bottle. 'I'll give him the second half,' she said. 'And then put him down again.'

He seemed to have grown in the time he'd been here, Aurora thought as she fed him, and she looked into eyes that could not be called navy any more.

They were black.

'Your father,' Aurora said, 'is the most complicated man I know.'

She looked at her son for a very long time.

At the long fingers that clutched hers as she fed him.

At his lashes, which she had already counted.

Then at the perfect dent in his jaw.

'I love him and I believe he loves me...' she whispered, and her breath hitched. 'Not a hundred percent as yet, and not as fiercely as I love him, but, my dear son, I do believe he is trying to love our little family.'

She knew eight years of rejection could not be eradicated in one night.

Aurora padded back to the bedroom and Nico could see that she had cried. It twisted him up inside that his cold, unwilling heart had hurt her.

'We'll build a house in Silibri,' Nico said as she climbed back into bed.

'And you will fly back to Rome...'

'No,' Nico said, '*we* will fly back to Rome. We will be based in Silibri, though.'

'No.'

Her emphatic *no* surprised them both. It was immediate, even though she had never dared to give a future with Nico true thought.

Aurora loved Silibri very much, but though there were so many decent memories she could think of, there were old hurts that resided there for Nico, and current ones for Aurora too, for her parents had turned their backs when she had needed them the most.

'We'll be based here, Nico,' she said. 'I want to sleep most nights in the bed where Gabe was made, and I want to wake to the Villa Borghese Park outside my window.'

'You're sure?'

'Very,' Aurora said, and then thought about it some more. 'We'll go back often,' she added, and then she looked over to him. 'And, of course, I would like to manage the temple weddings.'

'You don't give in, do you?'

'Never,' Aurora said. 'Not when I know I am right.'

She had tried to give up on their love so many times and to let Nico go. She thought of her tears, and the coin-toss at the Trevi Fountain when she had begged to be made love to in Rome.

'I want that job, Nico.'

'Then you shall have it.'

'I don't want favours, though,' she said as she lay in his bed. 'I really am the best for that role.'

She was also, Aurora knew, the best for his heart.

CHAPTER SIXTEEN

'LISTEN TO ME, NICO...'

Of all the bizarre moments in Nico's life, this possibly earned top billing: Pino giving him marital advice.

As it turned out, Nico *wasn't* the last in his family.

He still had many of them. Not blood relatives, perhaps, but neither would he introduce them as friends, for they were so much more.

'You have to keep the romance,' Pino said. 'I have been married to Rosa for thirty years, so listen when I give you advice. Even if it has not been a good day, you have to find a way to enjoy the night.'

'I can do that.' Nico nodded.

'And you have to dance,' Francesca added. 'Often.'

But Nico dismissed that suggestion with a shake of his head. 'I don't dance.'

It was three hours until sunset, and while Aurora was having all her treatments in the oratory, he was in the café on the hill with the Silibri contingent.

'Aurora can dance. She can dance very well,' Francesca said. 'You cannot let her down.'

And who knew that Vincenzo just happened to have been a ballroom champion, or a tango master, or something along those lines, a decade ago?

But Vincenzo wasn't a kind teacher.

Vincenzo was impatient, and exacting, and Nico could never have imagined he would spend the hours before his wedding dancing with a man in a butter-scotch suit.

'And there will be the tarantella,' Francesca said.

Nico frowned. He'd rather avoided weddings.

Until now.

Luigi had been brought in for this very special day, but instead of an elegant chignon, or snaky curls, Aurora chose to wear her hair loose and long.

Her make-up was for the most part subtle, but she asked Luigi to go to town with the eyeliner.

'Not just yet,' Luigi said, and glanced up. 'There's a surprise for you!'

'What?'

And then through the doors came Antonietta.

'Oh!'

'Don't cry,' Antonietta warned as they embraced.

She wanted to, though, for it had been four long years with just the occasional message in between. 'I never thought you'd come today!' Aurora said.

'I nearly didn't,' Antonietta admitted. 'But I could not stay away from your wedding.'

'Have you seen any of your family since you've been back?'

'Don't worry about that now,' Antonietta said. 'You have a wedding to attend. I'm going to head down to the ruins, but I just wanted to give you a kiss and offer my best wishes. Now, in case I don't stay for the party after, here...' She handed Aurora a little silver medal. 'For you to carry with you today.'

It was a French good luck charm: *Bonheur*, the little medal said.

'It means happiness,' Antonietta explained. 'That is my wish for you.'

Aurora thought back to that night on the hillside, watching the fires coming for them, and the wise counsel her friend had given her when she had told her to go home.

Aurora was so glad she had.

'I will carry it with me for ever. And I wish the same for you,' Aurora said.

But she felt the fragile shoulders beneath her hand and looked into her friend's sad eyes. It was an almost futile wish, Aurora was sure.

No!

She would never give up on her friend.

'We are going to catch up properly soon,' Aurora said as tears sparkled in her eyes. 'Even if I have to come to France to do so.'

'You *will* have to come to France,' Antonietta said, 'for I am no longer welcome here.' And then she recovered. 'Get on with your wedding! Your Nico is waiting...'

'My heart is waiting,' Aurora corrected. 'And I will tell this only to you. I think he almost loves me. And I believe that Nico will be the best father in the world.'

She blew at an escaped curl that Luigi would have to attend to in a moment. But right now she spoke honestly to her friend.

'He tells me that I am mad to doubt him...'

'Aurora...' Antonietta said.

She braced herself for a pep talk from her friend, for Antonietta to tell her that of *course* she was not mad. That of *course* she should enter this marriage with a reasonable nugget of doubt as to Nico's love.

But Antonietta had long ago thrown away the script.

'You *are* mad,' Antonietta said. 'Nico loves you. Why can't you just accept it?'

It was a good question.

It had been wonderful to see her friend, although Aurora was very pleased that Luigi hadn't applied the eyeliner before Antonietta had arrived.

'You are ready,' Luigi said to the bride.

He had indeed waved his magic wand—but not too much, for it was happiness that shone through on this day.

'Oh, Aurora...' Her father beamed when he saw her. 'This is the best day of my life,' he said. 'I always knew he was right for you...'

It would be easy for her to hold a grudge. But her parents doted on Gabe and had been all over Aurora from the second they'd found out that the baby was Nico's. They seemed to have conveniently forgotten that they had forced their pregnant daughter to leave home.

Forgiveness was not always the easier path. It was spiky and it stung as you trod on old hurts and raged internally.

'It's not worth it, Aurora,' Nico had said as he'd held her hands and she had sobbed in frustration.

And she had looked up to a master. She had looked up to and learned from a man who had been beaten, but who had risen.

Yes, forgiveness was a spiky path, but if you pushed on and through it you got to those bulrushes, waiting to be snapped so that a million seeds of kindness could escape...

And so, instead of pointing out the hurts her father had caused, when Bruno said he had always known Nico was the one for his daughter, Aurora smiled and agreed. 'You did always say that, Pa.'

It was better to be kind today.

And it was easy to be happy.

Especially when Nadia and Antonio ran in, laughing, carrying a small posy of the freshly picked wild flowers that Aurora would carry.

'You look pretty,' Nadia said.

'So do you,' Aurora said. She smiled and looked at Antonio. 'And you look so handsome! Your *mamma* is going to be so proud when she sees you at the temple ruins.'

Nico had arranged for them to come to the wedding, and they were both Aurora's flower-pickers and her little escorts on the walk to the temple.

And as she walked towards the ruins on her father's arm the resentment slid away, for there was nowhere more calming nor more beautiful than the temple ruins at sunset…

Aurora had been absolutely right about the staff uniforms, because Persian Orange was the colour of this night.

As well as cinnamon, and gold, plus a thousand unnamed shades of orange with which the sky blazed.

And orange did not give Nico a headache tonight.

Pino nudged him needlessly, to say that his bride was here.

Her dress was white, and fell in heavy drapes, and to Nico she looked like a goddess walking towards him.

Aurora cared not for the eyebrow-raises of certain people in the village, who were clucking behind their hands at the audacity of a single mother wearing white.

It was *her* wedding.

The day of which she had dreamt.

Only it was better than her dreams. For in those they

had not been at the temple, and Nico had not smiled at his bride the way he did on this day approaching night.

In her earlier dreams Nico had been a whole lot younger and perhaps, she conceded, just a touch less certain. On this new night and for evermore she was his chosen one. Of that she was ninety-nine-point-nine percent certain.

The whisper of doubt was so tiny in comparison that sense and hope combined to make her believe that Nico wanted this just as much as she did.

'Aurora and Nico,' said the celebrant, 'we stand today amidst these ancient ruins to celebrate your unending love.'

And it *was* both unending and without a clear beginning, for neither could quite pin down when their love had commenced.

When she'd used to open the door and tease him with 'Hello, husband'?

Or when Nico had denied to himself the fact that tears had pooled in her eyes when he had told her he would never marry?

Had there been love there that night on her father's sofa?

And had it returned again on the night Gabe had been made?

Or had it never left them?

It was Nico who answered as he pushed the ring on her finger. 'I have always loved you.'

First he had loved her like a sister, and for a while they had failed as friends. But they were friends now. And they were lovers and partners and parents too.

'And I always shall,' Nico said, looking right into those dark velvet eyes. There was nothing more beautiful than this beautiful Sicilian woman.

And now it was Aurora's turn to speak, and to push her ring onto his finger. 'I tried so hard not to love you,' she told him, and the world. 'I can stop fighting with myself now. I love you, Nico Caruso.'

'And I love *you*, Aurora Eloise Caruso.'

'Finally!' She smiled as her groom kissed his bride.

Nico was not a sociable person, and Aurora was not expecting a wild party. But back at the hotel the champagne flowed, and he accepted the many congratulations and danced with his bride.

Nico *danced*!

He pulled her in, he twirled her—and he even, to Aurora's delight, dipped her.

She laughed. 'Where did you learn that?' she asked. And even before the burn of jealousy could take her over, that he might have learned it in the arms of another woman, Nico halted her.

'Vincenzo taught me.'

'No!'

'*Sì!*'

The Silibri contingent saw the smiles and the near-kiss and started clinking their spoons on their glasses, demanding that Nico and Aurora proceed.

Oh, his kiss was heaven.

Just heavenly.

Deep and slow and loving.

And Aurora was starting to let go of that tiny little percentage of worry that Nico might not be as on board with this as she.

She could never be an actress, she knew, for she let her emotions carry her away. While Nico, on the other hand...

But this kiss was both silk and velvet, and it was at her own wedding party, which she had dreamed of.

It was Aurora who wanted to leave and go to bed…

But then it started.

A huge circle was forming, and she and Nico were being pushed into the middle.

'The tarantella,' Aurora informed him, still sure that weddings were not his thing.

'I know what it is, Aurora.'

He spun her as the circle moved in and out, with laughter and dancing, friends and family. The music pushed them to dance faster, and Nico never missed a beat.

Nico pulled her into him, and even in the midst of a circle full of joy and laughter he read in the woman he loved a sense of duty.

No glass would go unfilled tonight.

And no smile would be unreturned.

In a few moments he would take her upstairs and make love to her, as expected, but there was no sense of duty there.

How did he tell this complex woman that neither guilt nor duty could have him dancing the tarantella with such glee tonight?

Nico even held her hands as they were jumping. Stood in the middle of a circle doing silly jumping claps as the accordion insisted they jump some more.

This was a husband she had never seen before.

And Aurora really had to get him to a bed!

'My wife is tired,' Nico explained as they left. 'Party on.'

Aurora kissed her tiny son, who had been an absolute angel and would be treated like a prince in her parents' home tonight.

'I love you,' she said to Gabe. 'And I love your father so, so much.'

'Come on,' Nico said, and he took her hand.

There would be celebrations aplenty tonight, if he knew this lot, but right now he wanted his wife alone.

He led her up the winding stairs and she went to walk through the cloister, but he pulled her back. 'This way.'

'Aren't we staying in the Temple Suite?' Aurora checked, for it was the suite they both loved and the view that felt like theirs.

'Not tonight,' Nico said. 'In case you've forgotten, this is our honeymoon.'

Oh!

For all she had pored over the pictures and been on board with the renovations, she had a blind spot when it came to the Honeymoon Suite. So certain that she would never stay there.

Or, worse, that she might be there with a reluctant groom.

But now she stepped in and it was Aurora who gasped—for she had seen it by day, but never at night.

It was one Silibri's best-kept secrets.

'Oh, Nico!'

The glass domed ceiling revealed the stars and the Sicilian night sky.

'And do you know,' Nico said, 'that there are steps down to a private beach?'

'I wrote the brochure, Nico,' she teased.

But in truth she was in awe. How did a boy from Silibri, even if he'd inherited the land, do all this?

For there was magic in this building.

'It should be called the Starlight Suite,' Aurora said. 'And you know I'm right.'

'Of course you are,' Nico said, 'and that is why I have a present for you.'

Aurora frowned as he went over to a tray, where an ice bucket was cooling a bottle of champagne, but it was not that which he brought over. Instead it was a small pouch that he handed to her.

'Keys?' Aurora frowned as they fell into her palm. 'Is this to your home in Rome? Because I thought that was all electronic—'

'Aurora, look at them.'

They were old keys. One was thick and heavy, the type you might use to open a gate.

The gate at the side of her *nonna*'s house…

'Nico?' She did not understand. 'You've bought Nonna's house?'

'I bought your *nonna*'s house many months ago— through a third party, so your father wouldn't know it was me. Aurora, the only draw about my staying in Silibri was the thought that at night I would come home to you…'

Aurora looked at the heavy keys she held in her palm and laughed. 'Nico, the only thing that kept me sane in Silibri was the fact that one day I would marry you.'

'I love you,' he told her again. Aurora had always been his fabled wife.

'You really bought the cottage?'

She held the keys now. Or rather, they shared them.

'I bought the cottage, Aurora. At the time I didn't know why, but I do now—I guess I didn't want that dream of being with you to die completely.'

'But…' She looked at him. 'You said you could think of nothing worse than living opposite my parents.'

'And I still can't,' Nico admitted. 'But for holidays, and for things like Christmas, when there are too many

Messinas in your parents' house, we can just head over the road to our own little home. And for the times when we are fed up with the hotel...'

And Aurora's tiny, grating percentage of doubt faded under a million Sicilian stars and the softest kiss.

'Tomorrow,' Nico said as he removed her dress and her pretty underwear, 'we will take the steps down to the beach and I am going to have you in the water.'

'What about now?' She liked the thought of a naked swim, but Nico was already laying her down.

'No, no,' he said, and parted her legs, ready to dive into her. 'For tonight, all you have to do is look to the stars.'

* * * * *

A DARK
SICILIAN SECRET

JANE PORTER

For the fabulous Megan Crane
You've been an amazing friend.
I can't imagine my life without you!

CHAPTER ONE

PEACE.

Finally.

Jillian Smith drew a deep breath as she walked along the jagged cliff overlooking the stormy Pacific Ocean, relishing the fresh air, stunning scenery and a rare moment of freedom. Things were definitely looking up.

She hadn't seen Vittorio's men in over nine months and she was certain that if she was careful, they'd never find her here, in this small, private coastal town just a few miles outside Carmel, California.

For one, she didn't use her name, Jillian Smith, anymore. She had a new identity, April Holliday, and a new look— blonde, tan, as if she were a California native instead of a striking brunette from Detroit. Not that Vitt knew she was from Detroit.

Nor could he know. It was imperative she keep Vittorio, the father of her baby, as far away from her as possible.

He was so dangerous. Such a threat. To her. To Joe. To everything she held dear. She'd loved him, had come so close to imagining a future with him, only to discover that he wasn't a hero...wasn't a knight in shining armor but a man like her father. A man who'd made his fortune in organized crime.

Jillian drew a short breath, aware of the tension balling in her shoulders. Relax, she told herself. There's no reason to be afraid. The danger's behind you now. Vitt doesn't know where you are. He can't take the baby from you. You're safe. Everything's good.

She paused along the cliff to stare out at the dark blue water crested with foam. The waves were big today and they crashed against the dark rocks below with power and passion. The sea seemed angry, almost inconsolable, and for a moment she felt the same way.

She'd loved Vitt. And maybe they'd been together only two weeks, but in those two weeks she'd imagined a life with him. Imagined so many possibilities for them.

But then the truth emerged. He wasn't a hero—no prince on a white stallion—but a terrifying villain.

The first raindrops began to fall and she pushed back her long blond hair from her face, determined to put the past behind her and focus on the present as well as Joe's future. And Joe would have a great future. She'd make sure he had everything she'd never known—stability, security, a happy home.

Already she'd found a darling rental house just a quarter mile down the road on a quiet cul-de-sac. She'd gotten an amazing job at the Highlands Inn, one of the premier hotels on the Northern California coast, assisting with their marketing and sales. And best of all, she'd found excellent child care so she could work. In fact, lovely Hannah was with Joe now.

The rain pelted down, and the brisk wind whipped at her hair, tugging at her black fisherman's sweater, but she welcomed the fierce weather, and loved its intensity. She couldn't help smiling at the ocean, and the endless horizon, imagining life's possibilities.

"Thinking of jumping, Jill?" A deep male voice spoke behind her.

Her smile vanished as she stiffened in shock, recognizing the smooth, accented voice immediately.

Vittorio.

She hadn't heard his voice in nearly a year, but Vitt's was impossible to forget. Deep and calm, his voice was pitched to dominate life—whether it be man or nature—and it did.

He did.

But then, Vittorio Marcello d'Severano was a force of nature, a human being that inspired awe or fear in virtually everyone.

"There are solutions," he added softly, so softly that Jillian shuddered, and took a nervous step away from him, putting her closer to the cliff's edge. Her unsteady footstep sent loose rocks tumbling from the craggy point to the cove below. The falling rocks sounded like her heart shattering and Jill's throat squeezed closed.

Just when she'd felt secure.

Just when she'd thought they were safe.

Unbelievable. Impossible.

"None that I would find acceptable," she answered flatly, turning slightly but avoiding looking him in the face. She knew better than to look at Vitt closely, much less meet his gaze. Vittorio was a magician, a virtual snake charmer. He could get anyone to do anything just by smiling.

He was that handsome.

He was that powerful.

"Is that all you have to say to me after months of cat-and-mouse games?"

The rain fell harder, drenching Jillian's thick knit sweater so that it ran with rivulets of water. "I believe everything has already been said. I can't think of anything I've forgotten," she retorted, her chin tilted in defiance even though her legs shook beneath her. She was torn between fury and terror. Vittorio was just a man, and yet he could, and would, destroy her world given the chance.

And no one would stop him.

"I can. Let me suggest you begin with an apology," he said almost gently. "It would be a start."

Jillian threw back her shoulders and steeled herself against that deep, husky voice of his, forcing her gaze to his throat. What harm could there be in that? And yet it was impossible to look at his throat—strong and bronzed by sun—without seeing the square chin or the broad shoulders encased in charcoal-black.

And even limiting herself to that very narrow region, her stomach plummeted. Because Vittorio was still everything that overwhelmed her. Impossibly physical and primal, he was the true alpha male. No one was stronger. No one more powerful. She'd tumbled into his bed within hours of meeting him and she'd never done that before. For God's sake, she'd never even come close to making love before but something about Vitt made her drop her guard. With him, she felt safe. Near him, she'd felt secure.

"If anyone ought to apologize, it should be you."

"Me?"

"You misrepresented yourself, Vittorio—"

"Never."

"—and you've hunted me like an animal for the past eleven months," she said, her voice hard, her tone clipped. She would not fall to her knees. She would not beg. She would fight him to the bitter end.

He shrugged. "You chose to run. You had my son. What else did you expect me to do?"

"It must thrill you to have such power over helpless women and children!" she flashed, raising her voice to be heard over the wind and the great angry walls of water crashing onto the beach below.

"You're far from helpless, Jill. You're one of the strongest, shrewdest women I've ever met, with the skills of a professional con artist."

"I'm not a con artist."

"Then why the alias of April Holliday? And how did you manage to create such a persona? It takes money and connections to pull off what you nearly pulled off—"

"*Nearly.* That is the key word, isn't it?"

He shrugged again. "That's for another discussion. Right now I'd like to get out of the rain—"

"You're free to go."

"I'm going nowhere without you. And I don't like you standing so close to the edge of the cliff. Come away. You worry me," he said, extending a hand to her.

She ignored his hand, and glanced up instead, her gaze taking in the long, lean jaw, the angled cheekbone, the very sensual lips above his firm chin, and all it took was that one glance for her to go hot, then cold, and hot all over again.

"And you terrify me," she answered bitterly, looking swiftly away, knowing that his lips had kissed her everywhere, exploring her body with mind-blowing detail. He'd brought her to her first orgasm with his mouth and tongue and she'd been mortified when she'd screamed as she came. She hadn't imagined pleasure so intense or sensation so strong. She'd never known anything could shatter her control. But then, she hadn't ever imagined a man like Vittorio.

But the truth was, she wasn't terrified of him. She was terrified of herself when around him. Because in Bellagio, Vittorio undid her. With just one look, he weakened her resolve. One kiss, and he shattered her independence. From the first time they'd made love, she wanted him far too much, realizing she needed him more than she'd ever needed anyone.

"You're ridiculous," he chided, his tone exasperated. "Have I ever hurt you, or laid a hand on you—other than to pleasure you?"

She closed her eyes as her legs wobbled beneath her. During their two weeks together, two incredible weeks, he had only shown her kindness, and tenderness, and passion. Yes, he'd had his secrets. He'd been mysterious. But she'd ignored her concerns and followed her heart. "No."

"But you ran. And worse, you've kept my only child, my son, from me. How is that fair?"

She couldn't answer because already his voice was doing that strange seduction, where he peeled away her rigid control, stripping away her defenses. He'd done it that very first day she'd met him in the hotel lobby in Istanbul. One introduction, one brief conversation, one invitation to dinner and then she lost her head completely. Took leave from her job. Moved into his villa at Lake Como. Imagined she was in love…something Jillian didn't even believe in. Romantic love was silly and foolish and destructive. Romantic love was for other people, people who didn't know better. She'd thought she knew better.

But then came Vitt, and there went sanity, reason, self-preservation.

Oh, he was too dangerous for words.

He'd destroy her. And Joe.

But no, she wouldn't let him have Joe. Wouldn't let Vitt turn Joe into a man like him.

"He's not Sicilian, Vittorio. He's American. And a baby and my son."

"I've indulged you this past year, given you time alone together, but now it's my turn—"

"No!" Jillian pressed her nails into her palms, barely maintaining control. "You can't have him, you can't."

She swayed on the lip of the cliff, aware that the rain was making the soil a soggy, unstable mess, but she'd never go to Vittorio, nor would she give in to him. Far better to tumble backward into space than let Vittorio have Joe. Because at least Joe was safe with Hannah. Hannah knew if anything happened to Jillian, she was to take Joe to Cynthia, her college roommate in Bellevue, Washington. Cynthia had agreed to be Joe's guardian should the need arise and Jillian had formal papers drawn, clearing the way for adoption. Because it was Jillian's fervent wish that Joe be raised by a loving family. A normal family. A family with no ties to organized crime.

A family unlike her own.

A family unlike Vittorio's.

"Jill, give me your hand now. That ledge could give way any moment."

"I don't care. Not if it means I can protect my son."

"Protect him from whom, *cara*? Protect him from what?"

The concerned note in his voice drew tears to her eyes and her heart lurched within her chest. It took all of her strength to harden herself against him. He'd fooled her once, but she wouldn't be fooled again. She was smarter. She was older. And she was a mother now. Jillian wouldn't be swayed by warmth or tenderness, seduction or pleasure. This was about Joe, and only about Joe. His safety. His survival. His future.

This could have been avoided if she'd only known who she was dealing with when she accepted Vitt's dinner invitation twenty months ago.

If she'd only understood the implications of that date.

But she hadn't. Instead she'd cast Vittorio as Prince Charming and put him on a white horse and believed he was going to save her. Or at the very least, take her to an extravagant, romantic dinner and make her feel like a princess for a night.

The extravagant dinner turned into a fantasy romance. He made her feel so beautiful and desirable that she tumbled eagerly into his bed. He hadn't disappointed. He'd been an incredible lover and even now she could remember how his body had felt against hers.

She remembered the warm satin of his skin stretched over dense, sinewy muscle. Remembered his lean narrow hips and the black crisp hair low on his belly. Remembered the sensation of him extending her arms and holding her still as he slowly thrust into her and then even more slowly withdrew.

He knew how to use his body. He knew a woman's body. He'd quickly mastered hers.

For two blissful weeks she'd imagined she was falling in love with him, and fantasized about living with him, making a life with him, making a home. Yes, there were moments Vittorio was called away to take calls at strange hours, but she'd discounted those calls, telling herself it was just business, or the time difference, and that he was a CEO of a large international company so he had to work at all hours of the day.

He'd told her about his company, too, and she was fascinated by his newest acquisition—the purchase of three venerable, five-star hotels in Eastern Europe—and she'd fantasized about leaving her hotel job in Turkey and going to work for Vitt, helping him overhaul his newest hotels. After all, hotel management was her area of expertise, and she imagined them traveling the world together, exploring, working, making love.

And then on day fourteen, one of Vitt's young housemaids shattered her illusions with the whispered question, "You're not afraid of the *Mafioso*?"

Mafioso.

The word chilled Jillian's blood.

"Who?" Jill asked, striving to sound casual as the maid's eyes darted toward the bathroom door where Vittorio was showering. The maid was only there to bring fresh towels but apparently her curiosity had got the best of her.

"Your man," the maid answered, handing off the stack of plush white towels. "Signor d'Severano."

"He isn't—"

"*Sì*. Everyone knows." And then the maid disappeared, hurrying away like a frightened field mouse.

And then the pieces fell into place. Of course. It all added up. Why hadn't she seen it before? Vittorio's immense wealth. His lavish lifestyle. His strange, secretive phone calls.

Jillian had wanted to throw up. Instead she used her phone to do a quick internet search while Vittorio dressed and the d'Severano name pulled up pages and pages of links and stories and photos.

The maid had been right. Vittorio d'Severano, of Catania, Sicily, was a very famous man. Famous, for all the wrong reasons.

Jillian ran away that very afternoon, taking just her passport and purse and leaving everything else behind. Clothes, shoes, coats—they could all be replaced. But freedom? Safety? Sanity? Those could not.

Jillian gave up everything that day. She gave notice at the hotel, gave up her apartment, left Europe and all her friends, vanishing as if she'd never existed.

She knew how to do that, too. It was something she'd learned at twelve when her family was taken into the American government's Witness Protection Program. Since twelve she'd been an imposter of her former self.

Jillian became Heather Purcell in Banff, Canada, and worked for four months as a hotel operator at the Fairmont Hotel at Lake Louise in the Canadian Rockies. It was there in Alberta, Canada that she'd discovered she was pregnant.

"You had to know I'd eventually catch you," he added kindly. "You had to know I'd win."

Trapped. The word rushed at her, just as the relentless waves crashed onto the sand. But she wasn't a quitter. She was a fighter. And she wouldn't give up. She'd learned through hard experience to be tough, and had been fighting like mad ever since she discovered she was pregnant to protect her child from a life that would destroy him, because Jillian knew that life. Jillian's father had once lived that life, dragging them all into hell with him.

The rain fell harder, slashes of cold wind and water that drenched, chilling her to the bone, but Vitt looked sleek and polished and unperturbed. But then, Vitt always looked sleek, and polished, and unperturbed. It's what had drawn her to him in the beginning. That and his beautiful face.

"But you haven't won," she said from between chattering teeth. "Because you don't have him, and you can torture me, or kill me, or whatever it is you do to people, but I won't ever tell you where he is—"

"Why would I ever want to hurt you? You're the mother of my son, my only child, and therefore precious to me."

"I know what I am to you. Dispensable. You made that more than clear eleven months ago when you sent your thugs after me."

"My men are hardly thugs, and you've turned me into an adversary, *cara*, by keeping my son from me." Vittorio's voice momentarily hardened to match the set of his lean, hard jaw before easing again. "But I'm willing to put aside our differences for our son's sake. So, please, come. I don't like you standing so close to the edge. It's not safe."

"And you are?"

His dark gaze raked the cliff and her shivering, rain-soaked figure. "I suppose it depends on your definition. But I'm not interested in semantics. It's time to get out of the cold." And with a decisive step toward her, he shot out his hand, reaching for hers.

But Jillian couldn't, wouldn't, let him touch her. Not now, not ever again. She leaned away, pulling back so violently that she lost her footing, crying out as she fell. Vittorio, blessed with quick reflexes, grabbed her wrist and held on tight.

For a split second she dangled in midair, nothing beneath

her but the beach and crashing waves, and then her fingers wrapped around his wrist and she squeezed tight.

He could save her.

He would, too.

Vitt hauled her back up from over the edge, pulling her onto her feet and into his arms.

She shuddered as her body came into contact with his. Even wet, he was big and solid and overwhelming. So very overwhelming and she collapsed against him, needing, *craving* warmth and security and safety.

His arm wrapped around her tightly, holding her firmly against him. He felt good. Warm. Real.

For a moment she imagined he might still possibly have feelings for her. For a moment she imagined that maybe they could find a way to raise Joe together, and then reality crashed into her.

Was she mad? Had she lost her senses completely?

There was no way they could be together, no way to raise Joe together. She could not allow Joe to be drawn into the d'Severano world, and yet as Vittorio's oldest son, it's what would be expected of him. And expected of Vitt.

Anguish and heartbreak beat at her. "I can't do this, Vitt," she choked, as he wrapped an arm around her waist, holding her steady against him. "I won't be part of your life. I can't."

He slid his palm across her cheek, pushing heavy blond hair back from her cold face. His hand was warm, so warm, and the caress sent a shiver through her.

"And what is so wrong about my life?" he asked, his voice pitched low.

For a moment she could think of nothing. What could be wrong when Vitt held her so securely? How could feeling good be bad?

Her cheek tingled from his touch and her insides did crazy

flips. She struggled to put together a coherent sentence. "You know," she whispered, thinking of her father, his ties to the Detroit mob and the terrible consequences for all of them, although no one had paid more dearly than her sister.

"Explain it to me."

"I can't." She trembled against him, acutely aware of every place his body pressed against hers. His chest against her breasts. His hips tight against her pelvis. His thighs against her thighs. The contact was both exquisite and excruciating. Her body loved it, him. Her body wanted so much more. Her mind, though, revolted.

"Why not?" He stroked her hair over her shoulders into smooth wet waves down her back.

She drew back to look into his eyes. It was a mistake, as her heart turned over. He was beautiful. Beyond beautiful. But also so very lethal. He could destroy her with the blink of his eyes and no one would stop him. "You know who you are," she whispered. "You know what you do."

The edge of his full sensual mouth lifted, and he tucked a tendril of hair behind her ear, his fingertips lingering a moment against the back of the sensitive lobe. "It appears that you've tried and convicted me without giving me an opportunity to prove my innocence, because I am innocent, *cara*. I am not the man you imagine me to be."

"You deny you are Vittorio d'Severano? Head of the d'Severano family of Catania, Sicily?"

"Of course I do not deny my family or my heritage. I love my family and am responsible for my family. But how is being a d'Severano a crime?"

She held his gaze. "The d'Severano family fills pages and pages of history books. Blackmail, extortion, racketeering... and those are the misdemeanors."

"Every family has a skeleton in the closet—"

"Yours has at least a hundred!"

His dark eyes glittered, the brown irises flecked with gold. "Do not disparage my family. I have nothing but respect for my family. And yes, we are a very old Sicilian family. We can even trace our ancestors back a thousand years. Something I don't think you can do, Jill Smith."

She winced at the way he said her name. He made her feel common and cheap. But wasn't that his point? He was Vittorio d'Severano and she was no one.

He was right, of course. She was insignificant, and she had no one she could turn to, no one strong enough, powerful enough to protect her, because who would fight the mafia for her? Who would take on Vittorio, when not even the American and Italian government could bring him down?

But even knowing the odds, she still had to fight, because what were her options? Let Vittorio take Joe from her? Never. Not in a million years.

Which brought her to her senses. What was she doing in his arms, her body taut against his? It was insanity, that's what it was, and she fought to regain control. Jillian struggled against his chest. "You forget yourself," she gritted. "This is America, not Sicily and I do not belong to you. Let go."

He released her and she took a step away, and then another, walking blindly in the downpour in the opposite direction of her house because she'd never lead Vitt there. Never in a million years.

"Where are you going?" he called after her.

"Continuing with my walk. Need the exercise."

"I'll join you."

"Please don't."

But he followed her anyway, although at a more leisurely pace.

Gut churning, mind whirling, Jillian splashed through puddles as she walked, trying to figure out how to lose Vitt, how to keep him from discovering Joe's whereabouts.

She hadn't brought her cell phone with her, so she couldn't call Hannah and warn her. She hadn't brought money, either, so it wasn't as if she could catch a cab from town.

And so she just kept walking, and the rain kept coming, and Vitt continued following.

"How far are you planning on going, Jill?" he asked her, as they approached an intersection and the pathway turned into a sidewalk with a four-way stoplight.

"Until I'm tired," she answered, worried that the light remained red while his limousine purred just feet away.

The limousine continued to the corner and made a partial turn, blocking the intersection. Blocking her access to the crosswalk. Suddenly the doors of the black limousine opened and two of Vitt's bodyguards emerged.

In any other situation she might have laughed. Who but Vitt would have bodyguards that dressed like Italian fashion models? His men wore elegant suits, exquisite leather shoes and belts, and shaded their eyes with the latest in designer stylish sunglasses. They were sophisticated and well groomed and didn't blend in. They had never blended in. But Vittorio had to know that. Vittorio Marcello d'Severano left nothing to chance.

The bodyguards watched her with professional interest. They were clearly waiting for a signal from Vitt, a signal he had yet to give.

"Tell them to move," Jillian said, turning to look at Vitt.

"But I just told them to stop there."

"Yes, but I can't cross the street with them blocking the way."

"I know. But we can't just walk all day. We have things we have to discuss. Decisions that must be made."

"Such as?"

"How we're going to manage joint custody of our son—"

"We're not. He's mine."

"And which country he'll attend school in."

"The States. He's American."

"As well as Sicilian," Vitt countered softly. "As well as half mine. You can not legally keep him from me."

"Nor can you legally take him from me."

"Which I wouldn't do." He patted his chest. "Fortunately, I have excellent legal counsel, and have spent the past few months working with the best American and Sicilian attorneys. Everything's been handled. I've taken care of the paperwork. The documentation is here. You've had him the first eleven months of his life. I'm entitled to the next."

"What?"

He nodded. "We're to share him equally, or, *cara*, darling, you risk losing him completely."

"Never!"

"You'll be found an unfit mother should you try to run off with him again. And you don't want to be found in contempt of the court. It would seriously damage your chances of ever getting custody back."

Jillian stared at Vitt in horror. "You're making that up."

"I'd never lie to you. And I never have. If we step into the car, I'll show you the paperwork where it's dry."

He made it sound so simple. Just step into his car...just look at the papers...

He must think she'd forgotten just how powerful he was. He must think she didn't remember how seductive and attractive she'd found him.

If she took that one small step, climbed into his car, she feared she'd never be safe—or sane—again.

Jillian swallowed hard, her senses already overloaded. Tall and broad-shouldered, Vitt was undeniably attractive, but twenty months ago she'd fallen for more than his body. She'd loved his mind. He was brilliant. Probably the most intelligent man she'd ever met and she'd enjoyed talking to him more than she'd enjoyed talking to anyone.

Vitt could discuss politics and economics, history and culture, arts and sciences. He'd traveled extensively and obviously had loads of money, but he'd played no games. He'd been warm, sensual—and except for the odd strange phone call, and the sudden secret meetings—he'd been totally available.

And like a love-starved puppy, she'd lapped it all up, soaking it in.

Seeing him again reminded her of just how much she'd liked him and wanted him.

Seeing him again made her realize she'd never be immune to him. "I don't trust you," she said, her voice husky with emotion.

"The problem in a nutshell."

"Don't mock me."

"I'm not. But your lack of trust has created terrible problems for both of us."

She looked away, bit her lip hard, so hard it drew blood. "I want to see the paperwork, but I won't get into your car," she said steeling herself, suppressing all emotion. "Don't try to make me."

Vittorio was still walking toward her and he slid his hands into his black coat's pockets. "I didn't want it this way, *cara*. I didn't want it hard on you." He was just a foot away now and she scrambled to the side. He moved past her, heading to the open limousine door. "But if you insist," he added with an eloquent shrug, "then so be it. We'll do it this way."

Vittorio ducked his head and slid into the backseat of the car with its tinted windows. Jillian watched as one of the bodyguards climbed into the car and then the other. Vitt's men weren't coming for her after all. They were going to leave her alone.

She should have felt relief. Instead she felt fear and dread claw at her throat.

Something was wrong, very, very wrong, because Vittorio would never give up, which meant, if he was leaving her here, and letting her go, he'd already won.

He had Joe. He'd found her son.

Stomach heaving, she rushed toward the car, throwing herself at the door to prevent it from closing. "What have you done?"

Vitt looked at her from the interior of the car. The car's yellow-white light cast hard shadows on his face, making his eyes look almost black and his expression fierce. "It's what you wanted."

"What I want is for my son, my baby, to be with me. That's what I want—"

"No, you had that opportunity and you turned it down. You said you wanted to be left alone. I am leaving you…alone."

Jillian didn't remember moving or launching herself at him, but suddenly she was in the car and the limousine was moving and she was sitting on the black leather seat, next to Vittorio with his two thugs on the seat across from theirs.

"Calm yourself," Vittorio repeated. "Joseph is fine. He's in my safekeeping and with the court's permission, will be flying to Paterno with me tonight."

Jillian's stomach rose and fell and panicked, she searched Vitt's cycs for the truth. "You're bluffing."

"No, *cara*, I'm not bluffing. We had an early lunch together, Joseph and I. He's a delightful little boy, full of charm and intelligence, although I wouldn't put him in yellow again. It doesn't suit him."

For a moment she couldn't breathe. Nor could she think. Everything within her froze, and died a little bit.

She'd dressed Joe in a golden-yellow T-shirt this morning and tiny adorable blue jeans. She'd thought he looked like sunshine and it'd made her smile and kiss his neck where he smelled so sweet. "What have you done with him?"

"Besides treat him to a healthy lunch and ask that he be put down for a nap? Nothing. Should I have?"

"Vittorio." Her voice was hoarse, anguished. "This isn't a game."

"You've made it one, Jillian. You've only yourself to blame."

"What about Hannah?" she asked, referring to her wonderful new sitter, a sitter she'd found two months ago just after she'd rented the house. "Is she with him?"

"She is, but you don't need her anymore. We'll get a proper nanny in Sicily, someone who will help teach Joseph his native language."

"But I like Hannah—"

"As do I. She's been a very good employee. Has done everything I've asked of her."

A cold, sick sensation rushed through her, making her want to throw up. With a trembling hand Jillian wiped the rain from her eyes. "What do you mean, *you've* asked of her?"

Vittorio's mouth curved, which only made his handsome face look harder, fiercer. "She worked for me. But of course you weren't to know that."

CHAPTER TWO

SHE was sitting as far from him as she could on the limousine's black leather seat. Vitt had expected that. She was upset. As well she should be.

He'd just turned her world upside down. As they'd both known he would.

Nothing so far today had surprised him. Jill was the one in shock. Water dripped from her thick sweater and the ends of her hair, and her teeth chattered despite the fact the heater blasted hot air all over them. He found the temperature stifling, but left the heater on high for her, thinking it was the least he could do considering the circumstances.

His limousine had done a U-turn and was approaching the private road off the scenic coastal Highway 1 that led to her cul-de-sac.

Jill's rental house was small, brown, with very 1950s architecture, which meant nondescript. It was a house surrounded by soaring evergreens. A house with a plain asphalt driveway. A house that would draw no attention. Jill was smart, far smarter than he'd given her credit for, but once he understood her, once he understood how her mind worked, it was easy to lead her right into the palm of his hand.

The house.

The nanny.

The job opportunity.

He'd known she was in Monterey County for the past four months, but he didn't want to frighten her away until all his plans were in place. And to help her feel safe, secure, he'd wooed her into complacency by posting the rental house information on a coffee shop bulletin board where she went every day to get her latte. Thirty people called on the house before she finally did. He'd turned thirty people down before Jill made the call, and asked to see the house.

She toured the house with one of his company employees, a lovely woman named Susan who worked for him in his San Francisco commercial real estate office. It was Susan who casually mentioned the job opportunity at the Highlands Inn, an opportunity created for her as he owned the hotel, along with another thirty others spread over the globe.

Jillian had interviewed for the job, and while chatting with the hotel's resource manager, the manager dropped into the conversation that she was just about to let her nanny go as her children were now all of school age, and did Jillian know of anyone looking for excellent, but inexpensive, child care?

Jillian pounced.

The trap had been set.

Jillian was his.

In hindsight, it sounded easy. In truth, it'd been excruciating. He'd wanted to rush in and seize his child, know his child, help raise his son. But he didn't. He waited, fighting his own impatience, knowing that everything he did was watched.

The d'Severano name was a double-edged sword. People knew and feared his family. His grandfather had once been the don of one of the most powerful, influential crime families in the world. His family had been intimately involved with the *Mafioso* for generations. But that was the past. Vittorio's business ventures were all completely legal, and they'd remain legal.

"Shall we go to your house so you can change?" he asked.

"I'm fine."

"But aren't we close?"

"No."

"You don't live near here?"

"No," she repeated, staring out the tinted window toward the street.

He gazed out to the street, too. It was a blur outside the window. Rain drummed down, dancing onto the asphalt. It'd been raining the day he'd met her in Turkey, too. Absolutely pouring outside.

And so instead of taking the car to his next meeting, he lingered in the lobby waiting for the rain to let up. It was while he was waiting Jill crossed the lobby, high heels clicking on the polished marble floor.

He'd known from the moment he saw her across the lobby of the Ciragan Palace Hotel in Istanbul she was beautiful, and she'd shown remarkable intelligence during their first dinner date in the Caviar Bar Russian Restaurant, but he had no idea she could be so resourceful. This woman sitting next to him was street-smart. Savvy. Far savvier than many of the businessmen he regularly dealt with.

"I know your house is close, but if you don't want to go and collect anything…" He allowed his voice to drift off, giving her the opportunity to speak up.

Instead she lifted her chin and her fine, pale jaw tightened. "No."

"Then we can go straight to the airport, and I'll have your house emptied and your possessions packed and stored."

He'd gotten her attention now. Her head snapped around, her eyes blazed at him. "My house is none of your business!" she snapped furiously.

"But it is. Who else would have reduced the rent on an ocean-view home from fifty-six hundred a month to fourteen hundred for a single, unwed mother, with no references or credit, and her young son? I own the house. And you, *cara*, are my tenant."

He saw the moment his words registered, saw it in the widening of her eyes and then the clenching of her jaw.

"*Your* house?" she choked.

He shrugged. "My house. My nanny. My hotel."

"What do you mean, *your* hotel? I've never stayed at an expensive hotel—"

"But you've been employed by one the past sixty days, haven't you?" He smiled faintly. "The Highlands Inn is part of my International Prestige Collection. Or did you not check that on Google?"

Her lips parted. And her brown eyes practically shot daggers. *Brown* eyes. So very interesting. Her eyes had been a dark sapphire-blue some twenty months ago.

"You set me up," she whispered.

"What did you expect? That I'd let you get away with abducting my son?"

"I didn't abduct him. I carried him, gave birth to him, loved him—"

"Good. And now you can love him from the comfort and security of my home in Sicily."

"I will not live in Sicily."

"Fine. You can come and go, and visit us whenever you'd like, but the courts have agreed that based on your erratic behavior, and your inability to provide financially for the child, Joseph will make his permanent home in Paterno with me."

"But I have provided for him! I've always managed—"

"With my help, yes. You forget, *cara*, that the courts are fully aware that I provided you with a home, a job and child care. They understand you couldn't have survived without me."

Her hands balled into fists. "That's not true. I was fine. We were both doing fine!"

"So you say."

She fell back against the seat. "You tricked me."

"I did what I had to do to be with my son."

"And now that you have him?"

"He'll live in Paterno at my family home."

"What about me?"

"You will live with us until he's eighteen and then when he leaves for university, you can go, too. You'll be free to travel, buy a new home, start a new life, but until then, you will live with us in my home."

Jillian dug her nails into her palms. "I'm a prisoner?"

His gaze settled on her pale face, studying the high cheekbones, straight nose, full lips and strong chin. "Absolutely not. You're free to come and go, but Joseph will remain with me, to be raised by me."

"So he's the prisoner?"

"He's an infant, and my son. He needs guidance, and protection."

"From your enemies?"

He regarded her steadily. "I have no enemies."

"Except for me," she said beneath her breath.

"You didn't used to be." He spoke the words just as softly, and her color stormed her face, staining her cheeks a hot pink, a clear indication that she also remembered how responsive she'd been in his bed.

A translucent bead of water fell from a tendril at her brow to her temple. With an impatient swipe of her fingers she knocked the water from her face but not before he noticed how her hand trembled.

She was flustered. Good. She should be. He was furious. Beyond furious. Jillian had hidden her pregnancy, until she had accidentally bumped into one of his employees while taking the baby for a walk. On hearing the news, he'd worked out the dates and rung her immediately. Jillian had the gall to first deny the baby was his, and then when he demanded a DNA test, she ran from him, keeping his son from him for nearly the entire first year of Joseph's life.

Jill should be punished. And there would be consequences.

"In fact, I can still see you at the wheel of my new Ferrari in Bellagio," he added. "You loved driving it, didn't you? But then you loved everything about our time together at the villa in Lake Como. Including spending my money."

"You make it sound like I had a thing for your money."

"Didn't you?" he countered, signaling his driver to move on.

"No!" she answered fiercely, as fresh pink color darkened her cheekbones, highlighting the shape of her delicate face. "Your money meant nothing to me. It still doesn't."

"So you didn't enjoy the private jet, the villa, the servants, the car?"

"Things don't impress me," she threw at him, averting her head once more, giving him a glimpse of her neck and nape.

Her skin was pale, creamy, flawless, and his gaze traveled slowly over her, studying her elegant features and the mass of blond hair that hung in damp loose waves over her shoulders. The blond hair color was something new as well.

"I see. You were there for me." He studied her lazily, as though trying to decide if he liked her better as a glossy chestnut brunette or this California beach-girl blonde, but his lazy, relaxed demeanor was a façade, because on the inside he was wound hard, and tight.

Never in his life had he been played the way she played him. Never. It still astonished him. Jill Smith had seemed so innocent. Sweet. Pure. God, he'd misjudged her. But now he knew, and he'd never be foolish enough to make that mistake again. "You cared for me."

She met his gaze directly, her chin lifting. "I did care for you."

"Past tense."

Her eyes looked enormous but she didn't back down. "Past tense."

He glanced briefly out the window at the twisted, gnarled limbs of a cypress tree before focusing on her. "So what changed, *Jill Smith*?" he asked, emphasizing her name because her name, like the rest of her life, was invented. Jillian Smith didn't exist. Jillian Smith was a fabrication. A very good one, but a fabrication nonetheless.

Her lies had made it difficult to track her down, but he was persistent, and he'd succeeded.

Now all that was left was bending her to his will to ensure his son's health, wealth and happiness.

"Nothing happened."

"No? Nothing happened?" One black eyebrow lifted quizzically.

"No."

"No one whispered in your ear? No one told you something that sent you packing?"

Her jaw dropped a little before she snapped it closed, and yet even then she looked sick. Scared. He wondered if that's what she felt that day in Bellagio when his young housemaid told Jill he was part of the mafia. Silly housemaid to talk of things she knew little about. Silly girl to think he wouldn't find out. His staff had to know there were security cameras everywhere.

"What did you do to her?" Jill whispered hoarsely.

"Fired her." And then he rolled his eyes at Jill's expression. "You think I'd hurt an eighteen-year-old girl for saying the word *Mafioso*? Ridiculous. That just proves how little you know of me. I am not a cruel man. I do not hurt people, or give orders to have people hurt. That's barbaric."

And still she looked at him warily, her emotions volatile as fear, anxiety and uncertainty flitted across her face one after the other. "So you really do mean to take me to Sicily with you?"

"Yes," he answered decisively.

"And you won't keep me from Joe?"

"Not as long as you cooperate."

A tiny pulse jumped at the base of her throat. "What does that mean?"

"It means you'll cooperate. You'll do what I ask you to do cheerfully, pleasantly and immediately."

Apparently she didn't like the sound of that as her brown eyes shot daggers at him. "And if I don't?"

"You will be sent packing."

"You can't do that."

"No?" His dark gaze met hers and held for long, tense seconds. "You will be living in my home, in my country, among my family and my people. Who will stop me? Hmm?"

She inhaled sharply. "You can't use Joe as a weapon against me," she whispered, her voice failing her.

"But isn't that what you did to me?"

"I was trying to protect him—"

"From me, yes, I figured that out. But Jill, what a serious, terrible, tactical error."

Her gaze searched his, a deep line of worry between her eyebrows. "And if I *cooperate* for seventeen years?"

"You'll remain with us, enjoy my protection, wealth and all the privileges of being part of the d'Severano family."

"And yet if I stand by and *cooperate*, you'll succeed at turning him into one of you."

"You make us sound like a horde of vampires."

"You're not much different, are you?"

"According to today's popular culture, vampires are in."

"Not with me."

"You're anti vampire?"

"I'm anti bullies, thugs and thieves. I'm anti predators. Anti organized crime. Anti anyone who forces other people to their knees."

"È gran pazzia lu cuntrastari cu du nun pô vinciri nè appattari," he quoted, then translated the Sicilian proverb for her benefit, "It's insane to oppose when you can neither win nor compromise." The corner of his mouth quirked. "You're either shockingly brave or stupid, Jill, considering you have so much at stake."

"A great deal is at stake. We're talking about the life of a little boy. What we do now will impact him forever."

"Exactly so."

"Which is why I can't just roll over, Vittorio, and pretend that who you are, and what you do, is good. Your values and morals aren't mine—"

He'd heard enough, more than enough, actually, and tuning out the rest of her speech, he gestured to one of his men, who then tapped the glass partition, getting the chauffeur's attention. The driver immediately slowed and pulled off the highway onto the rain-lashed shoulder.

"It's a shame that we couldn't come to an understanding, but I suppose it's better now than later," he said calmly, knowing he was just about to destroy what was left of her world. "I did want this to work out. I think we could have made it work. Unfortunately, I can see it's not going to happen. So let's make the break now and be done with it. No point in dragging the pain out." He leaned to the side, opened the back door. "Goodbye, Jill."

Her lips parted with surprise. "What?"

"Your house is just a half mile back. Not far, but certainly not comfortable in the rain. Do be careful. The pavement is undoubtedly slippery."

She crumpled into the seat, her expression one of horror. "Vittorio," she protested, her voice strangled.

She looked hurt and bewildered. Shattered. But of course she'd be dramatic. Everything she said and did was extreme. But he'd had enough of her dishonesty and distortions. He despised lies and he'd worked too damn hard to restore respectability to his family to allow anyone, much less Jill Smith with her questionable morals and secretive past, to dishonor the d'Severano family.

"Jillian, come. Let's be honest. How can we possibly hope to raise our son together when you dislike me so very much? I want him to be safe and loved, not torn between us. But you would hurt him. You've turned me into a monster and you'd try to turn him against me—"

"I wouldn't."

She was grasping at straws and they both knew it.

"You already have. You've lied to me. You've run from me. You've promised to meet me and then you never showed. But then, you never meant to show. It was just a ruse to allow you to escape. With *my* son." He drew a slow breath, suppressing the anger and shame he'd felt when she'd tricked him following Joseph's birth, playing him, manipulating him for months. No one did that and got away with it. No one. Why should she? "Joseph will be one next month and today is the first time I've ever held him. And you call me the monster?"

She flinched, visibly shaken, and her eyes looked enormous in her now ashen face. For a moment he almost felt sorry for her. Almost, but not quite, because she'd hurt him, humiliated him, and made his life a living hell.

His child. *His.* Kept from him. Who did that? What kind of woman did that?

He gestured carelessly, his tone one of boredom. "Do us both a favor, Jill, and step out of the car—"

"Never."

"I'm going straight to the airport," he continued as if she hadn't spoken. "We have a flight plan in place. I don't have time to waste."

She sat very tall on the seat, her slim shoulders square. "I won't get out."

"Jill."

She shook her head. "I won't leave him. I would never leave him."

"And I won't play these games."

"There are no games. I promise."

"You made promises in the past—"

"I was scared."

"And you're not now?" he retorted, mocking her.

Jill's teeth were chattering again and she bundled her arms over her stomach, holding herself tightly as if afraid she'd disintegrate any moment. "Not scared," she said from between her teeth. "Terrified. Please. Please. No games. No trouble. I will cooperate. I will make this work. I will do everything you ask. I swear."

His dark gaze pinned her, held her captive. "I am out of patience, Jill."

"Yes."

His voice dropped even lower. "There will be no second chances. One misstep, one mistake, one small fib, and you're gone. Forever."

She was nodding, frantically nodding, and tears slid from the corners of her eye.

He refused to care. Refused to feel anything for her. She had it coming. Every little bit of hurt, heartbreak and misery. He'd trusted her. Had cared for her. More than he'd cared for any woman in years.

Twenty months ago he'd actually thought she was the one. The only one. The one he'd marry and cherish for the rest of his life. Which was absurd as he wasn't the impulsive kind.

He'd never met any woman he could imagine as his wife, but somehow he'd wanted her.

He'd wanted to love her, protect her, forever.

And then she ran, and lied, and cut his heart to pieces.

"Whatever you want," she choked, "whatever you say."

She was practically begging now, and he'd thought perhaps it would make him feel better. It didn't.

He'd never treated a woman harshly in his life.

He'd never reduced a woman to this. Nor should he have had to.

Vittorio could hardly look at her. Her lower lip trembled and tears shimmered on her cheeks. She made him feel like a savage, like the monster she'd portrayed him to be, but he was no monster. He'd spent his entire life healing wounds inflicted by previous generations. He'd battled to build back his father's company after his father had been tragically injured and the company had been forced to file for bankruptcy. But he battled for his father. He battled for his family. He would prove to the world that the d'Severanos were good people. "I won't take you out of the country by force."

"You're not taking me by force. I'm choosing to go. I'm begging to go. Please, Vitt. Let me travel with my son."

Something snapped inside of him and he reached for her, one hand wrapping around her wrist, while the other slid behind her neck, his palm against her nape, his fingers and thumb shaping her beautiful jaw. "*Our* son," he ground out. "He's not yours. He's ours. We both made him. We made him together in an act of love, not violence, and he is to be raised with love, not violence. Do you understand?"

"Yes."

Brown or blue, her eyes were mesmerizing, brilliant with raw emotion. He'd thought she was everything he'd ever wanted. He'd thought they'd be able to grow old together. "From now on there is no yours or mine," he continued roughly. "There is only ours. There is only one family. And that is the d'Severanos."

She nodded her head jerkily. "Yes."

And then because there was so much sadness in her eyes, he did the only thing he could think of—he kissed her. But it wasn't a tender kiss and it wasn't to comfort. He kissed her fiercely, taking her lips the way he'd now taken control of her life. She'd had her chance. They'd tried it her way. Now it was his.

The hard, punishing kiss didn't ease his anger. If anything, it made him want more. Her mouth was so soft, and her lips quivered beneath the pressure of his. Angling her head back, he ruthlessly parted her mouth, his tongue taking and tasting the sweetness inside.

Jillian shuddered against him, her fingers splayed against his chest and when he caught her tongue in his mouth, sucking on the tip, she whimpered, her back arching, her resistance melting.

He knew the moment she surrendered, felt the yielding of her mouth, the softness in her body. He could have her then and there if he wanted. If they'd been alone, he would have stripped her clothes off her to prove it. Instead he stroked her breast once, just to make her shiver and dance against him, and then he let her go, watching as she tumbled back against the leather seat.

"Airport," he drawled, adjusting the cuffs on his dress shirt. "We're late."

Approaching Monterey's executive airport Jillian felt as though she'd swallowed broken glass. Every breath she drew hurt. Every time she swallowed she wanted to cry.

She'd failed Joe.

Failed to protect him. Failed to save him.

His life would never be the same now, and it was her fault. Her stupidity.

She should have never left him with Hannah today. Should have never trusted Hannah in the first place.

But Hannah had seemed an answer to prayer; perfect in every way. Her résumé showed that she'd been a preschool teacher with a degree in early education and years of experience working with infants and toddlers. Her letters of recommendation said that her family was local and respected. Best of all, Hannah was cheap compared to nannies advertising services in the paper which made Jillian jump at the chance to have Hannah come work for her.

But Hannah's trickery was nothing compared to Jillian's self-disgust. When Vitt kissed her she'd practically melted in his arms.

There were no words to express her self-loathing.

And so her heart ached while her mouth burned, her lips swollen and sensitive.

Nauseated by her behavior, she dug her nails into her palms. Hadn't she learned anything? How could she respond to Vittorio when she now knew the kind of man he was. Her father had been the same, although he'd been affiliated with a Detroit crime family not Sicilian, but her father had been so ambitious. Her father's ambition had destroyed their lives. How could she possibly imagine Vittorio was any different?

She couldn't.

Pulling through the airport's security gate, Jill caught a glimpse of a white-and-burgundy Boeing 737 on the runway. Vitt's jet, she thought, her stomach free-falling. It was the same jet they'd flown from Istanbul to Milan, before taking a helicopter to the Bellagio villa at Lake Como.

Her stomach did another nosedive and she inhaled sharply, fighting hysteria, as the limousine pulled up next to the jet on the tarmac.

Vitt owned a half-dozen planes, including smaller jets, but this was his personal favorite. He liked traveling with his staff and security detail. He'd told her en route to Lake Como that comfort was essential while traveling, thus the jet's staff quarters, two bedrooms, dining room, luxurious living room and snug but gourmet kitchen that could prepare everything from espresso to a five-course meal.

The limo doors opened and Vittorio climbed from the car but didn't wait for her. Instead he walked toward the jet's stairs knowing she had little choice but to follow.

Apprehension filled her as she followed Vittorio's broad back up the jet stairs. What if Joe wasn't here? What if Vitt had been just toying with her? What if, she agonized, moving past the kitchen and dining room to the living room where her heart seized with relief.

There he was. Her baby. Her world.

Joe sat on a quilt on the floor playing with colorful foam blocks. He still wore his sunshine-yellow shirt and tiny blue jeans and was laughing as a dark-haired woman stacked the blocks into a tower for Joe to knock over.

Suddenly he looked up, caught sight of her and smiled. "Mama."

Jillian rushed to him and scooped him up into her arms. He was small and warm and he fit her body perfectly. And just having him in her arms soothed some of the fire inside her chest. She'd felt like she was dying but now, with Joe in her arms, she felt whole.

This child was everything to her. Life, breath, hope, happiness. And even if Vitt didn't believe her, every decision she made was to ensure Joe's safety, security and well-being.

Cuddling him to her chest, she stroked her baby's soft black hair and then his small compact back. For the first time in an hour she could breathe. As long as she was with Joe everything would be okay. She could handle anything, absolutely anything, except losing him.

Aware that the others were watching, Jillian glanced up into Vitt's face. His dark gaze was shuttered, his expression inscrutable, and it struck Jillian that in the last hour everything had radically changed. Joe's life, indeed her life, would never be the same.

As if able to read her thoughts, Vittorio gestured for the young woman to take the baby. Jillian started to protest but Vitt held up a warning finger.

"This isn't the time," he said, his brusque tone allowing no argument. "We're both wet and we need to change so we can depart. And then once we're airborne, we'll discuss what we'll tell our families."

CHAPTER THREE

JILLIAN stood inside the jet's plush, tone-on-tone bedroom, listening to the door close softly behind her, knowing it was but a whisper of sound and yet inside her head it resonated with the force of a prison cell door.

She was in so much trouble. And she'd brought all this trouble down on Joe's head, too.

And now they were en route to Paterno, Sicily, the home of the d'Severano family, and the center of their power.

Everyone in Paterno would be loyal to Vittorio. Everyone in the village would watch her, spy on her and report back to Vittorio.

Inside her head she heard the sound of a key turning, locking.

Trapped. She was trapped. And the worst of it was that Vittorio didn't know who she was, nor could she let him discover the truth.

God only knew what he'd do if he, the head of the most powerful crime family in the world, found out her real name? Her real identity?

He'd destroy her. He'd have to. It was the code. Their law. Her father had betrayed the d'Severano family, and the d'Severano family would demand vengeance. They'd wanted blood. They'd taken her sister Katie's. They'd insist on hers.

But what about Joe? What would happen to him in this power struggle?

Thinking of Joe snapped Jillian out of her fog of misery. She couldn't panic. She had to clear her head. Be smart. And she could be smart. She'd proven before she'd inherited her father's cunning. Now her life depended on staying calm. Remaining focused. But to remain focused, she'd have to control her emotions, something she found next to impossible when she was around Vittorio.

On her feet, Jillian opened her battered black suitcase on the bedroom's sturdy luggage rack. Her clothes had all been meticulously folded when they'd been placed in the suitcase. Who had done that? Who had taken that much time to pack for her? And then she shuddered, not wanting to think of anyone going through her things, touching her clothes, folding her intimate garments. It made her feel exposed. Stripped bare.

But not totally bare, she reminded herself fiercely, peeling off her wet clothes and changing into dry black pants and a soft gray knit top. Vitt knew a lot, but he didn't know everything. He didn't know who she really was, or who her father was, and he wasn't going to find out.

Jillian stared hard at her reflection in the mirror as she dragged a comb through her still-damp hair.

She'd been a redhead until she was twelve and had loved her hair. It'd reached the small of her back and the soft, loose curls had always drawn attention. Her father used to loop the curls around his finger and call her Rapunzel. Her sixth-grade art teacher had said she would have inspired the great Renaissance artists. And her mother cried when the government insisted on cutting her hair off and then dyeing the shorn locks a mousy brown.

She'd cried, too, but in secret. Because losing her hair hurt, but losing herself was worse. And they hadn't just cut her hair off, they'd taken everything else, too.

Her name.

Her home.

Her sense of self.

No longer was she Alessia Giordano, but an invented name. She was a no one and would remain a no one for the rest of her life.

A hand rapped on the outside of the bedroom door. "Have you changed?"

It was Vittorio's deep smooth voice and it sent a shudder of alarm through her. She squeezed the comb hard as she glanced at the closed door. "Yes," she said, forcing herself to speak.

"We take off in two minutes."

So this was all really happening. There would be no government agent breaking down the door to rescue her. There would be no last-minute reprieve.

Jill's hand shook as she set the comb down. "I'm on my way," she answered, and then lifting her chin, she squared her shoulders and stiffened her backbone.

She would do this. She'd been through worse. She could play Vitt's game. As long as Joe was happy and healthy, there was nothing Vitt could throw at her that she couldn't handle.

Leaving the serenity of her bedroom, she entered the luxurious living area. Vitt was already there, standing near a cluster of chairs on the far side of the room.

Vitt looked polished and elegant, dressed in a dark suit and white dress shirt, appearing as if he'd had an hour to shower, shave and dress instead of just minutes. How he did it was beyond her. Perhaps just having a strong, beautiful face made everything easy. She didn't know. She'd never found life easy.

"You look comfortable," he said, taking note of her simple black trousers and plain gray knit top.

She flushed, aware that he was really commenting on her

dowdiness, and self-consciously she tugged the hem of her cotton top lower.

"Mom-wear," she answered huskily, defensively, hating that she suddenly felt ashamed of her appearance, fully conscious that her clothes were old and cheaply made. He'd hit on a sore spot, too, because she was secretly, quietly passionate about fashion. She loved that beautiful well-tailored clothes could make you feel beautiful, too.

"Which is very practical of you," he said soothingly—which was actually far from soothing. "Now please, join me here," he added, gesturing to the tall honey suede chair next to his.

She hesitated for a fraction of a second, her gaze locking with his. His dark eyes stared back at her and after a moment the corners of his mouth lifted. It wasn't a smile. Instead it was a challenge. He'd thrown down the gauntlet earlier and she'd accepted.

"I'd love to," she answered, forcing a smile, and gracefully sliding into the chair covered in the softest, most supple leather she'd ever touched. But then Italy was the design capital of the world; why shouldn't everything Vittorio owned be exquisite?

She felt his inspection as she buckled her seat belt and crossed one leg over the other. She was trying hard to act nonchalant but on the inside her heart hammered like mad and her head suddenly felt woozy. Tall, broad-shouldered and devastatingly attractive, Vittorio seemed to suck all the oxygen from the room, leaving her gasping for air.

He was too strong.

Too physical.

Too imposing.

The fact that he was also one of the most powerful, influential men in the world hardly seemed fair considering all his other gifts.

Her fingers curled into her palms, nails digging into her skin. This was insane. And this charade would surely push her over the edge.

"I've ordered champagne," he said, taking the seat on the left of hers. "We'll have a glass now, and then another to celebrate once we level off."

How cold he was. How cruel. But why shouldn't he celebrate? He'd succeeded in cornering her, trapping her and claiming his son. She peeled her lips back from her teeth in an attempt to smile but the effort actually hurt. Her heart felt like it was breaking. "Haven't had champagne since Bellagio. I suppose we've now come full circle."

"But back then you were a stunning, voluptuous brunette with straight chestnut hair and Elizabeth Taylor's violet-blue eyes. Now you're the quintessential California beach girl. Blonde, lean, tan. An impressive transformation. Quite the master at disguise."

"I'm glad my resourcefulness impressed you," she answered with a tight smile before turning her head to stare out the plane window.

She hadn't wanted to be so resourceful. She'd been a dreamy little girl, sheltered, pampered, protected. Her parents had been wealthy middle-class Americans. She'd attended an exclusive Catholic girls' school. Her Detroit suburb had been lined with old trees and sprawling mansions.

Nothing in her life had prepared her for the revelation that her father wasn't merely a member of an underground organization, but a traitor within the organization. He was despised by all and when he testified against his organization, he put his entire family in danger.

Overnight twelve-year-old Jillian had been torn from her school, her friends, her community.

Jillian had struggled in their new life, with the new identities. The moves were hard. The isolation at times unbearable.

But over the years she'd settled into being these other people, playing the necessary part.

Her younger sister Katie wasn't as skillful. Nor was Katie as disciplined, or focused. Two and a half years ago—just eight months before Jillian met Vitt in Turkey—Katie had fallen in love with a handsome stranger, a grad student at Illinois University, and feeling safe, had revealed who she really was. She ended up paying for that misplaced trust with her life.

Jillian wouldn't make the same mistake. Jillian had learned that there could be no trusting handsome strangers, least of all men with connections to the mob.

Jillian's throat ached, remembering. She'd been devastated by Katie's death. The phone call from her mother giving her the news had been the most horrific phone call of her life. Even now, Jillian still felt shattered.

Jillian had been the big sister. It had been her job to protect Katie.

She hadn't, though.

And now Jillian had Joe, only this time Jillian would not fail. She would do the right thing. She would protect Joe with her life.

"Jill. Your glass."

Jillian jerked her head around to see the flight attendant standing before her with a flute of champagne. Vittorio already had his. Ruthlessly she smothered the memories of Katie and her family, killing the emotion inside her, smashing down the grief. She couldn't change the past. She could only move forward.

Her eyes felt hot and gritty. She blinked hard, blinking away unshed tears as she took the champagne flute. "Thank you."

The flight attendant disappeared, leaving them alone and Vittorio lifted his glass, dark eyes gleaming above high, bronzed cheekbones, the stiff, formal collar of his black suit contrasting the devastating sensuality of his mouth. "I propose a toast."

She lifted her glass, heavy, so heavy at heart, and waited for him to finish the toast.

He let her wait, too, making her hold her glass high, making her wonder what he'd say.

The jet's engines came to life. Jillian tensed, realizing soon they'd be airborne. Soon she'd never be able to escape.

And then smiling without smiling, Vittorio touched his glass to the rim of hers. "To the future," he said, "and our lives together."

Her heart fell, crashing into her ribs. Was he jesting? What kind of life would there be when there was no love, trust or respect between them?

Again her eyes burned, but once more she squashed the pain with a cool, hard smile. "To Joe," she said instead, changing the toast, her voice as brittle as her smile.

"To Joseph," he agreed. "The son we made together."

They drank.

She swallowed, the cold, slightly sweet, slightly tart champagne fizzing and warming all the way down.

She glanced down into her glass, watching tiny bubbles rise to the surface, admiring the champagne's pale gold color against the cut crystal stemware. Champagne in crystal was almost magical. She'd once loved how a glass of fine champagne could make her feel elegant. Beautiful.

She'd confessed that to Vitt, too, and for one week he'd ordered her champagne every night before dinner.

Did he remember? Is that why he'd ordered champagne now?

Her head jerked up and she looked into his eyes. His expression was shuttered. She could see nothing there.

But once, even briefly, there had been something between

them. Once they'd made love to each other as if their hearts had mattered.

"Feel beautiful now?" Vittorio asked lazily, watching her with those dark inscrutable eyes of his.

So he did remember. "Like a princess," she answered.

"And we're living a fairy tale," he replied mockingly.

She looked away, focused on a point across the cabin. How could she not have seen who he was? How could she not have realized that behind his charm and his stunning good looks was a man of stunning power?

"Can I please go get Joe?" she said, fighting to keep her tone neutral. "We're about to take off and I'd be more comfortable flying if he were here with me."

"But he's fine where he is. Maria is taking good care of him."

Jillian drew a deep breath, then slowly exhaled. Had she heard Vitt right? Was he making decisions for her? Was he deciding how and when she was to see her own son?

She fought the wave of nausea rolling through her. "I miss him, Vitt. I haven't spent much time with him today—"

"—because you left him. You regularly left him."

Again her insides lurched. "I had to work."

"You didn't. You could have come to me. I would have supported you, made sure you could have stayed home with him."

The floor vibrated beneath Jillian's feet. "I wanted the best for Joe. I wanted him to have what I didn't—security. Stability—"

"And you think running and hiding and living with false identities is the way to accomplish that?"

"Joe wouldn't have a false identity."

"He already did! You told Hannah that all of his medical records were listed as Michael Holliday. That when you enrolled him in preschool, he'd be called Mike."

Jillian flushed and shifted in her seat. He was right, and it did sound awful when put like that. "It hadn't happened yet," she said softly, uncomfortably. "It was just a thought."

"No. It wasn't just a thought. It was your idea of a good plan."

She flinched, stung by his mocking tone. He didn't understand that to protect Joe she had to think like a survivor. She had to be aware of danger, had to consider all the different possibilities. "Perhaps I've made mistakes," she said huskily, tears roughening her voice, but she wouldn't cry. Not here, not now, not in front of her enemy. "But I only wanted the best for him."

"And now he has it. His mother and father together under one roof. What a lucky little boy."

God, he was awful and hateful, bent on making her suffer. She blinked and ground her jaw together until she knew she had her emotions under control. "So can our lucky boy join us? Can he sit with his mother and father as the plane takes off?"

Vitt studied her pale face and hard, tight jaw for a long moment before reaching out to smooth a pale blond strand of hair back from her face. She shied away from his touch but he didn't comment on it. Instead he smiled at her almost kindly. "Our son is quite comfortable and sleeping soundly in an infant cot in the staff room. Maria will bring him to us when he wakes."

The jet began to move, rolling forward on the tarmac. "Please, Vitt. Please let me have him. I want him. I *need* him with me."

"Even though he's sleeping in his cot?"

She'd had her life ripped apart by her father's deceit. Her only sister had been killed in an accident the police termed "suspicious," yet they'd never brought charges against anyone. Her mother, terrified of further reprisal, had broken off all contact. Jillian's only anchor in life was Joe. He was the reason, and the only reason, she'd been able to survive so many blows. "Yes."

Vittorio studied her for a long, silent moment. "You really wish for me to have him woken up just so you can hold him?"

She heard condescension in his voice. Condescension and disbelief. Because what kind of woman would put her needs before her child's?

"No," she choked, lifting a hand to shield her eyes so he couldn't see her tears. "No. You're right. I don't want to wake him. It is his naptime. He should sleep."

Again Vitt subjected her to his scrutiny. "Sometimes it is difficult to do the right thing, but I have found that difficult or not, doing the right thing is the only real option."

The jet was moving faster now, racing down the runway, picking up speed by the second. Within moments the jet's front wheels left the ground and then the back wheels. They were airborne.

Dark pine trees dotted the ground. The blue of the Pacific Ocean came into view. In less than an hour they'd leave California far behind. In eleven hours they'd be in Sicily, in his world, and Joe, her baby, her child, would be living in Vitt's home.

And if Joe were to live in Vitt's home, where would she live? Would Vittorio keep her nearby, or would he set her up in her own house or apartment, someplace close by but not in his immediate household?

During the two weeks they'd spent together in Bellagio, Vitt had told Jillian a great deal about the twelfth-century Norman castle the d'Severano family called home. His family hadn't always owned the property. Apparently his great-grandfather had purchased the crumbling fortress in the early 1900s and each generation since had spent a fortune restoring sections at a time. Over half the *castello* still remained uninhabitable but Vittorio had said that was part of the charm.

Twenty months ago she'd been anxious to see this historic property. Now it was the last place she wanted to visit.

"My family is old-fashioned," Vitt said, breaking the silence. "And my mother is extremely devout. At first she might seem cold, and unapproachable, but given time, she will grow to accept you. But you must give her time. She is slow to embrace change."

This sounded far from encouraging, Jillian thought, turning from the view of the deep blue Pacific Ocean to look at him. "Is she upset with you for having a child out of wedlock?"

"She doesn't know."

Jillian's eyes widened. "What?"

He shook his head. "I haven't told her. Or anyone else in my family." He saw her expression and shrugged. "There was no reason to share such news. You were hiding from me. I didn't have legal access to him yet. But it's a different situation now."

"And now?"

"Now it is a joyful occasion. My wife and son return home with me. Everything is good. Everything is as it should be."

His wife and son…

His wife and son…

His *wife*.

Her heart hammered relentlessly and her hand shook as she clutched the flute. Is this why he'd ordered the champagne? "So that is the story we're to tell them."

"It won't be a story."

She exhaled in a painful rush. It was both a protest and a prayer. *"Vittorio."*

"My captain has the authority to marry us in-flight, allowing us to land in Sicily in the morning as husband and wife."

"That's crazy," she whispered, her fingers clenched so tightly around the flute's fragile stem that the tips had begun to go numb.

"Why is it crazy? We arrive married, stepping off the plane as a family. Joseph is no longer illegitimate. You are my wife. Problem solved."

Problem solved? Problem multiplied.

Her head spun. She was dizzy with the shock of it. Marriage was so serious, so binding, and even more so among the *Mafioso*. Once you were part of the family, there was no way out. At least not alive. "Your family has never heard of me, and then to produce me from thin air, introducing me as your wife, and Joe as your son—?"

"It would be the truth."

"They'll never accept us this way, Vittorio, surely you can see that. Especially your mother. She'll be hurt that you've kept her in the dark, and suspicious as to why you're only introducing us now. She'll have so many questions—why was there no proper courtship or wedding? Why didn't you tell her about the pregnancy or Joe's birth? You're bringing him to Sicily at nearly a year old. You know that won't go over well."

His eyes never strayed from her face, a faint smile playing at the corners of his lips. "And what would you rather me tell her? The truth? That you ran away when my eighteen-year-old maid told you I was a member of the mafia? That you then hid your pregnancy from me, and then kept my son from me after his birth? Would that be better, Jill?"

She stared into his dark eyes with the flecks of amber around the black pupil. He might be smiling but his expression was one of utter resolve. He was not going to relent. "No," she said after a moment.

"So we have to come up with a suitable story, one that compromises our integrity as little as possible, because I don't like lying to family. I don't believe in lying, much less deceiving my father and mother. But I have a son to think of and I would sacrifice everything to ensure his well-being."

And looking at him, at the steely determination in those dark eyes fringed by the thickest, blackest of lashes, she believed him. But she also believed that there was always more than one way to accomplish something. Life was full of possibilities. There were always options, and those needed to be considered. "You don't need to marry me to introduce Joe as your son. He is your son. He will always be your son—"

"Your point being?"

"That it would be easier for both you, and Joe, if you didn't marry me. Introduce me as Joe's mother. Let your mother think the worst…that I'm a floozy, or a gold digger, or whatever. But at least this way she'll be mad at me, rather than at you."

One of his dark eyebrows lifted. "How good of you to martyr yourself on our behalf. It's gratifying to know you do still have feelings for me."

"That's not what I mean."

"What did you mean?"

Jillian flushed. "That she'll be angry."

"Undoubtedly." He shrugged philosophically. "But I am an adult, a man and the head of my family. I do not answer to my mother, and nor should you fear her. As long as you play your part of the doting wife, she'll eventually be happy."

The words *doting wife* echoed loudly in her head. Jillian's throat sealed closed. What else would she be? After all, she was the eldest daughter of a famous Detroit mobster. Why shouldn't she be married to the head of the Sicilian mob?

And then she pictured her sister, followed by an explosion of color. Her sister's blue, blue eyes. The red-and-gold flames of the car burning. The black-and-white ink of the newspaper article covering twenty-one-year-old Katie Smith's death.

At least her sister died quickly.

At least she hadn't seen it coming.

"Surely there are other options we could explore," she said after a moment. "Roles that would require less acting…roles that would be less of a stretch."

"And what role would that be? My son's nanny? My mistress? My what, Jill Smith? Just what role would you now choose to play in life?"

"Joe's mother."

"And you may. Provided you're married to *Joe*'s father."

She cringed at the way he said *Joe*. He meant for her to cringe, too.

"My family has a disreputable history, a history you've thrown in my face. But my father has worked hard to change the past, and I've continued his fight. We've worked too hard, sacrificed too much, to have Joseph inherit scorn or scandal. No one is to know he was born out of wedlock," Vittorio continued quietly. "He is not to grow up marked by shame."

They were still climbing but Vittorio downed what was left of his champagne and ignoring the seat belt sign, rose.

"The ceremony will take place in the next half hour, before the baby wakes," he said, looking down at her. "Find something appropriate in your suitcase for the ceremony, something elegant and festive. Something that could pass for celebratory. I don't expect you to wear white, but silver, gold or cream would be nice. After all, we'll want good memories to help us remember our special day."

CHAPTER FOUR

JILLIAN fumed in her cabin as she confronted her open suitcase. Silver, gold or cream? Something celebratory for their ceremony?

Ha! He was out of his mind. His power had clearly gone to his head. There was no way she was going to dress up in a sparkly party dress for their vows. Because this wasn't a special occasion and she wasn't celebrating.

He was the one insisting on the wedding. He was the one forcing her hand.

Fine. Force her. But she wouldn't meet him dressed up like a shiny doll without a mind of her own.

No, she'd dress for the occasion her way. Which meant she'd find the plainest, drabbest, darkest dress she owned and wear that for their vows. A dull, dowdy black outfit should convey quite nicely how she felt about their nuptials.

Jillian allowed herself the faintest of smiles as she dragged a high-necked black blouse and a long gray skirt from the bottom of her suitcase. Perfect. Gray and black. Perfect colors for mourning.

Thirty minutes later, Vittorio stood in the center of the jet's living room holding Jill's hands as he recited his vows. His chief pilot, the jet's captain, performed the simple service.

Jill, he noted, had dressed as if she was attending a funeral, replacing her gray knit top with a severe high-collared black blouse and the black pants with a long, narrow, charcoal-gray skirt.

She wore the blouse buttoned high on her neck and her pale hair had been pulled back into a low knot at the back of her head. She wore no jewelry or makeup and couldn't have looked more miserable if she'd tried.

But she did go through with the ceremony, speaking her vows in a clear, almost defiant voice, and holding her hand steady so he could slip the ring onto her fourth finger.

And now his captain concluded the service, pronouncing them man and wife.

The captain didn't linger. With his mission accomplished, he returned to the cockpit, leaving Vitt and Jill to celebrate together.

The flight attendant appeared with more champagne, and a silver platter of delicate appetizers. Vittorio ate and drank, but Jill touched nothing. It didn't particularly trouble him. This wasn't a love marriage—it was about duty, commitment and responsibility, as well as restoring honor to his family.

"Jill d'Severano," he said, trying it out as he studied her pallor and her brown eyes that looked far too big for her small face. "Mrs. Vittorio d'Severano."

She lifted her chin, her expression pained. Apparently she wasn't very fond of the name.

"I wish I could say the worst was over," he added thoughtfully, "but tomorrow won't be easy. Nor will the day after that. But in a week's time the shock will wear off and acceptance will begin."

"It's going to take me more than a week to get used to being your wife," she answered tartly.

He laughed. "I was referring to my mother, and how she'll react to you. But I suppose you're right. You must be in shock, too. How were you to know this morning when you woke, that twelve hours later you'd be on a plane to Sicily, married to me?"

Fire flashed in her eyes. "Your empathy is touching."

"My empathy allows me to protect you instead of crushing you. You should be grateful for that."

She opened her mouth to speak but then closed it, shaking her head in silent, seething frustration.

She looked like a nun at a funeral. A nun minus the wimple. She was buttoned and closed and as emotionally distant as possible. But this was his wedding day, too, and he wouldn't let her do this to him, wouldn't have her play victim, all numb and cold, not when she'd created this situation. And not when he'd worked so damn hard to fix it.

"Unbutton your blouse," he told her, aware that his voice was hard, aware that he sounded every bit as cold as she looked. "You have the softness of a dried up old prune."

She held his gaze. "I like prunes."

"I don't."

"I'm sorry."

"If you were, you'd unbutton your blouse a little, smile a little, act like this isn't the worst day of your life."

"When it really is."

"I should have left you on the side of the road when I had the chance!"

"Too late. You brought me along. Married me. We're now husband and wife."

"And wives are to submit to their husbands."

"To believe that, you must also believe that husbands are to submit to the Church. But somehow I doubt you submit to anyone," she retorted, her eyes huge, her jaw tightly clenched.

His temper flared. She was *not* the injured party. She could not be allowed to play the victim, either. He was the one who'd been cheated. He was the one who'd been kept from his son.

"Do it," he ordered brusquely, "just unbutton a couple of buttons or I'll do it myself."

"We're to consummate the marriage here?" she flashed. "Right now?"

"It hadn't been my intention, but if you're eager—"

"Not at all."

"—and desirous of being my obedient, obliging wife—"

"That's the furthest thing from my mind."

"—then you can pleasure me. I appreciate that you are so sensitive to my needs."

She flushed furiously, her pale cheeks flooding with bright crimson color. "You have many needs, if I recall."

He took a step toward her. "And you begged for it every single time."

Undaunted, she took a step toward him. "You flatter yourself."

"No, if you recall, you flattered me. You were amazed at what my body could do and how I could make you feel. You wanted to know if all men were as well endowed as me, and if others could last so long. You were nearly always reverent when you took me into your mouth—"

"I was tired of being a virgin. I wanted knowledge and experience. You gave it to me. But I've been with other men now. I know what others can do, and oh, can they do."

He took another step toward her and once again she moved closer, chin lifted, eyes bright and challenging. She was deliberately provoking him, daring him to lose control. He was getting close to losing control, too, intensely aware of the hot lick of testosterone, and the primitive drive of an animal hunting prey.

"And what can they do?" he murmured, so very aroused.

She held her ground, chin high, eyes bright as she breathed

in and out in short, jerky gasps that made her breasts rise and fall beneath the ugly black blouse. Her cheeks were a vivid pink. "They make me moan and scream," she threw at him.

"Really?"

"Mmm. And the good ones can make me come multiple times."

This was a fine wedding day, wasn't it? "You've really gotten around."

"Why not? I wasn't your woman."

"But you are now." He reached out an arm, and catching her low around her waist, drew her toward him.

And with his body hot, his groin hard, he roughly slipped his finger between the buttons at her breastbone and popped the first button off. "Just as you always will be," he said, moving down a button and popping that one off, too. "So let's dispense with this blouse, shall we?"

Her lips now were nearly as pink as her cheeks. "Why don't you just lift my skirt and get this over with?"

She spit the words at him as if she could shame him.

He wouldn't be shamed though. He remembered how they'd been together. Intense, physical, passionate.

"Why rush our pleasure?" he asked, reaching out to touch one of the loose blond waves that now fell past her shoulders.

She stared him in the eye, her expression disdainful. "You wouldn't know how to pleasure me if you tried."

"Why do you want to provoke me?"

"Not trying to. Just stating facts."

Facts. His lip curled ever so slightly.

Despite everything, she was still determined to play a game with him, something he found both disturbing and intriguing.

She was either incredibly brave or ridiculously foolish. He wasn't a man to toy with. She had to know that. So why dangle her adventures with other men before him? Why throw his so-called inadequacies in his face?

Brave or foolish, she did intrigue him.

She'd intrigued him in Istanbul and then she'd intrigued him in Bellagio and now here she was, cornered on his plane, his ring on her finger, mocking him. Challenging him. Attempting to defy him.

Interesting, so interesting because so few people tried to defy him, much less a slim scrap of woman who didn't even reach his shoulder. Jill Smith was a complete enigma. She was small and fine-boned and yet so very fierce. She had a heart-shaped face, heartbreakingly high cheekbones and fire in her eyes. She flung her head back as if she were a tigress and to draw blood she talked of other men.

Of other men pleasuring her. Of other men making her moan and scream.

He should want to crush her. He should want to teach her a lesson.

But he didn't. Because he also knew that beneath her fire and fury there was terrible sadness.

He'd sensed it that first night they were together and then nearly every night after they'd made love, she would wrap her arms tightly around him and cling tight. Clinging as if her life depended on it.

He held her against him, her cheek pressed to his chest, and he'd stroke her hair again and again until she fell asleep.

Some nights he felt tears on his chest.

Some nights he felt her take a deep shuddering breath.

But always the sadness, and always his aching need to help her. To save her. To protect her.

That's when he knew he loved her. That's when he imagined marrying her.

He'd marry her and give her a new life, a better life. She could start over as a d'Severano with him.

And now she was, his wife but under totally different circumstances. Which intrigued his mind but left his heart cold.

"I see," he said evenly. "This is your idea of foreplay. You want me to talk dirty, manhandle you a bit, before dominating you in bed."

Two spots of pink color bloomed high in her cheeks. "You're crass."

He felt his lips curve in an unfeeling smile. "And you were the one that suggested I lift your skirt and get it over with. Would you prefer I do it here, against the wall, or would you rather I bend you over the armrest and take you from behind? I do remember you enjoyed it on your knees—"

"Did enjoy," she interrupted tightly, "past tense. Because I will never enjoy sex with you now—"

"Stop. Save the protests for someone who might believe them. I know better. You have always been hot and eager in my bed, and even if you've been with a hundred men since, I know you'll be just as hot and eager again."

Her eyes burned. Her cheeks turned crimson. "I couldn't—"

"You could. *Easily.*"

And to prove his point, he cupped her jaw and dropped his head to brush his lips over the warm satin of her cheek and down to the corner of her mouth. His mouth barely touched hers and yet he felt her lower lip quiver, heard her soft inhale. He kissed her again, just as lightly, a kiss that just grazed her lips, a kiss that was fleeting, teasing.

He could tell she was trying to remain rigid, trying to pretend she was indifferent to him and yet he could feel her rapid pulse in the hollow beneath her ear and the sizzling heat of her skin. She wasn't just warm, she was almost feverish to the touch, and her lips, which had been so tightly closed a moment ago, were parted now. She was breathing in those shallow little gasps that he'd always found erotic.

Instead of kissing her again, he reached inside her torn blouse and plucked aside her bra to cup one bare breast. Her skin felt like hot satin and his body, already hard, throbbed.

He strummed the taut nipple, and then rolled it between his fingers. She arched and inhaled and he pulled her against him, grinding his hips to hers so that she could feel the weight and heat of his erection, rubbing the trapped length between her thighs. She shuddered and arched and moaned.

The moan was what drove him out of his mind. That soft kittenlike cry, a mew of bewildered pleasure, severed all rational thought, annihilating control.

He flicked up her skirt, ran a hand up the inside of her thigh, feeling the quiver in her leg as his palm caressed the taut smooth muscle. He ran his hand up, up until it reached the elastic band of her panty.

He felt the damp heat of her before he'd even touched her there. She was hot, wildly hot, and when he stroked his thumb over the outside of the thin cotton fabric, she jerked and shuddered. She was still as sensitive as he remembered. He stroked her again, brushing the tender clit, watching her whimper and squirm.

She wanted him. And he was her husband. And while he hadn't planned on taking her here, now, like this, the primal male in him recognized that he could, and should. Because she was his. Because she now would always be his.

Sliding a finger beneath the elastic, he stroked her without the cotton barrier, and she was slick and silky and warm, so very, very warm.

He plunged his finger into her damp hot core and heard her sigh and felt her muscles tighten around his finger. He remained still, reveling in her tightness, and her softness, but she was impatient and she bucked against him, wanting friction, needing sensation.

He stroked her, once, again and then with two fingers and

still she arched, and still she whimpered, and they both knew it wasn't enough. It would never be enough. Not between them. Theirs was a physical relationship, an intense relationship, one founded on chemistry, desire and possession.

He'd possess her now, and he'd start with his mouth.

The ugly gray skirt had a loose elastic waistband and he tugged it to her feet in one swift motion. Her panties followed, and then he stripped off her shoes. She was half-naked and trembling but she wasn't afraid. He knew her better than that. Jill, his bride, was trembling with need.

Lifting her, he positioned her over the arm of the suede chair and pressed her back down, putting her butt high in the air. She was completely bare down there, something he liked, finding it erotic to have so much skin exposed. He ran a hand over her cheek, toward the cleft and then down to the soft, plump outer lips between her thighs.

She tensed and quivered as he caressed the cleft again, teasing the swollen flesh until she swung her hips in desperation.

He parted her legs wider, kneeled behind her and took the taut aching bud of her clit in his mouth, alternately sucking and licking until she began pleading with him to mount her, take her. He refused. He wanted her to buck and squirm, beg and groan until she shattered against his mouth and he could taste her surrender on his tongue.

"Please, Vitt," she panted, as his hands held her thighs apart and his tongue stroked and jabbed and then sucked and bit. "Please, please."

But he wouldn't fill her, wouldn't please her until he'd pleased himself by making her come this way. And so he licked her, covering her soft, wet, silky skin with his mouth, sucking harder, flicking the tip of his tongue over the delicate ridge until she broke, crying out as she climaxed in wave after wave, her body shuddering helplessly.

He knew he was a barbarian when he freed himself without taking off his slacks, pulling his length instead from his zipper. Fully dressed, he plunged into her hot, wet sheath while she was still shuddering. It was raw and primitive to mount her this way, but his body was hard and tight and about to explode. With his hands on her hips he held her firmly, taking her with deep long thrusts. He groaned at the pleasure, even as he hated himself for being ruthless. In his heart he knew a woman needed more tenderness. In his heart he'd wanted once to love her, not merely possess her, but possess her he did.

He was feeling even more barbaric as he neared his own climax, certain her body was sensitive, and then as he stiffened, the pressure building, she arched back against him, chest jutting, head thrown back as she came again, crying out even louder than she had before.

He came inside of her, emptying his seed into her and it crossed his mind that this was how it'd happened before. There'd been no protection the first time—although they'd used it every other time—but it'd taken just that one time. Perhaps it'd happen again.

Finished, drained, he slowly withdrew from her, his emotions as numb as his body was exhausted. He expected he'd feel something—pleasure, remorse, relief—instead he felt pain.

Pain.

How could that be? And why? Why should he hurt when she'd been the one to wrong him?

Infuriated by the thick dark emotions churning inside of him, emotions so heavy and aching he couldn't even begin to understand, he reached out and slapped one cheek of her round pert ass. "I think I'm going to like the married life."

And then, emotions wild on the inside, he tucked himself back into his trousers, zipped his slacks and walked out, leaving her to pull herself together on her own.

For a moment after he left, Jillian did nothing. Her legs were jelly. Her limbs shook. It was as if a bomb had exploded and she'd been left in the shattered aftermath.

Seconds passed and then she roused herself, forcing herself to move. Biting her lip, Jill straightened and began to gather her clothes strewn across the cabin floor, stepping into her panties, then her skirt before holding the torn blouse closed.

Numb, so numb, she walked quickly to her room, air bottled in her lungs, her throat raw from holding in all the emotion.

But in her room a tear fell, and then another, and she dashed them away with a furious fist.

She hated that she cried, but she cried not out of pain, or helplessness, or despair, but fury.

Fury with herself. Fury with him. Fury that she enjoyed the lovemaking as much as she had. Because she had. So very, very much.

Yet how could that be possible?

How could she allow herself to feel anything with him, much less pleasure?

And God forgive her, it'd been exquisite.

His hands, his tongue, his mouth…she shuddered with pleasure all over again even as her mind railed against her body.

She was weak.

She was pathctic.

And she'd loved it all—the wildness, the rawness, the passion. It'd been primitive and carnal and hot. Very, very hot. She could still feel the heat of his skin on hers, the weight of his body, the pressure of his hands. He'd held her, shaped her, taken her as if she were his to possess, and apparently she was. Because instead of shutting him down, she'd become hotter and wetter, responding to him with a feverish desperation.

Horrible.

For a moment Jillian felt like her father—a traitor. She'd betrayed herself. Her father had betrayed his mob family. And maybe their sins weren't of the same magnitude, but still, the genetic link was there, as well as the same weakness of character.

Her stomach cramped at the thought. She couldn't bear the idea that she was like her father. He'd hurt so many people. He'd destroyed their family. She refused to be like him.

Walking into the small ensuite bath, Jillian let her clothes fall and then stepped into the narrow shower, turning the water on full force. It was cold. She felt icy. But icy and cold was so much better than the last lingering effects of her feverish desire.

Taking the bar of French lavender soap, she scrubbed her skin, washing away Vittorio's scent and imprint, telling herself she was not his, that she did not belong to him even though everything inside her whispered, *you will always want him.*

She feared it was true. Despite everything, there was something about him that connected with her. Something about him that mattered so much to her.

Biting her lip, she rinsed her thighs as she felt the soreness inside, where Vitt had been. He was large and he'd taken her hard and this was the first time she'd had sex since Joe's birth.

But Vittorio didn't know that. Vittorio thought she'd been with dozens of men because that's what she'd told him.

Scalding tears burned the back of her eyes but she wouldn't let them fall. Instead she tipped her head back and let the water course down, drumming strength into her, drumming confidence.

There'd be no more tears.

She needed to be focused and smart and think about what would happen when they reached Sicily.

She was entering Vittorio's world tomorrow morning, arriving in Catania as his wife. That should make her feel protected. Respected.

Unfortunately the rushed ceremony made her feel exactly the opposite. The ceremony did not seem binding. Never mind honorable. Maybe the marriage gave Joe Vittorio's name, but it did nothing to ease her fears, or her sense of isolation.

She was still vulnerable.

In Sicily, she'd need Vittorio's protection.

How to get his protection and his family's respect? It wouldn't be with a quickie wedding, she knew that much. If Vitt's mother was as devout as Vitt said she was, she'd never accept Jillian as her daughter-in-law, not unless she believed their union had been sanctioned by the church. But how could their union be blessed by the church, if they hadn't even married in a church, or by a priest?

Her stomach did another nervous flip as she realized she needed a public acknowledgment that she and Vitt had indeed exchanged vows, and that they viewed their vows as holy and binding.

Which meant they needed a church wedding.

Fast.

Jillian dressed and blew dry her hair with care. She was just putting on earrings when a knock sounded on the door and she opened the door to discover Maria in the hall with Joe.

"Mama," he said, smiling and reaching for her.

What a lovely surprise! Jillian took her baby from Maria and hugged him tight. His small sturdy arms wrapped around her neck and she kissed his neck, his cheek, loving the sweet smell of him. Her baby. Her boy.

"*Signore*, Signor d'Severano has said dinner will be served in fifteen minutes."

"We're dining with Joe?"

Maria shook her head. "I do not think so. I believe it is just you and Signor, although he thought Joseph could join you for the first few minutes."

"Come in, then. I'm almost ready. Just need to finish styling my hair."

In front of the mirror in the bathroom, Jillian gathered her blond hair, shaping and pinning it into a soft French twist before stepping back to examine her reflection. With her fair hair up, and in the soft silver knit top and dark pewter slacks, she could almost pass for elegant. The top and slacks were big on her, items left over from her transition wardrobe following Joe's birth, but with pink lipstick, silver bangles on her wrist and a sophisticated hairstyle, she looked polished. Serene. Strong.

Serene and strong was good, because when she joined Vittorio for dinner, she had a purpose.

She was going to convince Vittorio that they needed to marry again, but this time in a beautiful ceremony in his hometown, in his family's church, in front of his community of family and friends.

She wasn't sure how he'd react to the proposed ceremony. She only knew she had to convince him it was necessary.

Finished dressing, Jillian thanked Maria for taking care of Joe and then carried her son to the dining room. Vittorio joined her almost immediately and she watched as he entered the room in a crisp white dress shirt with dark tailored trousers. His black hair was again damp and neatly combed, his hard, handsome features set.

She should hate him. She should.

She couldn't.

Because just looking at him, she wanted him all over again. Just seeing his beautiful face with that chiseled jaw and full, sensual mouth made her body warm.

Was it only an hour ago he'd parted her legs and covered her most sensitive skin with his lips? She remembered the way he'd sucked and licked and tasted her. It'd been wanton lovemaking. So very carnal. And yet it'd been exquisite, too. Who knew such pleasure was possible?

Yet desire came with a price. And hadn't she learned by now that those who needed others gave up power?

And wasn't she sick of being powerless?

Ever since she was a child, she'd been at the mercy of others. First, her father. Then, the government. Between twelve and twenty they'd lived in five different states with four different identities. Each new identity required a new image, a new name, a new history.

At first it'd been difficult to remember the script. Lee Black of Ashford, Oregon. Carol Cooper from Fountain Hills, Arizona. Anne Johnson, Fredericksburg, Texas. Jillian Smith, Visalia, California.

And then it stopped being hard, because she stopped caring. It was easier not to try to fit in. Easier not to make friends. Why bother to make friends when you'd soon have to leave them without a word of explanation, or the hope of ever seeing them again? In the government's Witness Protection Program there was no such thing as change of address cards, forwarding phone numbers, email exchanges. In the Witness Protection Program you simply vanished into thin air.

That lack of stability, and lack of control, transformed her from the innocent, sheltered little girl she'd been, a girl who'd adored her father, a girl who'd felt so very safe, into the woman she was today.

From the time she'd left home to go to college, she'd had one goal—to be completely independent. She'd gone to graduate school after finishing Gonzaga University to earn a master's degree in hospitality management, an advanced degree in the hotel and tourism industry, thinking it was a practical study, one that would catapult her to the top. Because the one thing she'd always wanted was power of her own. Power to choose. Power to travel. Power to become someone else.

And she'd come so close to having that power and freedom. In Istanbul she'd been delighted by her job, her apartment, her clever circle of friends. But then she'd met Vittorio, and accepted his dinner invitation and her life had never been the same.

She'd given up everything that one night without even knowing it.

"I still can't get over the fact that you're blonde," he said, approaching her.

"It doesn't please you?" she said, shifting Joe in her arms.

"It wasn't done to please me." As he neared her, his dark eyes met hers and held. "It was done to hide from me. It was done to keep him from me," he added, nodding at Joe.

She held her ground, refusing to be intimidated. "True."

"And you're not the least apologetic."

"I did what I thought was necessary," she answered, aware that Joe was watching his father with obvious fascination. "But that's behind us. We must close the door on the past. Now you're my husband. My protector. I have nothing to fear with you at my side."

He looked at her for a long moment. "And you have nothing to fear as long as you are honest with me." His dark eyes burned her with searing intensity. "As long as I can trust you."

And then he held his arms out for his son.

CHAPTER FIVE

As JILLIAN relinquished Joe, her lips curved in a terrible self-mocking smile.

She had nothing to fear as long as she was honest with Vitt.

Which meant she had everything to fear because she could never be honest with him. She could never share her past with him, at least, not until she knew she was safe with him. Not until she knew she could trust him, because she'd be trusting him with her life.

It was that simple, because her secrets were that dangerous.

Look at what had happened to Katie. She'd shared the wrong thing with the wrong person and it'd killed her. Jillian couldn't make the same mistake. Not when Joe needed her so much.

But watching Vittorio hold her son—*their* son—Jillian marveled over the fact that Joe didn't cry or go rigid when Vitt took him from her. If anything Joe looked supremely comfortable, as well as extremely content in Vitt's arms. It was the strangest thing, too, because Joe was never relaxed with strangers, and even less with men, as he'd been around so few in his first year of life. Yet here he was, held securely against Vitt's broad chest, nonchalantly studying his chubby baby hands as if this sort of thing happened every day.

Remarkable.

Extraordinary.

Vittorio and Joseph already fit together. And they certainly looked like they belonged together. Both had the same dark glossy hair, although Joe's was baby-fine, and the same intensity of expression, even though Joe's eyes were blue and Vitt's amber brown.

"You've held babies before," Jillian said, trying to come to terms with her intensely ambivalent emotions. None of this was supposed to have happened. Being here, like this, was her worst fear and yet nothing terrible had happened yet. Maybe nothing terrible would.

"I have four nieces and three nephews and I've held each one within hours of his or her birth," he answered.

The overhead light played off Vitt's sculpted cheekbones, strong nose and angular jaw. On someone else the nose might have been too long, the bridge too broken, but on him it was perfect. Vitt's eyes, shaded by that dark slash of eyebrow, and the curve of his full sensual mouth, were almost too beautiful. He needed a nose of character, and he had one.

"Your brothers and sisters live close then?" she asked, forcing her attention from his arresting face to the conversation. She would soon meet his family, and tomorrow she'd be expected to live amongst them. Who would have thought any of this possible?

Vitt dipped his head, pressed a kiss to Joe's temple. "Two do. The other two are in different countries. But I'm always there when a baby arrives. Nothing is more important than family."

She swallowed hard, hit by a wave of loss. Those were the very same words her father used to say when she was a little girl.

His two favorite expressions had been "There's nothing

more important than family" and "Family is everything." Only he hadn't meant it.

Or maybe once he'd meant it, before he'd become consumed by greed and reckless ambition.

"I agree," she said softly, hating the awful emotions churning inside of her. Growing up she'd been a daddy's girl. He'd adored her and she'd loved him deeply in return. He'd been such a handsome, gregarious father. Outgoing. Charming. Full of jokes and laughter.

And then it all changed, virtually overnight. Her father, learning he'd be arrested and prosecuted for a long laundry list of crimes, cut a deal with the feds and confessed his part, and everyone else's role in organized crime. He saved himself but sold his crime family out.

He should have gone to prison. Because even fourteen years after her father confessed everything to the government, revealing everything he knew, and giving up everyone he'd known, he remained hated and hunted. He'd done the unthinkable. He'd turned on his people, and the mob had turned on him.

"Are you feeling all right?" Vitt asked, shifting Joe in his arms and scrutinizing her face.

She tried to smile but her eyes burned and acid rose up in her throat. Discovering at twelve that the father she'd loved more than life itself, was a thief, a traitor and a coward, had broken her heart. She'd lived with shame every day since. "I'm fine."

"Do you need some mineral water?"

Did she need mineral water? No. She needed forgiveness. She needed peace. She needed grace. And most of all she needed to forget she was Frank Giordano's daughter. But married to Vittorio, she could never forget. Married to Vittorio, she'd never be forgiven. "That sounds like a good idea."

He took a couple steps, pressed a button on the wall and in seconds the flight attendant appeared. "Yes, sir?"

"A mineral water, and some crackers or dry biscuits."

The flight attendant disappeared to fulfill the request and Vitt drew a chair from the table. "Come, Jill, sit, before you faint."

Perhaps if he knew the truth now, perhaps if she confessed everything right away, he'd possibly forgive her. Perhaps he'd even understand…because surely, he wouldn't really hurt her…she couldn't believe he would hurt her, not after their two weeks together in Bellagio….

Katie flashed to mind.

Had Katie thought the same thing about her new boyfriend, Marco, the handsome law student she'd wanted to bring home to meet Mom and Dad? Had Marco made her believe that she was safe? That he could be trusted? Had she opened up and shared everything, thinking she'd finally found someone who would protect her?

Her eyes burned gritty and pain rolled through Jillian, hard, heavy, sharp, obliterating everything but a desperate determination to survive. To survive at all costs. And to make sure her son did, too.

So even if Vittorio wouldn't hurt her, Jillian knew there could be no confessing, no pleading of innocence or begging for protection. Instead she'd play the role she'd agreed to play.

She gave Vittorio a calm, steady look, maintaining the steely façade she'd so carefully cultivated over the past year and a half. "Feeling guilty for treating me so callously earlier?" she asked, taking the offered chair.

He gazed down at her, black eyebrow arching slightly. "You practically wept with pleasure. I'm glad I could still satisfy you."

She crossed her legs, feeling the tenderness between. "Is

this how our relationship is going to be? You take what you want, when you want, and I comply?"

"But of course. You're my wife."

"Yet you make me feel like your whore."

The moment the words left her mouth she knew she'd said the wrong thing. She didn't even need Vittorio to speak to know she'd blundered. The ugly words hung there, suspended, between them.

Did she really feel like a whore?

Or had he merely possessed her the way he knew best— thoroughly and totally?

She opened her mouth to retract the words but was cut short by the appearance of the flight attendant who'd arrived with a small bottle of Perrier, a glass and a plate of crackers balanced on a silver tray. The attendant was pretty and professional and until now had been extremely poised, but her expression faltered as she sensed the mood.

The mood wasn't good.

The mood would be even worse when she left.

The pretty brunette placed the silver tray on the table near Jillian's elbow and then Vittorio transferred Joe into her arms. "Have Maria feed him dinner," he said, giving his son a comforting pat on the back. "Tell Maria we'll be sure to see him before he goes to bed."

And then they were alone again, and in the silence and stillness Jillian felt panic. She'd said too much, perhaps pushed him too far.

With a shaking hand she poured the bubbling water into her short crystal glass. The water tumbled and splashed.

"Whore?" Vittorio repeated softly.

She couldn't speak. She didn't know where to look. The atmosphere weighed heavily on her, thick and tense.

"That's a horrendous thing to say," he said.

She bent her head.

"Do not ever use that word again," he added furiously. "You're my son's mother and my wife and I will not have you demean yourself—or our relationship—in that manner."

Her stomach churned and Jillian swallowed compulsively, fighting the nausea. Relationship? What relationship? There was no relationship. He was the dictator, the emperor, the ruler. She was his prisoner, his captive, his slave. He had utter and complete control and she would be lucky to survive the next week, much less a month with him.

Jillian drew another breath, gulping fresh air into her lungs. "We do not have much of a relationship."

"Then we'll build one."

She averted her head, bit her lip, holding back the hot retort that burned within her.

"We'll start over," he added. "Tonight. Now. Let's begin again."

She looked at him swiftly, and the intensity in his expression burned her. She flashed back to their lovemaking earlier and she shivered at the flood of erotic memories. It'd been so hot between them. Scorching.

She felt scorched all over again by the heat and desire in his dark eyes. Her whole body responded, breasts aching, nipples tightening.

"Easier said than done," she answered huskily, mesmerized by the chemistry between them. That sizzling physical connection was always there, and it'd been that way from the beginning.

He smiled at her, a lazy, sexy, smoldering smile. "Why didn't you wear this to the ceremony?" he asked, reaching out to touch her silver top. "This would have been far more suitable," he added, letting his finger slip down, stroking from her shoulder over one peaked breast.

His finger lingered on the tight, taut nipple.

She inhaled quickly at the sharp stab of sensation between her thighs. "Not for me," she said.

"Why not?"

She took another quick breath. "I was angry. Little girls do not dream of marrying in secret, shameful ceremonies on airplanes."

"Shameful?"

"There were no witnesses. No family. No friends. Our son wasn't even there."

Vitt's hand fell away and his brow furrowed. "The goal wasn't to have a formal wedding, but to join us together. The goal was to protect Joseph and give him my name."

"I understand. But you asked me why I didn't wear something more festive, and I told you. I didn't feel good about our wedding. It didn't feel right."

He studied her for a long moment. "What would have felt better? A church wedding?"

"Yes."

"I didn't think you were religious."

"I was raised Catholic."

"You never told me."

"You never asked."

For a long moment he said nothing. Then he rose and paced the room silently for several minutes. Finally he paused and looked at her. "The vows are binding, regardless of where we said them."

"I understand."

He frowned at her, clearly uncomfortable. "But you were disappointed by our ceremony?"

She licked her lips. "Yes."

"You used the word *shameful.*"

"It just felt that way. It was so…rushed and hush-hush. We don't even have any pictures to show Joe when he's older. And I can't help but think that one day he'll want to know how we met, and what our wedding was like. How will he feel when we've no wedding photographs to show him?"

"That's ridiculous," Vittorio said, moving to the narrow sideboard to pour himself a neat shot of whiskey.

"I know. I'm just being foolish. Not all weddings are music and candles and flowers with your friends and family gathered around. And just because I imagined a certain kind of wedding doesn't mean I needed it. Joe is what's important. Joe should be our only concern—" She broke off as the jet suddenly shuddered in a pocket of turbulence.

Holding her breath, Jillian watched the water slosh wildly in her glass. For several moments the jet bounced, up, down, up, down, and the glass and bottle on the table rattled and danced toward the edge of the table, and then just as abruptly the turbulence ceased.

All was smooth again but Jillian's heart still raced. "I hate turbulence," she whispered, mouth dry.

"It's over."

"I know, but I still hate it."

"But if we didn't have turbulence, we'd never appreciate a smooth flight."

Their dinner was a strange meal, an almost painfully civilized meal, with Vittorio playing the role of attentive host. They discussed only safe topics—their mutual love of Turkey, favorite European cities, the stunning Dalmatian coast as if both were determined to put their best foot forward.

Could they really start fresh? Could they make their relationship work?

"We're not entirely incompatible," he said just moments later, as if he could read the emotions flitting over her face. "We both like sex and apparently still enjoy it together."

She felt as though he'd dashed cold water over her head. "And that's enough for you?"

His dark eyes met hers. "It wouldn't be, but we also have Joseph and we share responsibility for him."

And that was a terribly important responsibility. Jillian couldn't imagine anything else ever being so important. "Yes."

Vitt continued to hold her gaze. "Maybe another ceremony wouldn't be a bad idea. Maybe we should renew our vows at the chapel, and include our families. It would be good to have them on our side."

"They won't be now?"

"No. Not entirely."

"Why not?"

His mouth quirked. "You're not Sicilian."

They left the small elegant dining room for the staff room and found Joe happily playing with a set of toy cars with one of Vitt's bodyguards. Maria watched from an armchair nearby.

Looking at Joe it struck Jillian that in Vitt's world Joe was royalty. He was treated like a young prince. Protected. Pampered. He was the heir to his father's throne.

It was both a terrible truth and a heartbreaking reality. Joe was no longer her baby, her son. He'd already become Joseph d'Severano, inheriting all the power, wealth and control that accompanied the d'Severano name.

They stayed in the staff room for a few minutes and Vittorio talked to his bodyguards as if they were close friends. And maybe they were. Then conversation ended, he swung Joe into his arms and led the way to Jillian's room where the baby's travel cot had been set up.

Her tiny plush bedroom felt absolutely claustrophobic with Vittorio there. She did her best to pretend he wasn't watching every move she made. Acting as natural as possible, Jillian gave Joe a sponge bath and then dressed him in his footed, zippered sleeper for bed.

Vitt half smiled at Joe's bright blue footed pajamas. "Babies all over the world must wear these."

"Snug sleepwear is essential," she answered, fastening the little flap that covered the zipper head. "You don't want a baby to get tangled up or in trouble."

For a moment Vitt was silent, his powerful body still. "Was it hard raising him on your own?"

"Yes." She looked up at him, her expression rueful. "Especially in the beginning. I was so tired. So terribly sleep-deprived."

"Did you have anyone to help you?"

She shook her head. "No."

"Not even your mother?"

"I haven't seen her in years."

Vittorio watched as she expertly juggled Joe on her hip and prepared a bottle. "So there never were any worries? He's given you no fits? No scares?"

"I didn't say that. I worried about him every single night. For the first six months of his life I woke again and again during the night to make sure he was safe, to make sure he was breathing. I was absolutely terrified that when I closed my eyes, something would happen to him."

"You mean like SIDS?"

She nodded. "You probably think that's silly."

"Not at all." He reached out a hand and held it over Joe, as if bestowing a blessing. "One of my cousins lost his son to SIDS. It was devastating."

"I can't imagine anything more horrible," she said, holding Joe closer.

"Neither can I."

Jillian struggled to wrap her mind around such a tragedy. "Did your cousin have other children?"

"A little girl. She was almost three at the time." Vittorio

shook his head. "Christopher lost his life six months later. It was a very hard time in the family."

Jillian shivered at the grim direction their conversation had taken even as Vitt's words stirred a ghost of a memory.

Years ago a young Sicilian immigrant named Christopher had died in Detroit after her father accused him of double-crossing Detroit's crime family. Christopher claimed he was innocent, without any connections to organized crime, but it didn't save him. "How...how did he die?"

"He was shot."

"Where...where did it happen?"

"In the States."

"I know, but *where*?"

Vitt gave her a hard look. "Does it matter?"

She shook her head, but on the inside, she knew it did matter. It mattered too much.

"Were you serious about having us renew our vows in the d'Severano chapel?" she asked, suddenly desperate to change the subject.

"Yes." He suddenly smiled. "Provided you don't wear black again."

She couldn't resist his smile. "I won't. I promise."

"Good." He stood there another moment, tall, broad, imposing, considering her. "I suppose that means we better get you a proper dress."

"No—"

"Yes. If we're going to do this again, we better do it right, which means making sure it's the wedding every girl dreams of."

He left them then, excusing himself to get some work done, and after he'd gone, Jillian gave Joe a bottle and then tucked him into his travel cot.

But after putting Joe to bed, she didn't know what to do with herself. Was she supposed to join Vittorio? Was she sup-

posed to stay here? What did one do when you were married
but didn't feel like a wife?

She ended up staying with Joe. After dimming the lights
as much as she could, she curled up on the bed to watch him
sleep.

Awake, Joe stole her heart. Sleeping, Joe broke it. He looked
peaceful and impossibly sweet in his little cot with his arms
stretched out above his head. His soft skin was flushed pink
and his long eyelashes rested in dark crescents on his round
cheeks.

Hard to believe that just a year ago she was pregnant
with him. Hard to believe life could change so much in one
year. From birth to boy in just eleven months. Impossible.
Magical.

Although the early weeks of her pregnancy weren't magical. Those weeks were filled with panic, and denial.

In the beginning, she didn't believe she was pregnant. She
didn't feel pregnant. She didn't feel like anything, certainly
not as though she was carrying a child, much less Vittorio's
child.

There were times she nearly convinced herself that it wasn't
so. She hadn't changed her clothes size. She didn't have any
cravings. She didn't feel queasy or headachy or emotional. But
her period never came, and her breasts grew fuller, heavier,
and her flat, taut belly took a gently rounded shape. Finally
she went to the doctor and he told her everything she needed
to know. She was approximately seventeen weeks, the baby
had a strong heartbeat, development looked good, and unless
the doctor was mistaken, it appeared to be a boy.

A boy.

Another male d'Severano.

In that moment, lying there in the paper gown, with the
ultrasound machine at her side, she vowed her son would never
become his father. She vowed her baby would not become

her father, either. Her baby, this unborn son, would have a normal life. A happy life. A life as far from organized crime as possible.

For the rest of the pregnancy she felt secure, confident she'd made the right decision.

She felt so confident, she left Banff when she reached her seventh month, returning to the States so that when Joe was born he'd be American.

Jillian settled on Bellingham, Washington, a university town just across the border from Canada. She found a reasonably priced apartment close to Fair Haven, Bellingham's charming historic district filled with coffeehouses, bookstores and antiques shops.

Joe's birth was uncomplicated and she returned to her apartment ready for the next phase of her life.

But then fate intervened.

Just a month after Joe's birth, Jillian was pushing him in his stroller, enjoying the May sunshine when she bumped into a woman she'd worked with in Istanbul. The woman had neither been a friend nor foe, just an acquaintance, but they both exclaimed at the amazing coincidence of meeting like this, so far from Turkey, in the most northwest corner of the United States.

Jillian had initially been alarmed by the meeting but realized the woman knew nothing about her relationship with Vittorio and therefore would have no stories to tell.

Jillian was wrong.

Within a week of bumping into her former colleague, Jillian received the first phone call from Vittorio. He'd heard about the baby. He wanted to know if the baby was his.

She told him no.

But he persisted, demanded a DNA test.

She ran.

He chased.

And that began the ten months of cat-and-mouse games.

If she hadn't bumped into that woman from the Ciragan Palace Hotel, Vittorio might never have found out about their son.

That had been her hope. That had been her plan.

The jet's bedroom door noiselessly opened and Vittorio stood in the doorway, his face shadowy in the dim lighting. "He's asleep?" Vitt asked quietly.

"Yes."

"Then come. Maria will be here any moment to spend the night with him—"

"I don't want to leave him!" she whispered.

"He'll be fine."

"Vitt, please. I've never slept away from him—"

"You'll have to sooner or later."

She glanced down at her baby in his blue pajamas. Her heart ached. "But not yet."

He studied her a moment, his expression inscrutable. "That's fine. We'll both sleep here then."

She'd thought at first he was joking—Vittorio was a man who loved his creature comforts—but it turned out he was serious, and left to go to his room to change into pajamas.

While Vittorio was gone, she slipped into the only nightgown she owned, a pink floral-sprigged flannel gown with a ruffled neckline, buttons down the front, and a long hem. It'd been a perfect gown for breast-feeding but it was far from glamorous or sexy.

Jillian brushed her teeth quickly and was just scooting into bed when Vittorio returned in dark gray pajama pants and a black silk robe. He glanced at her huddled in the bed and smiled briefly before turning out the light.

Nervously she turned on her side to face Joe's cot. With her eyes closed, she listened to Vitt approach, her ears straining to catch every sound he made from his heavy footsteps to the tug on the covers to the soft thud of his robe falling to the floor.

She felt the bed give on his side, felt the covers tug and then the warmth of his powerful body settle next to hers.

For a moment she couldn't breathe. She'd dreamed of this, of him, so many times since she'd run away from his villa in Bellagio, wanting so badly what she couldn't have.

Because she couldn't have him. It wasn't sane. He posed danger to her at every level.

But what was that expression? The heart wants what the heart wants?

And her heart had wanted him. Her heart had always wanted him.

"You can breathe," he said quietly, his voice pitched so only she could hear.

"I am."

"Barely."

She smiled in the dark even as her chest ached with fierce emotion. This was the Vittorio she'd wanted. This was the man who'd made her feel extraordinarily loved. "You don't need to worry about me," she whispered.

"Oh, but I think I do." His arm slid around her and he pulled her close against him. She felt his lips brush the back of her head. "Now relax. Sleep. Tomorrow will be here before you know it."

Miraculously, she did sleep. She must have drifted off right away because the next time she stirred, she was alone in the bed. Frowning, Jillian glanced at the clock on the narrow bedside table. Six hours had passed since she'd closed her eyes. Amazing because she never slept deeply, not anymore.

A soft knock sounded on the door and then the door opened. Maria entered with a tray. "Signor sent you coffee and juice and a breakfast pastry. He thought you might want something to eat before we land."

Jillian sat up, glanced at Joe who was stirring in his cot. "We're landing soon?"

Maria nodded and placed the tray next to Jillian on the bed. "In less than an hour."

Maria took Joe to the staff room to feed and dress him so that Jillian could have her coffee and dress in privacy.

Privacy felt like a luxury, Jillian thought as she nibbled on the breakfast roll between sips of coffee. But that was Vittorio's way—affluence, luxury, comfort. She'd forgotten just how posh his lifestyle was. She'd forgotten how decadent she'd felt in Bellagio in his lakeside villa with the stunning views of the mountains.

Dressed, she headed for the main cabin where Vittorio waited for her. "Did you sleep okay?" he asked her as she took a seat in one of the honey leather chairs opposite his.

"I did. Better than I have in months. Thank you."

"I didn't remember you being such a restless sleeper," he said, his long black eyelashes dropping to conceal his eyes. "You kicked and thrashed half of the night."

"Is that why you left so early this morning?"

"I stayed with you all night, only leaving so that I could have Maria bring you breakfast."

She flushed. "I didn't know."

"Yes. Apparently there's a great deal you don't know." He paused, studied her thoughtfully. "Just as there are many things I need to understand about you."

CHAPTER SIX

JILLIAN did not ask what he meant and Maria arrived with Joe just as the seat belt sign flashed on.

Jillian gratefully took Joe onto her lap and wrapped her arms around him. Blinding sunlight poured through the jet windows as the Boeing 737 dropped lower and lower until the jet's wheels finally touched ground. Once on the runway, she dropped a kiss on the top of her son's head, happy they'd landed safely.

As she kissed him, his cloud of soft black hair tickled her nose and she breathed in his sweet baby scent.

Feeling Vittorio's gaze, she glanced up, her eyes locking with his. He was sitting across the aisle from her and yet she could practically feel him. He had such a strong presence, a very physical energy that made her body hum even now.

"You have shadows under your eyes," he said.

"I shouldn't. I actually slept well last night."

"It sounds like you don't get a lot of sleep."

She shifted Joe in her arms. "Babies wake up a lot at night. And then of course, there's my need to check on him."

"You should have had more help with him."

Jillian knew what he was really saying—that if she'd come to him, she would have had help, she wouldn't have had to struggle on her own.

"It will be easier for you to sleep when Joseph is in his

own crib, in his own room," he added. "And he does have his own room at my house. There's space for Maria to sleep in the nursery should we need her to—"

"I like having Joe close at night," she interrupted. "I can't imagine not having him there."

"And I can't imagine making love to my wife if my son is present." His voice was firm, decisive. "Joseph will be fine in his own room. Trust me."

"So you've had a baby before?" she flashed, angered that he'd again start making decisions not just for Joe, but for her.

"No. But I can read a how-to-raise-a-baby book just as well as you, and I do have all those nieces and nephews."

She bit her lip to keep from replying sharply, and still struggling with her temper, turned her head to look out the window. It was a gorgeous clear morning. The sun was still rising and the sky stretched overhead, a lucid, cloudless blue. "You said I looked tired," she said. "Should I put some makeup on?"

"That's not necessary. You look fine. Just be yourself."

Ah, there was the dilemma. After falling into Vittorio's arms after so many months of running from him and fearing him, Jillian didn't even know who she was anymore. "As if it were that easy."

"It's not?"

Her lips twisted wryly. "No."

"Why not?"

She wanted to tell him she'd lived too many different lives in too many places. She wanted to share that more than once she'd sat frozen in a classroom or the cafeteria, terrified to open her mouth in the event she said the wrong thing. In the event she'd forgotten her part.

Lee. Carol. Anne. Jillian.

"Why isn't it?" Vitt asked, repeating his question.

She turned toward him, seeing his black tailored trousers,

the white shirt, the expensive black blazer. But then everything about him oozed money, success. "You've always lived in one place, and been raised around the same people. You've never had to be anyone but Vittorio d'Severano. It was different for me."

"You moved a lot when you were growing up?"

"Yes."

"Your father was in the military?"

She nearly laughed. Her father in the service? Her father an honorable man? *"No."*

"What did he do?"

Lied. Cheated. Backstabbed. But she couldn't say that. "Business. Sales. Things like that."

The jet had stopped taxiing to park at a small executive terminal.

"You never wanted to work with him?" Vitt asked, ignoring his flight crew as they prepared the aircraft for deplaning.

"No." She felt Joe wiggle on her lap, his small body warm and compact against hers and she glanced down at him, thinking there was so much she wanted for him, so much she wanted to give him if only she had the chance.

"What about you?" she asked Vitt as he unbuckled his seat belt and got to his feet. "Did your father expect you to go to work for him?"

Vitt towered above her, his expression somber. For a long moment he was silent before he gave his head a brief shake. "No. In fact, the opposite was true. He begged me to go somewhere else, do something different, but I wouldn't."

Her forehead furrowed. "Why not?"

Vitt shrugged as he reached for Joe and swung him into his arms. "I was a d'Severano. And my father needed me."

The door opened and sunlight filled the front cabin. Vittorio waited at the head of the stairs for Jillian before descending the staircase. Jillian descended more slowly, cautious in her high heels. She actually felt pulled together this morning in her brown sheath dress and chocolate suede pumps. All she needed was a great pair of sunglasses and she could pretend she was a movie star.

Vittorio's hand was on the small of her back as they started across the tarmac. A line of black town cars waited, each with tinted glass. Vittorio almost always traveled with escorts and bodyguards. He was rich. And he was a d'Severano. Therefore he could never be too careful.

They were nearly to the cars when a door opened on one of the black sedans. A slim blonde woman emerged.

Vittorio stopped in his tracks, his expression hardening. "She never listens," he said, shaking his head. "I told her not to come."

Jillian shot a swift glance at the sophisticated blonde in the pale blue suit. "Who is she?"

He sighed. "My mother."

Jillian stiffened. "Your mother?"

"She's what I like to call an independent thinker."

Until this moment, Jillian had been almost excited about arriving in Catania. She enjoyed travel and usually loved the moment she stepped off an airplane, thrilled by the sense of freedom and possibilities that came from being somewhere new. Every place had a different feel and unique energy. But all sense of wonder abruptly disappeared.

Vittorio's hand remained on her back. "This might be rough," he said. "But just remind yourself that you will survive."

Her heart fell. His mother sounded awful. "You're telling me her bark is worse than her bite?"

"No." His full sensual mouth twisted, dark eyes narrowed. "I'm telling you that no one yet has died from her bite."

"And that is really not very comforting."

He smiled suddenly, dark eyes glinting with humor before

he dropped a kiss on her lips. "Oh, she also thinks we're radiantly happy, and completely in love. Can you manage that?"

She pressed her lips together, mouth tingling from his brief kiss. She wished he'd kiss her again. There was something dangerously addictive about his mouth. "I'll try."

He smiled again. "Good luck." And then they were walking once more, closing the distance between them and the waiting cars.

Jillian's high heels made faint clicking sounds on the tarmac but her gaze was fixed on Vittorio's mother. She looked youthful, even glamorous in her ice-blue suit trimmed in a blue, aqua and cream braid, and matching high heels the same color. She wore her hair in a loose chignon, a style which highlighted her elegant features.

Jillian stood back as Vitt embraced her warmly and then introduced her to his son. How could this woman be Vitt's mother?

But Vitt was turning to Jillian now, and extending a hand. "*Madre*, this is my wife, Jill," he said, drawing Jillian all the way forward. "Jill, my mother, Theresa d'Severano."

Up close Jillian could see that Theresa d'Severano wasn't quite as young as Jillian had first thought, but neither did she look like a woman in her mid-fifties. Jillian didn't know if it was genetics or technology, but Theresa could have easily passed for Vitt's sister.

Suddenly Jillian didn't feel as pulled together as she had just a few minutes ago and wished she'd taken the time to put on a little makeup before stepping off the plane. But it was too late for lipstick. All she could do was make the best impression possible. Summoning her confidence as well as a warm smile, Jillian extended her hand. "It's a pleasure to meet you, Mrs. d'Severano."

Theresa gave her a long, level look, the expression in her

blue eyes cool. She ignored Jillian's hand. "You're the woman that trapped Vittorio."

So that's what they think happened. Vittorio, the adored oldest son and the apple of his mother's eye, had been ensnared by a villainous American gold digger. Jillian only wished she was half as sneaky and manipulative as his family imagined.

She dropped her hand and struggled to keep her smile. "I've heard a lot about you."

His mother's smile turned positively glacial. "Odd. I never heard a word about you."

Vittorio gestured toward the car. "Mother, why don't we continue our conversation on the drive home?" he suggested pleasantly even though his mouth was set hard.

His mother patted his arm. "Why don't you and the baby take one car, and Jill and I will take another? This way she and I can spend a little bit of time getting to know each other."

Jillian swallowed, thinking it was one of the worst ideas she'd ever heard but she couldn't very well say that.

"Jill?" Vitt said, looking at her. "What do you prefer?"

It was good of him to give her a choice. It sounded like the right thing to say, but clearly he didn't understand that Jillian couldn't refuse his mother's suggestion without appearing ungracious. She forced a smile. "I'd love to ride with your mother," she said. "Sounds like fun."

"It's probably a good idea," he agreed smoothly. "This way you'll have an ally on your side before you meet the rest of the family."

Jillian then had no choice but to follow his mother into her black sedan, even as her gaze strayed to her baby in Vitt's arms. She should be with Vitt and Joe. She should be traveling with them, not Vitt's mom.

"Have you ever been to Sicily?" Theresa asked as they each took position on opposite ends of the leather seat.

The chauffeur started the car and pulled away from the other sedans. Jillian forced herself to focus on Vitt's mother. The interior of the car was dark and cool and she needed a moment for her eyes to adjust after the bright morning sunlight. "No. I'm sorry I haven't."

Theresa tapped her nails on the door's metal handle. "Is your family Sicilian?"

"No."

"Italian?"

Her father was, yes, but she couldn't tell Theresa that. "German and Scottish, with a dab of Irish and a hint of French."

His mother regarded her steadily, her focus sharp. "You've been to Bellagio."

"Yes."

"The villa is beautiful."

"Extraordinary."

"Did you drive his Lamborghini?"

"No, the Ferrari."

"It's a nice life, isn't it? The cars, the houses, expensive jewelry."

They were back to the perception that Jillian was a gold digger. Jillian didn't know whether she should laugh or cry. She cared about many things, but money wasn't one of them. "You do your Vittorio a disservice. He's brilliant, devastatingly attractive and without a doubt, the most complex man I've ever met."

"But the money *is* nice."

Jillian kept her expression pleasant. "If I wanted a rich husband, I could have had a rich husband without the complications of a difficult family."

Theresa stiffened, her eyes narrowing as she fell silent.

Jillian realized she'd probably made a gross tactical error, but there was no going back now. All she could do was try to hold her own, push on and see this brutal conversation to the end. "But my family is no better," she said awkwardly, trying to make amends. "They don't approve of Vitt any more than you approve of me."

"You make it sound like you and Vittorio are two star-crossed lovers."

She shrugged lightly. "I suppose there are shades of Romeo and Juliet in our story, but hopefully without the tragic ending."

"Why don't your parents approve of Vittorio?"

Ah, Theresa didn't like that, did she? "They're aware that he and I come from different backgrounds, and perhaps have different values."

Theresa sat very still, her hands motionless in her lap. "Different values?"

"As you just pointed out, I'm neither Sicilian or Italian, and although I was raised Catholic, I rarely go to Mass now and yet from what I understand, your family is quite devout."

"So why did he marry you?"

"Love."

Theresa stared at her for the longest moment before smiling mockingly. "And you actually expect me to believe any of that drivel?"

Jillian opened her mouth to protest, but Theresa leaned toward Jillian and calmly, ruthlessly continued, "You don't think I have my own connections? You don't think I ask questions? I know you only just got married. And I know you didn't want to marry my son—you only married him to keep your son."

Jillian bit down into her lip, stunned.

But Theresa wasn't done yet. Her cool blue gaze swept Jillian's ashen face. "You can play whatever game you want to play with Vittorio, Jill, but don't play games with me." She paused, before bluntly saying, "Your entire relationship is a sham, isn't it?"

"No."

"It seems like one to me—"

"But it's not your relationship. It's mine. I adore Vittorio. I always have."

"So why am I only meeting you now, a year after my grandson's birth?"

Jillian sat tall, her chin tilted up. "I don't see how that is any of your business."

"I'm his mother!"

"And I'm his wife."

The rest of the trip passed in tense silence. Twenty-five minutes after leaving Catania, they reached Vittorio's hometown of Paterno. Catania, Sicily's second largest city, was crowded and noisy, a sprawling urban city with a questionable reputation, whereas small, serene Paterno lay surrounded by citrus orchards with the protective tower and walls of the d'Severano family's Norman castle standing guard.

It was a bright, clear morning with a stunning blue sky and the drive from the outskirts of Paterno to the castle entrance provided breathtaking views of both Mt Etna and the Simeto Valley.

Jillian and Theresa arrived first at the castle and were just stepping from their car, smoothing skirts and adjusting hemlines without once looking at each other, when the second black sedan arrived. Emerging from the back of his sedan, Vitt lifted Joseph out and then joined his mother and Jillian before the stone steps that led to the castle's massive front doors.

"How was the drive?" he asked, glancing from his mother's stony expression to the tight press of Jillian's lips.

"Good," Jillian said, her voice cracking.

"Not my choice of words, but we're both here, aren't we?" his mother retorted, one of her elegant winged eyebrows arching higher before turning around and walking away, her thin back ramrod-straight.

Vittorio watched his mother climb the pale stone stairs before turning back to Jill. "Sounds like an interesting trip," he said drily, eyes glinting again.

Of course he'd find his mother amusing. "It was," she agreed, taking Joe from Vitt and giving him a kiss.

"Did she ask a lot of questions?"

"Yes."

"Was she direct?"

"As well as rude." She took a deep breath, shook her head. "She doesn't like me at all."

"She doesn't know you."

"Well, she certainly doesn't think we should be together."

"You felt the same way yesterday," he retorted with a smile. "Now enough about my mother. Let me show you and Joseph around your new home."

From the immense twelfth-century walls, Jillian had imagined the interior would be dark and severe. Instead the castle had the feel of an airy Mediterranean villa. Everything was light and bright, walls and upholstery and floors all finished in cool, calming shades of white, sea-foam green and ethereal blue.

Because Joe was growing tired, Vittorio kept the tour brief, but Jillian didn't need a lot of description to be dazzled by Vitt's home. There was a sensual beauty to his castle, a warmth that permeated the old stones, thick walls and high-ceilinged rooms.

As they climbed stairs into towers, crossed terraces to view private gardens, Jillian caught whiffs of the heady perfume from the flowering citrus groves below the castle and felt the warmth of the gentle April sunshine as it cascaded over the weathered rock walls and surfaces.

Returning to the impressive staircase, they arrived on the third floor consisting of Vitt's suite of rooms and the newly renovated nursery for their son.

Jillian paused inside the nursery door, eyes widening at the charming ocean theme. The airy, spacious nursery had a wall of windows flooding the carpeted floor with sunshine and bright light reflected off the walls painted with fanciful fish. "You did all this for Joe?"

"Why wouldn't I?"

"I mean, it's just so perfect…."

"Did you think I wouldn't provide for my son?"

"No! Of course not." She shifted Joe in her arms. "I've never once questioned your desire or ability to provide for Joe. I know you could give him anything."

"As long as it's material."

She fell silent, realizing she'd said the wrong thing.

"Because that's all I'm good for," he added in the same velvet soft tone. "Money. Connections. Prestige."

She blushed. "You're putting words in my mouth," she protested huskily, setting a wiggling Joe on his feet. The baby had spotted the sapphire dolphin rocking horse in the corner and was toddling fast toward the dolphin to climb on its back.

"But isn't the money and prestige part true? You wanted me, enjoyed me, until you discovered I wasn't your perfect prince and then you ran from me, disappearing without a word."

"I'm sorry. Forgive me."

"Apology not accepted."

"Please, Vitt."

"Please, what? This nursery has sat here empty for ten months. For ten months I searched for you, spending hundreds of thousands of dollars hiring investigators and detectives and following up on every lead possible. For ten months I waited to meet my son." He leaned against one of the bookcases flanking the tall paned glass windows, his strong profile silhouetted by the bright sunlight. "And every day I thought, the only reason my son isn't here, is because you, Jill Smith, wouldn't let him."

She felt her face grow hot. Put like that, she was a horrible person. But he didn't know the whole story, and as much as she wanted to tell him, she didn't think she could. At least not yet. At least, not until she knew for a fact that she could trust him. "I am sorry, Vittorio."

He made a rough disgusted sound. "Let's be honest. You're not sorry you kept Joseph from me. You're sorry I found you. Only you're too much a coward to admit it."

Jillian's face burned with shame, because Vittorio was right. She was a coward. A pathetic coward. But if it meant she could protect Joe, and remain with Joe, then she'd do whatever she had to. "Maybe," she admitted softly.

"Why did you do it, Jill? Why keep my son from me? You had to know I'd be good to him. You had to know I'd love him. I always treated you well. You trusted me, too, and when you slept, you always slept close to me, pressed to my side."

She hated how her eyes suddenly felt gritty and dry. She hated that she could still remember how she'd felt with him, too. Loved. Safe. So very secure. "That was before," she answered faintly.

"Before?" he repeated, as if amused. Faint creases appeared at the corner of his eyes.

"Yes."

"Before what?"

He was still smiling but she realized she'd misread him. He wasn't amused. He was far from amused.

Jillian held her breath, the air bottled in her lungs, aware that she was walking on thin ice and she had no idea how to extract herself.

But Vittorio wasn't waiting for the ice to crack. He was going to shatter it himself. The corner of his mouth lifted. "Before you invented a world where I played the villain?"

She stared across the room at him. "I invented nothing. I dreamed up nothing. It's all there, Vittorio. It's all there on the internet."

"It's not true."

"There are dozens of stories and articles, Vitt."

"And you believe everything you read on the internet?"

"Not always."

"But you believed this...whatever it was you read about me?"

"Why would people lie?"

He studied her with his dark, fathomless eyes, the sensual curve of his mouth making her feel hurt and longing and desire and pain.

She'd loved his mouth, loved the shape of that mouth and everything it made her feel—physically, emotionally. He'd always made her feel so much and until she'd discovered the truth about him, it'd been so good. She'd felt so good. After so many years she'd felt whole. And then the truth emerged and she shattered all over again.

"Why indeed?" he mocked.

She waited for him to say something else. Waited for him to explain or defend or help her make sense of this life of his. He didn't.

She balled her hands into fists. "So now's your chance. Tell me. Tell me the truth. Are you...?"

"Am I what?"

"You know."

His head tipped to the side. "Do you realize you're in danger of sounding obsessive?"

His mockery infuriated her. "This is serious," she snapped.

"You've watched too many Hollywood movies."

"I know what I know."

"And just what do you know, *Jill*? You seem to be an expert on masquerades and games and charades."

She shivered at his tone. What if he knew more than she thought he did? What if he knew what she hadn't wanted him to know?

What then?

And what would he do with the information?

But she wouldn't let herself go there, not now, not yet. Instead she locked her knees for courage. "I know Sicily has a long, complicated history with the mafia. I know that the Italian government has tried for years to rid Sicily of the mafia but without great success."

"And why do you think?" he asked, watching her from beneath his thickly fringed lashes.

"Because by all reports, the mafia leaders are very clever."

He held her gaze, his dark eyes searching hers. "Or perhaps the mafia does not exist."

So that's how he wanted to do this. They were to pretend she was misinformed, confused, off base.

He wanted her to believe the mafia didn't exist. He was asking her to accept that organized crime was a Hollywood fabrication. He was asking the impossible.

She wasn't that girl. She knew better. She knew the truth.

Jillian had lived through things, experienced things most people only read about in books or watched on TV. Her father, while presenting a charming face to the world, had the callous heart of a killer. Her *father*.

"Is that what you want me to believe?" she choked.

"You must have had one miserable childhood, because you're completely incapable of trusting another."

"I'm completely incapable of trusting you."

"Just me?"

"Just you," she retorted, even though it was a lie. She didn't trust many people. She certainly didn't trust powerful men and still didn't know why she'd decided to trust Vitt nearly two years ago.

"Why?"

"You know why."

"The *Mafioso* thing again?" he asked, sounding bored.

"Yes, that. It's never gone away. It will never go away—"

"Which is a dilemma, isn't it? Because now you're my wife. Married to the mob. What will you do?"

"I don't know," she answered, throwing her head back, temper blazing even as tears shimmered in her eyes. "None of this was supposed to happen. It's the worst thing that could have happened."

"Why?"

"Because it'd kill me, Vitt, it would if my son grew up and became someone like you."

CHAPTER SEVEN

IT'D kill me if my son grew up and became someone like you.

It'd been two hours since Jillian had said the words but they still echoed in Vitt's head.

It would kill her if her son were like him…it would kill her…

Unbelievably hurtful words, especially considering they came from the mother of his child.

The worst of it was that she didn't know him. She couldn't seem to see who he really was. But he wasn't used to explaining himself, or opening his family or life to scrutiny.

Frankly, he didn't care what people thought of him. And he answered to no one.

Because no one could touch him, although in the beginning everyone had tried. Prime ministers, presidents, parliaments, governments. Police in every country.

But what could they do to him? To the d'Severano family? What crime had he committed? What crime could they pin on his father? None.

Yet Vittorio was still feared, hated, loved and loathed. He didn't even try to justify his behavior, or contradict the rumors or lies anymore. It was a waste of time, a waste of energy. Life was short. He would love it.

And yet Jill's words had struck a nerve. A very sensitive

nerve. Because he was not a bad man, or an evil man, or a violent man. He, like his father, had spent his life righting past wrongs, as well as building new relationships with people, businesses, world leaders.

He did have family members who were connected to the mafia, but he wasn't one of them. Nor was his father. Nor would his son be.

Because you didn't have to be crooked to be powerful. And you didn't have to resort to pressure or violence to be influential. His success stemmed directly from his work ethic, his focus and his value system.

So let Jill Smith, the twenty-six year old American he'd just made his wife, say what she wanted. He knew the truth. He knew who he was. He knew what he was.

But in his heart, her words did hurt.

Jillian held Joe's hand as they walked in the rose garden after his afternoon nap. He toddled happily from bush to bush, savoring the sunshine and colorful petals and sweet scent of the antique roses.

Jillian talked to him and crouched down to help him smell different blossoms but her insides churned, her heart felt heavy.

She'd said something awful to Vitt earlier and she couldn't forget what she'd said, or Vitt's expression as she'd said it.

It'd kill me if he were to grow up and become like you....
Such cruel, hurtful words.

But she hadn't meant to hurt him. She was just being honest. Just sharing her fear.

Her father's crimes still horrified her, and she believed more than ever that the world needed good people. The world needed men who were strong. Courageous.

Compassionate.

That's the kind of man she wanted Joe to be one day. That's

the kind of man she'd thought Vitt was. Until she'd looked the d'Severanos up on Google ánd found out the truth.

Crouching next to a pink rosebush, Jillian held a soft open flower up for Joe to smell it. He pressed his face into the petals. "Mmm," he said.

"Smells good, doesn't it?" she said.

He smiled up at her, his eyes deeply blue, his expression trusting.

Her heart ached all over again. She owed Vittorio an apology. She needed to let him know she'd been wrong to say something so unkind, especially in front of their son. Hopefully she could talk to him before they met his family for dinner. She wouldn't feel better until she apologized.

Footsteps sounded on the walk and Jillian looked up to see Maria approach.

"Is it time for dinner already?" Jillian asked.

Maria shook her head. "Signor sent me to tell you that he is not eating at home tonight. He said that he'll have dinner sent to you and Joe in your suite, and that you'll meet his family tomorrow."

Jillian straightened. "Did he say when he'd be back?"

The nanny shook her head. "No. But he may not return tonight. It's possible he'll remain in Catania until tomorrow."

Jillian's heart fell. "What?"

"He has a big apartment there, not far from his office. I've never seen it but I've heard that it's at the top of a building and very nice. In English I think you call it a penthouse." Maria bobbed her head and then excused herself, returning to the house.

For a moment Jillian just watched Maria walk and then driven by some dark, murky emotion, Jillian scooped up Joe and chased after Maria. "Is Signor still here?" she asked, catching up with Maria just inside the door.

The castle felt cool and shadowy after the afternoon sun.

"I think so," Maria answered. "He might even still be up-stairs."

Jillian left Joe with Maria and dashed up the stairs, her high heels tapping against the polished stone floor. She reached their bedroom just as Vittorio was turning off the light.

"Where are you going?" she asked breathlessly.

"To Catania. I have some business to take care of."

"You're going to your office?"

"Does it matter?"

She searched his dark eyes yet his expression was so completely shuttered she couldn't see what he was thinking. "Yes."

"I will be going to my office, yes, among other places."

"Do you conduct most of your meetings at the office?"

"Not necessarily." He gazed down at her, lips curling in a sardonic smile. "Worried that I'll be conducting illicit business in dark alleys, Jill?"

"No."

There was a moment of tense silence before Vittorio shook his head. "And you call me a liar." His smile grew, his dark eyes glittering with anger. "But I don't have time for this, as interesting as it is. Have a good night. Don't wait up for me. I'm not sure when I'll return."

"You're not coming back tonight?"

"I don't know. Haven't decided."

"Vitt," she protested, reaching out to touch his coat sleeve.

He glanced down at her hand resting on his dark coat and then into her face. "Don't even try to pretend that you'll miss me, Jill."

She flushed, her cheeks burning with heat. "It's only our first night here. I don't know anyone. I barely know my way around."

"You have our son. You know Maria. That should be

enough." He paused, considered her. "It has to be enough. Because that's all you really have."

She felt as if he'd slapped her. Her eyes watered. Her blush deepened, her skin burning from her chest to her brow. "You don't need to be cruel."

"I see. You can say whatever you want, but I have to play nice?"

"I'm sorry about earlier—"

"No you're not. You're never sorry. You're spoiled and self-ish and incredibly self-centered. And since you're so big on the truth, let me tell you the truth. You are the absolute last woman in the world I would have picked to be my wife."

"You didn't used to think that—"

"Because I didn't know you. But I do now."

She buried her hands behind her back as tears filled her eyes, and then pressed her lips together to keep them from trembling.

"Truth hurts," he said bitterly, "doesn't it?"

"I never meant to hurt you," she said, "but you're enjoying being cruel."

"I don't enjoy being cruel. But I will give it to you straight. This isn't the kind of marriage I envisioned, just as you aren't the kind of wife I wanted. But it doesn't matter now. I deal in reality, not in fantasy or fairy tales. We slept together. You became pregnant. I accept my responsibility."

How could he be so cold when her heart felt as though it were on fire? "How good of you," she murmured. "How very mature."

He shrugged. "There's no love here between us. There never will be, at least, not now. So we will focus on our son. We'll sleep together on occasion. Have sex when the mood strikes. Put on a good face in front of my family. But that's it. Understand? That's all you'll get from me, and that's all I want from you."

She blinked, looked away, battled to keep control because it felt like he was taking a knife to her, again and again. "Stop it."

"Stop what?"

"Torturing me."

"Torturing you is the last thing on my mind. I'm merely clarifying our relationship, defining the parameters before we have to function in front of my family and the rest of the world."

"And those parameters?"

"You belong to me in the bedroom. The rest of your life is your own."

"I am not an object."

"Agreed. You are my wife. You will fulfill your conjugal duties. But you are free to shop, and travel, and make female friends of your choosing."

"Female?" she flashed, glancing up at him, tears still matting her lashes.

"Only female. I will tear apart any man that comes within ten feet of you. You are my wife. You are a d'Severano. You'd best remember that."

"You must enjoy having so much power when I have none."

"You don't need power. You have me."

"To think for me, speak for me and force me to lie in your bed!"

"I shall never need force to get you into my bed. I proved that point yesterday. But if you'd care for a refresher—"

"Not necessary, but thank you."

He smiled mockingly and reached for his tie, loosening it slightly. "Maybe I do have time for a quickie."

"No."

"No?"

The pale green bedroom walls felt as though they were

about to close in. "I mean, not like this. Not a quickie. It won't be right."

"And what would be right? Romance? Candles? Soft music in the background?"

"You're so angry."

"I am."

She trembled inwardly, not out of fear, but shock and pain. She didn't want him angry with her, not like this, not when they'd once been so happy together. Maybe they only had two weeks, but those two weeks had been the happiest of her life and she wondered if they could maybe be happy again. If they could just sort out their past. If they could just figure out the future. How they'd do that, she didn't know, but she had to have hope. Had to believe they could make a real marriage out of this, otherwise, how did one live in a loveless marriage? How did one live with so much? How would she survive the next seventeen years?

"I don't want you angry, Vittorio. And I do want to fix this…make amends. I don't know how yet, but will you at least let me try?"

For an endless stretch of time he said nothing. Then he reached out to her, his palm sliding down her neck, his fingers curving to fit her nape with his thumb at her earlobe. "And how would you do that?" he murmured huskily, stroking the hollow beneath her earlobe.

Her pulse leaped at his touch. She licked her lips as her mouth dried. "I would try to remind you that we can be good together. That we could be happy."

"Where?"

"Anywhere."

His dark eyes held hers, the brown irises hot, glowing with tiny shards of amber and gold. "Does that include the bedroom?"

"Yes."

"You're offering me your body."

"Yes," she answered, her voice low.

His dark eyes flared with heat and immediate carnal desire. "And what will you do for me when I am in your bed?"

He was binding her heart with a chain. "Whatever it is you want your wife to do."

Vitt's hand slid down her neck to her collarbone and then over the middle of her chest, into the V between her breasts. "Anything I want?"

His hand was warm, so warm on her chest. Her breasts swelled, heavy, her nipples hardening. "You said I was to be obedient."

"What a good wife you intend to be," he taunted, clasping her jaw in both his hands, lifting her face to his. He held her face up, examining every inch as if she were a beautiful thing he'd bought at market and he was now eager to inspect his purchase. After an endless, scorching scrutiny, he dipped his head, covered her lips with his, and kissed her deeply. His tongue probed her mouth, tasting, savoring the softness and heat within.

Jillian shuddered, heat exploding in her middle, coursing through her veins.

His tongue stroked the inside of her lower lip, flaming nerve endings everywhere. His teeth, straight, white, nipped at her lip and heat flared from her womb to her limbs.

She was melting, dissolving in his hands.

And then he drew her tongue into his mouth and sucked the tip, the sucking sensation tight and rhythmic, reminding her of his body thrusting into hers, making her back arch, her hips tilt, her body shaping to his.

His hands slid up into her hair, his fingers dragging across her scalp. He was waking her, warming her, fanning the empty aching need.

And still he kissed her, his knee parting her thighs, pressing up against her sensitive flesh and she grew hot, wet, needy in response.

Jillian slid her hands up his chest, feeling his heart beat beneath her hands as she kissed him back, her skin hot and sensitive, her body taut with desire.

Long moments passed and then he lifted his head. He gazed down into her eyes a long moment and stroked her flushed, warm cheek. "I think I will claim what is mine."

He unzipped her dress and peeled it off over her head before unhooking her bra and casting it on top of the discarded dress. Her panties followed along with her slim chocolate heels.

Once he had her naked, he dropped her not all that gently onto the enormous bed. With his dark gaze fixed on her, he shed his own clothes and then joined her on the bed, pushing her back to straddle her hips.

This time there was no foreplay. This was a lesson in ownership, a display of possession. He possessed her, too, stretching her out beneath him, his hands holding her wrists down above her head, his chest crushing her full breasts, his strong thighs holding her slim thighs apart as he entered her, and then filled her, driving deep into her body, again and again.

She was warm and slick, his shaft thick and hard, and he stroked her relentlessly, creating a maddening friction that was so pleasurable it almost caused pain.

With each of his thrusts she tightened her inner muscles around him, wanting to hold him, wanting to keep him with her in an attempt to meet that wonderful and yet terrible need he created.

As he filled her, her head spun, and her senses swam with the dizzying pleasure of it all. Making love to him had always made her emotions feel wildly out of control. Today was no different. She craved him. She hated him. She needed him. She wanted him. She wanted him like she'd never wanted anyone or anything. And when together like this, skin against skin, warmth to warmth, heartbeat to heartbeat, she didn't think she could possibly ever want anything more.

This was intimacy, and closeness, connection as she'd never known it. Together like this, she felt whole. Comforted. Cherished. The lovemaking was such perfection it made her eyes sting and her heart ache. She never wanted it to end. Not even tonight.

Long before she was ready, her body betrayed her, nerves and muscles coiling into an explosive physical climax that triggered his. She sighed as he released into her, her body still sensitive and shuddering with pleasure. How could sex be so right with him when everything else was so wrong?

For a moment she allowed herself to relax into him, savoring the feel of his hard, lean body. And then he withdrew.

As always, she felt bereft.

As always her heart ached, wanting, needing more.

He turned onto his side, pulled her up against him, his arm over her chest holding her close to him. She let him, too, because when they were together like this, she did need him. She needed him more than she'd ever needed anyone. Her life had been lonely. Her father's problems had eclipsed everyone else's needs. When Vittorio loved—even if only with his body—she felt good. And safe. Safer than she felt with anyone else.

But sex, even slow and leisurely, didn't last forever. It always ended. And the afterglow always ended. And then she was swamped with all the overwhelming emotions again.

Emptiness. Pain. Hopelessness. Sadness.

And so when he wrapped his arm around her, his forearm warm and snug against her breast, she unsteadily exhaled and inhaled and exhaled again to keep the tears from falling.

How could she mistrust him and yet need him so much?

How could he make her feel so vulnerable? No one else made her feel this way. Why did he?

* * *

Lying in the bedroom's semidarkness, with the last lingering rays of sunlight fading from the sky, Vittorio felt Jill's chest rise and fall, a silent hiccup of emotion that she never acknowledged, and always refused to discuss. Suppressing a sigh, he drew her small frame closer to him, her soft round breasts pressed to his arm.

She was so full of secrets and her secrets wore on her. He'd known many men who lived in the shadows, clandestine lives filled with cloak-and-dagger games, but those men reveled in their furtive behavior, thriving on danger, thriving on power. Jill didn't.

He'd once wished she'd tell him what troubled her. He no longer cared. Or that's what he told himself.

But when her narrow rib cage rose and fell with a deep shuddering breath, his own chest grew tight.

In Bellagio everything had been easy between them. Not just the sex, but the connection, the conversation, the friendship they'd been building. He'd trusted her. He'd believed she was honest, true and real.

Turned out nothing about her was honest or real. Not her name. Not her past. Not even her hair color.

His meeting tonight was with one of his detectives. The detective had learned what he'd called "significant details" of Jill's past.

Tonight in Catania he'd discover who she really was.

Tonight could change everything.

And so he held her closer, held her as if he could possibly keep bad news from changing the fragile tie between them.

Maybe in his own way, he still loved her a little.

"When I first saw you on the cliff, I thought perhaps you were wearing a wig," he said quietly, his voice rough with passion and emotion he'd never share. "But it's not a wig. You dyed it."

She lay still in his arms. "Yes."

"How have you perfected so many different disguises?"

"Theater. I performed in all the high school plays and musicals. I loved it so much that I went to Gonzaga as a theater arts major."

"I thought you studied hotel management."

"I did. I graduated with a degree in hotel management, but initially I wanted to be an actress."

"Why?"

She took a deep slow breath. Her voice wasn't entirely steady. "I wanted to be someone else."

Vittorio stayed with her another half hour and then wordlessly he pulled away and left the bed. She lay on her side facing the wall listening to Vittorio dress.

He was leaving.

Leaving her.

She told herself she didn't care. She squeezed her eyes closed, trying to ignore the slide of fabric and the scrape of zipper. Then came a moment of quiet. She felt Vitt's hesitation. Felt him standing over the bed, gazing down at her. She didn't turn to him, or speak. She kept her eyes closed pretending to sleep.

Then he walked away and the bedroom door opened. She opened her eyes then, looked toward the door and the hallway. A ray of light fell across the bedroom floor and she glimpsed Vittorio's hard, handsome profile and his shoulder before the door closed, shrouding the bedroom in darkness once again.

For long minutes she lay on her back, thinking but not thinking. Feeling but not feeling. Doing her best to close her own door on her inner turmoil.

She couldn't let herself feel. Couldn't analyze a single emotion. Couldn't go inward because if she did, she'd fall apart.

Every time she was with Vitt it felt so right, so why did it have to be so wrong?

* * *

In Catania Vittorio met with the American private investigator at his office. It was nine o'clock and the office was closed, all lights off except for the executive suite that housed Vittorio's office.

The detective, a former FBI agent, sat across the desk from Vitt, a notepad open on his lap, telling Vitt everything he'd discovered.

He'd discovered a great deal.

It required all of Vitt's self-control to remain seated with his expression neutral while the detective revealed everything he'd discovered about Vittorio's new wife.

April Holliday wasn't Jillian's only alias. Jillian Smith was an alias, as well. There were three other aliases before she had become Jillian Smith at age sixteen.

She'd been in the U.S. government's witness protection program for fourteen years, had moved numerous times and changed her looks and name repeatedly because her family's safety had been repeatedly compromised.

"She had four different identities on file with the government," the detective said, glancing briefly at his notes. "She was creating that fifth one—April Holliday—when we located her in Carmel. But April Holliday wasn't a government-issued identity. It was one she'd created on her own to hide from you."

Vitt's brow lowered. "Is she still part of the witness protection program?"

"She is supposed to be. The rest of her family still is."

"Where is her family?"

"Parents are in Florida. The exact location isn't known."

"Who are they?"

The detective shook his head. "That is the one piece of information missing from her file." He leaned forward, slid a sheet of paper across the desk toward Vittorio. On the paper he'd listed all of Jill's aliases, including her schools and studies and the different addresses from the time she was twelve until now. "There is nothing I could find that gives her birth name, or her parents' original names. Like Jillian, her family goes by Smith, and has used Smith for a number of years. We do know that the entire family, a family of four—mother, father and two daughters—was placed in the program fourteen years ago but we don't know why."

Vittorio calmly studied the paper in his hand, his relaxed features revealing none of his inner tension. There was a reason Jill had run from him in Bellagio. She'd heard the word *Mafioso* whispered and disappeared like a thief in the night. And she'd kept running until he'd found her. But she remained terrified of him. She'd made it clear she didn't trust him, or believe that he wasn't connected to the mafia. She'd said so several times.

She had to be linked to the mob herself. Had to have insider knowledge. Why else would she be so completely unable to trust him?

"There is nothing here of her original identity," he said, glancing at the former FBI agent. "According to this paper, she didn't even exist before she was twelve."

"That's right. Everything in her file that would link her to a birth name, birthplace, or birth date was completely erased."

Vitt kept his expression neutral. "Is this normal protocol for the United States' protection program?"

"No."

"But you've seen this before?"

The detective hesitated. "Yes. There are two incidences when I've seen this happen—when the government is protecting a foreign spy, or a high-ranking member of an organized crime family."

There it was. The connection to organized crime. Vitt had

known it in his gut, but wondered why it'd taken him so long to see it.

"So what do you think we're dealing with?" Vitt asked, sounding bored.

"She's the daughter of an American mob boss."

Vitt felt hard and cold all the way through. It's what he'd been thinking, but somehow it sounded a thousand times worse spoken aloud. "Are there many in the American government's witness protection program?"

"A half dozen."

"Anyone you view a particular threat?"

"One or two, although Frankie Giordano is the one the government is most protective of. He sold out the entire Detroit operation, and Detroit was linked to nearly every other operation."

Vitt nodded slowly. "Which means Giordano gave up everyone."

"Yes."

"If his whereabouts were discovered, he'd be a dead man."

The detective closed his notebook. "As would his family."

CHAPTER EIGHT

JILLIAN woke up with sunlight pouring through the windows. She hadn't drawn the drapes last night when she'd gone to bed. Instead she'd stayed up late, leafing through Italian *Vogue* and French *Elle*, magazines Maria had loaned her, waiting for Vittorio to return.

He hadn't, though.

He'd remained out all night. Or if he had returned, he'd slept elsewhere.

The fact that he'd stayed away worried her. He'd been so upset with her yesterday. And she knew she deserved his anger, but she was also desperate to patch things up. She didn't know how to live in his house and be shunned by him.

Jillian bathed and dressed quickly before heading to Joe's nursery to check on him. He wasn't there so she went in search of him, knowing he had to be with Maria.

But he wasn't with Maria. He was with his father having breakfast on the terrace just off the dining room.

The soft pink-tinged morning light painted the terrace's pale stones rose and gold. Large clay pots lined the terrace, and beyond the balustrade the valley and snow-capped Mt Etna dominated the view.

"Good morning," Jillian said huskily, turning her back on green-and-yellow hills dotted with orchards and farmhouses to face Vitt and Joe.

"'Morning," Vitt answered, breaking up a breakfast roll into little pieces for Joe who sat in a tall antique high chair at Vitt's elbow.

She noticed that he barely looked at her and his tone bordered on cold. "May I join you?" she asked uncertainly even as she leaned over to give Joe a kiss.

"It's your home," he said, sounding completely disinterested.

She breathed in Joe's warmth and baby scent for courage before straightening and taking a seat at the glass-topped table.

Kitchen staff immediately appeared to place another setting for her and offer her a choice of espresso or American style drip coffee. Jillian chose the drip coffee and then clutched her hands in her lap to hide her nervousness.

"When did you get back?" she asked, struggling to keep her voice light and normal.

"Last night."

Her heart fell and ridiculous tears burned the back of her eyes. So where had he slept? And why hadn't he come to their room? "How did your meeting go?"

"It was interesting."

"That's good." She forced her lips up into a brittle smile and then caught Joe's eye. He was staring at her as he fed himself a bite of the bread. She smiled more warmly even as her eyes felt grittier, saltier. Please God, don't let her cry.

"Tell me about your family," Vitt said abruptly, leaning back in his chair. "You never talk about them."

"I…I'm not sure what you want to know."

"Tell me about your father. You said he was a businessman. Sales, I think you said."

She nodded woodenly. "Yes."

"And you moved a lot growing up?"

"Yes."

His eyes narrowed a fraction. "Where were you born?"

"De—" Jillian broke off, bit her tongue, realizing she'd come dangerously close to telling him the very things the government had insisted she never share. "Dallas."

"Dallas?" he repeated, head tipping to the side. "Which hospital?"

"I don't remember. I'd have to ask my mother."

"And where is she?"

"In a retirement community in Florida."

"We should invite them out for our wedding."

"They don't...they don't...like to fly."

"Don't you want your father to give you away?"

She squirmed. "Of course I would, but they don't travel much and they wouldn't be comfortable here."

His lips curved. "Here in our home?"

"No."

"You mean, here in Sicily?"

"No. That's not what I mean."

"So what do you mean, Jill?"

Completely flustered, she bit down into her lower lip, chewed the tender skin. "I'm not close with my parents," she said at last. "I haven't seen them in years."

"They've never met Joseph then?"

She shook her head. "They don't even know he exists."

"I'm shocked."

"We're not all close-knit Sicilian families that dine together every night."

"Those big noisy meals keep the generations tight."

"I can't even imagine." Jillian had been raised without an extended family. Her mother's family had cut her off after she married Jillian's father against their wishes. Her father had been an only son and he'd left home at eighteen to make his fortune in the big city. He'd never bothered to introduce his wife and or children to his parents, even though they only lived six hours south of Detroit. "I don't even know if I have cousins and I've never met my grandparents."

"Are they still alive?"

"I don't know." She made a small sound, a hiccup of laughter tinged by frustration. "I believe both my grandmothers and one of my grandfathers might still be alive, but they were never part of our life."

"Why not?"

She smiled up at Vitt's kitchen staff for refilling her coffee. "I don't know for sure but I think my father had a big ego and far too much pride. I think my mother, having lost her parents when she married my father against their wishes, was terrified of losing my father so she supported him on everything, which meant we didn't see grandparents, we didn't do big family holidays. It was always just us, the four of us, Mom, Dad, Katie and me."

"Where does she live?"

"She's…she's—" Jillian broke off, looked away, unable to finish the thought. *Gone.* Katie's gone. Everything in Jillian's life seemed to be about the past. Past tense. Past self. Past life. What she needed was new. What she needed was a future. "Dead. She died. A couple years ago. Katie was only twenty-one."

"I'm sorry."

She looked at him, the pain in her eyes giving away far more than she knew. "I am, too."

Vittorio watched Jill's expression as she talked about her family. Emotions flickered over her face and yet the expression in her eyes never changed. Her eyes revealed grief. Total loss.

"I do think we need to make an effort to include your parents in our wedding. If we set the ceremony for a week from today—next Saturday—we should have plenty of time to invite them and arrange their travel," he said. "Should we

place a call to them before dinner? We can make it a confer-
ence call, get everyone on the line."

She took a quick sip from her coffee cup. "I don't know if
they'll be around. They might be away...traveling."

"I thought you said they didn't like to travel."

"They don't like to fly. Or travel far."

He smiled at her kindly. "You seem nervous. Why would
you be nervous?"

"I'm not. I'm just..." she struggled to smile with quiver-
ing lips "...overwhelmed. Weddings and castles and change.
There's just been a lot of change, Vittorio. I confess, my head
is spinning."

"I think you just need something to focus on, like picking
out flowers and cake and a bridal gown for the ceremony. My
mother is handling the guest list. I will take care of the dinner.
You just need to select your gown, music, favorite colors, that
sort of thing."

She'd been the one to suggest a formal wedding. She'd been
the one to say they needed something public to cement their
relationship but suddenly it all seemed very risky. "We're
not thinking a big wedding, are we? Just something small,
intimate and elegant?"

"I might be wrong, but I believe the guest list has gotten
rather extensive. Since Catania is a small place, everyone
knows everyone and it was hard for my mother to limit the
guest list. But we can try to keep the church ceremony small
and invite everyone else to the party after."

Jillian felt increasingly queasy as he talked. Why had she
suggested another ceremony? Why hadn't she realized that it
could end up big, which would end up attracting a great deal
of attention? "Perhaps we should postpone the ceremony a
little longer, give us more time to plan."

"With everyone pitching in, a week will give us more than
enough time—" He broke off as his mother approached and

got to his feet to pull a chair out for her at the table. "Good morning, Mother," he said, dropping a kiss on her cheek. "You have perfect timing. We were just talking about the plans for next Saturday."

"Have you told her about the appointments with the designers?" Theresa asked him, dropping into a chair at the table and crossing one leg over the other. This morning Theresa wore an ivory pantsuit with gold buttons and delicate chains. Her heels were very high, accenting her fashionably slim figure.

"I haven't heard yet," Jillian said, with a glance down at her own uninspiring navy slacks and navy-and-cream striped top. She felt so dowdy next to Vitt's mother, and knew it really was time for a wardrobe update. Less matronly clothes. More stylish and form-fitting.

"You will be meeting with three of our top Italian designers later," Theresa said smoothly. "One arrived last night, two are flying in from Milan this morning. They will each meet with you for a half hour and then work up a design. Each designer will have a sketch to show you before they leave tomorrow. You get to select your favorite gown and then the winning design will be made this week in time for the ceremony next Saturday."

Jillian's eyes grew round. "That sounds incredibly extravagant."

"It's an extravagant ceremony," Theresa replied sharply, "but that's what I understood you wanted."

Jillian turned to Vittorio. "I didn't say I wanted an expensive wedding. And I certainly don't need three different designers flying in to work up three different designs for me to choose from. One designer would have been more than sufficient!"

He shrugged. "You did say you wanted a beautiful dress."

"Yes, but even an off-the-rack gown can be beautiful."

"Because you buy your clothes off the rack," Theresa

said with a sniff. "If you wore couture, you'd know the difference."

"But I don't, and I'm grateful everyone is trying to make the wedding special, but simple is good. Simple can be lovely." Jillian extended a hand toward Vitt. "We can do simple, can't we?"

"It's your wedding," he said, pushing his chair back and getting to his feet. "You're free to do whatever you want."

"I thought it was our wedding," she countered, watching as he ruffled Joe's dark hair, a gentleness in Vitt's eyes as he looked at his son.

She'd never seen that expression before. So much tenderness. A look of pure protection.

He really loved Joe, she realized. He truly wanted to be a father.

"It is our wedding," he answered, "but it's supposed to be your dream wedding. I don't care about the particulars as long as you, me and the priest are there."

Joe was looking up at Vitt now, a gummy smile lighting up his face. Vitt glanced down, caught Joe's cherubic smile and grinned. "Let me change that to you, me, Joseph and the priest," Vitt amended, touching Joe's cheek before walking away.

Jillian watched Vittorio's back for a moment before realizing Theresa was closely watching her. Blushing faintly beneath her mother-in-law's scrutiny, Jillian sat taller and turned to face her. "Thank you for your help in arranging everything. I do appreciate it."

"It was all Vittorio's doing," Theresa answered with a careless wave of her hand. "I told him the designers in Catania would do but he has his own ideas. Always has."

Jillian didn't know what to say to that and rose to get Joe from his high chair.

"So what do you think of the house?" Theresa asked, clearly determined to fill the silence.

"You have a beautiful home," Jillian said, sitting down again with Joe on her lap.

"It's Vittorio's home. He's just kind enough to allow us to live in one of the wings here."

"But I thought the castle had been in the family for nearly a hundred years?"

"It had." Theresa paused, lips pursed a moment as she chose her words. "My husband experienced a reversal of fortune fifteen years ago. We lost everything, including this place. Vittorio dropped out of university to take a job to help us out. He worked very, very hard. There were a lot of problems and a lot of debt. But six years ago he was able to buy the castle back, along with that beautiful villa in Bellagio."

Jillian glanced around the sunlight-dappled terrace with the pots of white roses and lavender wisteria. "I had no idea."

Theresa shrugged. "Vittorio would never tell you something like that. He never takes credit for any of the good things he does—and he does many. But that's how his father is, too. My husband, Salvatore, never thinks of himself. His family has always come first."

"It sounds as if you've had a good marriage."

For the first time since meeting her Theresa genuinely smiled. "I couldn't live without him." And on that note, she got to her feet and headed back into the house.

Jillian spent some time with Joe, and then when he went down for his morning nap, she met with the first of the three fashion designers.

One of the designers was a woman, the other two were men, and all three were so excessively polite that Jillian wondered what they'd been told by Vittorio.

Each designer took measurements. Two asked her questions about what she'd like in a bridal gown, while the third, one of the men, said he had the perfect design in mind and he'd show her later once he'd completed the sketch.

While the three designers retreated to various wings of the castle, Jillian was summoned to the castle's large modern kitchen finished in white marble and commercial-grade stainless steel appliances, to meet with a famous pastry chef from New York flown out just to make the wedding cake. The chef had brought samples of six different cake flavors, along with various icings and fillings.

Jillian sampled bite after bite and narrowed the selection down to three—white chocolate cake with a raspberry filling, a butter cake with lemon cream, and chocolate cake with chocolate mousse—but then didn't want to make the final decision without input from Vittorio. But he'd gone out for the day.

The chef suggested they use all three combinations with each layer of the cake being unique. Jillian agreed and left it to the chef to come up with the overall design.

"Traditional, unusual, colorful, classic, architectural?" the chef asked, trying to swiftly understand Jillian's personal style and vision for the wedding.

"I don't know," she confessed. "I hadn't planned on a big wedding, but it's turning out to be quite formal, so I suppose the cake should be classic. Elegant. Vittorio is very sophisticated. He has tremendous style. I think the cake should at least reflect that."

The pastry chef scribbled some notes, showed Jillian a book of photographs showing elaborately decorated cakes in all kinds of colors, shapes and tiers. They were all beautiful, Jillian told him, and she'd be happy with any of them.

While Jillian was still poring over the photo album, Theresa entered the castle's spacious kitchen to let Jillian know the florist was waiting in the dining room to discuss flowers for the wedding and dinner.

Jillian, who'd felt so unsure of herself during the cake tasting, felt far more comfortable talking with the florist. She'd worked with many florists over the years during her career in the hospitality industry and with a little guidance from the florist, quickly chose a theme of fragrant white gardenias, creamy white roses, contrasted by the silver-gray stems of lamb's ear for softness and texture. The florist suggested weaving in some delicate silver beads for a hint of sheen in the table arrangements, and then for Jillian's bouquet, the florist thought the long stems should be tied with a pale silver satin ribbon for a little extra sophistication.

Jillian loved the idea, and could suddenly see the wedding she wanted—charcoal, black and ivory colors—with lots of candlelight and glamour.

Jillian dragged the florist back to the kitchen where the pastry chef had just finished packing up his dishes and samples and photo albums. She introduced the florist to the chef so they could compare notes, which was perfect since Theresa appeared to announce that the designers were ready to meet with her and she needed to come immediately.

As Jillian and Theresa climbed the stairs to return to the sunny sitting room on the second floor, Theresa warned Jillian not to make any decisions on the different designs until she'd seen all the sketches. "You could easily change your mind several times, so study each design and think about what you want, because this is your day."

They'd paused outside the sitting room with its pale blue walls and white linen-upholstered furniture. "Thank you," Jillian said warmly. "You've done so much for me. I can't even express my gratitude—"

"It's him," Theresa said bluntly. "This is what Vittorio wants for you, and so I support him and am trying to arrange a beautiful wedding and ceremony. But you, I don't know you, and I don't know why you've kept Vittorio from his son for the past year, but no one has asked my opinion, nor will Vittorio ever. He is a man, and he makes his own decisions, and I appreciate that. However, let me give you a little motherly advice. Do not disrespect Vittorio, and do not disrespect this family, because it will not be tolerated. Indiscretions will not be forgiven, either. As Vittorio's wife, you are to bring honor and respect to the family. And if you can't do that, you have no business being here. Do you understand?"

The warmth inside Jillian faded, leaving her chilled. She stiffly nodded her head. "Yes."

"Good," Theresa said more lightly. "Now let's have a look at the bridal gown designs and see which one you prefer."

Jillian spent the next hour dutifully studying the sketches and talking to the designers, but her heart was no longer in it. For a brief moment she'd gotten excited about the wedding. For a brief moment while consulting with the florist she'd felt like a real bride making real decisions about her dream wedding, but Theresa's stern warning outside the sitting room had brought Jillian crashing back to earth.

This was not a normal wedding. Their ceremony next Saturday was not going to be a happy day.

With a heavy heart, Jillian gazed at each of the three sketches again—one dress looked like a princess ball gown with layers and layers of tulle and delicate pearl beading, another looked like a fitted ivory satin negligee with a daringly low back and snug shoulder straps, and the third was a slim empire-style dress made of white chiffon, topped with a jeweled bodice and a matching Cleopatra-style jeweled collar.

All three bridal gowns were stunning, all three were glamorous and all three would cost a fortune.

"They're all beautiful," Jillian said, going from one to the other and around again without making a decision. "I could wear any one of them."

"Yes, dear, but you can only have one, and the designers

need to go home and get to work," Theresa said coolly. "So which gown is it to be?"

Jillian lightly ran her fingertips over the sketch in her hand. It was the ball gown sketch, the one that looked most like the kind of dress Cinderella would have worn the night she met the prince.

The first night Jillian had gone to dinner with Vitt she'd thought him a prince.

That first night she'd been so sure there would be happily-ever-after.

She set aside the ball gown design to look at the satin 1930s glamour gown. The dress looked like something a rich man would have his mistress wear. It spoke of sex and seduction and money.

And then there was the chiffon empire-style dress with the jeweled bodice and collar. The embroidery and jewels looked modern and yet the chiffon added softness, making her think of the silvery fuzzy lamb's ear leaves tucked among the fragrant white flower blossoms.

These three gowns were all so fancy, so showy, she couldn't actually imagine wearing any of them.

Yet she couldn't say that to the designers. She couldn't hurt their feelings.

She flipped through the female fashion designer's sketch-book, pausing briefly at a sketch she hadn't been shown. It was a strapless ivory silk gown with a full ruched silk skirt without any embellishment other than a sage green satin ribbon at the waist. The green satin ribbon had been tied into a soft bow and the ends dangled all the way to the skirt's hem.

It was simple, maybe too simple, which is why Jillian hadn't been shown it, but she loved the color green, and the ruched ball skirt with the organza overlay.

"I like that one best," a deep male voice, a very calm voice, said from behind her shoulder. "It looks like you."

She glanced over her shoulder at Vittorio, tears shimmering in her eyes. "You think so?"

He nodded and reached out to catch one of the tears before it fell. "Why are you sad?"

"She's not sad," Theresa said sharply, "and you're not supposed to be here. The gown is supposed to be kept secret—"

"We're already married, Mother. This is a renewal of vows for the benefit of our family." He leaned over the back of the couch, took the sketchpad with the color drawing of the ivory gown and green ribbon and held it up. "Who did this one?"

The female designer raised her hand. "It's mine."

"This is the one Jill wants," Vitt told her. He nodded to the other designers. "Thank you for coming today. As promised, you will be well compensated for the consultation. Thank you everyone, and now we must say goodbye as Jill and I have someplace we have to be."

Jillian lifted her head, met Vitt's gaze. He nodded slightly. She rose and together they left the room.

"Where are we going?" she murmured as they started down the stairs.

"Out. Away. I thought we could both use some air, and time to ourselves." He glanced down at her as they reached the bottom stair. "Would you like that?"

"Very much."

"Good. So would I."

CHAPTER NINE

VITTORIO opened the front door to the front steps and sunshine flooded the stone entry. The air felt fresh, the sky was blue with just a few wispy clouds, and a cream two-seater convertible sports car gleamed in the circular driveway.

"That's a beautiful car," she said, descending the steps to examine the car's flowing lines from the curving panoramic windshield to the sleek rear end. "Has to be a 1950s design," she added.

"Good eye. 1955," he said, smiling at her. "A Lancia Aurelia."

"Don't they call these B24 Spiders?"

Vittorio laughed softly as he opened the passenger door for her. "They do. How did you know?"

She glanced admiringly into the interior with its dark red leather seats and dash. "My dad loved cars. He was always buying new cars and living in Detroit—" She broke off, horrified by what she'd just revealed and then panicked, she babbled on as she slid into the passenger seat. "Dad still watches car auctions on TV."

Vittorio closed the door behind her and moved to the driver's seat. "You never mentioned your father's interest at Bellagio."

She glanced up at the chiseled features of his face to see if he'd caught her slip, but Vittorio looked relaxed, his expression almost happy. "I didn't realize you liked old cars, too," she said, thinking that her mention of Detroit hadn't registered, "because all of your cars at the lake villa were new."

"And what do you prefer?" he asked, closing his door.

"I do love classic cars best."

"Sounds like you are your father's daughter," he said, starting the car.

Jillian grew hot, her skin prickly. She'd definitely been her father's daughter the first twelve years of her life. She'd loved his energy and charm and ready laugh. "Growing up I was very close to him," she said quietly. "I was proud of being a Daddy's girl."

"What changed?" Vittorio asked, shifting gears and heading down the driveway to the castle's impressive gates.

She was silent a long moment as Vittorio pulled away from the Normandy castle with its turret and tower to head down the drive toward town.

The sun shone brightly and Jillian lifted a hand to shield her eyes. "His job," she said at length. "He had problems at work."

"What sort of problems?" Vitt asked, sliding on a pair of sunglasses.

"Financial."

Vitt shot her a glance. "Did he embezzle money?"

"No. At least, I don't think so. We never talked about it at home. My father wasn't open and my mother didn't ask questions. They had a very traditional marriage. Dad was the head of the family and made all the decisions. It was Mom's job to agree with him."

Vitt shot her a brief glance. "You're nothing like your mother."

She laughed despite herself. "No, I'm not. Maybe that's why we're not close." But then her smile disappeared as she thought of her sister, a beautiful brunette who'd taken after their mother. Mom and Katie had been close, practically been best friends. "My sister and Mom talked every single day though, sometimes three or four times a day. Even when Katie was at college she called Mom to get her advice, ask her opinion. I used to tell Katie to grow up, become independent but she said Mom needed her, and now, looking back, I realize Katie was probably right. Mom hasn't had much of a life."

"When is the last time you saw them then? Your sister's funeral?"

Jillian dug her nails into her hands and looked away. "I wasn't able to make the funeral."

"What?"

She felt Vitt's stare and she lifted her shoulders. "I was in Switzerland working. There was no graveside service. Mom and Dad just took Katie's ashes home."

"That's just strange."

"As I said, we're not close." She turned to look at him, eyes huge in her pale face. "I haven't seen them since I graduated from college, and that was five years ago."

"Don't you want to see them?"

"Yes." Her voice broke. She swallowed hard. "But there are reasons we don't get together, and I have to respect those reasons." Jillian grabbed her long hair in her hand to keep it from blowing in her face. "I'm not saying it's easy, because it's not. I wanted to go home and see them after Katie's death. I wanted to be with the people who loved Katie as much as I did, but I couldn't go, and I grieved on my own, and it was horrible." She blinked back tears. "But then I changed jobs and moved from Zurich to Istanbul and that helped. Helped distract me from always thinking about losing Katie."

Vittorio glanced at her again, his sunglasses hiding his eyes and yet from the set of his mouth she knew he was thinking over every word she'd said.

She'd said a lot, too.

"Can we talk about something else?" she said huskily. "Talking about my family just makes me miss Katie even more."

They drove along the lower slopes of Mount Etna, passing through acres of black lava only to arrive at terraced fields of vineyards and almond and hazelnut groves.

They stopped at Roman ruins an hour and a half outside Paterno and Vittorio held her hand as they walked down stone stairs cut from the hillside to the bottom of what once must have been a very grand amphitheater. In places the rows of stone seats climbed perfectly up the grassy hillside. In other areas the stones had been broken and toppled and lay in pieces on the ground.

"Can you imagine attending a play or a concert here?" Jillian asked, doing a slow circle to fully savor the amphitheater's grandeur.

"Now and then concerts are still performed here. It doesn't happen often anymore—the last time was ten years ago—but it's a magical thing to have the theatre come alive, with all the performers lit by moonlight and candlelight."

Jillian sat down on a stone bench that was still largely intact. "We're in a field with a secret Roman amphitheater that's just an hour from your home. I'm jealous!"

"It is beautiful. And the amazing thing is, we have ruins like this all over Sicily. Every couple of miles you'll find the tumbled stones of a Doric temple, Byzantine church, Norman castle, Greek and Roman amphitheaters. But the ruins aren't merely in the countryside. Our cities are filled with ancient gates and bridges, tombs and altars. We have two thousand years of history on this island, and it's all created the strong, modern Sicilian character."

"You're proud to be Sicilian," she said, looking up at him.

Vittorio nodded. "Very proud. Sicilians haven't just been

shaped by thousands of years of different cultures and rulers, but also by the land and weather. Here in Sicily we have six months of perfect warm weather followed by months of torrential rains. The interior of the island is dry, rocky and arid, while our exterior is one of endless coastlines with picturesque beach towns and breathtaking views. We're surrounded by water and yet at the center is our Mount Etna, Europe's largest, most active volcano."

"A place of extremes," she said.

"Exactly so," he agreed, extending a hand to her. "Shall we go so I can show you more?"

They stopped in Bronte, enjoying a simple meal in the restaurant's charming, shady courtyard before Vittorio ducked into a boutique and emerged with a silk scarf and pair of sunglasses. "For your hair," he said, tying the scarf under her chin. "And your eyes," he added, slipping the sunglasses onto her nose.

Touched by his thoughtful gesture, she rose on tiptoe and kissed him. "Thank you."

He gazed down at her for a long moment, a small muscle pulling in his jaw. "My pleasure."

And then they were climbing into the Lancia sports car and heading to Paterno. Riding home in the sleek two-seater convertible, Jillian felt very chic in her sunglasses and scarf. "This was a really nice afternoon," she commented as he slowed to allow a shepherd and his flock of sheep to cross the road.

"It still is," he agreed, dark eyes holding hers, before focusing again on the road. As he drove they sat in silence, mellowed by their meal, the warmth of the sun and the scenic drive.

It wasn't until they were on the outskirts of Paterno that Vittorio spoke again. "I want to call your parents when we return and personally invite them to the wedding. I will let them know that I can handle all arrangements, and have a plane at their disposal—"

"Vitt, not this again!"

"Jill, you are their only daughter."

"Maybe, but they won't come. They just won't."

He shot her a swift glance. "How do you know if you haven't asked them?"

"Because I know them!"

"But I don't, and if we're to be a family, I want to know them, and I'd think they'd want to get to know me."

"They don't. It sounds dreadful put like that, but it's the truth. They don't want to know anyone anymore, not after Katie's boyfriend—" She broke off, bit down hard into her lip, astonished that she would once again say so much.

He shot her a swift glance. "What did Katie's boyfriend do?"

Jillian closed her eyes, hating herself.

"Jill?" he demanded.

She looked at him, expression stricken. "Marco hurt her."

"*He* was the one that killed her?"

"Yes." She ducked her head, studied her laced fingers, remembered how when she and Katie were young they'd hold hands when they crossed the street. Held hands when Katie got scared. Tears burned her eyes, but they were nothing compared to the emotion tearing up her heart. "So now my parents don't go anywhere or meet anyone. They just live in their little house in Fort Lauderdale and soak up the sun and maybe play a round of golf."

For a moment Vittorio said nothing and then he spoke quietly, flatly. "I am not Marco. I would never hurt you, or your family—"

"That may be, but we will not call them. I will not call them."

"Then I will." He glanced at her. "I have their number, Jill. Home and cellular."

She turned her face away from him, jaw set. He didn't know. He didn't understand. "Don't do it, Vitt. It's not a good idea. You *have* to trust me on this one."

"Like you trust me?" he retorted.

She stiffened, her spine rigid.

"Your parents are important," he added. "They're not just your parents, but they're Joseph's grandparents and they should be part of his life."

"But I don't want them in Joe's life! He's not safe with them in his life. Leave them in Florida. It's where they belong."

"How can you be so bitter?"

"Because you don't know what my father put us through!"

"What did he put you through?"

"Hell." Then she smiled bitterly to hide the hot lance of pain. It had been hell, too. Her childhood had been so happy that she hadn't even been prepared for the terrible things that happened when she turned twelve. Couldn't have imagined that she'd be ripped from that idyllic, sheltered childhood and thrust into a world of constant fear. To know that your father was a hated and hunted man…to live believing your family was in constant danger…to go to bed every night thinking it might be your last…

"Your teeth are chattering," Vitt said.

They were, too, but that's because she was freezing. "I'm cold."

"It's eighty-four degrees out."

"So?"

"You're not cold. You're afraid."

"Why would I be afraid?"

Vitt abruptly pulled over to the side of the road and shifted into Park. Unbuckling his seat belt he turned all the way in his seat, his body angled forward to face her. "You're afraid because if I call your parents, it will reveal all your secrets and all your lies—"

"I have no secrets!"

His jaw flexed. His nostrils flared. He looked as if he was barely keeping his temper in check. "You have one hour to make that call, or I will."

Vittorio shifted into Drive and steered the Lancia Aurelia back onto the highway.

Jillian sat with her hands clenched in her lap. For a moment she felt nothing. Not even panic. And then slowly her head filled with noise, a buzzing sound that became a roar.

He'd found something out. Something important. Otherwise why would he want to call her parents personally? Why would he be so determined to speak to them, introduce himself, meet them personally?

Instinct and self-preservation told her that this wasn't a courtesy call. This phone call had nothing to do with playing the gracious bridegroom. He was cementing his power.

He was ensuring security.

He was going after the truth. And he was going after the truth because he didn't trust her.

Smart man, she thought, swallowing around the lump in her throat.

Blinking back hot tears, she stared blindly out the car onto the fields dotted with stone walls as they drove the rest of the distance in agonizing silence.

Pulling up before the castle, Vittorio shifted into Park even as Jillian was throwing open the car door and jumping out. "You're down to forty minutes, Jill. You have forty minutes to decide what you want to do. I'll be in the library waiting for you."

"I've nothing to tell you!"

"That's a shame. Because you have so much to lose."

Jillian turned and ran up the steps into the house, and didn't stop running until she'd reached the nursery where Joe was sleeping.

Maria put a finger to her lips when Jillian burst into the room. The shades were down, darkening the room and Jillian nodded as she continued to the crib. She had to see Joe, had to see him as only then could she believe everything would be okay.

Jillian stared down at him, taking in his flushed cheeks and his rosy lips. He'd never looked more angelic. "Did he have a good day?" she whispered to Maria.

"Yes. He played and played and he ate a lot and we also went for walks."

Jillian's chest squeezed. She longed to reach out and touch him but she didn't dare wake him. Instead she smiled at Maria and went to her room, where she changed from her navy striped top and slacks into a simple white linen dress. She ran a comb through her hair and then turned away from the mirror. Don't be scared, she told herself, heading for the stairs.

Reaching the library on the second floor, Jillian wiped her now damp palms on the sides of her dress before opening the library door. "What do you want to know?" she asked.

"Everything," he said as she stepped into the room.

She closed the door behind her before approaching his desk where he'd been typing something on his laptop computer. "But you know everything."

"Do I, *Jill*?"

"Yes. I have no secrets. My dad's a jerk. My mom's weak. My sister's dead. What else is there?"

"Then who, *cara*, is Anne? And Carol? And Lee?" He caught her expression and smiled grimly. "Yes, my wife of many identities. Who are you really?"

"How long have you known about the different identities?"

"Since yesterday. But I had suspicions before."

She nodded. "Then you know everything…"

"I don't know why, and I don't know who you were before you went into the government's witness protection program, but I have my suspicions."

Jillian startled and he nodded. "I'd wager this castle that your father is linked to organized crime," Vitt continued, "and I'd bet my Lancia that he's a mob boss from Detroit, a man who confessed everything he knew to the FBI to save himself from going to prison."

He smiled and gestured to the phone. "Now I just need you to confirm it for me."

She swayed on her feet. "I can't, Vitt."

"Can't or won't?"

"Both."

"Then I will, and once I call them, and let them know you're here with me, I'm confident they'll tell me what I need to know—"

"They won't."

"Not even if they think you're in trouble?"

She laughed. "God, no! They didn't when Marco kidnapped Katie, so why would they do it for me?"

"Is that how your sister died?"

She made a low tormented sound. "The tragic thing is that they didn't even want Katie. They wanted my father. But my father wouldn't dream of sacrificing himself for anyone else, much less his daughter."

"And so she died."

"In a car bomb. Can you believe that? She thought she was free to go. She thought she'd escaped the danger. Instead they blew her up as she started her car." Jillian dragged her fist across her face, rubbing away tears before they fell. "The police called it an accident. But everyone on the inside knew it wasn't an accident. And so the government stepped in and Mom and Dad were moved to yet another location. I didn't change my name, but I did change jobs, going from Switzerland to Turkey."

"And it was in Turkey you met me."

She nodded. "I thought you were perfect for me, too. Until I discovered who you were. So I ran. Just as I've been running for my life ever since I was twelve."

He rose from behind his desk and went to her, caught her hands in his and drew her toward him. "You don't have to be afraid—not here, not anymore."

"I wish I could believe that. I really do."

"Why can't you?"

"Because bad things happen when we let our guard down. Katie let her guard down—"

"You're not Katie," he interrupted, lifting her hand with her wedding ring to his mouth and kissing her ring finger and then her palm. "You will never be Katie, and I promise that nothing will happen to you if you trust me. I can protect you. And my family will protect you. Always."

Her gaze clung to his. She wanted to believe him, she really did, because she needed to believe in someone, needed to believe the world could be a good place, and a safe place. Her world had often felt very dark and harsh and cold and yet whenever she was with Vitt, she felt warm.

She felt safe.

"Kiss me," she whispered. "Kiss me and make all these bad feelings go away."

"That's the smartest thing I've heard you say all day," he murmured, lifting her face to cover her mouth with his. He kissed her slowly, deeply, lips drawing from hers an immediate and almost feverish response.

She needed him.

She needed him desperately.

For the longest time she'd felt as if she was drowning but

maybe he could save her. Maybe he was strong enough, smart enough...

Hope blazed to life. Hope and heat kindling into hot desire.

With his mouth on hers, Vittorio walked her backward across the library until she felt the dark paneled door against her hips.

He leaned past her, turned the lock on the door, and then moved closer, his tall, lithe, firm body pressing into her.

She loved the feel of his body against her and the warm hard ridge of his erection rubbing against her inner thighs. She wanted him and she groaned against his mouth.

"Careful, *cara*, or I will take you here," he warned, teeth nipping at her soft, swollen lower lip.

"Good," she answered, her body trembling with need.

"Don't tempt me," he said, his warm breath caressing her skin as his lips brushed the curve of her ear and then lower to the tender hollow below. "Because I'm dangerously close to losing control."

She turned so that her lips brushed his. "Lose it."

"Don't say that. You don't know how I feel. I'm angry, Jill, I'm angry and frustrated and I don't want to hurt you—"

"I'm not afraid of a little pain."

"Stop it," he growled. "Don't talk that way."

"Then take me and make me forget everything but you and me and being here together right now."

"I cannot fight you, and me." He tugged the hem of her white linen dress toward her hips and put his hand between her legs. "But don't say I didn't warn you."

Jillian felt as though she'd burst into fire on the inside. Her body felt wild. Her nerves explosive. She arched against Vittorio, demanding more.

He stroked over her cream silk panty, stroking the soft feminine shape of her.

She gasped and tipped her head against the door, giving herself over to exquisite sensation as hot, silvery shots of electricity burst through her, tightening her nipples and melting her core.

He lifted the edge of the panty, moving beneath the thin satin band to slide his fingers beneath the fabric, to run his fingers against her, then between the folds to the softest, warmest part of her. His fingers felt slick against her, which meant she was wet. Very wet.

Her mouth dried as he rubbed her between two fingers and she rocked helplessly against his hand, responding with not just her body, but also her heart.

With him she was safe. With him she was home. There could never be any other place she belonged but with him.

"You're mine," he ground out, his voice husky in her ear. "And I'm going to fill you and make you mine, and you will always be mine."

"Yes." Because of course she was his. She'd always been his. It was inevitable from the very first meeting in the hotel lobby. Fate brought them together, and it was up to fate to keep them together.

She heard him unzip his trousers as he freed himself, and then with one hand he pressed the head of his hot, hard erection against the wet entrance to her body.

He teased her for a moment with the tip, rubbing it across her wetness, and then up and down over her softness until she panted with need. And once she moaned his name, he plunged inside of her, filling her all the way.

She sucked in air, and held it bottled in her lungs as her heart seemed to burst open inside of her.

She loved him.

She did.

He and Joe were everything. Life, breath, hope. She circled

his neck with her arms, pressed her lips to his. "I need you forever," she whispered.

"You have me forever," he answered.

Tears burned her eyes. "Promise."

"I promise."

"No matter what?"

"No matter what." He lifted her against the wall, hooking her leg over his arm to thrust into her even deeper, stretching her, filling her, making her one with him.

She gasped at the fullness of them together, overwhelmed by the warmth and the dizzying emotions and intense sensation. He thrust into her again and again, and with each thrust she knew he was making her his.

But then he'd known from the very beginning that she needed this hard, physical coupling to feel loved.

Making love with Vittorio always made her feel loved, but she needed it now more than ever when everything felt so unpredictable, when their connection felt so fragile.

She buried her fingers in his cool, crisp hair, pressed her face to his neck, her lips to his warm fragrant skin, aware of each long, measured stroke of him taking her, filling her. With each thrust he edged her closer and closer to that point of no return, pushing her past reason and control until she shattered in a thousand pieces. He climaxed as she came, and dipping his head he covered her mouth with his, swallowing her scream in a kiss.

CHAPTER TEN

WITH one arm still braced against the wall, Vittorio slowly withdrew, and struggled to catch his breath as Jill slid down the door to sit in a boneless heap on the floor.

Tucking himself back into his trousers, he drew up the zipper knowing his body had found release but his emotions were tangled, pleasure diminished by sorrow.

She'd been through so much. She'd lived through chaos and betrayal, grief and pain.

Her pain hurt him. He should have comforted her, not taken her savagely against the wall.

He understood why she used sex as a paste or plaster to smooth problems over, but why did he? He knew sex solved nothing. Sex just masked problems until they revealed themselves again.

Dark, wrenching emotion filled him as he glanced down at her. She sat on the floor and leaned against the dark paneled door. Her thick blond hair tumbled over her shoulders in disheveled curls, her white linen dress was creased around her slim hips, and her long bare legs stretched before her making her look fragile and so very vulnerable.

Because she was vulnerable. Heartbreakingly vulnerable. And now that he understood her secrets and pain, he wondered how she'd endured it. How she could lose so much—family, friends, home—and yet be so strong. So determined to make a good life for their son.

His lingering frustration morphed into admiration. She was such a fighter. Such a complex woman. Intelligent, sensual, mysterious, stubborn. Very, very stubborn.

His chest tightened as his gaze met hers. She looked up at him with enormous eyes. Whether she had brown eyes, or blue eyes, pink or purple, it didn't matter. They were beautiful. She was beautiful. And he had never wanted her more.

Or needed to protect her more.

She did need him, too. He understood that now. She needed him not just for protection, but love, and patience and compassion. Jill was battered and bruised from fourteen years of fear and intimidation. It would take time for her to learn to trust people again. Hopefully she could trust him.

Hopefully she understood that she was safe with him. Hopefully she understood that here in Paterno she was finally safe. Home.

Crouching next to her, he buried his hand in her tangled curls and gently lifted her face to his. Her eyes shone, glimmering with tears.

"Don't cry, *cara*. No one will hurt you ever again. I promise you that," he said huskily, angered that her father had failed to protect his daughters, angered that the government had failed to protect her sister. "I will protect you. I will always protect you."

Emotion darkened her eyes. "But you don't even know who I am."

He stared deep into her eyes, looking so intently that he felt as if he could see the shy little girl inside the woman. "You are Jillian d'Severano. Joe's mother and my wife."

Her eyes turned liquid and she blinked hard. "Would you feel the same way if you knew my father was Frank Giordano?"

For a moment Vittorio couldn't breathe. His mind darkened. Frank Giordano was the scum of the scum. A man so selfish and self-serving he'd turned on his own organization to keep himself from serving time. "Frankie's your father?"

She nodded and tears clung to her lower lashes. "I'm sorry."

"Not your fault," he said, voice sharper than he intended. He'd wondered these past two days if she was possibly related to Frankie Giordano. He'd hoped, even prayed she wasn't. There was a lot of bad blood between his family and Frank Giordano. Very bad blood. His father would be sick that Vitt had married Frank's daughter.

"You're upset," she whispered, reading his expression.

"You didn't commit any crimes, Jill. You are not responsible for your father."

"But I am." She ground her teeth together. "I am responsible for my family's name, just the way you are responsible for yours. And I know I'm not the kind of person your family would want you to marry. I know they'd be horrified to discover Joe was the grandson of Frank Giordano—"

He cut off her tortured words with a kiss because he couldn't bear to hear more. Because she was right. His family had fought for twenty years to escape the taint of being connected to the mafia, and having the daughter of Detroit's most infamous mob boss be Vittorio's wife wouldn't help the d'Severano reputation, but Vitt had chosen her because he loved her.

He loved her.

The truth exploded within him, searing his mind and heart. He'd loved her all this time. It was love that drove him to search for her after she disappeared without a word from the villa in Bellagio. It was love twisted with pain when he discovered that Jill had given birth to a son.

He knew the child was his.

Just as he'd known from the first time he spotted Jill in the hotel lobby in Istanbul that she was meant for him.

Her lips quivered beneath his and her mouth tasted salty from her tears.

"Shh." He comforted her, his hand cupping her face, caressing her warm flushed cheek. "It's okay. I promise you, everything is okay."

"I will always be a danger to your family," she whispered against his mouth, her voice faint, unsteady.

He drew back to look into her eyes. "You are not a danger—"

"There are bad people out there, Vittorio. Bad people who are determined to find my father."

"Then they'll have to go through me, *cara*, because they cannot have you. They can not touch you. I make that promise to you as a d'Severano, and a d'Severano always keeps his word."

She gazed up at him, torn between hope and concern. "Will your family feel the same way?"

"This is my home. You are my wife. If anyone in my family has a problem with you or your past, they don't need to come here—"

"Vittorio!"

"I mean it. Yes, I've worked hard to restore the d'Severano honor and fortune, and I will never regret the sacrifices I made to take care of my family, but my loyalty is to you, and our son."

Jill reached up to lightly touch his face, her fingers infinitely gentle on his cheek and jaw. "You really mean that?"

"I do." He nodded and rose, and then held a hand out to her to assist Jill to her feet. "And while I don't like keeping secrets from my family, I don't think it's necessary we share your background with everyone at dinner tonight. I'll find a way to break the news, and I will do it soon, but this evening isn't the time."

"I'm meeting the family tonight?"

He nodded, his mouth quirking. "My sisters are having fits that they haven't met you yet, and my father is very eager to meet my wife. It'll be a large group—uncles, aunts, cousins—can you handle that?"

She nodded. "Yes."

"Good." He unlocked the door, started to open it, then stopped. "So what is your real name, since we know it's not really Jill Smith?"

"Alessia," she said softly. "But I haven't been Alessia for fourteen years. I'm Jillian now, and that's who I want to be."

"Then that's who you will be. So go shower and dress and try to relax, because I should warn you, my sisters are a lot like my mother—strong, talkative, rather intense—but hopefully a little more friendly."

Jillian's head spun as she climbed the stairs to their master suite on the third floor. She'd done it, she thought, reaching the bedroom and closing the door.

She'd told him. She'd told him the truth and nothing horrible had happened.

The planets hadn't collided.

No stars had fallen from the sky.

No scary men had jumped out of bushes and snatched her away.

Maybe all the bad things were behind her. Maybe, she thought, stripping off her dress and stepping beneath the showerhead with the faucets turned on full force, just maybe, everything would be okay.

Relief swept through her as the water beat down, first icy, then scalding until she finally adjusted the water to the perfect temperature.

Mind spinning, she soaped up, shampooed her hair and rinsed off all while thinking that her fears seemed so silly now. Why hadn't she trusted Vitt sooner?

Why had she thought he'd be like her father?

How tragic that she hadn't trusted him before. It would have saved them all so much heartache as well as lost time together.

Once dry, Jill styled her hair, then applied makeup, before slipping into the simple black cocktail dress hanging in the closet.

She felt like a different woman as she tugged up the dress's zipper. It was such a relief to have shared the truth with someone. Such a relief to know she wasn't alone. Keeping the secret had been a crushing burden and suddenly she felt lighter. Freer. Happier.

Twisting her hair into a silky chignon she stared at her reflection in the master bathroom's enormous mirror, her brown eyes smiling shyly, her mouth curving uncertainly.

He knew the truth about her, knew she was Frank Giordano's daughter, and he hadn't pulled away in disgust.

But having him just accept the truth wasn't enough. She wanted his love. She wanted his heart.

Yet how could he love her if he didn't know her? She needed him to know her, the real her, the woman who was falling in love with him.

Looking hard at her pale reflection, Jillian took a deep breath and removed one contact lens, and then the other, taking the brown colored lenses out to reveal her natural eye color—a vivid, and rather startling, turquoise green.

Moving to the sink, she washed the brown contact lenses down the drain and then washed her hands, all the while looking at her heart-shaped face with the high cheekbones, aristocratic nose and strong chin.

This is you, she told her reflection, this is you without artifice and make-believe. This is the you Vitt needs to see.

She didn't know how Vitt would react when he saw her eyes had changed color again but at least tonight when he saw her face, he would see her real face. He'd finally see her.

Vittorio rapped on the bathroom door. "My family is gathered downstairs and waiting."

"I'm ready," she said, opening the door and stepping out, wondering how long it'd take him to notice what she'd done.

He tipped his head, studied her. He'd noticed the change immediately. "You look...different."

"Is it my hair? I can take it down."

"It's not your hair."

"Maybe it's the dress. It's a little big."

"Everything in your wardrobe is big."

"I never bought new clothes after I had Joe. But I don't mind. And no one's really going to be looking at me tonight, right?"

He smiled with his eyes. "Keep telling yourself that if it makes you feel better." And then he drew a velvet pouch from his pocket. "But maybe this will add a little sparkle and shine to your black frock."

Shyly she bent her head forward so that he could fasten the elaborate gold clasp at the back of her neck. The choker was snug, the strands heavy with precious stones.

"Turn around," he said.

She did, and for a moment he said nothing and then he tipped her chin up with one finger. "Green eyes tonight."

She nodded.

"How did you know you'd be getting emeralds?" he asked, sounding amused.

"I didn't."

"You just decided to swap out your colored lenses tonight?"

She fingered the precious jewels at her throat. "I decided I was tired of hiding, so I threw away the contacts."

"Your real eye color is green?"

She nodded.

"And what is your real hair color? Red?" he guessed.

"How did you know?"

He'd been smiling but his smile died. "It's the one color you've never been." Vitt reached out to her smooth chignon and touched the twisted strands at her nape. "My wife has red hair and green eyes. How odd to think I've never really known her."

"But you have. This—" and she gestured to her face and body "—this is the real me. The only me. The one you met in Istanbul. The one you took to the villa. The one who had your baby."

"Good. Because you are the one I wanted in Istanbul, and you are the one I loved in Bellagio, and you are the one I want to help raise our son." Then he took her hand in his, kissed her hand, before tucking it in the crook of his arm.

Together they descended the staircase and entered the grand dining room with the pale blue-and-cream frescoes on the walls. Jillian stiffened in the doorway when everyone turned to look at them.

"I know it's a lot of people," Vitt murmured reassuringly, "but just be yourself and everyone will love you."

She nodded, even as she pressed her hand tighter into the crook of his arm.

They hadn't made much progress into the room before two attractive women moved toward them.

"My sisters," Vitt said beneath his breath. "They take after my mother. Just do your best."

"That's not comforting at all," she answered in a whisper.

Vittorio made the introductions. "Bianca and Carlina, I'd like you to meet Jill, my wife. Jill, this is Carlina, the youngest of my sisters, and Bianca, the oldest. Guiliana isn't here. She lives in Europe with her family."

The four of them made small talk for a few minutes before Bianca and Carlina came up with an excuse to get Jillian alone. Knowing his sisters wouldn't be satisfied until they'd had their time with her, he allowed them to drag her off toward a private corner. He in the meantime went to greet his paternal grandmother who was already sitting in her chair at the table.

He stooped to give her a kiss. She was small and rather frail but her mind remained sharp. "Nonna, how are you?" he asked, sitting down in a chair close to hers and taking her hands in his.

"The sun was shining today and I am alive. What could be better?"

Vitt grinned. "Not much, Nonnie."

His grandmother nodded at Jillian, who was still in the corner with his sisters. "How did this happen?"

"The baby?"

She narrowed her eyes. "I know how babies are made. I had nine of them. But how is it we are only meeting your family now?"

He shrugged. "There were problems. We're working them out."

"Good. Children need their mother and father together in one house."

"I agree."

She tipped her head, considering Jillian. "She's Italian, isn't she? Maybe even Sicilian. Look at her nose, the cheekbones, you can see it in her face."

His grandmother was smart. He smiled at her and patted her hand. "Would you like to meet her?"

"Why do you think I'm here?"

Laughing softly, he rose to get Jill, but before he could pry Jill away from his sisters, his mother entered the dining room then, pushing his father's wheelchair.

Vitt hadn't seen his father since arriving home and approached his father right away, bending over the wheelchair to kiss his father on the cheek. "Father, you look well. What have you been doing? Chasing *Madre* around the bedroom?"

His father's dark eyes shone, and his mouth pulled into a smile. "Impudent dog," his father said, his voice distorted by the ventilator helping him breathe.

Vittorio had always admired his father, but one of the things he enjoyed most about his father was his sense of humor. "Everyone tells me I take after you."

Salvatore rolled his eyes before looking toward the corner. "Is that your wife talking to your sisters?"

"Yes."

"Go get her. I'm anxious to meet her."

Jillian startled when Vitt suddenly touched her low on her back. "My father wants to meet you," he said quietly as he drew her away from the others. "He speaks with difficulty, and it's not always easy to understand him, so please be patient," he said, leading her across the room to where his father sat.

Jillian's breath caught in her throat as she spotted the family resemblance between Vitt and his father. Salvatore d'Severano was tall like Vitt, and very broad-shouldered, and while probably once powerfully built, he was now thin, his body stooped, the muscles connecting his large frame slack from years of atrophy.

But while his body appeared frail, his dark eyes burned with a fierce intelligence and his intense gaze seemed to see everything as she approached his wheelchair.

"Did he have a stroke?" she asked, suddenly terribly nervous.

"No. He was shot. It left him paralyzed."

"He's a quadriplegic?"

"Yes."

And then they'd arrived at Salvatore's side and Vittorio again made the introductions. "Father, this is my wife, Jill. Jill, this is my father, Salvatore d'Severano."

"Hello, Mr. d'Severano," she said. "It's a pleasure to meet you."

"There's no mister here," he answered gruffly. "You are my daughter now. Welcome to the family."

"Thank you." Her voice was pitched low. "That means a great deal to me."

He looked at her with dark searching eyes. "If you are happy, why do you cry?"

"I'm not crying," she denied, blinking hard to keep her eyes dry.

"Has my son made you so very unhappy?"

"No."

"I may be paralyzed, but I'm no fool."

"I promise you, it's not Vitt. He's been very good considering...considering..."

"Considering all the drama?" Salvatore finished for her, eyes watering with the effort it cost him to speak.

She nodded.

His brow furrowed. "You look so very familiar. I can't help but think I know you."

She shook her head. "I would have remembered you."

"Perhaps I know your family. You are Sicilian, aren't you?"

"No. American."

"Yes, but your family is Italian, from Sicily, I am sure of it."

Again Jillian shook her head but then her composure cracked and murmuring excuses, she slipped from the room, rushing past everyone to push through the hall door to the outside terrace. It was a quiet night, the terrace lit by just the moon. Jillian paced back and forth before leaning against the stone balustrade to draw great gasps of air into her lungs.

Of course her family was Italian, and she still took pride in her Italian heritage. But her father...

She was so ashamed of her father. And so disgusted, too.

He'd sacrificed Katie to save his own skin. How could he do that to her? How could he do that to all of them?

What kind of monster was he?

"What did my father say?" Vittorio asked quietly from behind her, his footsteps so silent she hadn't even heard him approach.

She shook her head. "Nothing."

"Then why are you so upset?"

She turned to face him. "He was so kind to me, but he wouldn't be if he knew who my father was."

"He probably wouldn't like who your father was, but he wouldn't hold it against you, *cara*. My father is a bigger man than that."

"How did he get hurt?"

Vittorio leaned against the balustrade next to her. "He decided to leave the mafia."

"So they shot him?"

"Yes."

"How old were you when it happened?"

"Seventeen."

"Just a teenager!"

"Yes."

She heard something in his voice that made her look closely at him and she saw the shadow of grief in his eyes. "It must have been terrible for you."

"It was."

She waited for him to say more, hoped he'd say more

because she so badly wanted to understand him, but he didn't.

Instead he straightened, and held out a hand to her. "Come, *cara*, let's return to the house, join the others again. Tonight is supposed to be a celebration, a chance to welcome you into the family. There will be plenty of opportunities to talk about the past, but tonight is about the present and our plans for the future."

Hand in hand they returned to the dining room where everyone was just taking their places at the long tables. Jillian was disappointed to discover that she and Vittorio would not be sitting next to each other but across the large square table from each other.

But Vittorio did not neglect her during the lengthy meal. Instead she felt his eyes on her time and again, and more than once she felt as though he was seducing her with his warm gaze, using his dizzying physical presence to arouse her, weaken her, make her want him.

He didn't realize she always wanted him.

He didn't realize she would always want him as she'd fallen in love with him. Hopelessly in love.

While the family talked, switching easily between Italian, Sicilian and English for Jillian's benefit, she tried to imagine life without Vittorio but couldn't.

Looking at him now talk with his grandmother, remembering the way he held Joe, as well as the way he made love to her, she wondered how she could have ever thought him dangerous. Wondered how she could have doubted his integrity.

Vitt suddenly looked up, caught her gaze, and smiled a slow, intensely physical smile that made her grow hot and cold. He was so incredibly sexual. He did things to her that she couldn't imagine any other man doing. And she liked how Vitt took her, possessed her, making her feel as if she really, truly belonged with him.

As if she were really, truly his woman.

As if she really, truly had a place here.

And she did want to belong to him, as well as belong here. It'd been years since she'd had a place to call home, much less a stable family.

Hours later when they were finally alone in their bedroom, Vittorio locked the door and dimmed the lights and Jillian smiled shyly. "You read my mind," she said, moving toward him and unzipping her dress as she walked.

He'd been unfastening the buttons on his shirt but his hands stilled as her dress slid to her hips and then she stepped out of it.

Her pulse drummed as she unhooked her black lace bra and then dropped it on the floor next to her cocktail dress. She felt Vitt's heavy-lidded gaze focus on her full, bare breasts, and her nipples tightened, puckering, and then his gaze dropped lower as she peeled off her black silk panties.

The air felt cool on her naked body and for a moment she wanted to cover herself but she didn't. Instead she held her ground and stood before him in just her black high heels and the emerald choker. She let him look, let him get his fill, before she slowly approached him.

His dark eyes burned her as she pushed him backward to sit on the edge of the bed. Her hands shook as she finished unbuttoning his shirt and pushed the soft cotton fabric over his shoulders and down his arms. As she freed his arms he reached out, palmed one of her breasts. Jillian shivered with pleasure, her legs like jelly.

She'd meant to be the one seducing him. She'd meant to show him she could give him the same pleasure he gave her, but Vittorio caught her in his arms, and rolled her onto her back and kissed her deeply, thoroughly. It was the way he used to kiss her before she'd run away from him, before she'd hid the pregnancy from him, before everything had become so awful.

She loved the kiss. She loved him. "Vittorio," she whispered against his mouth, burying her hands in his thick dark hair. He felt so good. He felt like everything she wanted and needed.

He pulled away to remove his trousers and then once naked, he stretched out over her, kissing her again, and then lower on her neck, and then down to her breasts where his tongue bathed and flicked one taut nipple, then the other.

He reached down between her thighs, discovered she was wet and then used his damp fingers to caress her, playing with the sensitive nub until she squirmed against his hand.

"You are always so greedy," he murmured in amusement as he stroked her again, apparently enjoying how her body shuddered and jerked against his.

"It's greedy to want you?"

"It's greedy to rush me," he answered.

"I can't help it. I just want you. Not an orgasm. Just you."

"That I can do."

She closed her eyes as his powerful thighs pushed her legs open wider. His erection was long and heavy and she felt it brush against her, and then Vittorio was entering her, stretching her to accommodate him.

She loved this moment when they became one, loved the feeling of possession and connection. So much of her life she felt alone, but when they were together like this, she felt whole and peaceful.

He slowly began to move in her and her hands stroked the length of his back, his skin warm and satin smooth beneath her palms. His body was hard and lean, beautifully muscled and she relished the width of his back, the smallness of his waist, the leanness of his hips and the small strong muscles in his butt.

She ran her hands over his butt, feeling the muscles tighten with each thrust of his powerful hips even as she pressed her mouth to his chest, his neck and his jaw. He smelled so good. He felt even better. *I love you,* she thought, as his hard strong body pushed her to the pinnacle of pleasure. *I will love you forever.*

CHAPTER ELEVEN

THEY'D made love again during the night and Jillian woke early the next morning still wrapped in Vittorio's arms.

It was the most amazing feeling in the world to wake in his arms. The most amazing thing to feel so safe. So loved. Because in his arms, against his warm chest, she felt loved. She felt perfect.

This was perfect. He was perfect. They could make this work, they could.

Turning in Vitt's arms, she pressed her cheek to his firm chest, her thighs brushing his. Closing her eyes she listened to the steady beat of his heart. She loved listening to his heart. It made everything simple and real. He was a man. She was a woman. And they fit together.

"What are you thinking about, *cara*?" Vitt's deep voice asked, rumbling through her.

"You. Me. Us. Everything."

"All without coffee?" he teased, lifting a hand to stroke her hair.

"Mmm." She smiled, snuggled closer, sliding one of her bare legs between his. "I loved last night. Thank you."

"My family was delighted to meet you too."

She giggled against him. "You know that's not what I mean. I was referring to us. Making love. It felt really good. It felt like it used to."

Vittorio continued to slowly, lazily stroke her hair, his hand running from the top of her head all the way down to her back. "It was good."

She felt like a cat beneath his caress and she arched a little with the pleasure. "I did like meeting your family though. And I adored your grandmother, as well as your father. You look so much like your father. Do you hear that often?"

"I do," Vitt agreed.

She pictured his father and the wheelchair with the ventilator tucked beneath. "Where was he shot?"

"He took a bullet in the back. Well, five actually, but the one that severed his spinal column was the one that nearly killed him." He paused. "Thank God it didn't. But he was in and out of hospitals for the next two years. Sometimes he still gets very sick."

She struggled to process what he'd told her. "But who actually shot him?"

"A member of the *cosca*," he said, using the Italian word for a Mafia clan or association. "As I told you last night, he wanted out. I was seventeen, the age many men join the brotherhood, but he made it clear that I wouldn't, nor would any of my children."

"I didn't think you could just walk away."

"You can't."

She heard the pain in his voice and moved closer. "What happened?"

He tensed. "My father announced he'd no longer be part of any criminal activity. He made it clear he would no longer extort money or provide kickbacks." Vittorio paused, stared up at the ceiling, deep lines etched next to his mouth. "We were all at dinner one night in Catania. My father and mother, my grandparents, my uncles, their wives, a few cousins and me. They called all the men out of the restaurant. My father knew what would happen. After all, he'd been a member for years, just as my grandfather had been. He told everyone to stay put, that he alone would go out. My grandfather and uncle refused to let him go alone.

"They shot them all," Vitt said bluntly. "My father threw himself over Giovanni, his younger brother, to shield him but it didn't matter. One of the bullets that struck my father, passed through him and killed Giovanni instantly. My father alone survived. It's a miracle he did."

"And then your family was finally free?" she asked, her voice husky with emotion.

"There was a huge public outcry. Everyone knew us in Catania. Everyone knew what had been done. People were livid. Even members of the association were uncomfortable with what happened. I think the taking of two lives, and the maiming of my father, satisfied the clan's need to make a statement. Enough blood had been shed. We were left alone."

She pushed up on her elbow to look down on Vittorio.

"Your father saved you."

He swallowed roughly. "He did."

His face was etched in such hard lines of pain that it made her heart ache. Gently she kissed his jaw, and his chin, and then his mouth. "I wish your father was my father. He's such a brave man."

Vitt reached for her, drew her up onto his chest and kissed her back. "But he is your father now, and you are part of this family now. We are one. You must believe that."

They kissed and then made love slowly, leisurely before falling back asleep for another hour. But finally they rose and showered together before collecting Joe from the nursery to take him to have breakfast with them.

They were in the middle of having breakfast when Theresa appeared, dressed in tailored cream slacks and a gold knit tank with a rope of crystals, pearls and small gold beads around her neck. She looked polished, wealthy and very angry.

"You had a phone call, Jillian," Theresa said shortly, "on the house phone. I wasn't about to chase you down so I took the number. You're to call him back. He said soon."

She handed Jillian a piece of paper. "It's not anyone working on the wedding. I know, because I asked him. Who else did you give our number to?"

Jillian shook her head. "No one."

"Must have been someone, because he called." Theresa smiled but even that was chilly. "Oh, and he's American. Apparently a friend with an urgent problem. Do call him back, but in the future, I'd prefer it if your friends used your wireless number."

Jillian felt Vitt's gaze and she turned to him. "I can't imagine who'd call."

"Go find out," he said, unconcerned. "Joe and I will be here waiting."

Jillian was troubled as she dialed the number Theresa had written down. She couldn't imagine who would call her at the d'Severano's Paterno castle. No one knew she was here. No one could possibly have the d'Severanos' number.

The phone rang three times before a man answered. "Hello?" he said.

"This is Jillian d'Severano returning your call. Whom am I speaking with?"

"A friend."

Her skin suddenly crawled. "My friends have names. What is yours?"

"Does it matter?"

"Yes, it does."

"In that case you can call me Mark, or Marco, whichever you prefer."

Jillian's legs nearly went out beneath her. Marco was the name of Katie's boyfriend. "Marco, you say?"

"That's what your sister called me."

She sank down on the white slipcovered couch in the sitting room. Her head spun. She felt close to fainting. "How… how… did you find me?"

"I have friends in high places. Police. CIA. FBI." He laughed a little. "Heck, I might even be a friend in a high place. I guess you never know, which is why it's important to know who your friends are."

"What do you want?"

"I'm sure you know what I want. It's what I—we—have always wanted. It's not very much. A few numbers. One little street address. And you're done."

"I'm sorry, I don't follow."

"I want your father's address."

"I don't know it."

He snorted. "You expect me to believe that?"

"It's the truth."

"But you could get it for me."

"I couldn't. He doesn't share it with me. I don't see him. I have no contact with him—"

"Those are excuses. I'm not interested in excuses. None of us are. What you need to do is think out of the box. Get creative. Invite him to your wedding. I am sure he'd be delighted by a trip to Italy if you asked him nicely."

Jillian's stomach rose, acid filled her throat. Marco knew too much. He was far too connected. Which made her wonder how he'd traced her here. "My father and I haven't talked in years."

"That's a shame, because you have so much at stake. Your baby…your husband…your new family."

She bent over, nauseated. "Don't threaten me."

"Then don't be stupid. You know what happened to Katie."

Briefly she closed her eyes, remembering Katie's violent death, remembering her own grief. Jill couldn't lose anyone else. Her heart couldn't bear the pain. "I would need time," she said, her voice low and broken.

"You don't have time. And you're not to involve your husband. He's not part of this. He's not to know about this. And should he find out, trust me, there will be *devastating* consequences."

Then he hung up.

Jillian slowly, numbly set the phone down and sat frozen on the edge of the couch.

For the past twenty months she'd been afraid of Vitt, terrified of his mafia connections, but Vitt wasn't a threat. He'd never been a threat. The threat was her family. The threat was her father's past. His choices. His actions. *Her* father was the danger. And as long as her father was alive, he'd always put the rest of them in danger.

But Jillian knew she could never turn on her father. Could never sell him out.

Something else would have to happen.

Something else would have to change to keep Vittorio and her baby safe.

Jillian returned to the breakfast room, but Vittorio was gone, just Theresa and Joe remained.

"Where's Vitt?" Jillian asked, scooping Joe up from his high chair.

"I don't know. He left the breakfast room not long after you did."

Jillian kissed Joe. "We'll go find him then," she said, struggling to keep her voice natural, to make everything seem normal. "See what he has planned for the day."

Theresa tipped her head back to look at Jillian. "This friend who called…he's not an old boyfriend, is he?"

"No." Again Jillian's stomach rose in protest. "Absolutely not."

"Who was he, then?"

"An acquaintance of my sister's. Just calling to check in."

"On our house phone?"

"He'd heard about the wedding."

"So he was calling to congratulate you?"

Jillian felt swamped by grief. "Yes."

"How good of him."

"Yes."

"Well, as long as that's the truth. Because you know Vittorio. He can't abide dishonesty." Then Theresa pushed back her chair, rose from the table and patted Joe's back before walking out.

For a moment after Theresa left Jillian couldn't move. She stood in the middle of the breakfast room, absolutely shell-shocked. Although sunshine still poured through the tall windows, splashing light across the tiled floor, Jillian couldn't focus. Couldn't see.

In less than five minutes Marco had turned her world inside out. In less than five minutes Marco had stripped away her security, and her hope.

Jillian wasn't sure her legs would hold her as she carried Joe up the stairs from the breakfast room to the nursery on the third floor.

Her heart thudded. Her teeth chattered. Her mind raced, thoughts spinning wildly in every direction.

What would she do now?

What could she do?

She had no idea how Marco had found her. But he had. And now that he had, she put everyone here in danger.

Like Katie before her, Marco's people would use her, make her a tool for destruction.

But she couldn't risk Vittorio's family's safety. And there was no way she'd ever hurt Vitt.

Not when she loved him. Not when he was the one person who'd reached out to her, helped her, loved her.

Because in her heart, she did feel loved. In her heart, she knew he'd do anything for her.

But she needed Vitt alive and strong for Joe. Because Joe, as a d'Severano, would need guidance. Joe would need the wisdom and courage of his father.

Drawing Joe closer against her breast, she breathed him in, smelling his sweetness, aware of his softness. She would never put her baby in danger. She would never compromise his safety in any way.

There was only one thing she could do.

Only one decision to be made.

She had to go. It was the only way.

Tears filmed her eyes and she blinked to clear her vision as she reached the top step. Joe stared into her face with concern and patted her cheek. "Mama," he said, his baby hand against her face, "Mama."

"It's okay," she soothed him, kissing his small palm. "Daddy loves you. Momma loves you. Everyone loves you."

Entering the nursery, Jillian found Maria folding Joe's clothes. At first glance, Jillian thought Maria must have done his laundry, but then she realized Maria was putting everything of Joe's into a suitcase.

Had Vittorio found out about Marco's call?

Was Vittorio sending them away?

"What are you doing?" Jillian asked Maria.

"Signor told me to pack the baby's things."

Jillian's legs shook. "Why?"

"He said that you were going on a trip."

"Me?"

Maria nodded, and Joe impatiently kicked, wanting to be put down. Numbly Jillian set him on his feet and just like the first day he was here, he raced toward his toys, pulling out a stuffed floppy dog off the bookshelf to squeeze to his chest.

Jillian drew a shallow breath. "When did he say that?"

"Five minutes ago. Maybe ten. He came into the nursery and told me to pack because the three of you were going away on holiday for a few days. Going to Capri, I think he said."

Relief coursed through her veins. "Capri?" Jillian repeated.

Maria folded another one of Joe's little T-shirts and added it to the stack in the suitcase. "He wants you to relax before the wedding. It's a pre-honeymoon honeymoon."

A pre-honeymoon honeymoon, to Capri no less. Vitt's thoughtfulness staggered her, aware that he knew it was one of the places she'd always wanted to go but had not yet been.

Shaking her head, Jillian looked off, across the bright nursery with its cheerful colors and fanciful fish. She loved this nursery almost as much as Joe did. It was such a perfect room for a little boy to call his own. "Maria, can I leave Joe here with you while I go talk to Signor?"

Maria smiled. "Of course."

Jillian left the nursery and headed down the hall for the bedroom she shared with Vitt.

The room was dimly lit as the curtains had been drawn against the morning sun. In the darkened room the large canopy bed looked massive and the antique wardrobe in the corner appeared to almost topple over. A suitcase lay open on the bed and Vitt's clothes were stacked in a neat pile in half of it.

Inside the bedroom she heard the sound of running water coming from the ensuite bathroom. Vitt was showering. Humming.

He sounded so happy.

It was such a small thing, but somehow it stole her breath, and practically brought her to her knees.

She couldn't hurt him. She couldn't do it. But just being here with him put everyone at risk.

And then the sound of running water stopped. Vitt had finished his shower.

Jillian put a hand to her middle. For a moment she felt so physically sick she thought she'd lose her breakfast right there on the elegant green-and-cream rug. But she couldn't afford to get sick. She had to keep herself together, had to talk to Vitt.

Gritting her teeth against the acid rising up in her throat, she opened the door and entered the bathroom.

Vitt was standing at the far end of the white marble room, naked, hard muscles glistening, with just a white towel wrapped neatly around his lean hips.

The long mirror over the double sinks was cloudy with steam and steam still wafted from the large white marble shower.

Vitt reached for another towel and began drying his thick hair. "How's your friend?" he asked, rubbing the towel over his wet hair.

"Good."

"Everything okay?"

She looked at him, knew she loved him, knew she'd do anything for him, just as she'd do anything for Joe. They were her family. They were hers to cherish. "Yes."

Vitt grinned as he dragged the towel over the back of his head. "Mother was worrying he was an old boyfriend."

Vitt's boyish grin nearly broke her heart. Jillian forced a smile. "She was wrong."

"I told her that."

Jillian exhaled hard. "It was an old friend of Katie's actually. He'd heard about the wedding. Wanted to offer his congratulations."

"Did you invite him?"

"No."

"Why not? He's welcome to attend."

Jillian turned away, close to throwing up. She couldn't do this. Couldn't pretend everything was fine when her heart was breaking. "He's not someone I'm close to." She ran a shaky hand through her hair, pushing it back from her face. "Maria's packing Joe's things. She said you're taking us to Capri for a few days."

Vitt draped the damp towel he'd used on his hair on a towel bar. "You weren't supposed to know," he said.

She stared at his broad, muscular back, his skin lightly golden, loving him more now, in this moment, than she'd ever loved him. "I'm still surprised. And delighted. We're really going to Capri?"

"Yes." He turned, glanced at her in the mirror, his dark eyes locking with hers. "You said you'd never been."

"You remembered."

"I remember everything."

Hot tears pricked her eyes but she wouldn't cry. Not now. Not when she had to be strong. "Thank you."

"The trip sounds all right?"

"Heavenly," she said, meaning it, because all she wanted was to be with Vittorio. All she wanted was time with him. To make love with him. To have a life with him. "When do we leave?"

"Soon. I've a quick meeting in Catania, and then my driver will bring you and Joe to meet me at the airport. We'll fly out at noon. Can you manage that?"

"Easily. What should I pack for the trip?"

"Nothing. I'm buying you a new wardrobe there."

"You're serious?"

"Your clothes are horrendous. And you are absolutely gorgeous and I can't have my beautiful bride running around in mom-wear…even if she is the mother of my son."

Her heart ached, and she swallowed around the lump filling her throat. "I don't need that much. A few pretty dresses, yes, maybe a wrap to cover a new swimsuit, but I don't need more than that, not when I have you."

His dark gaze met hers in the mirror again. "You really are happy with me?"

"Yes."

"You don't feel as if I've forced you into this?"

"No." She felt like she was dying on the inside. Her heart seemed to be coming apart, twisting, writhing, bursting into little bits of nothing. "So I'll pack a few things and then see you at the airport."

"In ninety minutes. My driver will be waiting downstairs for you. As soon as you're ready, jump in the car." He walked toward her, dropped a kiss on her lips, stroked her cheek and then again, smiling into her eyes. "Green eyes," he murmured. "I love them."

"Thank you."

"You're going to love Capri."

She rose up on tiptoe to brush her mouth against his. His warm mouth sent a tingle down her back. "I know I will if you're there."

"See you soon," he said.

"See you soon," she answered, grateful she had the acting skills to hide the fact that her heart was breaking.

After Vittorio dressed and left, Jillian packed the few things she had into the battered green suitcase, an old suitcase that reminded her of a bruised avocado. As she packed, she tried not to think about what she was doing, or what was happening, or where she'd be going. Because she wasn't going to Capri and she wouldn't be meeting Vittorio.

Instead she was using the opportunity to leave Vittorio.

And she'd be leaving Joe here with Vitt.

Her insides writhed with pain at the idea of it, so she jammed her emotions down, suppressing them with all her strength.

She wasn't going to think right now. She wasn't going to feel. She was just going to put one foot in front of the other and do what she had to.

Suitcase packed, she carried it to the top of the stairs, knowing that Maria and Joe were waiting for her by the front door. But before she headed down, she went to the nursery, peeked inside for one last time.

This is it, she thought, glancing around, trying to remember all the details. The color blue. The painted fish. The crisp white bookshelves.

This is where Joe would sleep at night, safe, secure, protected.

This is where he'd grow up, adored, loved.

It was good that she was leaving him here. It was good he'd be raised by such a strong, moral, compassionate father.

Now all she had to do was go. Her bag was packed. The car was waiting. The only thing remaining was to walk out the door, and close it, and leave her husband and baby behind.

Imagining walking away from Joe made her knees buckle. She put out a hand, touched the wall, took a deep shuddering breath.

You can do this, she told herself. *You have to.*

Joe was too innocent and beautiful for the life she'd lived these past fourteen years. Joe was too innocent to be caught up in her family's darkness and turmoil.

With a last glance around the bright cheerful nursery, she saw how the warm sunlight shone through the windows and fell onto the crib. The light was good. The warmth even better. Leaving Joe here was the right thing to do.

Jillian went down the stairs to the front door where Maria was waiting with Joe and the luggage. The lump in her throat was beyond horrendous. It was murder to swallow and her eyes felt scalded but she would not let the tears fall.

Vittorio would be angry. He'd be so furious that she'd left

them. But she hoped one day he'd understand. She hoped one day he'd realize she was doing this to protect them, not hurt them.

"I've one last thing to do," Jillian told Maria, her voice cracking. "Can you take the baby for a quick walk around the terrace? Let him touch the roses. He loves the flowers. And then he and I will go."

Jill didn't kiss Joe, or make a sound, as Maria carried Joe out, because God knew, she couldn't leave if Joe started crying. But Joe didn't cry. He was happy to go outside, loved the pretty roses, and as Maria carried him, he looked over Maria's shoulder and smiled at his mother, waving, *bye-bye*.

Bye-bye.

Bye-bye, my love. Bye-bye, my baby. For a split second Jillian nearly screamed with the pain. She couldn't do this. She couldn't. There was no way...

And then she lifted her hand and smiled and waved back to her boy. Bye-bye, my heart.

And as the door to the terrace closed behind Maria, Jillian picked up her own suitcase, leaving Joe's two small bags on the gleaming floor, and headed out the front door to climb into the car.

Vittorio wrapped up his meeting early and headed straight for the executive airport, anxious to see Jillian and Joe and be on their way for their three-day holiday. But on reaching the airport in Catania, he discovered his driver hadn't arrived yet.

He waited ten minutes then called his driver. His driver immediately answered. "How far away are you?" Vitt asked, glancing at his watch.

"I've just returned to Paterno," his driver said. "I dropped Signore off at the airport."

"But I'm at the airport. I've been here. The jet's fueled and waiting."

"Signore said I was to take her to the public airport."

"What?"

"She said there had been a change of plans."

A change of plans? Why would there be a change of plans? Vittorio reeled from shock and struggled to speak. "Where is my son?"

"Here in Paterno, at home."

Thank God. Vittorio exhaled. "But the Signore?"

"She is gone."

Vittorio immediately jumped into his car and drove home, unable to believe that Jillian had really gone.

As he drove through the gates of his estate, he played his last conversation with Jillian over and over in his head. She'd said she was looking forward to Capri. Said she was happy with him.

So why would she leave?

In the house, he dropped keys on the ornate sideboard in the hall next to the vase of fresh flowers and stood frozen in place.

How could everything have changed so quickly? Just hours ago everything had seemed so perfect he'd planned an impromptu getaway to his favorite five-star hotel in Capri. But just hours later, Jillian was gone and she'd abandoned him, abandoned their son.

Why?

How?

Something must have happened. Something must have driven her away. But what? Or more accurately, who?

He replayed the morning's events over in his head one more time, picturing waking up with her, making love, showering, breakfast, his mother's appearance…

The phone call.

The phone call.

Someone had said something to her. Scared her. Threatened her. Chased her off.

He'd find out who called the house. There were ways to trace numbers. Even unlisted numbers.

He climbed the stairs to the library, determined to find out everything he could when he heard the sound of his father's wheelchair down the hall.

Vitt paused at the top of the stairs and spotted his father waiting for him at the door of the library. But his father wasn't the only one in the wheelchair. Eleven-month-old Joseph lay on his grandfather's chest, his thumb in his mouth, sound asleep.

"Where has she gone?" Salvatore asked Vittorio.

"I don't know."

"Why would she leave her son?"

"I don't know that, either."

His father stared at him hard. "Has she done this before?"

"Never."

"Then why now?" his father demanded.

"I don't know. But trust me, I'm going to find out."

Jillian had purchased a last-minute seat on an Air Italia flight from Catania to Heathrow. From Heathrow she'd catch the cheapest flight she could to the States. Where in the States she didn't know. She'd figure that part out later. It was hard enough just leaving Vittorio and Joe behind in Sicily without thinking of the vast Atlantic Ocean separating them.

The flight attendant on Air Italia offered Jillian snacks and drinks but Jillian shook her head, unable to speak, almost catatonic with despair.

What had she done? How could she have left them both? Why hadn't she gone straight to Vittorio and told him everything?

Because you're scared, a little voice whispered. You're scared that if you make a mistake, you could lose the people you love.

And she did love Vitt, just as she loved Joe. She loved them so much she wanted to be brave and strong and do what Salvatore had done—sacrifice herself for the good of his family, but how it hurt. It hurt so bad she wasn't sure she could survive it.

Arriving in Heathrow, Jillian purchased the cheapest ticket she could on a U.S. airline, which ended up being to Houston, Texas.

She didn't want to go to Houston. But she didn't know where else to go. The problem was, she didn't want to go to the States. She wanted to jump back on a plane for Catania. She wanted to tell Vittorio she couldn't live without him and yet she was so afraid of him being hurt. For the two hours before her flight, Jillian wandered around the international terminal in a fog.

Nothing about leaving Paterno felt right.

Nothing about leaving Joe and Vittorio felt right.

But what else could she do?

What else should she have done?

She should have talked to Vitt. She should have trusted him, because somewhere inside of her she knew he could handle the very real things she was afraid of. Look at his father. Look at what he'd gone through in his own life. He wasn't a man who crumbled in the face of adversity. He was a man who met it head on. Fierce. Tough. Unflinching.

Instead she'd tried to handle everything on her own, the way she had for the past fourteen years.

But her way didn't work. Her way meant she was lonely. Her way meant leaving everyone she loved behind.

There had to be a better way. Because this way was hell. It was madness.

It was breaking her heart.

She'd had enough of heartbreak and madness. She'd suffered through far too much pain.

If only she could reach Vitt. If only she could call him before it was too late. He might be angry but she thought perhaps he'd understand. Perhaps he'd realize she was trying to do the right thing, trying to be strong, trying to be independent, which in this case, seemed to be absolutely wrong.

If only she knew how to trust better. If only she could trust him…

And then it hit her. She did.

Jillian raced to find a bank of phones, but there weren't many in the airport, not with so many people carrying their own phones now. Finally she found a cluster of phones, but as she picked up the receiver she realized she didn't even know Vittorio's number, nor did she have a number for his family.

What about his office in Catania? Surely that would be listed. She called information and gave him the d'Severano name, asking if they had any businesses by that listing. They did not. And then she ran out of ideas, because she didn't know the name of his company.

Just as she hadn't taken the time to really know Vitt.

There was so much she'd do differently given the chance. So much she wanted to know, so many things she wanted to do with him.

Travel, explore, talk, make love.

Have more kids.

An announcement sounded through the terminal that Continental Airlines was now boarding their afternoon flight to Houston.

Heart in her mouth, she watched the other passengers line up at the gate. She watched all two hundred passengers board, but her legs wouldn't move. She couldn't line up. Couldn't do it.

The gate personnel were finished boarding but they didn't close the door. Instead the gate agent paged her. "Jillian Smith, this is your final call. Jillian Smith, your final call for Continental Airlines Flight 52."

Jillian glanced down at the boarding pass crumpled in her damp hand, and then at the gate agent, and realized that even though her initial reaction was to leave her family to protect them, she knew it was the wrong one.

Family didn't leave family.

Family didn't betray family.

Family protected family.

And Jillian needed hers.

It struck her that she didn't have to run anymore. She didn't have to be afraid. She had Vittorio. He was smart. He was strong. And he could be trusted.

Eyes burning, throat aching, she picked up her small carry-on bag and turned her back on fear, and walked through the terminal, past security, out the airport terminal to the curb.

It was twilight and the sky was lavender and gray. Jillian stood on the curb trying to figure out how she'd get back to Catania and what she'd say to Vitt once she got there when a deep voice spoke behind her.

"Thinking of going somewhere?"

Vittorio.

Usually deep and calm, his voice sounded rough and as if he was in pain.

She turned to face the man who'd turned her life upside down in the best way possible. He looked tall and handsome and worried. He looked so very dear. It didn't hurt that he had a small boy in his arms that meant everything to her.

"Yes," she said, tears filling her eyes as she looked at the two people she loved most in the world. "I want to go home."

For fourteen years she'd had to take care of herself. For

fourteen years she'd had to pretend she didn't need anything from anyone, when in truth, she needed everything.

Love, comfort, tenderness, support.

"I want to go home with you. Please take me back to Paterno," she choked.

The haunted expression lifted from Vittorio's dark eyes and then he slowly smiled. "I hoped you'd say that."

"Oh, Vitt, I don't know what I'm doing. I just know that I got scared, but I'm so tired of being scared, Vitt. I'm so tired of running and looking over my shoulder and worrying the bad guys will find me."

"I guess one found you this morning," Vitt said, wrapping his free arm around her, bringing her close to him.

"Yes." She pressed her cheek to his chest, feeling the warmth of her husband and son. "But I should have come to you, Vitt. I should have told you. You wouldn't have panicked. You would have known what to do."

"Marco can't hurt you," Vitt answered, brushing his lips across her brow as his arm squeezed tighter around her waist. "The FBI were able to trace his call. It came from near a cell tower in downtown Detroit and the Detroit police arrested him an hour ago. The police have been looking for him since your sister's death, and now they have him. He's going away for a long time. He won't ever be able to threaten you again."

Jillian's lips curved in a watery smile. "So you did know what to do."

"I'm a d'Severano, *cara*. I know how to take care of my family."

His deep voice rumbled through her, his tone fierce, proud. "Am I still your family?"

"Forever."

Tears filled her eyes. Her chest grew tight and she struggled to take a breath. "I'm sorry I didn't trust you. I'm sorry I didn't come to you right away. I was just so scared he'd hurt you or Joe or someone else in your family—"

Vitt reached up to wipe her tears away. "I understand. Just as I understand you've had no one to be there for you since you were a little girl. But we'll work on trust, and we'll learn to be a strong family together, yes?"

"Yes." She blinked to clear her vision. "So you're not mad at me?"

"Of course not."

Joe wiggled in Vittorio's arms, and reached out with both arms to Jillian. "Mama."

Jillian looked up, over Joe's head, to Vitt. "Can I hold him?"

"You better. Your little boy cried for you endlessly on the plane. Fortunately it was my own plane so no one complained."

Jillian didn't know whether to laugh or cry. And then she laughed because Vittorio had the most amazing way of making her feel good. With him, life was the way she'd always dreamed it should be.

"Can we go home now?" she asked.

"Most definitely."

EPILOGUE

ELEVEN-and-a-half-month-old Joseph was supposed to be the ring boy, but he refused to walk down the aisle in his miniature black suit to the front of the d'Severano chapel where Vitt waited in his elegant black tuxedo. Instead Joseph walked down the aisle swinging his pillow in circles before stopping at his grandfather's wheelchair at the outside of the wooden pews.

"Up," he said to Salvatore, dropping his pillow. "Up, Papa," he repeated, wanting to be put on his grandfather's lap, because in his nine days in Paterno he'd learned to love many things and many people but his grandfather Salvatore was probably his favorite.

His grandmother Theresa put a hand on Joseph's shoulder and tried to steer her grandson toward the front of the chapel, but Joseph squawked in protest.

Checking his smile, Vitt stepped down from the stone steps before the altar and placed his son on his father's lap.

"Vittorio," his mother said softly, reprovingly, slim and chic as ever in a pale silvery-gray fitted gown.

Vitt shrugged. "It's his day, too. He should sit where he wants, and if he wants his grandfather, who am I to say no?"

Salvatore smiled at Vitt and then down at Joseph as the little boy squirmed to get closer to Salvatore's chest.

Vittorio clapped his father on the shoulder and then returned to the front of the church as the string quartet played the first bright notes by Vivaldi.

Jillian appeared in the arched doors at the back of the chapel. The ends of the pews were decorated with flowers. The old stone chapel glowed with candlelight. Guests crowded the pews but Jillian only had eyes for Vittorio who looked impossibly handsome in his black tux and white dress shirt with the white tie.

Hers, she thought, on a quick breath. He was hers. And she knew he'd always be hers.

Her lover. Her partner. Her husband.

She walked down the aisle on her own, her ivory gown rustling, her legs shaking with every step, yet knowing that once she reached the front of the chapel she'd never be alone again. She'd have Vittorio. She'd have his family. They'd be a family.

Reaching the front of the chapel, Vitt stepped forward to take her hand. His beautiful face looked somber in the candlelight but then he smiled and love raced through her, love, desire and joy.

The ceremony passed in a blur, with Jillian seeing nothing but Vittorio's beautiful face and dark eyes. They said their vows, exchanged rings, kissed as her heart turned over.

She was home.

She finally belonged somewhere.

And then the ceremony was over and she was walking with Vittorio down the aisle. The chapel smelled of gardenias and orange blossoms and the soft candlelight reflected off the arched ceiling and the high stone walls. Faces smiled at them as they passed the crowded pews, but then they were alone in the small antechamber. It was dark and blissfully cool.

Vittorio dropped his head, kissed her and kissed her again.

"I love you," he said as the chapel bells pealed high overhead.

"Even though your family was shocked when you told them who I was yesterday?"

"They're fine. They're used to drama," he answered with a grin. "I don't know what we'd do without some excitement."

Jillian tried to smile but tears filled her eyes. "You're too good to me."

"Impossible. You deserve so much happiness."

"You've made me happier than I ever dreamed I could be."

"Good. I'm glad." He tipped her chin up so he could look into her eyes. "I have loved you since you walked through the lobby of the Ciragan Palace in your black management suit with your midheight heels. You were the picture of efficiency and yet somehow you stole my heart. I'd never thought about settling down and then suddenly all I wanted was to marry you and take care of you forever, and I mean that Jill Anne Carol Lee, I do."

She sniffed and laughed, her fragrant bouquet crushed between them. "You can just call me Jill. It's shorter."

"Not Alessia?"

Jillian shuddered. "Never Alessia. She's gone. Dead. But oh, I do like being your Jill. I like it more than anything."

He smoothed her crisp white veil back from her face and then caressed one of her dark red curls that rested on her bare collarbone. "And I love your green eyes and your red hair and your infamous family history," he said, before glancing over his shoulder, aware that any moment the doors would open and family and friends would pour out. "I love everything about you."

Jillian laughed and lifted her lips for him to kiss her, and then kiss her again. "Good," she murmured against his lips, "because you've got me now."

"Finally." He gazed down at her, his dark eyes holding hers for an endless moment before he whispered in Sicilian. *"T'amu bidduzza." I love you, beautiful.*

Eyes stinging, heart overflowing, she reached up, touched Vitt's lean bronzed cheek, dazzled by joy. "I can't believe it."

"Believe what?"

"I've come home." Her voice broke, her expression one of wonder. "I've finally come home, haven't I?"

"You have," he answered, dropping his head to kiss her deeply, even as the chapel doors burst open and their family and friends surged out to celebrate their love.

OUT NOW!

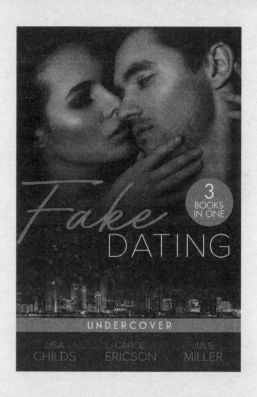

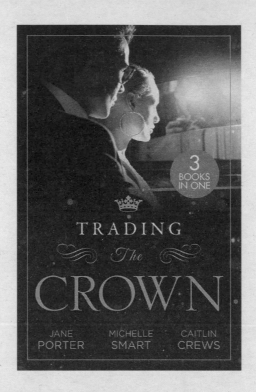

MILLS & BOON

HEROES

At Your Service

Experience all the excitement of a
gripping thriller, with an intense romance
at its heart. Resourceful, true-to-life
women and strong, fearless men face
danger and desire – a killer combination!

Eight Heroes stories published every month, find them all at:

millsandboon.co.uk

MILLS & BOON

Desire

Indulge in secrets and scandal, intense drama and plenty of sizzling hot action with powerful and passionate heroes who have it all: wealth, status, good looks…everything but the right woman.